THE BOYS IN THE BRAZOS RIVER BOTTOM

PETER L. SCAMARDO II

ISBN 978-1-7375404-0-3

To my grandparents, Pete and Camella, the family they created, the countless cousins, and the stories we will continue to share.

FOREWORD

When the Sicilians first came to the strange, flat land that was Texas, the Brazos River was there to greet them. They saw it as a sign. The arm of God stretching across the fields. A river that would protect them, sustain them, and allow their families to prosper in this unfamiliar country.

MAY 1969

THE BOYS

The calf spasmed under the boys' grip. A patch of dust had gotten sucked into Matt's throat, and the shocking dryness that surrounded his vocal cords led to a rough expulsion of saliva and soot. Regardless, the resulting cough distracted Matt from the task at hand.

The calf had felt a moment of freedom and in an instant imagined shedding off the human hands and dashing back to its mother on all five feet.

The boys had almost driven into a ditch when they first spotted the calf earlier that week. By all accounts it was a normal calf, one more part of the herd. The notable shine on its fur told the boys it had been born only a few days prior, but they could not stop looking at the legs. The knock-kneed skeletal legs that looked incapable of holding up anything, let alone a sixty-pound baby cow.

The calf had five legs. Four normal ones and an extra, limp appendage, coming out of its left shoulder. With each step the extra leg slapped against the calf's body and looked as if it would snap off at any moment.

Matt thought he was going to throw up when he first saw it. None of them could believe what they saw. Papa wasn't shocked by the news.

"We best be doing something about that," was his reply, before he continued reading that day's issue of the *Hearne Democrat*.

3

Matt thought it was only right to put the animal out of its misery. Whether that meant calling Uncle Frank LaCarpentera down from Highbank with his pistol or driving the newborn to the slaughterhouse, Matt wasn't sure, but he was damn sure the five-legger wasn't going to be a heifer or a bull of any value. He hadn't gotten close enough to see its sex.

Whatever he was expecting, he wasn't expecting Papa to go into the paddock and pick the calf up in his arms and carry it away as easily as he would a sack of flour.

Papa had gotten up before sunrise and guided the mother cow and her calf into one of the paddocks in the yard. An area of weeds, broken-down tractor parts, and a bevy of manure from the injured or sick cows that were kept there at various points of the year.

The three brothers had awoken to the sounds of frightened mooing as the calf and his mother brayed at each other from beyond the fences. Papa was in the backyard waiting for them, standing as if he was about to give a sermon.

"Get dressed, come on," was all that came out of his mouth.

Matt felt his gut tightening when he saw the calf braying in the lot adjacent to them. Numerous scenarios ran through his head about what Papa wanted them to do. He settled on Papa having them slaughter the calf themselves.

This was not out of the question. They had seen Nonno go into the smokehouse many times and come out with many a slaughtered pig. Perhaps it was the same with cattle.

The boys donned their button-down shirts, with long sleeves to keep the sun off their arms, blue jeans with mud capped knees, and work boots that had grown an inch in circumference from the dirt that had caked on all sides.

Only as they scampered down the back porch did they notice the device in Papa's hands. The rectangular thingamajigger was some sort of rifle, judging by the trigger and shoulder butt. But Papa didn't own any guns. The boys thought it was safe to assume Papa was the only farmer in the Bottom that did not own a single gun.

Regardless, on the very end of this thing was a hook where a piece of elastic string was stretched into a circle. Matt's stomach tightened again as he remembered what exactly the tool was used for.

The three of them marched from the back of the house, through the gate into the yard and down the gravel road to the paddock holding the deformed calf. Only when they were in the lot, with the calf nudging all of their hands to see which one of them had food, did Papa finally speak.

"Matthew, Joshua, get it down," were his instructions.

"Whatcha mean get it down?" Josh asked.

"Just what I said. You two hold it down and keep it steady. We're gonna get that leg off."

Matt saw Josh making a face as if to argue, or at least demand a further explanation about what was about to happen. Matt did the only thing he could do to stop Josh from speaking up, he wrapped his arms around the calf and started to heave. Josh saw what Matt was doing and went to help.

Matt stood at the head of the animal. He gripped tight, holding the front legs down, trying his hardest to keep the calf from struggling. Last thing they wanted was to risk it injuring its neck. It took all of Matt and Josh's body weight to keep the calf steady.

They looked at each other from across the animal's stomach. Without saying a word, they spoke to each other. Josh's eyes asked desperately, "What are we doing here?" Matt's roll of the eyes and shake of a head responded, "Just forget about it."

Matt had forced Josh's hand so fast that they never did get Papa to explain just what was going on. Yet the presence of the fifth leg was unavoidable. As the calf attempted to get free, the extra leg would swing up and down with each little wiggle. Had Matt been a few inches closer, he would've been clobbered by the hoof.

They should have known Papa would never have taken the easy road of just slaughtering the calf, Matt thought. Papa fancied himself a shepherd, even though he raised no sheep. Always looking out for his flock. Papa probably thought the calf could still grow to be a valuable steer, for they were now close enough to sex the calf, even with the birth defect. That's why Papa was the boss. He could always envision an animal's use further down the line.

But they had to do something about the leg.

It was clear the calf had no feeling in the leg, given how it flung every direction with each thrust. Papa must have seen this and feared each possible scenario of infection. It would be too easy for an older cow to gore the calf in a fight, or for a coyote to take a bite out of the extra leg. The calf would not notice the cut and the wound would fester. Then they would have a dead calf and nothing to show for it.

All this crossed Matt's head as he continued to spit dirt out of his mouth. His muscles were starting to tire as the calf never did let up. Matt glanced up to see what was taking so long. What he saw was Papa putting the tool in Tommy's hands.

The youngest of the three took it from Papa's hands and let Papa guide the butt into his armpit. Matt watched as Tommy rubbed his hands along the barrel and pulled back after touching a sticky substance. He held his hand up to his face and sniffed.

"Oh, Jesus Christ," Matt mumbled under his breath, making sure Papa could not hear him curse.

Papa stood so that he was right behind Tommy. The two of them towered over the calf as its bulging black eyes looked straight into theirs. Pupils wide, nostrils flaring, its mother screaming in the distance. A scared animal, nothing more. A part of Matt expected the mother cow to come rampaging through the gates to get its baby back. She didn't, but they could still hear her.

"You're afraid," Papa said.

"What?" Tommy asked.

"You're afraid of the calf, your arms are shaking."

6

"I mean . . ."

"You've got to stand tall," Papa interrupted. "If the calf can see you're afraid, then it's going to be afraid. It thinks you're trying to hurt it."

We probably are hurting it, Matt thought.

"Is this not going to hurt it?" Tommy asked.

"If we do it right the calf won't feel a thing," Papa said. "Now steady yourself."

"Why don't . . ."

"Hush," Papa interrupted. "You've got to do it."

Matt wanted to turn away. He didn't want to watch his little brother get pushed into something he didn't want to do. An all-too-common sight among the Ruggirellos. But he couldn't. The dirt was no place to shove his face, and he dared not look at the calf. All he could do was look up at Papa and Tommy.

He watched as the two of them slowed their breaths. Together, their bodies moved up and down as they steadied themselves. Matt swore he saw a shimmer flash across Tommy's eyes, but it disappeared just as fast.

Tommy licked his lips as he slowly stepped forward, looping the rubber band at the end of the tool around the calf's hoof and guiding it down to the deformed shoulder. Tommy and Papa took one more deep breath before pulling the trigger and watching as the rubber band snapped tight.

"Let him up!" Papa called.

Matt and Josh shot up to their feet with the speed of a pellet shot. The calf, still braying, got to its feet just as fast and started for the paddock gate. Matt, hands on hips as he caught his breath, looked over at Tommy. He looked as if he might start laughing at what he just did.

The purpose of the rubber band was to lock around the fifth leg's shoulder joint and cut off the circulation. Over time the leg would shrivel up and fall off without any harm to the calf, or at least that was the intention. However, no one ever stopped to explain to Tommy what the rubber band was meant to do.

The look on his face was more out of shock that he actually did the deed.

"Get the calf back with its mother," Papa said.

And that was that. Not another word. The boys could do nothing but say, "Yes, sir," and watch as he exited through the gate and to the white, two-story garage where his Ford truck had been parked. Almost like a ritual, they watched as Papa climbed in and turned the keys in the ignition, listening as the engine churned twice before a loud pop cascaded through the air and climaxed with the truck rocking back and forth as it chugged down the road.

The Mustang. At least that's what the boys called it. A little joke on their part. They knew Papa would never pay for such extravagance as a Ford Mustang. The fastest car in the country. So, they joked that the dark green, mud-scabbed beast of a truck was Papa's Mustang. The king of the farm roads.

Matt saw that Tommy's face had dropped with Papa's sudden departure, but not one of them commented on it. There was no point.

The matter was there was a five-legged calf in their possession that they had to return to its mother. Luckily, that came without any bodily harm to the four of them.

From there, the day proceeded like all the others. The three boys crammed inside Matt's own Ford truck. A white 1956 model that had since turned black from the farm roads. Matt drove them from field to field, opening up the irrigation wells one after another for miles on end and checking to make sure the water flowed out of the pipes unobstructed. It would be deep into the night before Matt, who worked the night shift, would come back to close those same wells.

There had been days where he had forgotten to close one or two pumps. The result was a flooded field that hampered the growth of the cotton.

Other tasks included checking the fences to see if the barbed wire had been cut or a post had broken. Papa and his neighbor, Mr. Francis DiRusso, were always in land battles. One was always claiming the other was encroaching on their land and cutting the other's fences. The boys were not about to slip up and create more trouble for Papa.

Apart from that, they made sure none of the cattle had gotten injured or that none of the pigs had gotten loose. They also made sure to brush and feed the horses, of which there were three.

Not one of the horses had inspiring names. They were Red, Scout, and Luke's Horse. Poor things were hardly ever ridden. They were kept for the rare days when a road would ice over, one of the rivers flooded, or a truck had broken-down. Papa didn't even want a third horse. Luke's Horse only came into their possession because one day a man named Luke asked if he could leave his horse on the farm as he drove into town for supplies. That man never did come back, but the horse stayed.

Overall, Ruggirello & Sons Farms consisted of over 3,000 acres of land.

Nonno and Nonna lived in the big house that marked the southernmost point of the property. The house was not large in the sense of height like one would find belonging to a doctor in the city, but it was spacious. That was where all the family gatherings were held.

In total, there were seven farms that Papa and Uncle Andrew managed. The two did not split their responsibilities evenly. Instead, their respective farms zigzagged all over the Bottom. Uncle Andrew's farms were more to the north, near his home at the Orange Grove, a patch of land called such for the oranges he grew on it. Papa, as the oldest child, had taken over leadership of the Home Farm, allowing Nonno to take advantage of retirement now that he was 70.

Add in the land that belonged to Nonno's brothers—Carlo, Rosario, and Giacomo—and the Ruggirellos owned thousands of acres on the road to Bryan.

All the Ruggirello land bumped side by side with the likes of the DiRussos, Devinos, Salvatores, and DiCarusos, other Sicilian families that had come to America looking for work and had set up farms of their own. The same could be said of almost every farm or ranch south of Hearne and north of Bryan. The Sicilians had arrived decades prior, trying to make a living as workers and now owned the land itself.

Despite their shared origins, they were not a friendly people. They all could trace their roots back to the towns and villages in Sicily, meaning those same cross-town rivalries carried over into the new country. Apart from the rare sight of a handshake at Sunday mass, everyone always had something to argue about.

Papa and Mr. DiRusso's arguments were a capsule of the entire Bottom. Someone was always trying to encroach on another's land, steal someone's bull, or claim someone had sabotaged a tractor.

This was the community that the boys grew up in. Matt was eighteen and would be starting his senior year at Hearne High School. Josh was sixteen and also went to Hearne. Tommy, only ten, still went to the primary school in Mumford.

Together, they lived in a white house adjacent to the Big House where Nonno and Nonna lived. The house sat on an elevated platform that prevented any flooding in the event of heavy rainfall. The Big House didn't worry about floods as it sat on a hill. They fenced the house in with two gates on either side, one leading to the vegetable garden, the other into the yard.

The house was nothing out of the ordinary, but it was theirs. It was Papa's wedding gift to Mama.

But their first year of marriage was spent living at Nonno's house, as if Papa had never moved out or gone to college. Mama was accustomed to living in a house full of people since she was the youngest of ten siblings, but she was ready to start her own family and have a place they could call home.

Papa commissioned the house to be built and paid for it with his own money, investing every dollar he had. Uncle Andrew once remarked that the house should have a name, like all the houses you hear about rich people owning.

Papa wanted no part of that.

Still, when the boys heard that story, they started calling their home Three Pecans. Mama's favorite book was *Gone with the Wind*. They had spotted her reading it up to thirty times in the last five years alone. Mama liked to say she grew up in the Old South, but Matt never thought that statement was accurate.

She mentioned that in the book there was this grand plantation house they go to called Twelve Oaks. The way Mama described it made it sound like the most amazing house in the world.

The boys knew their house didn't have twelve oak trees outside, but it did have three pecan trees.

There were also a handful of fig trees located around Three Pecans and the Big House, one of which sat right next to the garden entrance gate. It was the boys' first stop when they returned home that afternoon.

After parking Matt's truck in the garage, leaving space for the Mustang, the three ventured through the gates and caught sight of the fig trees. Without a word, they all looked at each other before sauntering over to check on the figs.

They were ripe.

They all shared one more glance before each plucked their own fig from the branches and busted open the fruit with their mouths. The Ruggirellos valued many things, but the figs were one of their cherished possessions.

The brothers found themselves so enraptured by the sweet fruit that they almost missed the sound of toes tapping against wood.

With figs still in hands and mouths, the three turned toward the house and found Susanna looking down at them with arms folded across her chest.

Susanna was that poor soul that fate determined to be the only girl in a litter of boys. Still, Susanna may have only been fourteen years old but she was more or less a second mother to them. When she spoke, they heard Mama's voice.

"Y'all should be ashamed of yourselves," Susanna said.

The boys did not answer as they were still swallowing the figs. Susanna continued to tap the toe of her black boot against the porch.

"Don't even think about coming inside yet," Susanna continued. "I can see y'all forgot to swing by the post office."

Matt immediately looked to the sky in frustration. That was another one of their tasks. Every three days the boys were tasked with driving by the post office to collect what mail had gathered up. That, and it also gave them a chance to pick up a copy of the *Hearne Democrat*.

"Go on," Susanna said. "Get going before Papa gets back. Give y'all time to think about eating figs before dinner."

"We're going," Matt said before trudging back toward his truck.

Josh and Tommy made two steps toward the house, but Susanna just huffed at them. They both looked up at her, then back at the dirt before following Matt back to the truck.

Once again, they climbed in and headed north on the farm-to-market road. The only benefit of this trip was the advantage of a paved road. Dirt and gravel were all that made up the farm roads, resulting in about one thousand micro bumps that sent the boys rocking with every turn of the tires.

The bumps and bruises on the top of their heads were from the times they drove over potholes that shot the truck three feet into the air and the boys' heads against the roof of the truck.

"Bet you an Army issue Jeep we don't beat Papa back," Josh said to Tommy.

"Bet you a Charger if we do," Tommy responded.

"I don't have a Charger," Josh said.

"I know," Tommy said, grinning as he looked out the front window.

The sun was still up but it was starting to make its curve. It would definitely be set by the time they got home, but that wasn't what they were afraid of. If Papa got back and the three of them were missing, there would be words.

For that reason, Matt was putting a little bit more pressure on the gas than he normally would. He would slow down whenever he saw a police cruiser coming around the bend, but would pick up speed the moment the troopers were out of sight.

Matt heard static and looked down to see Tommy fiddling with the radio. He was moving the dial back and forth and turning the knob to adjust the sound. Sometimes he would pick up the sound of a station, but the majority of time it was just static. Each time Tommy heard static, he would slump forward in disappointment.

"I know what you're looking for," Matt said. "You're not going to be able to get it out here."

"Well, can we go to the spot?" Tommy said.

"Not tonight," Matt said. "We're already behind."

"I don't see what you two get out of that station," Josh said, half leaning outside the passenger window. "Can't understand what they're saying half the time. Other half is nothing but noise."

"Oh, don't be so sour," Matt said.

"That's the best music in the country," Tommy added. "They said so."

"I ain't ever seen a list," Josh said. "You just gonna take the word of some man you've never met before?"

"Papa trusts the guys he hears on the news, he ain't ever met them," Tommy said.

Josh didn't respond. He just flashed the palm of his hand, signaling he was done with that conversation, leaning further out of the window. Matt thought Josh rather enjoyed the feeling of the wind against his face. It was a nice contrast to the heat on their skin during most of the day.

Tommy kept fiddling with the radio for a while longer but soon gave up on his search. For whatever reason, there was only one spot in the entire Bottom that could get that one signal.

"What's on your mind," Matt asked.

"Huh," Tommy replied.

"You're quiet," Matt said. "Quieter. So what's up?"

"Nothin."

"Come on."

Josh looked across the truck and made a face as if to say, "Why are you prodding?" But Tommy did speak.

"I guess, I was thinking about the calf," Tommy said.

"In what way?" Matt asked.

"I mean. I don't get why Papa had me do it. He could've done it so easily. Y'all could've too. And the longer we took, the more frightened the calf became. I thought for sure I was going to mess it up."

"But you didn't."

"Yeah," Tommy said, almost laughing. "Couldn't quite believe it."

"Well, that's probably the point," Matt said. "You had a job, you doubted yourself, but you succeeded. You're right, Papa or us could've done the job faster. That's not to say we've dealt with a five-legged calf before, but we know how to use that tool. Papa decided it was time for you to learn. Simple as that."

"Yeah, Tommy," Josh added. "There's a lot to learn with this job, what Papa does. Today was just one of those things, ya know."

Tommy nodded his head. Matt hoped his words did something to calm his little brother. He knew too well the feeling of Papa's lack of guidance. Communication was far from an open channel.

Matt and Josh never had such a talk.

"Just don't put your hands anywhere near your face after using that thing," Matt said.

"Why's that?" Tommy asked.

"It's what we use to castrate the cattle."

To Matt's relief, Tommy did not become nauseous at the revelation, but he did remain quiet for the rest of the trip.

MATT

They continued to speed up the winding road, passing several tractors, and crossing over two sets of railroad tracks. The sight of homes and storefronts in the distance told the boys they were close.

Had they been speeding, the boys would have exited Hearne just as quickly as they had reached it. About forty-five seconds is all they would have needed. But no, Matt made a couple of left turns and a right and the boys found themselves parked outside the Hearne Post Office.

"I didn't think you'd make it this time," the clerk said as Matt dashed through the door.

"What can I say . . . slipped our minds," Matt said, not so much in the mood to talk.

"You know I can't keep this place open forever."

"I know, I know."

"How're your parents? They still in good health? Haven't seen them around lately."

Matt was sometimes bugged by the type of people who just loved to talk. The clerk did not seem to notice Matt's tapping boot heel as he waited for the clerk to fetch their mail.

"Oh, they're fine. Just busy is all," Matt said.

"Well, that's alright," the clerk said, putting the mail on the counter, an abnormally large pile. "Be coming back soon though. I expect there's more on the way."

Matt took the mail, paid the clerk for a copy of that day's newspaper, and sped out the door just as fast.

Together they shot back into the street and onto the highway, resuming their high-speed trek down the country roads. By the time they got back to Three Pecans, The Mustang was nowhere to be seen.

"I win," Tommy said to Josh as they walked up to the gate adjacent to the garden.

"Yeah, yeah," was all Josh replied.

By now the sun had set, the wind had picked up, and the temperature had dropped drastically. Combined with having driven down the highway with the windows down, the only option with no air conditioning unit, the boys had gone from extreme heat to bitter cold blasting against their faces.

The result was that the sweat had dried all over their bodies and had formed a thick coat underneath their greasy heads.

The three of them climbed up the steps, leaving their boots on the porch so as not to dirty the inside of the house. There was no point in hosing them down, they were going to put the same ones on the very next day and get them just as dirty.

When they opened the door, the three were hit with the smell of frying chicken and green beans. There was a notable crackle from the stovetop as Mama flipped one piece of chicken onto its opposite side. Without even thinking, Matt, Josh, and Tommy all started drifting over to the kitchen.

There Mama stood, flipping the pieces of chicken while also stirring the green beans and a pot of mac and cheese. She was focused. Not one second did she step away from the stovetop to see who had come through the door. She stirred away, all the while listening to the CBS radio broadcast.

The interior of Three Pecans was simple. The main entrance was to the rear, a set of brownstone steps that opened into the hall at the center of the house. There was a door at the front, on the side of the house facing the highway, but that opened into Mama and Papa's bedroom.

17

To the right of the back entrance was the kitchen with a stovetop, oven, refrigerator, sink, and drying rack, all with easy access to one another. There was also a radio so Mama could listen to the news while cooking. One large, circular brown wood table sat in the center of the room with just enough chairs to seat the family. No more, no less.

The kitchen led to the living room, a space that was originally two rooms but then had the dividing wall broken to create one long room. The floor was carpeted, a sofa sat along the wall with a window, while Mama and Papa sat in cushioned chairs that faced both the television and the second radio set.

There they would sit, usually saying a rosary or some other prayer. When they weren't doing that, they were reading the newspaper. If they weren't reading the newspaper, they were listening to the radio or watching television.

They owned a television, but it was rarely used. They bought it to watch Pope Paul VI when he came to the United States four years prior. Mama had been so excited that she took a Polaroid photo of the children watching the pope on the television. The flash from the camera blurred out any image of the pope in the actual photo.

The right side of the house was the living space, while the left side of the house was where the bedrooms rested. None of the children had spacious rooms, but they each had their own room. Cabins would have been a more accurate description. The rooms were a bit of foresight on Papa's part when designing the house. He and Mama slept in the master bedroom to the west side of the house.

Their rooms were separated by the only bathroom in the house. A cramped space where everyone had to wait their turn. The room was so small that Tommy once burned himself on an exhaust pipe while waiting for his turn to brush his teeth.

There were two air conditioning units in the house, but Three Pecans was built with a window in every room that linked with a window on the opposite side of the house. Whenever a great wind would come by, it would pass through the entire house and cool everything it touched.

Susanna was in the dining room, setting the plates and silverware onto the table. Matt spotted a plate of sliced bread and was creeping toward it to steal a slice.

"Wash yourselves," Mama said, not looking up from her task.

She may not have greeted them, or even made eye contact, but Mama knew they were there. Mama knew everything that was going on inside and out of the home.

"You're all filthy," Mama said. "Go wash that gunk off before your father gets home."

There was no point arguing. The three boys suffered through their showering, donning pairs of less dirty jeans and almost identical short sleeved collared shirts. In the end it was all for naught.

The three gathered around the table, now fully loaded with food Mama had spent hours preparing. Odd enough, Mama looked like she had not sweated a bead despite standing over a hot stove. In contrast, Susanna constantly patted her forehead with a cloth to swipe away the sweat.

Placed in between the mound of fried chicken and bowl of macaroni and cheese was a pitcher filled to the brim with ice water. The pitcher just sat there, tinkling as the ice clinked against each other. Cool, well water to quench their thirst but just out of reach.

Not one of them dared reach forward to make their plates or even pour a cup of water. Stealing a slice of bread earlier was Matt's only shot at a snack of any kind. That window had shut. Now they waited.

No one said a word. Neither Mama nor Susanna had questions about how the boys' day had gone, nor did they share any interesting news they might have heard on the radio. The boys made no mention of the five-legged calf or the mail they had gathered. Mama had seen the mail on her chair, if not read it already.

Their silence was their combat. Every single one of their stomachs was tightening, even Mamas. Having stolen bites from the fig trees had proven to be the downfall of the boys. Their stomachs had felt the taste of sweet, hunger quenching food, and then it had disappeared. Now it wanted more. The strength they had held while traveling up and down the fields had vanished, all for a fig.

Matt did not know how Mama remained so upright, despite being as hungry as the rest of them. Praying was his best guess.

Matt's mind went down a different path. He thought about football. At first, he wasn't sure why. He didn't play. Papa wouldn't let any of them play. Papa played when he was a boy, then he injured his knee and stopped playing. He still loved the sport, never missed an Aggie home game. Baseball may have been an option for Matt, but baseball leagues were in the summer, and they had to be at the farm in the summer.

Why football? Matt asked himself. Hearne. They had been to Hearne. They had passed by the high school. It was about a month away before the football team began its summer workouts. Hearne was crap at football but people still came out to watch every Friday. The country folk lived for it. Many of them farmers' sons. Some might have a future doing other things. Many would likely end up right there in Hearne working the farms their families worked on or owned. Why football? They probably enjoyed it. That was the logical answer. Yes, the Texas sun threatened to melt them every time they stepped onto the field, but they had fun.

Still, there was that other factor. What if they were really good? What if they were better than anyone else who came through Hearne? What if the farming life was not for them? What if an Aggie scout or someone saw them play football one day and wanted to offer them a scholarship? A chance to go out and accomplish a dream. To carve their own path.

Matt wondered if he was thinking about football anymore.

Regardless, his mind had wandered, and the arms on the clock had continued to tick.

They all sat up at the sound of tires crunching against gravel. It came from the side of the house that sat along the paddock. The familiar roaring and rattling of the diesel engine left no question in the boys' minds that The Mustang had arrived.

Together they listened to the sound of heavy boots traveling from the side gate, through the back lot and up the steps to the side of the porch near the garden. One thud, then another announced that the dirty boots were discarded. The screen door closing and shut told them all that Papa was finally home.

Matt watched as Mama turned her head and glanced at Papa. He was on his way to shower when they locked eyes. The glance said everything. Even Papa had taken too long. They would do the right thing and wait for him to get home, but he would not have the benefit of showering before they ate.

Matt and the boys only prayed that the food would still be warm by the time Papa washed his hands, for he was permitted to do that, and sat down.

Tommy almost slipped up and started to reach for a piece of chicken when Papa finally did join them, but the nightly dance was not done yet. Together, they made the sign of the cross and held hands.

"Bless us, O Lord, and these, Thy gifts, which we are about to receive from Thy bounty," they said in unison. "Through Christ, our Lord. Amen."

They made the sign of the cross again and Papa remarked, "Now we can eat."

...

Everyone went to bed at 10 p.m., but Matt was only allowed a 30-minute nap. While everyone else was fast asleep, he had to prepare to work the night shift. Matt was to get in his truck to go close the wells they had opened earlier that day. Matt would be working until midnight.

One snore, two snores, three snores. Everyone was asleep. Everyone except Papa, who had already left to begin his part of the night shift. He threw off the covers, still dressed and went to put his school shoes on. With the tiniest of steps, Matt made his way out of the house and back toward his truck. After climbing inside he waited. He waited for one particular moment. The Union Pacific Line.

If any of the Ruggirellos were to step outside their door and travel fifty feet to the west, they would be standing on the set of railroad tracks just on the opposite side of the road. At several points during the day, but notably during the night, trains from Union Pacific would blast their horns and blaze down the way.

Their destinations were always a mystery to Matt and the others, but the trains demanded their attention whenever they stormed past. The sound and fury of the train caused the entirety of Three Pecans to rock. At night, the boys enjoyed it. If they managed to sleep through the horn, the rocking of the house would lull them into a deep sleep as if they were still in a crib.

Here, Matt sat in his truck, waiting, fingers clutched tightly around the keys as they sat in the ignition. Off in the distance, he heard the horn. Looking up, he saw the light from the engine shining in his direction.

Within moments, the Union Pacific train zoomed past like it had done every night for as long as Matt had been alive. At the exact moment it passed by Three Pecans, Matt turned the keys and his crusted Ford truck roared to life.

With the train still rattling past, clicking as it crossed over every piece of metal on the track, Matt took his truck onto the highway and just as quickly down the farm roads. Yet Matt did not go straight to the fields to close the wells. His journey took him eastward, over the bridge to cross the Little Brazos River and onto the sloping hill where the Ruggirellos kept one of their cattle pastures.

There, Matt drove the truck till he was right under the hill, nestled beside a set of pine trees. Putting the truck in park, Matt glanced down at the radio dial. He thought for a moment about Tommy, how this was his favorite spot on the entire farm for this exact reason.

Matt turned on the radio and moved the dial to station 550, KTSA San Antonio. The only station in America bringing listeners the Top 55 songs in the country when everyone else only had the Top 40.

That spot was the boys' best kept secret on the farm. Papa was not one to take part in the new era of music. The only thing the radio at home ever had on was the news, not by the children's wishes. The main music Papa and Mama would listen to was at mass. Sometimes if they were driving to Houston for the Livestock Show and someone like Frank Sinatra or Bing Crosby came on, they let the song play. Neither Papa nor Mama would sing along to it, but the fact they let it play at all told the boys they enjoyed the music.

KTSA was a welcome change of pace. The boys stumbled across it four years prior when they were feeding cattle. One of them was fiddling with the dial and all of a sudden, they heard The Beatles, Motown, Creedence Clearwater Revival, all these voices that had only sometimes slipped through the cracks of Papa's censorship.

Josh didn't care for it, but Matt and Tommy gravitated toward the station. It was the main reason Matt had started collecting 8-track tapes.

When Matt turned on the station, "Sugar, Sugar" by The Archies was playing. Matt sighed and turned the volume down so that the music was only a faint whisper in the background.

Matt was not up there to listen to music. He needed a calm place to think.

With hesitation he glanced at the glove box and the letters that lay inside it. Letters that had been addressed to him and him alone. Each one had gold-like lettering written across the surface. On all six of the letters was a seal on the top right corner that indicated it was an official letter from a university or college.

SMU, TCU, Rice, Baylor, Texas, and Texas A&M had all sent letters addressed to Matt. Each one contained the same subject: National Merit Scholar Program. The letters contained details on scholarships of varying sizes but all extreme amounts. All four-year scholarships.

Matt did not know how to fathom what he was reading. Outside of A&M, these were schools he had only heard of but never thought he would have the option of attending. He knew nothing about the schools except what their football teams had done that previous season.

He knew Papa would never consider any of this. A&M. It was always A&M. That's where Papa went to school, that's where Uncle Andrew went to school. Everyone in the Bottom had gone to A&M. Yet that was not the first thing to cross Matt's mind. He realized that was the case, and he pushed past it.

Again and again, Matt read over the details of the letters, comparing what each school had to offer. It gave him a thrill. He was being courted. But he knew he needed to find out more information.

Then another thought came to mind that did frighten him. The clerk had mentioned in passing that more letters were likely on the way. The ones Matt held in his hands were already offering a lot of money. He wondered who else might be wanting his signature.

JOSH

"I done told you all we wanted was some new tires for the tractors," Papa said. "It'll be picking season before we know it and I don't want my hands driving around with tires about to burst."

"I know, I know," Mr. Sullivan said.

Sullivan was the manager of a John Deere dealer outside of Bryan that the Ruggirellos went to for all their equipment. Sometimes this was to purchase a new plow, other times to just replace spare parts. These were days Papa always dreaded.

Papa always used his equipment until the last possible instance. Why? Because Sullivan was known to be difficult when it came to prices. Papa won every fight for a better deal, Sullivan always got frightened when a customer threatened to walk away.

Still, a trip to Sullivan's was never a short ordeal. On top of being difficult with giving them what they came there to get, he always tried to sell them something extra.

"But while I have you here, we just got a new supply of all-terrain vehicles," Sullivan added.

"I can see them with my own eyes," Papa said, glancing to his right at the line of trucks, tractors and trailers as well as the three wheeled all-terrain vehicles.

"I'm telling you, Paul, they're the thing of the future," Sullivan continued. "I see that truck of yours. It looks like it'll explode any minute."

"I'll tell ya, that truck of mine's seen me through the last fifteen years," Papa said.

"It's still gonna break down one day. When it does, you'll need an ATV ready to take you around the fields to keep watch on everyone while you find time to get a new tractor."

"What you want, is for me to buy a thing that I'll use possibly once in ten years. Let's say I do. Then I'll have to buy one of those attachable trailers to help carry supplies to and from the fields."

"Well, you'd want one designed for the ATV."

"Sullivan, if the day comes where I'll need an ATV, I'll come buy an ATV. But right now, I came to look at tires and that's the one thing I don't see in front of me."

Sullivan puffed his lips and breathed out through his teeth. This was the same face that Sullivan made every time he knew he failed to finish a deal.

With a wave of his hand, Sullivan called for one of his employees to take Papa around the shop to take a look at the tractor tires. These were not simple tires either. Not round pieces of rubber that any rascal could roll down the street. These were hulking behemoths that drove the cotton pickers during the most important parts of the year. If one of them was to fall on a person, nothing but mush would be left behind.

Josh had been standing by The Mustang for the entirety of Papa's discussion with Sullivan. Josh did not think Papa had a sadistic side to him, but he did notice how willing Papa was to start a conversation with Sullivan.

Every time they came to the shop, Papa would walk right up to the man and ask how he was doing. Sullivan would answer and then immediately go into his sales pitch. Now Papa bought something more often than he didn't, but it was never what Sullivan was pitching him or for the price Sullivan was asking for.

Today's incident, in particular, made him think about all the times Papa and Sullivan got into debates. Josh knew Papa was not about to buy any tires that day, nor was he going to place an order in advance for a new set.

Papa had only gone to the shop at the behest of Nonno, who himself relayed a message from Big Jake that some of the tires looked like they were starting to wear.

"Joshua, wait by the truck," Papa said as he walked off. "Only take a minute."

Josh knew it was going to be longer than a minute. Not one of the Ruggirellos was ever on time, extended family included. The mindset was, dinner is set for 7:30, eat at 8. Why? Well, it can't start without them.

Even if it wasn't for their untimeliness, Josh could easily see Papa toying with these people. Inspecting every tire they had in stock before up and deciding he was not going to buy anything that day.

So, Josh remained by the truck, leaning against the side and crossing his boots so that he looked like James Dean on the poster for *Giant*. Josh would've been fully content to remain there, standing in the heat with nothing but his crusted Aggie cap to keep the sun out of his face. By that point, a nice trickle of sweat was running down the back of his neck and cooling his entire body.

Then he heard the sound of boots against gravel and looked up to see Sullivan approaching him. Josh had no interest in speaking to the man, but did lift his cap to better see his acquaintance.

"Joshua, if I heard right," Sullivan said, extending his hand as he approached.

"Josh, that's what my brothers call me," Josh said as he shook Sullivan's hand. "Rest of my family calls me Joshua."

"Yes, yes. Like one does."

Josh nodded his head and kicked a rock off into the distance.

"Yes, I thought you had brothers," Sullivan said. "Where are the other two? Thought the three of you were inseparable."

"Papa sent Matt off to the co-op to purchase some feed," Josh said.

"Cattle feed?"

"Cattle feed. Horse grits. Stuff for the pigs, though I'm not really sure what they eat."

"Pigs eat anything."

"That's my point. So what do you buy pigs to eat if they'll eat anything? Can't just feed 'em shit if we're going to eat 'em eventually. Pardon my curse."

"No offense taken. So, why're you here and not with them?"

The incident had happened just the previous day. Papa had ordered a crop dusting on the Travis Farm and had sent the boys to the field in order to signal where the pilot was to fly. Some farmers in the Bottom would order a crop dusting without supervising the flyby, only to come home and find the pesticides sprayed in every spot imaginable except where they were supposed to go.

Matt, Josh, and Tommy all stood in different spots on the field and held flares when it was time to signal the flyby. When it was Josh's turn, he went a little off script. He held his flare and waved it to signal the pilot to fly by, but he took his time in getting out of the way. Josh stood there, staring down the rickety vessel as it came down from the heavens like a fighter jet on an attack run. He could hear Matt and Tommy shouting for him to get out of the way, but Josh would not move.

Josh waited until the crop duster was right above his head and the pesticides were ejecting into the air before stepping aside and watching as the plane continued its flight. He felt like he had run a mile.

"Papa didn't take the news lightly," Josh continued. "He won't say it's the reason, but he's got me lagging behind today for that little stunt. Doesn't want to take his eyes off me. It's whatever."

"Yeah, guess it's best to do what Papa says," Sullivan said.

Sullivan looked off at the distance for a moment. Josh could feel a sales pitch was coming.

"I heard that there's an entire lot of broken-down cars just sitting at the back of your farmhouse," Sullivan said.

"Sort of," Josh replied. "Now that Papa's running the Home Farm, he's let all the broken-down cars start to pile up. Nonno would have tossed them all years ago, but I guess it doesn't bother him."

"Any reason why it's just piled up?"

"Papa always says he's going to fix them. A car breaks down, 'Don't get rid of it. We'll fix it.' Then an entire year passes and the car is now covered in weeds and rusted and beyond all measure of repair. Worth absolutely nothing when Papa could've gotten a quick buck if he'd just given up on them."

"So, your father's always been cheap?"

Josh paused before replying, cocking his head at Sullivan.

"I don't think I like that word," he responded. "Papa remembers when he had nothing. He doesn't like to give up on something the first time its use has run out. Has the lot behind home become cluttered with cars, trucks, and tractors from the last three decades? Of course. But that shouldn't take away from the fact Papa wanted to try."

Sullivan took a step back with his hands in the air.

"I stand corrected," Sullivan said.

Josh blew hot air out of his nose.

"Though if your family ever gets in the spirit of cleaning up the joint, you could be sitting on a fortune," Sullivan said. "Yes, maybe some of it's only good for scrap metal, but there are collectors out there. Someone in town might be interested in a broken-down Model T, if they might be able to refurbish it."

"Well, there ain't no Model T, not that I can remember at least," Josh said.

"Well, there's bound to be something. You said cars from the last three decades."

"Yeah, that's true. Plenty of Ford trucks you don't see on the highway anymore. A couple of them definitely are from before the war. Some International Harvesters, Chevrolets, Oldsmobiles, Cadillacs, Mama's always loved Cadillacs. No foreign cars like Volkswagens or anything like that."

"Your daddy don't like foreign cars?"

"I can't imagine what use Papa would have for a '67 convertible Volkswagen Beetle in a place like Mumford."

"You sound like you know your cars."

Josh surrendered a grin.

"You could say that. I pick up an issue of *Autoweek* every now and then when we go to the grocer. They write good stuff."

"That's good to know about cars. Can't be taking your daddy's hand-me-downs all your life. Got a dream car?"

Josh paused to think for a moment. A part of him was surprised he was actually having a conversation with Sullivan, or at least being responsive to his quick-fire questions. The other half was sifting through the memory files of what he had been reading in the most recent issue of *Autoweek*.

He squinted as sun got into his eyes, questioning how much longer he wanted to tolerate speaking with Sullivan. Then again, Josh never shied away from talking about cars.

"I'd have to say a Shelby Mustang," Josh answered. "They just had photos of the latest models. Bright blue with white racing stripes. Clean as a whistle. The Thunderbird has a cool sounding name, but doesn't even come close."

"Hey, you'll probably end up driving one someday the way you're talking about it," Sullivan said.

"Nah, that ain't happening."

"Sure. There might not be a dealership in Mumford, but if you go up to Waco or down to Houston, I'm sure they've got 'em."

"People in Houston got money. No way Papa would ever spend money on a sports car. And if I had money for one, I don't think I could justify the expense."

"You're young, boy, there's no telling where you'll be in fifteen, twenty years."

"What are you, a fortune teller now?"

Sullivan just threw his hands up. Josh peered past him, wondering just how long Papa was going to spend bullshitting about tires he was not going to buy.

"What about Jeeps?" Sullivan asked.

"Jeeps? What would we do with a Jeep?" Josh asked.

"Not sure. Just thought I'd mention it. I've recently come into possession of a 1945 Jeep. The exact same model they used during the war but this one never saw action. It's in perfect condition."

"Ah. Well, I'm sure that's exciting."

"Yeah. I'm a bit of a collector myself. I like to collect memorabilia from the war. I already own a Colt .45 pistol, an M1 Carbine. Been trying to get my hands on a Thompson, but just haven't had any luck."

"I don't know anything about guns."

"No, no, I'm just talking. But I've got the Jeep and a General Motors truck, all Army issued. I've also got a motorcycle like the one Steve McQueen rode in *The Great Escape*. I go nuts for that stuff."

Steve McQueen did look awesome racing through the Austrian countryside, Josh thought. At first, he couldn't imagine having one himself. Then again, Josh thought it would be one hell of a rush riding one.

By this point, Papa was returning. As Josh had predicted, Papa announced that he would not be buying any tires that day. They'd be back when they needed to buy tires, but would not bite on Sullivan's proposal to debate the price right then and there.

Papa climbed into The Mustang but Sullivan had a quick word with Josh before he left.

"If you ever find the time to get rid of those cars, just let me know."

Josh gave Sullivan a thumbs-up and climbed inside the truck with Papa before the two of them sped off down the road.

They drove in complete silence for nearly the entire trip back to the farm. That was their way. Papa was not one for small talk. Josh had no interest in talking about the crops or the cattle. If he had tried to talk about cars, Papa would have held up his hand and gone, "That's enough of that." So, Josh settled for silence.

On the way back to the farm, they passed the gas station run by Mr. Woodyard. Woodyard was a simple man with a long face. Having sold what little land he owned decades ago, he had set up a gas station at the intersection between the farm-to-market roads on the way to Bryan. It was a simple, easy living. Most of his business was on Saturdays during the fall when the farmers drove into College Station to watch the Aggies play. Even then, it wasn't to get gas but to use the restroom or to buy candy.

Josh spotted the gas station coming up around the bend and a thought came to his head.

"Papa, can you stop up ahead real quick?" Josh asked.

"What for?" Papa asked.

"I've got to take a piss."

"You can't hold it a bit longer?"

"I've been holding it. Held it while I let Sullivan talk my ear off and while you were looking at tires. So, can we please just stop?"

Josh made sure not to take an accusatory tone with Papa. He knew he could never undermine Papa's decisions. He had to talk to him like an adult, with reason to his claims. Yes, he was trying to shame Papa for taking too long with the tires, but he could not say so outright.

As they pulled up to Mr. Woodyard's, Josh all but flew out of The Mustang and sprinted inside the shop.

That night, the boys helped themselves to a serving of hamburgers and green beans at the dinner table. At night, the three boys retreated into their rooms. Susanna stayed in her room until she was ready for bed. Tommy took the time to open up his chest of Matchbox and Hot Wheels toy cars. One by one he would pull them out, roll them between his fingers and then roll them across the floor as if they were real vehicles that come to life.

The cars were by far Tommy's most prized possessions. He had made a knack for talking Nonno into buying him one every time they went to the grocer. Nonno liked to spoil Tommy whenever he got the chance. Regardless, they were easy gifts for the baby of the family.

Josh waltzed into the room, uninvited and unannounced. He stood in the doorway, leaning against the frame as he looked down at Tommy.

"What?" Tommy asked, looking up at Josh.

"What was it you bet me? A Dodge Charger?"

"Yeah."

Without warning, Josh tossed a piece of rectangular plastic right into Tommy's lap. The shock caused him to drop whatever Chevrolet or Ford model he had been holding. They rolled to a halt against the wall as Tommy picked up the piece of plastic in his lap.

It was another HotWheels set. Sure enough, a Dodge Charger. It even had a picture of Steve McQueen on the front, even though it was the bad guy who drove a Charger in *Bullitt*, not Steve McQueen.

Tommy smiled up at Josh. Josh just saluted his brother and went off to his room. He made good on his debt.

TOMMY

Diamond, the family dog, was in a shouting match with the old white bull when Tommy returned to Three Pecans one afternoon. The boys had been given light assignments that day, driving around the fields before being sent to the paddock to feed the horses. Tommy got the benefit of going home early by virtue of being younger than the rest of them and still growing accustomed to working in the heat.

The old white bull acted like the guardian of Three Pecans. He remained inside the yard, so he did not actually reside in Three Pecans, but he kept a watchful eye on every truck, tractor, and train that passed in front of his view. No one entered without him knowing about it.

No one on the farm knew for sure how old the bull was. Some said he was twelve years old, others as old as twenty. He was always a titan on the field and had sired many heifers. Even as he had grown old and lost his ability to walk, he was still a Goliath of an animal, despite being a glorified watchdog.

The veterinarians had told Papa it would have been better to slaughter the bull, now that he had lost his usage and his knees could not carry his weight. For whatever reason, Papa could not bring himself to put the old bull down.

For the past year, the old bull spent parts of its days in shouting contests with Diamond. Whether they were having an actual conversation, or just screaming at each other, Tommy was not sure. But it was still a funny sight.

Diamond only barked at the old bull for as long as it took Tommy to reach the entrance gate. Once Diamond caught sight of him, he immediately ran to the fence and stood on his back legs so that he could lick Tommy's face from the opposite side.

Diamond had come into the Ruggirello's lives three years prior. Tommy had been riding with Papa one day when they spotted a cardboard box out near the Vitale Farm. Upon inspecting it, they found a puppy with fluffy orange and white fur and the largest smile you ever did see.

From that day on, he became part of the farm. With a few conditions. Papa made it clear that the dog would never step inside the house, that it was the boys' responsibility — by that, he meant it was Tommy's responsibility — to watch over the dog, feed it, and keep it clean. Moreover, when the dog died, Tommy would be responsible for burying it.

Tommy agreed to it right then and there in the carriage of The Mustang. The dog licked his hands every time Tommy ran his fingers through his fur. From day one, there was no doubt the dog belonged to Tommy.

He named the dog Diamond for the diamond-shaped patch of fur that rested between his shoulder blades. For three years he fed the dog, used his work money to buy dog food, washed the dog, and trimmed his fur whenever it got full of burrs or too bushy. Only during the winter, when the roads tended to freeze over, did Tommy let Diamond's fur grow to a perfect puff.

It was on their first trip to the veterinarian, when they had Diamond neutered, that the vet told the Ruggirello's that Diamond was a Great Pyrenees. A Spanish mountain dog. How such an animal ended up in Mumford, no one could say for certain, but the vet determined Diamond was a pure breed. Very valuable.

It took time for Tommy to train Diamond. He had the extra task of forcing a puppy to grow up, but eventually Diamond became loyal to the Ruggirellos. He would spend his days chasing bugs in the yard and barking at the old white bull, and in the nights, he would sleep on the porch as if it was his own bed.

They kept Diamond within the fenced area of Three Pecans. There was early discussion to keep Diamond at Terrano, the pasture the Ruggirellos owned near Benchley, to keep an eye on the cattle. Some thought if he was bred to guard sheep, maybe the same would work with cattle. That was a failed experiment.

So, inside the fences he remained, sprinting back and forth and around the sides of the house numerous times in a day. Mama was the one who argued for keeping him in the fences rather than the yard or with the cattle. She had seen too many dogs get run over on the highway.

When Diamond stood on his hind legs, he was almost an entire foot taller than Tommy. More often than not, Tommy would find himself knocked to the ground and covered by licks from Diamond. No one would ever come to Tommy's aid. Well, no human. It was the old white bull that would bray at the two of them when it thought Diamond had gone too far. Or at least that's what it appeared to be doing.

Each time the bull would bray, Diamond would jump off of Tommy, run to the bull and bark in its face.

"Having fun out there," Susanna called from the top of the porch.

Tommy rolled onto his side to look up at her. Susanna was standing there with a white cloth, polishing a pair of black shoes. Mama's shoes were his best guess.

"Only a little," Tommy said, turning back to look at Diamond, who was now sitting across from the white bull and wagging his tail. "I need to cut his hair."

"What was that?" Susanna asked, not clearly hearing him.

"His fur," Tommy said, speaking up. "Look at him."

At that moment, Diamond began scratching behind his ears and without a moment's pause rolled onto his back and rolled around in the grass.

"He's dying in this heat," Tommy said.

"And he's got fleas again," Susanna said. "I'd worry more about that than anything else. You let one of those fleas jump onto Mama and you'll never hear the end of it."

Tommy just sighed. "Well, only one thing to do."

Tommy stepped up onto the porch and walked to his bedroom window. Sliding it open, he reached inside and pulled out two strips of bacon from the pouch by his bed. By now, they were hard and crusted, but Diamond still loved them.

It took all of five seconds for Tommy to wave the strip of bacon in the air, for Diamond to halt all movement, turn, and notice the strip in his hand. Had Tommy kept his hand in the air, Diamond would have leapt seven feet off the ground in order to seize the crusted, savory meat. Tommy didn't give him the chance. Instead, he knelt down, so that he was at Diamond's height and let the dog seize the bacon.

With Tommy's other hand now gripped firm around the fur of Diamond's neck, for he did not wear a collar, he led him around to the back of the house with the allure of the second strip of bacon. Diamond figured out what was happening at one point and went limp. Such a big dog was so easily afraid of water and scissors.

Within minutes, he had Diamond chained to the back of the house. Tommy began clipping off as many chunks of hair as he could grab either with his hands or with the comb. The Ruggirellos had been smart enough to buy a pair of clippers solely for the dog, so there was no risk of excess fur from Diamond ending up in the kitchen when someone had to cut open a bag of flour.

Diamond would attempt to casually walk away every time Tommy stopped cutting, but Tommy would always pull him back with the chain. Diamond did not struggle when Tommy pulled him back. It was as if his walking away was his reminder that he did not agree with what Tommy was doing.

Once all the clipping was done, Tommy hosed Diamond down from head to toe with the hose. A cold stream of water can be refreshing on a hot summer day, especially in 90-degree heat. But Diamond looked miserable as his great poof of fur slumped against his body looking like he was made of aluminum foil.

Tommy went over Diamond again with the comb and this time, the dog glanced at him sideways as if to say, "How could you do this to me, Friend?"

"Sorry, pal," Tommy said as he continued brushing him with the comb. "But you're going to feel so much better once this is done."

At that moment the old white bull brayed, as if he was mocking Diamond, or in revenge for whatever Diamond had been shouting earlier.

Once the combing was done, Tommy poured the dish soap over Diamond's back and went about rubbing it in as many places as possible.

This was the one part Diamond enjoyed. Tommy and his soapy fingers ran all over Diamond's body until he was a soapy white mess. Diamond still tried to put up a stoic face. Standing tall, refusing to pant, not making eye contact. What gave him away was his tail. Every time Tommy would start, his tail would begin to wag. Slowly at first, then faster and faster.

"Yeah, you enjoy this, you can't hide it," Tommy said as he continued to rub. "You're gonna be all nice and clean now."

At that moment, Diamond started to pant. Even though it was probably from the heat, it always looked like he was smiling.

Susanna came around the porch just as Tommy was hosing the soap off of Diamond's back. Tommy looked up and saw she had a towel in her hand.

"Told Mama what you were doing," Susanna said. "Told me to bring you a towel."

"For the dog or for me?" Tommy asked.

"For the dog, obviously. You think a towel's going to clean all that gunk off of you? Don't think that soap is gonna get rid of your stink."

"Yeah, whatever."

Tommy continued hosing down the dog, being slapped in the face multiple times by water when Diamond would attempt to dry himself by shaking left and right. Susanna also got splashed, so she eagerly handed Tommy the towel to dry Diamond off. It did not completely dry Diamond, but it did enough for the sun to finish the job. Once Tommy was finished, he rewarded Diamond with the second strip of bacon he had taken from his room.

Tommy wagered he had cut ten pounds of hair off Diamond's body, because when he untied him from the chain, Diamond sprinted off in the distance at a speed only seen when Diamond had received a haircut.

To their annoyance, the dog also started rubbing the side of his head against the grass and dirt. The clean version of Diamond lasted all of ten seconds before there was once again mud and dirt trapped behind his ears and in the neck of his fur.

Once Diamond was done rubbing himself down, he ran over to the old white bull. From the other side of the house, Tommy and Susanna listened as Diamond barked at the bull and the old bull brayed back.

"All that work," Susanna said.

"Yup," Tommy replied. "He'll have fleas again by the end of the month. I'll just have to wash him again."

Tommy smiled up at Susanna before taking a seat on the porch.

"Have you talked to Matt at all?" Susanna asked.

"I talk with him every day," Tommy replied.

"That's not what I meant."

"Well, can you be more specific?"

"Like has he said if anything's wrong."

Tommy was puzzled by this question.

"No. He's been normal."

"He's not been quiet?"

"Matt's always quiet."

"Well, quieter?"

"Why all the questions? Who's wanting to know this?"

Susanna sighed, taking a seat in the rocking chair on the back porch.

"Mama's being inquisitive," Susanna answered. "She think's Matt's been awful quiet the last few days."

"Well, can't say I've noticed anything peculiar," Tommy said.

"Mama thinks there's something on Matt's mind he hasn't said."

"Has Mama thought about asking him herself?"

"If you think you or I are capable of giving Mama orders, you don't know our mother."

Susanna paused as she rocked back and forth in her chair.

"Those Dodge boys were here earlier today," Susanna continued.

"Who's that?" Tommy asked.

"You know, those no-good brothers from Hearne. The ones Matt ran off with that one night."

Tommy was too young to remember the night in question, but Mama was quick to bring up the Dodge boys whenever he or his brothers got into mischief. The Dodge boys were a pair of jocks. Matt had a knack for making friends with jocks. Matt would have played baseball with them had it not been for the farm work, but during school days he could talk with them for hours about sports.

Matt considered them friends, but they were not equals in the classroom. The Dodge boys were the kind of folk who would spend their entire life in the confines of Hearne. They may have been conscious of this fact as they made an effort to have as many parties as they could organize. Matt only went to one such gathering, but he never heard the end of it.

Matt led Mama and Papa to believe he was going to a pep rally before Hearne's first football game of the season. He had claimed pressure to go as it was his first year at the school. However, as it got deeper into the night, and Matt still hadn't come home, the Ruggirellos became concerned about his whereabouts.

When Papa drove into Hearne to find Matt, he learned there had been no pep rally. They were celebrating before the first game of the season, but they did so with a pasture party in one of the neighboring pastures. Several teens scattered at the sight of Papa lumbering through the grass, but he didn't bother with anyone else. At least not after he set eyes on the Oldsmobile.

There, he found Matt all groggy, with an empty bottle of Jack Daniels in the back seat.

The following day, they made Matt drink glass after glass of water until he was sick to his stomach. Matt never wanted to look at a bottle of alcohol after that. It may have been a one-time incident, but it kept Matt on the straight path ever since.

Matt didn't get his car back until the next summer.

"They wanted to talk to Matt, but I told him he wasn't here," Susanna said. "Also told them to scatter before Mama caught sight of them and told Papa. It did the trick."

"So that's why Mama's thinks something's going on?" Tommy asked.

"No, she had that thought before. But this didn't help anything."

"Well, I don't know if anything's going on with Matt. Simple as that."

At that moment, they heard Diamond barking again. It was the type of bark that alerted someone had pulled up to the house. Distinct from the bark of a truck that had sped off down the highway, or even the one Diamond used to speak with the old bull. It caused both Tommy and Susanna to stand up.

"It might be worth asking," Susanna said before heading toward the front porch.

It was Uncle Andrew. He had driven with his Chevy truck and parked right in front of Three Pecans. He stepped out of the truck with a small gray sack in his left hand, the sides covered with tiny black patches.

Tommy could not confirm this, but he was certain that Uncle Andrews' truck was twice the size of The Mustang or any of Papa's Fords.

Uncle Andrew stepped out of his truck, wearing his almost trademark white cowboy hat, and waved to Tommy and Susanna.

"Howdy," Uncle Andrew said with a smile.

Diamond barked again, this time at the sight of another ten-year-old boy walking around from the opposite side of the truck. It was Uncle Andrew's son, also named Andrew, but who everyone called Andy in order to distinguish the two. It was just one example of how Sicilians are too accustomed to recycling names.

Diamond had gone right up to the fence and was standing up in order to receive pets from both Uncle Andrew and Andy. Tommy and Susanna went up to greet them.

"What the heck are you doing here?" Tommy asked Andy from the opposite side of the fence.

"I could ask you the same thing," Andy replied. "Don't see your brothers or daddy hanging around here. Ain't you supposed to be workin?"

"Why ain't you out in the fields?"

"I'm with my daddy."

"That ain't no excuse. Coulda ridden with somebody."

"Whatever. Why you smell like wet dog, anyway?"

"You don't see the wet dog right in front of you?"

Only then did Andy stop and see the freshly clipped Diamond, now covered in mud but with a much thinner coat of fur.

Susanna beat Uncle Andrew to his question, telling him that Mama was napping and Papa was still out in the fields. Uncle

42

Andrew said he'd wait at the Big House as he needed to talk to Papa about something.

"What about?" Susanna asked.

"Well, I'd best wait to talk to him about it before I give all the details," Uncle Andrew said. "But it does have to do with what's in this here sack."

"You find gold?"

"Hah. If Id've found gold, I sure wish I wouldn't need your daddy's second opinion to tell me what I found."

"What is in the sack?" Tommy asked, taking a momentary pause from his back and forth with Andy.

Uncle Andrew paused for a moment. Looked into the sack, looked back at Tommy and Susanna with a coy smile.

"Ah, what the hell," he said. "A little peek won't hurt."

Uncle Andrew opened the sack and the two of them looked inside. In the sack was ten to twelve black rocks, all cubic shaped with jagged edges. They looked like any other rock someone might find on the riverbed in the Brazos, except they were jet black.

"What's so special about a bunch of rocks?" Tommy asked.

"Maybe nothing," Uncle Andrew said. "But give them a feel."

Doing as he was told, Tommy reached down and picked up one of the rocks. It was about the size of his palm, jet black, crusty, as if someone had stuck their hand in the ground and ripped it from the earth. What Tommy noticed was that the rock was shiny. It shined and there was a sticky coat around its entirety. It was gross and made Tommy want to put it back as quickly as possible.

"They're sticky," Tommy said.

"Exactly," Uncle Andrew said. "Made me confused as well when I first noticed it. Every single one of them has that same coating."

"You think Papa might know what it is?" Susanna asked.

"Well, it's more a prayer than a hope," Uncle Andrew said. "But I thought I'd check with Paul before I go running off to ask some stranger. I have my thoughts on what it might be, but I wanted to run it by him, too. Who better can we trust than our brothers, right, Tommy?"

Tommy just smiled and nodded to Uncle Andrew's proposition. It was true. When Tommy was hurting or having trouble at school, he always went to Matt or Josh before he went to Mama.

Susanna invited Uncle Andrew to come inside while they waited for Papa to come home. Given that it was a Saturday, there was hope that he would be back at a reasonable hour. Still, Papa always seemed to find something needed to be done, something needing to be fixed during his rounds of the farms.

Uncle Andrew had also brought a sack of potatoes for Nonna.

Regardless, Uncle Andrew gave the sack to Andy and told him to give it to Nonna. Tommy decided to tag along. He met the two of them at the gate to the garden, held it open for Uncle Andrew and then closed it as he stepped into the garden with Andy. He made sure to be quick to keep Diamond from getting out.

The garden acted as a pathway between Three Pecans and the Big House. It was Nonna's favorite thing—the joys of being able to look out her kitchen window and see any number of grandchildren sprinting toward her house.

As Tommy and Andy stepped past a series of carrots, tomatoes, cabbage, lettuce, and an assortment of peppers that filled the garden, they came across one of the fig trees. With an enormous grin on his face, Andy reached up to pull one of the figs off of the branches. Within moments, he would have had the thing stuffed into his face and all the sweetness sucked out, had it not been for Tommy elbowing him in the side.

Andy was about to say a word his parents would not have taken lightly to him saying, then he saw what Tommy was pointing at. With the fiercest of glares, Nonna was staring at them from her kitchen window.

44

THE BOYS IN THE BRAZOS RIVER BOTTOM

Regardless of whether she was cleaning plates or washing vegetables, she was looking at them the entire way. Andy knew he was caught and no figs were to be in his future. So, they marched on.

For a few steps, neither one said a word. Then Andy spoke.

"My dad's gonna be rich."

"Huh?" Tommy asked, more than a little confused.

"You heard me, my dad's going to be rich. We're going to be rich."

"And what makes you say that?"

"The rocks."

"What about 'em?"

"I heard Daddy talking with some of the Aggies that work for him."

Uncle Andrew always seemed to have a flow of both current students and recent graduates from A&M to help work the 1,500 acres he was responsible for.

"They think those rocks have something to do with oil," Andy continued.

"Oil?" Tommy asked.

"Yeah. Those rocks were just a handful from a whole area they found on Daddy's land. They crushed some of them with a hammer and all that was left was this thick black liquid. That sticky stuff you felt, that's just bits of what's inside leaking out."

"Did it smell like diesel?"

"Nah, ya idiot, it's oil. They've got to send it to some factory to turn it into diesel."

"I ain't no idiot. You just talk too much. Either way, that don't mean it's oil just cause it's a black liquid."

"What other type of black liquid you know about?"

Tommy stopped himself as they were walking up the sloped driveway toward the Big House's side entrance. He turned so that he was facing Andy.

"What difference does it make if it's oil or not?" Tommy said. "It ain't going to change anything."

"Horseshit, yes it would," Andy replied. "If it isn't oil and just some funky rocks my Daddy found, nobody gets hurt. But what if it is oil, and there's a mountain of it underneath the farm? If word spreads of that, there's going to be a lot of people wanting to pay our family for that oil."

"You're talking about a bunch of strangers coming onto our land and making trouble. I can't see Papa ever agreeing to something like that."

"You don't think he'd want that money?"

"I don't know. Papa has always preached about being grateful for what we have. Everything we got is what the family has earned. So, I don't know how Papa would react."

"If there's a mountain of oil on our land, that sounds like a blessing, if you ask me."

Andy then walked past Tommy and the two of them soon found themselves standing in Nonna's kitchen. From the moment they stepped inside, their eyes started to burn with the searing pain that only arises when onions are being cut. Remembering not to rub their eyes with their fingers, they blinked furiously and grabbed the nearest cloth to dab their closed eyelids.

"Serves you right for trying to eat a fig before dinner," Nonna said as she continued to chop away at her onion.

Nonna may have only been five-foot-four, but when she spoke, the family listened. She made a habit of jabbing her long fingernails into the backs of the children whenever someone misbehaved. It got their attention right quick.

She stood there at the kitchen island, now with her back turned to the window, continuing to chop the onions.

"Sorry, Nonna," the two of them said through tear-filled eyes.

Nonna looked over at the both of them. She looked at them standing there, looking like a miserable pair of sponges that were shriveling up under the sun.

"Alright you two, looks like you've suffered enough," Nonna said. "Come over here and give me a kiss."

The two grandchildren did as they were told.

"Come vai nipoti?" Nonna asked.

"Cosi cosi," Tommy replied.

"Bueno," Andy said.

"That's Spanish, Andrea," Nonna said. "We all must speak English, but don't mistake the two languages."

"Sorry, Nonna," Andy said. "What can I say, we hear more Spanish nowadays from the hands."

"Uh huh," was all Nonna replied.

It didn't take long for Nonna to put them to work. She still needed to chop the garlic and the celery. Stepping onto a pair of stools, Tommy and Andy got to work. They chopped their respective vegetables into the tiniest pieces possible, so small that once it was all added together in the pot, they would dissolve into the sauce.

That's what they were making, the Ruggirello family suga, a secret recipe to all those whose families did not come from Poggioreale, Sicily. In the pot, it would look like any other red sauce someone might buy in jars at the market, but the taste and the smell were unique to the creations of that one specific family.

Suga was a sauce best cooked slow. The more time it had to cook, the stronger, the better the taste would be. That's why they were making the suga an entire day before it was going to be used for a dish.

Tomorrow was Sunday dinner, the one time the vast majority of the family was all in one place. They needed a lot of suga.

Nonna got them to work so fast that Andy almost forgot to drop off the sack of potatoes.

JUNE 1969

MATT

Sunday may have been the day of rest, but that was in word only.

Each one of the Ruggirellos was still up at 6 a.m. every Sunday morning. Papa was up by five. Everyone had to be clean for Sunday mass, and they only had the one shower.

Matt wondered if Papa ever slept. They sometimes heard him snoring at night. There were some nights they could hear him shuffling on the wrap-around porch in his heavy-footed way. He was always up before everyone else, always showered and shaved. On Sundays, he went the extra mile of combing over his quickly thinning head of hair, given one could not wear hats in Church.

Regardless, by the time Matt and the others awoke, Papa was already fully dressed. His navy blazer was hanging on the coat rack and he was sitting back in his chair, reading the paper.

Even with how early Papa woke up, Mama was not far behind. Once Mama had showered, which was not a quick affair, it was a mad dash to see which child could get into the bathroom the fastest. There was no line established by birth order. If Matt slipped up and Tommy beat him into the shower, there was nothing he could do about it.

Regardless, the word of the day was cleanliness. During the week, they would have been seen covered in dirt, manure, possibly blood, and any number of pesticides, but on Sundays, they were to be as clean as a freshly washed baby.

The boys all were dressed like miniature versions of Papa. They wore white button-down dress shirts with either a red or maroon tie to strangle around their necks. They wore dress shoes that always cut against their ankles because they only wore them once a week and never had the chance to break them in.

Papa wore suit pants, but the boys were allowed to wear tan khakis that made the lower half of their bodies almost disappear in the sunlight. Tommy was still in the stage where he begged to wear his cowboy boots, the ones not used for work, but Mama would hear nothing of it.

Mama and Susanna wore identical white dresses, paired with white gloves and white hats that more or less sat on their heads rather than cover them. The only black part of their outfits was their shoes.

Normally, Matt would have shot out of his bed and gone directly to the shower. His body was already accustomed to waking up after Papa and Mama had showered and he always just managed to beat out his siblings. It was not to be the case that day.

When Matt awoke, his bedside lamp was still shining and a barrage of letters and papers were sitting on his chest. It was Diamond's barking that woke him up, never a good sign. Matt immediately saw that the sun was starting to rise outside and saw that the clock at his bedside table read 6:30.

"Shit," Matt said under his breath, still afraid to let either of his parents hear him cursing.

Matt immediately got up, stuffed all the envelopes and papers underneath his bedsheets and retrieved his Sunday clothes without ever taking a momentary pause. When he came into the living room, Papa and Mama were sitting in their chairs waiting for the children to finish washing.

In the bathroom, Josh was brushing his teeth and was all but fully dressed. Tommy was standing in the doorway waiting with his towel, meaning Susanna was already in the shower. There was

52

nothing Matt could do but lean against the side of the wall and wait for his turn.

Being the last person to shower meant Matt did not have time to wash as thoroughly as all the others. For whatever reason, the Ruggirellos insisted on attending 9 a.m. mass at St. Joseph's in Bryan. The same church offered masses at noon, 2 and 5 p.m., but none of those suited the Ruggirellos. They always wanted to hear God's words at the earliest available service.

As shown by their furious washing, mass was arguably the most important event in the Ruggirello family. So important, that they were not about to waste ninety minutes of cleaning themselves by climbing inside The Mustang. Instead, they took Mama's Cadillac.

The 1960 model was a Papa's ten-year wedding anniversary gift to Mama, something she could feel excited about driving, rather than be towed back and forth from town to farm in one of Nonno's old Fords.

Papa had to take the train to Detroit to pick it up and drive it back down. He later said it was a miserable traveling experience to be so far away.

The model looked like all other Cadillacs, long as hell, with pieces on the rear that looked like shark fins. Mama's was cloud white, and she made a commitment to having it washed every two weeks to get rid of all the dust and bugs that splatter on the windshield when driving between Bryan and Mumford.

The Cadillac is what they drove to Kyle Field on Saturdays to watch the Aggies play. Mama's car had the strongest radio and could pick up the Aggie broadcast in case they were late to the game, which happened more than regularly.

Despite Matt's late start, they all stepped outside and headed into the Cadillac right on schedule. They all made sure to not let Diamond anywhere near them, lest his free-flowing fur spread itself all over their freshly ironed clothes.

The Cadillac was the one car Papa was not permitted to drive, so he sat in the passenger seat. Susanna sat between Mama and Papa while the boys sat together in the back. Matt on the right, Josh on the left, and Tommy in the middle.

Matt leaned his head against the side of the car and only meant to rest his eyes for a moment. That moment must have turned into a couple of minutes, and Tommy had to nudge him awake.

"Matthew, your mother's trying to talk to you," Papa called back from the passenger seat.

"Sorry, I must've dozed off," Matt replied.

"Dozed off?" Mama said back, both chastising and inquisitive. "What you got to be dozing off for?"

"Had trouble falling asleep, is all," Matt said.

Mama didn't say anything in response, but Matt caught her glancing back at him through the rearview mirror. As if she was wanting to peel back his skin to find his secrets.

Matt also caught Tommy glancing up at him, something was on his mind too. Matt began to worry that he had been letting on.

Tommy was now looking at the radio in front of where Susanna was sitting. Without even asking, it was clear Tommy was thinking about the music. Sure, the beaten down Ford trucks could only pick up KTSA in that one specific spot, but Mama's Cadillac had a better radio.

At that moment, Mama had some country music station playing. The sound was not extreme, only background noise, but that did not make it any more enjoyable. The boys groaned in unison when the music first started playing. They may have been country boys, but they did not see the appeal in melodramatic guitar tunes.

Matt saw Tommy leaning forward to whisper into Susanna's ear, to ask her to change the station. He put his hand on Tommy's shoulder to stop him.

"It ain't worth it," Matt said.

The words looked like they crushed Tommy's spirit, as if he wanted one good thing out of such a tiring morning. The two of them slumped back in their seats and listened as the Cadillac transitioned from gravel roads to asphalt, alerting them that they were nearing town.

Ironically, Josh had fallen asleep on his side of the car, but no one bothered to check on him. Matt rubbed his eyes after seeing Josh passed out. Seeing that no one was keeping an eye on them any longer, Matt let himself close his eyes.

For a few moments, he listened to the rumbling of the car against the road, letting the car rock with every subtle bounce. Then he started to hum.

It was subtle at first. Nothing Mama or Papa could hear over the radio or the sound of the engine, but he was humming. At first it wasn't to any one tune, then it began to take shape. Matt wasn't sure what he was humming, but then he realized it was a song they had been listening to just the other day.

"Proud Mary" by Creedence Clearwater Revival.

As he continued to hum, Matt could all but see the lyrics about the Riverboat Queen keeping on rolling down the river. Soon, those words matched the humming. Then, Tommy caught on to what was happening. Both of them began to hum. Never too much for them to be noticed by anyone, but enough for the time to pass. To think about fun times listening to music through the countryside.

When they finally reached St. Joseph's, only a handful of cars were still in sight. Mass was the one time the Ruggirellos were early for anything.

Given that this was the one time the vast majority of the family was in the same place, the Ruggirellos took up almost an entire wing of the church.

Nonno and Nonna sat in the second aisle on the right-hand side, the first aisle was reserved for handicapped parishioners.

They sat with Nonno's brothers and sisters, along with their wives and husbands. Sicilian-Texans every one of them. Nonno was the only one that had been born in Sicily, although he was three years old when he immigrated and had no memories of the old country.

Behind them sat Papa and Mama and their children. From there, the rest of the family filed in. Uncle Andrew and Aunt Gertrude sat behind them, along with Andy, the twins Isabella and Charlotte, Henry and little Matty, all of three years old.

The church itself had a deep interior with a vast angled ceiling, a reference to Noah's ark, Matt was told. The church was made of dark red, almost maroon, wood on both the outside and the inside. A series of candles near the altar and at the front entrance were the main sources of light in the dark interior. The only sources of color were the stained-glass windows reflecting scenes from the Bible.

Various other cousins of the Ruggirellos filled up the church. These were the cousins who had their names incorrectly spelled at immigration, but who could still trace their roots back to Poggioreale.

There was the Ruggirellers, the Ruggellos, the Rugerios, and the Ruggirellis, which some claimed was the proper spelling in Sicily, though that was an area of heated debate. Tommy once asked Nonno why people always spelled their family name wrong. Nonno's answer confused Tommy.

"Well, Tommaso, I guess it causes people to turn dyslexic."

Nonno did not stop to explain what the word meant and Tommy never looked in his Funk & Wagnalls to find out, but every time he saw a cousin with a misspelled name, he thought of the word dyslexic.

The other Sicilian families all gathered in the church, as well. Given the Ruggirellos — and their incorrectly named cousins — made up the majority of the gathering, all the others sat on the left-hand side of the church. This was the sight of rare occasions where Papa and the others would share a friendly hand-shake with the neighboring farmers. Papa and Mr. DiRusso made eye contact from across the aisles but did not shake hands.

Even with their constant disputes, there was something about Church. It was a through line to the old country. Even as the families became more Americanized with each generation, and the Italian slipped further and further from their tongues, they did not want to forget where they came from. Even on the other side of the ocean, the Church would always be there.

There were no Irish-Catholics in the area to be found. The rich white men in Bryan, most of them doctors, were either Methodists or Baptists. To hear Mama talk about them, one would think they were a foreign species that sprung out of the water one day, yet not once had she attended a mass from either denomination.

The Anglo landowners that the Ruggirellos and many others had purchased their farms from had left the Bottom decades ago. Most of the Mexicans that worked in the area went to the Spanish mass at night, but a few would come during the regular masses to practice their English. The Sicilian families tolerated their pres-ence, but the two groups never had in-depth conversations.

Of those Sicilian families, the Ruggirellos' notable absence was Aunt Ella, Papa, and Uncle Andrew's only sister. She was the oldest of the three but had become estranged from the others. She had gone off and married a jeweler in New Orleans, giving birth to girls Grace and Chloe, who the rest of the family rarely saw.

No one in the family ever met the husband, so there was always suspicion of whether Aunt Ella had given birth out of wedlock or not. Maybe there had never been a husband. Aunt Ella returned to Mumford for a period after giving birth to Grace, her oldest. After that she bounced around between Waco, Houston and College Station, struggling to keep a job and drag-ging Grace and Chloe with her. Last they heard, she was somewhere in Houston, but even that was questionable.

Nonno and Nonna didn't talk about her much. There was a sense that they had been too lenient on Aunt Ella. Too forgiving of her actions as a child that paved the way for precociousness as a young adult. Still, there was a notion that their doors were always open to her. It was only a matter of time before they saw her again.

Matt looked across at Papa once they first made it to their seats. He had made a clean scan of all those in attendance and all those who came through the doors. Maybe he was looking for Aunt Ella, Matt thought.

They all stood and mass began. The choir began to sing, everyone followed suit. Monsignor Shepard and his deacon came down the center aisle, accompanied by the altar boys. One carried the wooden cross, the other carried the missal.

From there, the monsignor welcomed everyone, and they all made the sign of the cross and spread peace to those around them. The choir sang its songs, the members of the church stepped up to the altar for the daily readings, and everyone sang the responsorial songs. The monsignor read the gospel and preached his sermon.

It was only six years prior that the masses were spoken entirely in Latin. Those were the days that Matt truly blotted out what was being said in Church, never understanding a word of scripture. Still, the fact the mass was now in English did not solve the faults with its shepherd.

Matt was always on his best behavior in mass, but he could never remember a word of what was said in the sermons, or what message the monsignor was trying to relay. The monsignor spoke in this slow, crusty voice that made one think milk was going to spoil by the time he was done speaking.

His voice told all that the monsignor was not from the Brazos River Bottom. It sounded like a statue had come to life and was trying to figure out how people talked.

More than that, Matt felt the voice did not fit that of some-one who was supposed to be welcoming to an entire community. St. Joseph's shepherd was rather frightening.

There was some truth that the monsignor spoke in his slow, droning fashion so that the older members of the community would be able to follow, but that did not take away from the fact a simple sign of the cross took all of fifteen seconds to complete.

Yet even with Matt's thoughts, he knew they were pointless to bring up. Even as he sat there, closing his eyes momentarily to blot out what the monsignor was saying, praying that the sermon would end, he overheard Mama lean over to Tommy.

"Now that, that is a great message," Mama whispered in Tommy's ear. "Our monsignor is a great man, a good priest."

Tommy said nothing. That was how mass was. Mama could lean over to tell them something, but they could not speak up. Mama would make a handful of comments like this throughout the mass, praising the monsignor or how great the Church was or how important it was for men to become priests and serve God.

She would make these same comments at every mass they attended. When Matt was younger, she said them to him — when Josh was younger, she said them too. For whatever reason, they had grown up, and she stopped saying them to him. Now, she passed the words on to Tommy.

She never said them to Susanna.

Matt could not wait to get out of the mass, but there was nothing he could do to speed the process along. The fact that the entire family waited to be the last ones out of the church did not help anything. Nonno made sure no one left their aisles until the monsignor had walked to the end of the center aisle. Even then, the Ruggirellos made sure they were the last ones to shake hands with the monsignor. Matt did as well, though he never enjoyed touching the man's icy hands.

The other amazing thing about the family's voyage to Mass was the fact that they had been fasting the entire time. Despite making sure to eat a hearty breakfast every other morning, they did not eat a crumb on Sunday mornings.

However, their stomachs never grumbled on Sundays. Until that moment when mass had ended and they had stepped beyond the threshold of the church. At that exact moment, every single one of their stomachs uttered a roar as startling as a thunderbolt on a summer day.

The sound of the grumbling family was followed by a mad dash by all the children to their respective cars. It did nothing to speed their parents from getting into their drivers' seats, but it prevented any delays once they were ready to get going.

Papa and Mama never rushed to get into the Cadillac, even if their stomachs grumbled like all the others. There was always someone to talk to, some cousin to share news about, some friend who needed money. Matt sometimes wondered if more people spoke to Papa than they did the monsignor.

But return to the car, they did. Hunger moves everybody's spirit after a matter of time. This time, there were no naps in the back seat or humming of some of the country's top songs. Everyone was awake and alert and desperate to put some food in their stomachs.

Even while Uncle Andrew and Nonno and all the other cousins sped off back to their respective homes, Mama drove at a steady pace. Matt calmed himself, knowing that it was Nonna who was making Sunday lunch, which would become Sunday dinner, but that did not take away from his inability to not think about his grumbling stomach.

Eventually the entire Ruggirello family made its return to the Big House. The Cadillac was parked in the driveway for the Big House instead of the garage at Three Pecans, which was reserved for the trucks. The boys, and Susanna, all but flew out of the car the moment Mama put the car in park.

Throwing their blazers onto the coatrack and ripping off their ties, the boys marched through the front door. The four of them passed through the smoking room that no one ever smoked in, Matt rubbing his hand along the television and radio sets and walking over the orange rug stretched across the floor.

That room connected to the dining room. In truth, it was one large wing that acted as both the dining room and one of the living rooms. On the north side of the wing was a long dark wood table that could seat up to twelve people. Depending on how many grandchildren were in attendance, an extra plank could be brought in to extend the table. If that still proved insufficient, there was a smaller card table that they extended to the very end. Either way, everyone was promised a seat at the table.

Against the wall was a matching dresser where Nonna's silver and fine plates sat. It also acted as a station for all the desserts to be placed. A mirror hung along the wall so that the family could look at themselves eating like a photo out of *Life Magazine*.

Matt and the others kicked off their shoes by the doorway and ferried themselves through the entrance to the next room. There they stood in what was the official living room. The room did not have any radio or television sets, but there was a fireplace, another ornate rug, a large sofa, and a series of large windows that looked out into the open fields.

The courtyard was not much, a red brick-stone area with a fire pit on a hill, just in front of a row of oak trees. Beyond that was grass fields, but in those grass fields were a series of broken-down tractors, farm equipment, and a diesel tank that Papa used to refill the trucks. So, while the windows provided much light into the living space, it was not much of a view.

However, the courtyard was not their destination. Taking a sharp left turn, they all turned toward the kitchen, an area much more spacious than that of Three Pecans. The kitchen was complete with an oven, stove, refrigerator, countertop, a corner where a small dining table rested, and an island that on it sat an enormous tray of freshly baked fig cookies.

The boys, all at once, realized the error they had made in plucking the figs earlier in the week—they could not think far enough ahead. They prayed fig cookies would be included in a family meal. Only those who had gotten to cook with Nonna would know if the sweets were made.

Yet neither Tommy, nor Andy, had seen any sign that fig cookies were being cooked when they brought over the potatoes. Matt looked at his little brother, almost betrayed that he had not spilled the beans. Regardless, they helped themselves to the sweets, satisfying their grumbling stomachs at last.

Had they been left unchecked, the fifty some odd cookies would have vanished in moments. Yet when Matt was about to reach for his second cookie, Nonna appeared from beyond the island to slap at his hand.

"Do not rush," Nonna said. "One cookie per ten minutes. No sooner."

Nonna had been there the entire time, fiddling with an assortment of suga, noodles and cheese on the countertop. The meal of the day was lasagna. Nonno had rushed them home to allow her to go straight to work. Nonna didn't trust him to help her in the kitchen.

Layer by layer Nonna applied the sauce, noodles, ground beef, mozzarella, ricotta and repeat. She repeated this through two trays' worth until all ingredients had been used up. There was suga left over, there was always suga left over, but everything else was shoved into the creases of the three-inch thick trays.

Matt was in such a haze from hunger that he had not noticed Nonna standing there. That, and given the fact Nonna seemed to always be in the kitchen, Matt did not think twice about her being there. It did not take away from the sting that came with having the fig cookie slapped out of his hand.

Regardless, the meal continued like all other Sunday lunches. Nonna prepared the main meal, Mama had brought over a pecan pie she had baked, while Aunt Gertrude had delivered a bread pudding. There was this unwritten agreement that Nonna would make the main dish while the daughters-in-law would provide desserts.

They also brought along bread and salads, but the desserts were crucial. Even when the stomachs were full and the belt buckles were undone, there was always room for dessert.

"I gotta tell ya, Paul, I don't think the Aggies are gonna have a good year," Uncle Andrew said.

"Now why you talking like that?" Papa asked. "We can't go writing them off before they've even played a single game."

"I'm just saying, Darrell Royal's got a strong squad up in Austin from what I've heard. The Cotton Bowl feels like a lifetime ago."

Papa blew hot air out the side of his mouth. He didn't even like hearing the name Darrell Royal, or anyone else who went to Texas for that matter.

"If y'all want to talk about football," Nonno said, "y'all should be focused on Hearne. They haven't made the playoffs since Matteo's been there. Wouldn't that be exciting for his senior year."

Matt just grinned as he glanced up at Nonno, continuing to cut into his food.

"That would be something," Uncle Andrew said. "What about you, Josh? You thinking of trying out for the team?"

This may have been a bit of brotherly back and forth as Uncle Andrew seemed to pull back, expecting retaliation from Papa, the moment after he said the words. He was half laughing, half smiling.

"That's enough of that," Papa said.

Now and then there was a period of silence where the only noises were the clinking of silverware against dishes. For every chef, and particularly for Nonna, it was the sign that a great meal had been cooked.

"Andrew, I need you to check on the fence line sometime this week," Papa said between bites. "I wanna be sure the cattle don't get loose."

Uncle Andrew nodded in acknowledgment. It was not often that he was given tasks on the Home Farm.

"Have y'all heard about that new book that came out?" Aunt Gertrude asked. "I can't remember the name, but I heard there's this book about an Italian family in America that's on the *New York Times* bestseller list."

"Can't say that I have," Nonno said. "Last thing I heard on the news had to do with Vietnam."

That was the extent of the political talk at the table. Never a prime subject. Tommy and Andy had their own conversations next to each other and all the other grandchildren found their way to talking about one thing or another.

Matt remained quiet. He would answer when spoken to, but it was never about anything substantial. He was thankful no one questioned his quietness, at least that time. Though there were moments he saw Mama glancing his way, but said nothing.

Once the meal was finished, Nonno, Papa, and Uncle Andrew all departed to the "smoking room" sofa. As expected, they unbuckled their belts, leaned back on the sofa and promptly passed out. Nonna, Mama, and Aunt Gertrude went into the courtyard to talk, though Aunt Gertrude kept Little Matty with her, not keen to let the baby out of her sight.

The grandchildren wandered throughout the rest of the Big House. Some of them wandered into the guest bedroom, others to the master bedroom to see Nonno and Nonna's cream-green bathroom and pink telephone setup. Tommy drifted throughout the space, looking at the variety of old family photos and western-themed artwork that filled the main hallway.

They all went back for second and third helpings of the various desserts. The boys, in particular, wanted to enjoy the moment before going back to work the next day. Needless to say, the fig cookies all but vanished once the grownups retreated to their respective parts of the house.

Matt was the only one who remained put. He did his part in helping clear the table and slice portions of the lasagna into Nonna's Tupperware. There were always leftovers from Nonna's cooking. It would serve as their dinners.

But afterwards, after Matt had helped himself to a second serving of pie and bread pudding, Matt just sat at the table. He ran his fork back and forth over the crumbs on his plate to give the illusion that he was doing something, but Matt found he was stuck in his own head.

He had this image of the post office. He had this image of the Ruggirello mailbox stuffed to the brim with letters. Not letters of business that desperately needed Papa's attention. No. Letters from colleges and universities that wanted Matt's signature.

It had gotten to where Matt was getting letters from schools he had never heard of, in states he had never thought of traveling to, but what he found odd was he enjoyed it. Their presence frightened him, but he enjoyed the fact they wanted him. They were all but begging him to come to their school.

Yet he had not said a word of this to anyone.

The family lounged at the Big House until the sun was descending into the western part of the sky. Uncle Andrew was the first to gather up his family and depart. While their drive was not substantial, it was the longest of the family.

Once Nonno and Papa awoke from their slumbers, they continued to talk. Their conversation never wavered from topics of the farm. They mentioned crops, the amount of fertilizers still in supply, recent weather forecasts and what they predicted the season's intake would be.

By this point, Tommy and Josh had passed out on the sofas. Susanna had found time for a quick nap but was now awake and helping Nonna put away what dishes were still out. Matt had never found a moment to rest his eyes.

Matt was the one who had to stir Josh from his slumber and who was given the task of carrying Tommy back home. By the time they had said their goodbyes, it was 5 p.m. and the horizon was now an orange glow in the final hour of sunlight. It was the one moment of the day that resembled a painting, Matt thought.

They all shuffled their way back over to Three Pecans and back inside the house. Tommy was stirred long enough to change from his nice clothes into a relaxed pair of blue jeans and a white t-shirt. They had all gotten their shoes mildly dirty from the short crossing and the task of wiping all the dirt off fell to Matt. Why? Cause Mama told him to do it and you did not argue with Mama's command.

So, Matt sat there on the porch, scrubbing away at dress shoes and heels alike, first with a wet cloth, then shoe polish. He made sure to put them high on a shelf to dry and keep them out of reach of Diamond, but Matt did give the lovable dog plenty of scratches once he was finished. He also made sure to fill his food bowl, since someone had neglected to do that as well.

Sunday nights were a fascinating affair because it was the one night out of the week that saw no family dinner. The lunches had so filled their appetites that no one could think of cooking, sitting at the table, or eating anything of any creation. Had Mama made the time to prepare an entire second meal, they would have had heart attacks from clogged veins.

Instead, Sunday nights were the sight of snacking on crackers, grapes, bread and whatever leftovers the family found themselves able to prepare or warm up.

Crackers and cheese were Mama's go-to, though she always had a loaf of bread somewhere. Papa had a fascination with sardines that nobody understood. The Church only deemed they needed to fast from meat on Sundays, but Papa took that to include Fridays and Saturdays.

Papa would always tell Mama that they weren't supposed to eat meat on those days, she would tell him to hush. Still, that did

66

not stop Papa from fasting in his own manner. Hence the sardines. Not one member of the entire Ruggirello family enjoyed the taste of fish. Not even the most expensive of salmons. Yet Papa could always be found with a can of sardines not far behind.

...

Because there was no dinner, there was no call to come to the dinner table at any point. Meaning Matt retreated into his room, closed the door and continued to look over letters and letters.

Penn State, Stanford, Southern California, Pittsburgh, Syracuse. Places Matt wondered if he could even spot on a map. Some of them he had heard in passing from sports talk but nothing about academics. It was stirring. A part of him wanted them to stop, but another part wanted them to just keep coming. Matt wanted to know what far-off place might be looking for him in Mumford, Texas.

While Matt still did not know what to do with all the letters, they did succeed in lulling him to sleep. Somehow, his body must have remembered to hide them under his sheets cause when he was woken up some hour and a half later, they had all been stuffed underneath his buttocks.

There was no knock on the door, but the sound of the door opening and closing stirred Matt awake. It was Josh and Tommy. Tommy immediately sat on the floor and began fiddling with a pair of cars he had carried with him. Josh remained by the door, pressing it closed with his body weight, not even looking at Matt.

"What is it?" Matt asked.

Josh held up a finger, telling Matt not to say another word. Matt listened close. He could hear the buzzing sound of the television off in the distance. A little while after that came the sound of men talking in that unnatural way that newscasters talk to the camera.

Once Josh had confirmed the presence of the active television, he turned to face Matt.

"Well," Matt said. "Can I help y'all?"

"Is something going on with you?" Josh asked.

"Huh?"

"You've been quiet."

"Hell, I'm always quiet. Why say something stupid if you ain't got something to say?"

"You know what I mean. You been lock-lipped. Not said a word."

"I believe my previous statement still stands."

Josh groaned as he stepped forward. He looked down at Tommy playing with the Matchbox cars and slapped him on the side of the head. Not hard enough to seriously hurt him, but enough to get his attention.

The cars rolled underneath Matt's bedside table, and Tommy groaned at the sight. He glanced up at Josh and only then did Tommy remember why they had come into the room.

"I'm with you, I didn't think you were any quieter than normal," Tommy said. "But Mama thinks you've been acting strange. Susanna told me so."

Matt remembered Mama's gaze through the rearview mirror just that morning. Eyes that wanted to dig into his secrets.

"Yeah, I figured as much," Matt replied.

"So, come on then," Josh said. "If something's going on you should tell us, now."

"Well, nothing's happened, if that's what you're worried about," Matt said.

"It doesn't seem that way," Tommy said. "You have been looking at nothing quite a bit."

"What's that supposed to mean?" Matt asked.

"Like just staring out windows," Tommy said. "The cotton hasn't bloomed yet, there's nothing to look at."

"I mean…," Matt said, trailing off without an answer.

"Matt, come on," Josh said. "Papa and Mama aren't here. What's going on?"

Matt, still sitting on his bed, looked at his brothers for almost fifteen seconds without saying a word. He was weighing how much he should say with how much he believed they would keep to themselves.

"Alright," Matt said.

Matt then shot off into his explanatory tale. He called them back to the day they had forgotten to swing by the post office and how there was mail for Papa but also for him. That caught their attention.

Then came the revelation about the letters. One by one, Matt revealed the letters he had hidden under his sheets. There were about 35 letters in total. Josh and Tommy were just as bewildered by the amount in front of them and the names on the envelopes.

Yes, they knew SMU and Baylor, and were shocked to find anything related to the University of Texas in their home. They could hear Papa blowing out hot air just that evening. In Papa's mind there wasn't anything worse than a Texas Longhorn. No ounce of burnt orange could be found within fifty square miles of Three Pecans.

Regardless, they were just as surprised to find the likes of Ohio State and the University of Buffalo in and among the pile. For fifteen minutes, Josh and Tommy did not say a word. They just kept opening one letter after another and reading every word of typed black ink.

"What's a National Merit Scholar?" Tommy asked.

Josh also looked up at Matt, inquisitively.

"It's this competition they run through the schools," Matt said. "There's all these tests that you take in school in order to go to college. There's one you take as a sophomore that prepares you for the big one. Miss Salazar in English pulled me out to apply for it last year, but I hadn't thought much more about it after the fact. Apparently, they compare the results from that test with everyone in the country. If your scores then match the results from the big test, and you're one of however many, you're named a National Merit Scholar."

Tommy looked up at Matt for a few moments, then looked back at the paper in his hands, this one from Georgetown University, and then back at Matt.

"But what does that mean?" Tommy asked.

"It means Matt's one of the smartest people in the country," Josh said.

Those words hung in the air as all three gripped the heaviness of that statement.

"I don't know about that," Matt said.

"It does," Josh said. "You don't hear news that every kid in Hearne is getting all these envelopes."

"Wow," Tommy said, excitedly. "That's awesome."

Matt did not say anything, but he did start to curl in on himself as he sat cross-legged on the bed. He explained his gut feeling that more letters were likely just waiting in the mailbox. Josh didn't say anything, he just kept going over all the letters, again and again. Eventually, he just stood up and walked out of the room without any warning.

Matt and Tommy were confused, but Matt was more relieved that there was no call for Papa or Mama to come into his room.

"So, all these schools want you to come to them," Tommy said, more so trying to explain it to himself than actually asking a question.

"Right," Matt said.

"And they're going to pay you to go there?"

"Well . . . no. They're offering scholarships of different amounts. Rather than Papa have to pay money to the school, I would basically be going for free."

Even Tommy understood that was a big deal. At that point, Josh came back into the room and closed the door behind him. He had brought with him a map of the United States, that up until that point, had been hanging on a wall in his room. Matt looked at him, wondering why he had brought it with him.

Josh went letter by letter to read the locations of each school that was offering Matt a scholarship. With little yellow dots, he marked one after another on the map. There were ten markings in Texas alone, but his markings extended to California, the Midwest, the East Coast, pretty much every location one could think of in the country.

"You think you'd wanna go to these places?" Tommy asked, stunned at all the spots on the map.

"I doubt it," Matt said. "Not all of them at least. I ain't gonna go somewhere it snows. It's a pain enough when it snows down here, and that's nothing."

"Some of these look like they're in the middle of nowhere," Tommy said.

Matt didn't need to comment on those schools.

Tommy didn't vocalize it, but Matt could see a hesitant look on his face, the way Tommy's shoulders were hunched. The thought of being separated from his brother was something Tommy had not thought about. It made him uncomfortable.

Josh continued to put mark after mark on the map. It grew to the point that Matt and Tommy tired of it. They sat around the map, picking up what letters Josh had yet to go through. By the time they were finished there was a heavy amount of yellow markings. Matt figured by the next post office stop, there might be a marking on every state.

Together, they helped pin it to Matt's wall. He could not quite believe it. Parts of the country he never thought to see, who had no idea who he was apart from some numbers on a score sheet, yet here they were asking for him. They all just sat on the bed looking at the map.

"Now what?" Tommy asked.

"It doesn't really matter," Josh said. "Papa won't hear a word of it."

Matt said nothing, he just looked at the letters in his hand.

"Papa's been hard set on you going to A&M," Josh continued. "All of us."

"Well, that is where Papa went to school," Tommy said.

"It's where they all went to school, everyone but Nonno," Josh said. "Did A&M send a letter? I've forgotten."

Matt pulled through the letters to see. By now, they had all been spread out and far from categorized, but he did find the letter that A&M sent.

"They did," Matt said, opening the letter once more. "They were one of the schools offering full rides. I think it has something to do with being a Texas resident, if I read that right."

"Well, there you go, problem solved," Josh said. "Tell Papa about the A&M scholarship. They'll be thrilled. It's the school they want and they won't have to pay a dime of tuition."

"He has a point," Tommy said.

Matt still did not say anything. He just sat there, looking over the letter and looking up at the wall. About a million thoughts were running through his head. Possibly a million for each scrap of paper that now rested on his floor.

"I'm assuming you haven't told them," Josh said.

"No, I haven't," Matt answered.

"So, why the hesitation?"

"Because . . . because, you said it yourself. You don't hear about this happening to every student at Hearne."

Josh straightened his back. "What are you getting at?"

"I'm getting at the thought that maybe I should not brush all of this aside so quickly."

"You mean . . . you don't want to go to A&M?" Tommy asked.

"I'm saying, I've never had an alternative," Matt said. "I've always figured I'd go to A&M cause it's what Papa wanted. It's not like we've talked about it. Go to the school where Papa and Uncle Andrew went to school, that was the mindset."

"What's so wrong with that?" Josh asked. "It'll better prepare us for when we're older and have to do what Papa's doing now."

"There is nothing wrong with A&M," Matt finally said. "But . . . but what if I don't want to be a farmer?"

There was a moment of pause in their dialogue. Josh and Tommy did not know how to react to what Matt was saying.

"You don't wanna be a farmer?" Josh asked, almost confused that the words were coming out of his mouth.

"I don't know," Matt said. "Maybe I do. Maybe I don't. The point is, I don't know."

"But that's what Papa wants," Josh said. "It's obvious he's been preparing for you to take over one day. The same way Nonno prepared him."

"I get that, but when has he ever asked me?" Matt asked. "When has Papa asked what any one of us actually want to do?"

They all remained silent.

"But we're supposed to do what Papa and Mama say," Tommy said.

"Because we're their sons," Matt said. "But there's a difference in doing what you're told to do, and not making our own decisions."

"So what're you saying?" Josh asked. "You're gonna go off to school in Pennsylvania or Ohio and do something that's going to change the world."

"Fuck you," Matt said.

That really stopped the brothers in their tracks. Matt did not say the curse with any great anger or ferocity, but it did shock them. Matt did not curse in the open, ever.

"I didn't mean that," Matt said, genuinely sorry for the language. "But you insulted me."

"I insulted you?" Josh asked, baffled.

"You disregarded what I was saying," Matt continued. "I won't claim to be filled with high-flying ideas that are going to change the world. Nor do I think I'm smarter than you, or anyone in our family, for that matter. I don't even feel like I'm the smartest person in Hearne or the entire Bottom. But I'm sitting here with offers from schools I never thought I would even have the chance of attending.

"Yes, I know about Papa and Uncle Andrew and what they think about A&M, but I don't know it. Maybe A&M is my second home, but what if I'm miserable there? I've never even visited the campus."

"You've been to the games," Josh said.

"I've been to the stadiums," Matt said. "I know nothing of its classes or professors, of its graduates, what future its education could give me. I know as much of A&M as I know about all these other schools that have sent me their letters."

From then on, it was silence among the brothers. That was that. Matt had made up his mind. They could all see a confrontation between him and Papa would be in their future. Sadly, even Matt knew this could all be for nothing.

Josh did not say a word. He just stood up from the bed and walked out, closing the door to his own room on the way. Tommy did not leave as abruptly. He said nothing. He just sat there in silence with Matt. A part of him did not want to leave his brother without any second thought.

That night, the boys fell asleep running over the conversation they just had while also catching glimpses of what Mama and Papa were listening to on the news. A man was getting ready to go to the moon.

TOMMY

Tommy felt his legs shaking when he tried to walk the next day. His body was filled with so much tension that he felt as if he was walking through an abandoned neighborhood, frightened by what might be around the corner.

He was too aware of how tense Matt and Josh had gotten the night before. Neither had gone to bed with settled minds. A confrontation among family members was imminent, but Tommy was cautious of when his brothers would debate each other again. There was a heaviness climbing into Matt's truck. It was no longer a safe haven from stepping out onto the fields and pastures. The troubles did not stop at the car door.

They all stared straight ahead as Matt drove down the road. If they didn't look at each other, they wouldn't have to discuss their problems. Still, Tommy noticed Matt and Josh kept glancing at each other. For a moment, he thought they were snarling too.

They were so in their own world that neither had noticed Tommy switching the radio to KTSA 550.

The station was mainly static, with only a lyric or a guitar note every half hour, but they never made him change stations.

The day was a simple one, driving from field to field and opening irrigation wells.

At one point, they stopped to help Papa change a tire on his truck, but there was no conversation. Nor did any of them think that was the time or place to talk about the letters. Still, Tommy noticed that Matt and Josh's eyes continued to dart back and forth at each other.

At one point, Tommy did startle his brothers, or at least the radio did. They had been passing by the Big Brazos to the west, far from that secret spot on the hill, when all of a sudden, they were no longer listening to static.

It was Creedence Clearwater Revival, again. "Bad Moon Rising." It caused all of them to turn toward the center of the truck.

Matt stopped the truck when he heard the song come on. For the entire two minutes, they just sat there looking at the radio, listening to the guitar and the banjo and the voice warning of bad troubles on the way. Earthquakes and lightning did not sound like they would be in their future, but bad times today?

Tommy could feel his knees shaking again. He wasn't sure if he believed in omens, but at that moment, the song felt like one. Too much tension was being built up. Eventually, it would boil over.

Matt waited till the song was finished and not one second later, turned the radio off. He looked at Tommy and he looked at Josh, they said nothing.

"That's enough of that," was all Matt had to say.

Their day continued in similar silence, going back over the irrigation wells to make sure they were all open. Matt noticed the fuel tank was almost empty once they finished up, so rather than returning to Three Pecans, he drove his Ford to the field behind the Big House.

There, they parked the truck along the three-ton tank of diesel oil that rested in the field. So many tiny ounces of diesel had dripped from the nozzle over the years that the grass around the tank was dead. Tommy wagered that if they checked back in ten years, there might be a hole in the earth where the tank once stood.

The tank was an expense Nonno found worth it for the benefit of the farm. Rather than have any number of trucks drive to the nearest gas station time and time again, Nonno would fill the tank up with enough diesel to last the farm for an entire month. He would refill the tank every month, but it saved everyone else a great deal of trouble.

Matt was the first out of the truck, taking responsibility for filling up the Ford. Josh also hopped out to stretch his legs, pulling his cap down as he leaned against the truck. Tommy climbed out as well, not a fan of sitting in a boiling piece of metal without any air flowing through the windows. He stepped up on the rear tire and flung himself onto the side of the bed, letting his legs dangle over the side.

Tommy appreciated the simple moments where he could look across the sky and see the orange glow. Apart from the birds and the vultures, and one barn owl that appeared every four months, there were no distractions in the entire world.

Only the sound of tires against earth and a growling engine distracted him from what was happening. All three of the boys looked to their right and saw Nonno's bright red truck coming around the farm road from the Big House. It did not take them long to realize he was heading right toward them.

None of them moved to greet Nonno, but they did make sure they were facing him as he pulled up. Nonno was all smiles. He removed his white cowboy hat once he parked the truck. His clean-shaven head shimmered in the sunlight as he wiped sweat from his brow.

"Nipoti, come vai?" Nonno asked.

"Just filling up the truck is all," Matt answered.

"A successful day?" Nonno asked.

"We made sure to open the wells," Josh replied.

"Good, good. Have you seen your papa?" Nonno asked.

"Not since earlier when we helped him change a tire," Tommy answered.

"Only saw him for a moment," Josh said.

"Alright, I had gotten a call from the co-op that he had forgotten to pick up his meat from the butcher," Nonno replied. "Said the meat would spoil if he didn't come soon."

The boys were more than surprised by this. It was not like Papa to forget such a thing. A man as organized as him, as particular as him. It was shocking to hear he would forget about something as valuable as freshly slaughtered beef.

"We'll let him know when we see him later," Matt said.

"No, no. Just tell him I've gone to pick it up for him," Nonno said. "We have our own beef to pick up, as well."

"Is that where you're off to now?" Tommy asked.

"No, I'm actually off to deliver the Sunday meals," Nonno said.

With the inventions of tractors and cotton plows, a farm as large as one might find in the Brazos River Bottom could now be manned by a skeleton crew. A handful of men could easily keep an eye on hundreds of acres on any given day.

Given the amount of family members Nonno had at his disposal, there was little need to hire a great number of people. Granted, Nonno still had a handful of men in his employ. They lived on the road behind the Big House, right up against the first row of crops that mark the Home Farm. Truly they worked for Papa, but Nonno was their official boss.

The Ruggirellos did not go out of their way to be super friendly to the hands. They may have lived on the land, but they were not family. They were employees and as such kept a distance when not working. Still, Nonno and Nonna provided each hand with a tray from every Sunday meal.

"It seemed we all got carried away yesterday, and no one was given the task of delivering the meals," Nonno said. "So here I am."

"You want us to deliver them for you?" Tommy asked, trying to be helpful.

"No, that's alright," Nonno said. "But why don't you come with me, Tommaso? Just for the ride."

Tommy looked back at Josh and Matt. Neither of them seemed bothered by the suggestion. They treated Nonno's requests the same way they treated Papa's requests. They always did what was asked, yet Tommy was the one with doubts.

He did not show concern on his face, but he did not want to leave Matt and Josh alone. He was the only thing keeping them together the entire day. Tommy feared they would lash out if he was not there.

"Go ahead, Tommy," Matt said. "We'll tell Papa you're with Nonno. He won't mind."

Tommy looked at Matt, still trying to put on a brave face. But there was nothing he could do. Nonno had made his request, so he got in the truck.

Nonno's truck was unlike the others. A Ford, like the rest. Nonno's bright red truck had a massive carriage and enough lights on the front to light up a baseball field. Nonno had told stories of having to check on parts of the field in the middle of the night when he was a young man. Now as the boss, he wanted his truck to have enough lights to where darkness was never a problem.

From their current spot, the drive to the houses where the hands lived took all of ninety seconds. The houses were simple things. Wooden shacks on platforms. Many of them, at first glance, looked like they were moments away from collapsing in on themselves.

Tommy had once gotten into a fight with Andy about the houses. Andy kept saying that the houses were where they used to keep the slaves. Tommy was quick to point out that neither Nonno nor his father, Papa Paul, had owned slaves. Andy was just as quick to explain that Old Man Carson was the one who owned the slaves and built the houses.

"Them houses ain't 200 years old," was Tommy's final retort. A sharp end to their conversation. For even as uncomfortable as the houses looked, Andy could not argue that they were 200 years old.

There were four hands in total. At any time during the week, they could be spotted moving around the farms either in their own trucks or in the beds of Nonno or Papa's. In the evening, they could be found meandering to the Wagon Wheel, a tiny saloon built up between the highway and the railroad tracks and owned by the Ruggirellos. A place for hands from all the neighboring farms to go wet their gullets. Driving past it, the Wagon Wheel looked like any common shack, but inside was a bevy of alcohol.

There was Big Jake, a man they called such because his name was Jake and he was indeed big. Giant was the better descriptor. The tallest man Tommy had ever seen. When standing next to Big Jake, Tommy could not see the sun, that's how tall he was. In truth, he was over six and a half feet tall. Big Jake had come westward from Louisiana, looking for a new line of work after laying down railroad tracks.

Tommy had been fascinated by Big Jake from almost the moment he set eyes on him. At first, it was because Tommy thought he was black as coal dust. Then it was because of how strong he was. Big Jake could lift up a pipe that needed three men to carry and haul it over his shoulder. His arms and legs looked as large and as strong as such steel rods. When Tommy was even smaller, Big Jake would get him to grab his hand and he would do standing presses with Tommy as the weight.

Papa put a stop to that the first time he saw it happen. Mama also had a word or two about it.

Big Jake wasn't married, but he had a daughter named Liza, who was rarely seen. Tommy wondered what happened to Liza's mother, but never got around to asking.

"How are you, sir?" Big Jake asked as he approached the truck, rubbing his head with a cloth.

"Just fine, Jake," Nonno said. "Just brought you some of our food from Sunday."

"Thank you kindly. No doubt I'll put this to good use," Big Jake said with a laugh.

Big Jake's laugh seemed to ripple through his belly. Once the laughter ceased, Big Jake stepped closer to Nonno.

"There was one other thing I wanted to say. I've noticed Jim's been hitchhiking off to town some nights. Now I don't know what he's doing hitchhiking when he's got the Wagon Wheel right around the bend, but it don't look right."

Nonno glanced past Big Jake, toward Jim's house down the way. Jim was a white man, about ten years younger than Big Jake, at least. Jim was also tall, but skinny as a reed in comparison to Big Jake.

Jim was a quiet fellow. Polite. He would always say, "Yes, sir," whenever given a command, but he was quiet. A piece of mystery hung over all of the hands. Of the various faces who had passed through over the years, most of them just showed up at the Big House to ask for work and got work. As a result, Jim carried a bit of mystery as well.

"He done anything else suspicious?" Nonno asked.

"Nothing I've seen," Big Jake said. "He's beaten us every time we've played cards."

"You think you just might need to get better at cards?"

Nonno and Big Jake shared a laugh at the jest. He promised to keep an eye on Jim but told Big Jake it probably wasn't anything to worry about.

When Nonno pulled up to Jim's house, he did not begin an interrogation. Jim thanked Nonno for the food and that was that. Tommy wasn't sure if Nonno believed what Big Jake had told him, or if he was concerned about it. Either way, it wasn't at Nonno's forefront.

Then there were the two Mexicans, Ignacio and Epefanio. Ignacio was the younger, an athletic man in his mid-twenties. He spoke no English, but he made up for it in the fields.

The Ruggirellos never fully learned the connection, but Epefanio was somehow a distant cousin to Ignacio. It was through Epefanio that Ignacio learned there was work in Texas. When he showed up to ask for work, Nonno accepted him into the fold.

81

Tommy was certain that Ignacio's past life had something to do with horses. Every time Ignacio was sent to feed and groom them — or on the rare occasions when they were saddled — he would always be found singing a song into their ears. Every time, the horses would obey his every command.

On top of that, Tommy once saw Ignacio get to ride one of the horses out to the pasture. Tommy watched as Ignacio leapt onto the saddle with one bound. He slid onto the horse's back without ever having put his foot in the stirrup.

Without saying a word, Ignacio came out and accepted the offering from Nonno. There was something to appreciate about a hardworking man of few words. There definitely was nothing to complain about.

"¿Cuál era el antiguo trabajo de Ignacio?" Papa asked one afternoon.

"Un vaquero," Epefanio replied.

Epefanio was one of the longer tenured members of the farm hands. His house was only marginally bigger than those of the other hands, but he needed it. Epefanio lived with his wife Antonia and daughter Eva.

Epefanio came to Texas when he was eighteen years old and had worked under Old Man Carson when he still owned the farm. Every dollar he made was mailed directly back to his family in Oaxaca.

When Nonno bought the farm from Carson, Epefanio was one of the most seasoned workers and asked to stay and work. Nonno was more than happy to keep him on.

Now Epefanio was a man in his fifties and a husband of fifteen years to Antonia, a Bryan native of Mexican descent. As for their daughter, Eva, Tommy had seen her with his own eyes, unlike the fabled Liza.

Eva was a skinny, dark-skinned girl with black hair that seemed to ripple down her back like water over rocks. Whether she was seen dressed like a tomboy in blue jeans or a girl in a traditional dancing dress, there was no doubt that she was beautiful.

Her beauty had drawn the affection of Andy, who more than once talked Tommy's ears off about it. Andy thought she was the prettiest girl in the entire Bottom. Tommy had snarkily reminded him that the majority of the women in the Bottom were not beautiful.

Yet Andy would not be silenced. He would make several dares with Tommy, the loser having to walk up to Epefanio's door and ask Eva for a dance or have to steal her headkerchief to earn a chance to talk to her. Tommy never bit. For one, he knew Andy was the one who wanted to do all those things, and Tommy just thought it was stupid.

"If you wanna go talk to the girl, why don't you just go talk to her," Tommy had said. "She speaks English."

That was a fact. Eva went to junior high in Mumford and would attend Hearne when she got older, meaning she had to speak English. Epefanio was supportive of it. While Antonia knew English as well, she was not a great teacher. With Eva, Epefanio was able to learn and improve his English as Eva learned it.

"What's wrong with you? Ain't she the prettiest girl you ever did see around here?" Andy remarked.

"That she may be, but that don't mean I'm gonna go do a foolish thing around her on account of a dare," Tommy said.

Either way, it was clear Andy was more attracted to the girl than Tommy would ever be. Still, she was the one who came out to greet Nonno when his big red truck pulled up.

"Hello, Mr. Matthew," Eva said, calling Nonno by his Christian name.

"Good afternoon, Eva," Nonno replied. "Is your father home yet?"

"No, I'm not sure what's keeping him," Eva said. "Mother's gone into town to buy some flour."

"Ah, anything special on the menu?" Nonno asked, playfully.

"Nothing worthy of praise," Eva said with a smile. "Hello, Thomas."

Tommy smiled and nodded at her noticing him in the truck. "Hello," he said.

"Well, not to intrude on your mother's cooking, but please take this portion of our Sunday meal," Nonno said, handing the lasagna to her. "You don't need to eat it now, but we forgot to deliver it yesterday."

Eva smiled back as she looked at the tray. "I'll tell them about it when they get back. Thank you, Mr. Matthew."

"You're most welcome, good-bye now."

When all the trays were delivered, Nonno was ready to make the quick turn back to the Big House. Yet Tommy, sitting up in his seat, noticed the pile of burnt wood and ash at the very end of the row of houses. It used to be a little house of brown wood where Stella lived.

Stella had been the caretaker for Tommy and his siblings. She came to the Ruggirellos in 1951, the same year Matt was born. At first, she was hired to assist Mama around the house as she juggled being a new mother. Then, as the second, third, and fourth children came into the picture, Stella began to look after all four kids. Mama still cared for them and took care of the home, but when a baby started crying, it was Stella who rocked them.

Mama had so many children that Matt, Josh and Susanna all grew up with Stella at Three Pecans at various points. The family appreciated Stella so much that they built her a house on the Home Farm. Not one of the rundown shacks that the hands lived in. An actual house with fresh paint. Yet on New Year's Eve in 1962, something horrific happened. Some said it was arson, some said it was a rogue firework, but however it happened, Stella's home had caught fire and she perished inside.

It was the most brutal thing that ever happened on the farm. Even the DiRussos put aside their differences to help the Ruggirellos put out the fire.

Tommy only knew of Stella through the stories about her. He knew about the night of the fire and thought about it every time he saw the pile of wood, a sort of memorial to her, different from the actual memorial sight in the Bryan cemetery. So when he spotted it this time, he got Nonno to pull over.

Nonno seemed surprised at the request, but still stopped the truck. Tommy didn't say a word. For a moment, he forgot all about Matt and Josh and their feuding. He forgot all about the letters. Instead, he thought about a person he never got the chance to know. He chose to kneel down and say a prayer.

...

Nonno gave Tommy his peace and did not question his grandson when he got back in the truck. Turning south bound on the highway to resume their errand running, Tommy didn't say a word. He let his thoughts fill his head as he watched the rows run past the window.

Tommy was so distracted that he did not even notice Nonno switching on the radio. It was only when Tommy heard the vocals of Sly and the Family Stone that he looked back at the console. To his shock, but not horror, Nonno had turned the radio to KTSA 550.

"What?" Nonno asked, seeing Tommy's surprised face.

"I . . . You . . . I'm just surprised you can get that station," Tommy said.

"This, oh I only get it so often. On this road at this exact hour there's a chance. Love it. So many good songs."

"Really?"

"Yeah! Can't stand most country music."

As "Everyday People" sang out of the console, Tommy thought this was the most non-country song Nonno could have chosen.

"I'm just surprised, is all," Tommy said.

"I get that much," Nonno said. "I can see it on your face."

Tommy just looked straight ahead in response, even though he wanted to tap his feet to the beat of the music.

"So, tell me, Tommaso, why'd you do your little prayer there? I've never seen you do that before."

Tommy sighed. "Felt like hallowed ground. I felt like I needed to say something, but speaking it wouldn't be right. I've got a lot of thoughts right now and thought maybe praying would give clarity."

"Do you want to talk about those thoughts?"

Tommy had to stop himself from outright spilling his beans right then and there. He knew he shouldn't tell him about Matt. Nonno deserved to know, but Tommy wasn't going to be the one to say something that got everyone else in trouble. Because they would get in trouble if Papa learned they knew about it and did not say anything to him. Still, there were things Tommy wanted to know.

"Nonno, why did you want Papa to become a farmer?" Tommy asked.

Nonno looked across at Tommy, his face having dropped at the sound of the question.

"I never told your papa to become a farmer," Nonno said.

Tommy could hear the words repeating in his head. He pressed a hand to his temple, he had a headache. Tommy had come to believe the cycle of Ruggirello men working on farmland to be this long, unbroken chain strapped to their heels. The thought of no cycle even existing made Tommy's eyes bulge.

"What do you mean?" Tommy asked, not sure what else to say.

"I'm not sure how else I can clarify it—I never wanted your papa to become a farmer," Nonno said. "He chose that path for himself."

Tommy did not know what else to do but look out the front of the truck at the passing road. He felt like a broken-down radio set. While it appeared structurally sound, the wiring just was not there.

"I don't understand," Tommy said.

"I see that," Nonno replied. "Has he told you I wanted him to be a farmer?"

Tommy thought for a second.

"Well, no. I guess, I guess we all just figured that was the case."

"Hah, far from it. I know this path can be an unrewarding one. Far from glamorous."

"Then..."

"I became a farmer because that's what my papa did, your Papa Paul. I never got a chance to go to school. I didn't learn to read or write until I was eighteen, did you know that?"

"No."

"Yes indeed. Picture it, your nonno, eighteen years old, strapping," Nonno added a playful wink as he said that final characteristic. "But there I was, sitting in a tiny room with a bunch of children. Some not even five years old. It was one of the most humiliating things I ever did. I didn't want to do it. I was embarrassed. But my papa was right—it prepared me for now. Not only did it help me and your nonna teach our own children, but it taught me the value of an education."

"What do you mean?"

"I was held back by our circumstances. The American Dream is very hard to claim. And it cannot be claimed without an education. I realized farming life was the only option for me. Now, do I complain every morning when I wake up? No. I thank God for the fortune that has befallen me. Not only have I put roofs over all of y'all, but with his help we now claim the land itself. Land is the one thing that lasts. Everything else will fade, but the land will always be there. I guaranteed our family would have land to provide for us. But that did not mean I wanted my sons to be farmers."

"Then . . ."

"The only thing I wanted them to do was to go to school. They did that. They went to A&M, they got their degrees, and they learned English before they were eighteen. My boys could have chosen a life very different from this one. Your papa got a degree in petroleum engineering. Fresh out of college, and with no war to fight, was offered a job at Standard Oil Company of New Jersey. Ever heard of them?"

"Can't say I have."

"Well, have you ever noticed gas stations in Bryan and College Station with pumps labeled Esso?"

"Yeah."

"That's what Standard Oil became. That same company was ready to offer your daddy a well-paying managerial job, to oversee numerous wells in the southeast. He could've made more money than anyone in this family has ever seen."

"We would've been city boys."

"That's right. But you know what, your papa turned it down. And you best believe we questioned him when he did so. Not for our sake, but that was a major opportunity."

"So, why'd he turn it down?"

"He wanted to be a farmer, simple as that. Said it was in his blood. I never quite bought that."

Nonno took a long pause after that last moment. Tommy could not read what was going through his grandfather's mind. Tommy feared he had brought out some hidden feeling of disappointment that Nonno had repressed until that very moment. Tommy wondered if this was the first time he would see his grandfather cry.

"I don't think your papa ever forgave me for what happened with your Aunt Ella," Nonno continued. "I realized too late that I was too lenient with her. Much more lenient than I was with Paulo. I think the farming life was something he understood, something he knew how to control. He didn't want to see another Aunt Ella situation."

Tommy remained silent in his chair. Thinking again about Matt and his letters. Was Papa still in control? He asked. Was this another Aunt Ella situation?

"Why'd you ask me that anyway?" Nonno asked, catching Tommy off guard.

"Just . . . clarity is all," Tommy said, turning his head back out the window.

The two remained quiet for a little longer after that, listening to the rumble of the road as Nonno drove his Ford around the curves. The one thing that saved them from the silence was the radio. While they had forgotten it was playing during their conversation, the change of tune caught their attention.

It was Elvis. That hubba-hubba Tennessee drawl was unmistakable. Even Tommy could pick out Elvis if he heard him on the radio. "Suspicious Minds" was the song.

The following minutes featured Nonno and Tommy singing along to the song. It was an odd mixture of both wanting to break the silence, but also enjoying the song so much that they had to sing along. There was something about Elvis' voice. It was hard not to do your best impression when you heard it.

The drive from that point on was more relaxed. They passed the houses on the opposite side of the train tracks. The Russells were a family that lived in a compound with a gate and a forested driveway. The Russells were the only remaining former Anglo plantation owners that still resided in the Bottom, although they had long abandoned the farming life to become dentists and teachers. One of the older ladies still taught at Hearne and was notorious for speeding down the highways.

Everything went smoothly once they reached the co-op. Nonno picked up his own beef, as well as Papa's. Nonno threw in a Coca-Cola bottle as a treat for riding along with him. Of course, he got himself one too. They savored the sugar water as they drove all the way back to Three Pecans.

Yet after Nonno had driven to the Big House and after Tommy had shooed off Diamond, Tommy found himself standing in the living room only to catch the tail end of the conversation that had been taking place.

"I'll hear no more of this," Papa said.

JOSH

Matt and Josh watched Tommy disappear into Nonno's truck for quite some time. Even after Matt's Ford had been topped off with diesel, they still sat there watching the car go down the row of houses and then onto the highway. They could hear Diamond's barking off in the distance, but still they remained, standing on opposite sides of the truck.

"What?" Matt asked as he leaned against the diesel tank.

"What?" Josh asked right back.

"If you've got something to say, I'd rather you just say it."

Matt huffed through his nose. Josh mirrored his movements, not responding.

"Just get in the damn truck," Matt finally said.

Josh did as he was told and climbed into the passenger seat, though he was far from surprised when Matt drove the truck further up the highway rather than stopping at Three Pecans.

Matt drove past the Wilson, Bevins, and Carr farms. In truth, the boys never knew for sure which farms they were passing. They knew the general area that they were working on a given day, but they could never draw them on a map. Only Papa and Uncle Andrew could do that. The rest could mark out the entirety of the 3,000 acres the Ruggirellos possessed, but as far as where one farm ended and another began, the lines were blurred.

Regardless, Matt drove north and then passed over the railroad tracks to the western part of the Bottom. Matt was driving with no particular destination in sight, but he did bring the truck to a stop at Deliverance Farm. This was the farm that ran right next to the Big Brazos River. This was the one farm all the boys could mark on a map, because they all knew the story behind it.

Even before the railroad had placed its tracks in the Bottom, the land that makes up Deliverance Farm had a natural levy on its eastern border. This levy was a natural place for the railroad to build, essentially forming a wall of dirt and steel for the land. Added to the fact the land was also at a slight incline to the rest and Deliverance was more or less a fishbowl.

Every season when there would be heavy rains, the Big Brazos River would flood and overflow into the land. The levy meant that the water would take a substantial amount of time to drain, making the land into a pond for months at a time. The land was deemed worthless. So worthless that its former owner, a fellow named Crockett, was begging for people to buy it from him. All he wanted was pennies for his dimes.

Well, about a year into owning the former Carson plantation, Nonno had the idea of buying that land. Everyone said it was crazy.

It was a rare moment where no one in the family supported his idea. For one, they argued that Crockett was still wanting too much money for worthless land. This only added to the fact that no one could understand Nonno's reasoning for wanting to purchase land that was deemed worthless. By this time, the Ruggirellos were not fresh off the boat. They knew Texas and its nine-month summer. They knew how the crops reacted to conditions and how to get the best produce. Even Papa Paul saw Nonno's venture as nothing more than buying a pond.

Yet Nonno proved them all wrong. That planting season was a severe drought. With this being before irrigation wells were put in place, many of the farmers were never able to produce a crop. The Ruggirellos were the only family with a naturally irrigated farm thanks to the flooding the previous season.

Nonno's mother, Theodora, christened the farm Deliverance for bearing the fruit of her son's gamble and for being able to provide for the family when those around them suffered.

This was the piece of land that Matt parked his truck on, leaping out of the Ford as he did so. Josh, very much on the defensive, took his time in stepping out. Matt may not have been a fighting man, but he would have been a plank of boardwalk had he been reborn as a tree, but that did not mean Josh was not prepared for the worst. All he knew about fighting was from the comic books Nonno would slip into his stockings at Christmas time. They were no-good model to follow for an actual confrontation.

"What're you doing?" Matt asked when he crossed over and saw Josh standing there with fists bared.

"I'm being prepared," Josh said, still holding up his fists. "You're the one who drove us out here."

"God . . . what do you think this is, Cain and Abel?"

"I'm sure Abel wished he had second guessed himself."

"I'm not wanting a fight. So put your hands down."

Josh hesitated for a moment, but did drop his hands eventually, standing at ease.

"Alright, so what's going on?" Josh asked.

"I wanted a place I could be sure we wouldn't be overheard," Matt said.

"Well, you got it. Nothing here but the river. She does talk though."

Matt was unimpressed by Josh's jest.

"I'm gonna tell Papa," Matt finally said. "About all of it."

Josh tightened his lips and started to rock his head from side to side. This was the news he had been dreading. He had suspected it, but had not been prepared to act until after he had heard it from Matt's lips.

"I don't like it," Josh said.

"I hear ya, but you've got to stand with my decision," Matt said.

"No, I don't. Don't think you'll be the only one affected by this. You already know Mama suspects something, well I got a feeling Papa don't have a clue. If you drop a ball on him like this that you've been getting all this important mail and haven't said a word, he's gonna start second-guessing everything we do. He'll start thinking we've all got secrets."

"You're paranoid."

"I'm telling you Papa is paranoid."

"Well, maybe it's worth it. Maybe Papa needs a wake-up call."

Josh hunched over slightly; mouth agape as he just stared at Matt.

"Are you hearing yourself?" Josh asked. "Don't be actin' like we don't have a good thing here. You know damn well all that Papa's done for us."

"That I do," Matt said. "I say my prayers every time we go to Church. I thank God for helping Papa provide for us the way he has. He's the only reason I've done what I've done. That's why I need to tell him. My only mistake was not telling him sooner."

"You're damn right, that's why I'm saying forget about all the rest. I say we go to the post office right now, get there before they close. Act like you just got that letter in the mail, the one from A&M. What harm is a lie if it's a joyful one?"

"Cause there's nothing joyful about it."

"Hell, Matt. You say you know what Papa's given us, but you sound like a spoiled brat. Don't be thinking A&M's the end of the world. They got other degrees there than agriculture."

"That still doesn't mean it's the right fit. And now you're assuming Papa will just let me abandon the farming life."

"You're the oldest son, the firstborn, the golden boy. Mama always said you looked like a cherub as a baby, gold curls and everything. If anyone can get out of it, it's you. But I'm asking you not to."

Josh could feel himself almost on the edge of watering eyes when he said that last plea. He did not expect it, but that's what happened.

Josh could feel his stomach tightening with Matt's announcement. He knew it wasn't going to end well. Yes, he didn't want to see Matt get hurt, but he also feared repercussions for himself, Tommy, and Susanna. He did not believe Mama or Papa would become violent, but he knew they could hold grudges.

Even so, Josh could not deny a sense of jealousy had started to swell over him in the last twenty-four hours. He was right — Matt was the favorite. The successor. The Ruggirellos were very archaic in the sense of the oldest son taking command of the family, or at least Papa was, himself a first-born son. Josh felt confident that Papa was going to deny Matt's request within an instant of hearing his proposal, but Josh also knew he would never have that option. Whatever task was given to him, the answer would always be "Yes, sir." Why? Cause the second son always had to play catch up. The second son has to live up to how great the first-born is.

Josh had always known this about himself and had confessed several times about his inner conflict. Still, he feared this might be the moment it was exposed to Matt and the rest of the family.

Matt stood tall in front of his brother.

"I'm sorry, Josh," Matt said. "I've made up my mind. I've already decided I'll live with the consequences, whatever they be."

Josh tightened his lips again and clenched his eyes and fists. He did not curse, nor did he lash out. All he did was utter a whisper as he heaved a tremendous breath.

"But we have to live with those consequences too."

Again, Matt did not hear the comment and squeezed Josh's shoulder as he circled him to climb back into the truck. Josh realized he had lost, again. He could not stop Matt once his mind was made up. It reminded him of Papa. Defeated, he climbed back into the truck.

Papa, again, was not home once Matt and Josh made it back to Three Pecans. Susanna greeted them at the porch when she heard the sound of Diamond barking. She asked where Tommy was and they explained that he had gone to the co-op with Nonno.

"I told Paul ten times he needed to go pick up that beef," Mama said, overhearing what they had explained from outside. "Sometimes he can be so stupid."

"Well, Tommy should have it when he comes back," Josh said.

"Yes, but your father should've picked it up yesterday so we could eat it today," Mama said. "It's probably no-good now. You've got to cook that beef when it's fresh or it'll spoil."

"I'm sure it'll be fine," Matt said as he helped lay the silverware on the table.

Mama was already assuming whatever beef was waiting at the co-op had spoiled. Instead, she had prepared pork chops on the frying pan and had mashed potatoes along with boiled broccoli. The pork chops were gifted from Nonno, who had slaughtered the pigs himself before sending them to the butcher.

To the surprise of Matt and Josh, the unmistakable sound of The Mustang rolling to a halt reached their ears before Tommy burst through the doors.

Papa stepped inside, his boot-less feet still causing the floor to creak under his weight. He went to the kitchen sink and rolled up his plaid sleeves to the elbow to wash his hands. Josh looked over at Papa, his sweat crusted hairy arms hiding how pale his skin was underneath.

Papa's shirts were always soaked through with sweat, but the only parts of his body to get touched by the sun were his face and hands. One may think it counterintuitive to wear long-sleeved shirts in the burning summer, but it was the right choice. If they kept sweating, they would stay cool and could keep working. If the skin burned, they would be hampered. Regardless, Papa's hands were as crusted as overcooked bread, in contrast to the rest of his body.

Papa washed his face and ran his hands through his hair to further slick it back with the excess water. Without further delay, he took his seat at the table. After some questions and answers about Tommy's presence, they said their prayers and commenced with the meal.

They all shared the usual chitchat about any number of things, but also ate their meal in prolonged silence for periods at a time. Not an awkward silence, though Matt and Josh could feel their blood pumping faster with each tick of the clock, but a comfortable silence. The silence that comes when a family is taking in the pleasure of a good meal and not spoiling it with needless comments.

Josh did not notice if Matt was looking his way, but Josh kept darting his eyes between Matt and Papa. Josh could see it on the way, Matt was going to speak. Josh was only trying to prepare for when it would happen.

As it happened, Matt was sympathetic toward everyone else's desire to eat dinner. Had Matt gotten into his dialogue too early, everyone would have been sent off to their rooms only a third of the way through their meals. There was no scenario where Josh or Susanna got permission to eat in their rooms.

Even though Josh never relaxed, they finished their meals together. But with each clink of fork and knife against the plate, and with each bite of his dinner, Josh could feel his blood pound faster and faster. It seemed as if Josh looked across the table one moment and he looked down the next to find he had finished his dinner.

"Must have been good cooking, Violet," Papa said to Mama from across the table. "I ain't never seen Joshua eat that fast."

Josh wiped his mouth before speaking. "Guess I was just hungrier than expected," he said, coughing after the fact. "It was delicious, Mama."

"Well, thank you," Mama said. "But you best learn to savor those meals. Count your blessing that you don't have to race the rest of us for your portion of food."

"Yes ma'am," Josh replied.

Josh sat there, mopping up the potatoes on his plate with slices of bread and cleansing his palate with iced water. Josh saw that Papa was moments away from finishing his own plate. Then as Papa finished wiping his mouth with his napkin, and before the napkin even fell to the plate, Matt spoke up.

"Papa, there's something I've been meaning to tell you," Matt said.

Papa did not immediately respond as he was still swallowing the scraps of food he had just forked into his mouth. Josh spotted Mama lock her gaze on Matt when he spoke, though she said nothing.

"You do?" Papa asked, not sure what to make of Matt's speaking up.

"Yes, sir," Matt replied, somewhat timid.

"Joshua, help your sister clear the table," Mama said.

Josh had clinched his entire body once Matt spoke up. The moment had arrived. He had anticipated it so much that he had not even noticed Susanna get up and start to clear the table. Mama had saved a plate of food for Tommy but there were no more scraps of food to save. The two discarded the dishes into the kitchen sink and topped it off with soapy water, letting the bubbles billow to the surface.

"Well, what is it you wanted to say?" Papa asked as Josh had his back turned.

Susanna noticed Josh's face fade of all distinguishable colors as the conversation behind them began. She gently grabbed his arm and that seemed to break the trance. Josh responded by pulling her in the direction of their separate rooms.

Had Mama been not as focused, she might have called them to take their seats back at the dining table. As it stood, Josh deemed it safer for them to retreat to the doorframes of their bedrooms.

"I haven't been honest with y'all lately," Matt said.

Hearing those words made Mama and Papa angle their chairs so they better faced Matt. Josh could tell they were already imagining the worst possible scenarios.

"On my last few trips to the post office, I've been getting mail and haven't told you about it."

Mama sat up, preparing to speak, but Papa put his hand out. A sign to let Matt continue to talk.

"At the end of the school year, my teachers told me I was named a National Merit Scholar. I never mentioned it because I didn't think it meant anything other than a good test score. But a couple weeks ago, I started getting scholarship offers from schools. Some schools I'd never heard of, but letter after letter kept coming, are still coming. I was hesitant to bring this up before because I was overwhelmed by the volume, but I feel this is something we should look into."

Matt proceeded to list out all the schools that had sent him scholarship offers. He made sure to mention all the Texas schools, and where they were, but also the out-of-state schools, and where they were. Matt recalled some scholarship figures from memory but estimated with others. It was then that he went into his bedroom and retrieved every letter. Thirty-five in total. Mama and Papa got to see the sheer volume of offers he had received. Then, it was done. Matt had said all he could say. Every detail was put forward. What followed was silence.

The three of them just sat at the table and did not say a word. The only noises that passed through the house was the slightest sound of the ticking clock and a bray from the old white bull outside.

"I don't understand," Mama finally said.

Josh was not surprised that she was the one to break the silence.

"Why don't you want to go to A&M?" Mama continued.

"I'm not saying that, Mama," Matt responded.

"It sounds that way. What're you doing writing letters to all these places you ain't never heard of?"

"I didn't write to them. They wrote to me."

"Well, how'd they know where to send them?"

"From the test results. From the school. I don't know exactly. But that doesn't really matter."

"Well, how do you know these are real?"

Matt looked across the table with a look of exhaustion at his mother.

"I . . . faith, I would say," Matt said. "Faith that someone did not waste their time in preparing dozens of letters offering college funds without any clear reason."

"They could be trying to trick you to get our money," Mama said.

"Mama, that's what I'm saying. They're offering us money. In a sense."

"All because of a test result?"

"No, Mama. The test was how I got noticed. My grades are what earned the offers. The letters are my hard work paying off."

"Seems impersonal. Why don't they have someone come up here and talk to us in person, rather than sneaking letters to our children. I don't like no backdoor dealings."

"Mama, you're overthinking it . . ."

At this moment, a large, hairy, and scabbed paw raised itself up from the table. Papa, with his eyes still toward the table, held up his hand as if the spirit was compelling him to speak. He did not speak right away, but the motion silenced Matt right then and there.

"That's enough of that," Papa said, so low it might as well have been a whisper. "A&M is a good school. It's where everyone in this family has gone to school. We know they'll take care of y'all, and they'll prepare you for when you're grown and have to lead a life of your own. That's it."

Matt watched as Papa lowered his hand to the surface of the table. The tightness in his body made the motion feel long and excruciating, even if it only lasted two seconds. But the moment Papa's palm returned to the table, Matt spoke up.

"Papa, I'm not saying A&M isn't a good school," Matt said. "I'm saying why not look at others if one might be a better fit for me."

"That means you don't think A&M is a good fit," Papa replied.

"I'm saying I don't know one way or the other."

"And you think one of these places you've never heard of might be a better fit? I tell ya right now, that don't make any sense. Your Mama and I have done good to save money for you to go to school. No more needs to be said."

"Papa, don't think I'm not grateful for what you've done, but I don't just wanna throw away something I've earned from my hard work."

Papa did not say anything for a moment. He had yet to raise his chin and make eye contact with Matt. For now, they just sat across from each other, talking into the table.

"That's what I don't get," Papa said. "Why are we only just now hearing about this? I don't like that my son's been keeping secrets in my own home."

"I didn't say anything at first cause I wasn't sure what it all was," Matt said.

"But you have over 30 letters," Papa said. "This didn't just happen."

Matt paused. Josh saw that he was making fists with his hands, as if he was fighting what he was about to say.

"Well, if I'm being honest, Papa," Matt began, "I debated saying anything about this at all . . . because I thought you might disregard it entirely."

Papa was sitting up in his chair at this point, left arm reclining across the open chair by his side. A different man would have been smoking a cigarette or enjoying a glass of bourbon at that hour. Not Papa. Apart from a bit of fatigue, Papa was totally present.

"Well," Papa said, patting the table for a second. "Maybe it's right, I didn't know. It's foolishness. What point is there talking about running off to some school you don't know, towns you don't know, people you don't know? You don't really want to do it, it's just something different. Something that excites you. It's not real."

Matt's hands were now white around the edges. Blood may have started scratching against his nails if he were to open the palm.

"Papa, it is real," Matt said.

"Matthew," Papa said, but Matt continued.

"You don't want to acknowledge it cause you don't know what to make of it. Even I'm not sure what to make of it all sometimes. But it could be something big. It could be an opportunity."

"Matthew."

"Maybe I find something I didn't know about myself at one of these schools. Maybe I'll get to do something bigger than myself. And maybe I'm wrong. Maybe A&M is the right school for me. Maybe it's better if I stay home. The fact is I don't know, and I want to know. I feel it could be an opportunity and I think I earned the right to take it. I put the work in at school and I don't want to throw it away."

"Sietete!"

There was the word. The one word that told them all that the talking was done. Josh had never found the word written in any dictionary or Italian-to-English translation book, but they all knew it was Papa's word telling them that they were not to speak anymore. Papa had likely misheard the word for silence once and it had stuck with him as "Sietete." Now they knew what it meant.

"I'll hear no more of this," Papa said, sitting up in his chair. "This isn't like you, Matthew. Speaking out when you shouldn't. Acting like you know better than us. I'll hear no more."

It was at this moment that they heard the screen door open and close. They all turned toward it. Papa and Mama noticed Josh had been standing in his doorway the entire time, but they did not look at him. Tommy had finally come home, several slices of beef all wrapped in brown paper in his hands as he looked at what was going on in the living room.

In that moment of hesitation, where Papa did not charge off to his bedroom or to his sofa chair, Matt stood up and stomped his way out of the house.

"Matt?" Tommy asked as his brother passed him.

"Matthew! Where are you going?" Mama called from the porch steps, having followed him out.

One by one, they all trickled onto the porch and watched from a distance as Matt climbed into his hand-me-down Oldsmobile, turned the keys in the ignition and sped off down the road.

Papa did not rush after Matt. Instead, he strolled off the porch and to the front gate, putting his hand down to stop Diamond from jumping onto his legs. By that point, the family were all watching Matt's taillights as the Oldsmobile disappeared down the road.

"Are you not going to go after him?" Mama shouted at Papa from atop the porch.

"That wouldn't do any good," Papa said, only mildly raising his voice. "Then there'd just be two of us on the road late at night. Only risks the danger of a crash. Don't want that."

"So you're just gonna do nothing?"

"He's full of hot air. Just needs to blow it off. When he does, he'll come back here."

By then, Josh had drifted to Tommy's side. He looked up at his older brother.

"What happened?" Tommy asked, trying to speak softly enough that he would not be overheard.

103

"He told them," Josh answered. "Told them everything. And he didn't like the response he got."

"Oh. Well darn. So, he just ran off?"

"Looks like it."

"Where to?"

"Who knows."

"This is bad."

"No shit."

They looked to their right as Susanna walked over to them, arms folded across her chest as if she was the one who had been insulted.

"You two knew about this?" Susanna asked.

Josh and Tommy nodded their heads.

"Alright," Susanna said. "You'd best keep that information to yourself. No need for this to get worse than it already is."

"You all gone get to bed now," Papa said from below. "No need for y'all to be staying up for all this."

There was a moment of hesitation where the three siblings just stood on the porch, looking at each other. Josh knew he wanted to stay up and wait to see what happened to Matt, but he couldn't speak for the others. In the end, they all did as they were told and went off to bed. But not to sleep.

Josh had rolled right up against the wall of his bedroom and had cracked his window open ever so slightly so that he could hear what was being said outside. Mama and Papa had retrieved their newspapers from the house and were sitting in the rocking chairs.

"Oh, Paul, why don't you go looking for the boy?" Mama asked, more as a way to get him to act than actually asking a question.

"I done told you it wouldn't do any good," Papa replied.

"Ain't you worried about him?"

"Course I am, but this is a lesson. Can't just run off all angry like and expect us to come after him. Went looking for him once. He knows to come back."

Josh could hear Mama groan. Then there were a few moments of silence where the only noise was the creaking of the rocking chair.

"Do you want to talk about it?" Mama asked.

"Bout what?" Papa asked.

"About this whole, National Merit Scholar business."

"Oh gosh. Don't start that. This is what I'm saying. He runs off and we start to get sympathetic toward him. It doesn't work like that. We've known what's right for him. He can't be throwing this in at the last moment. Ain't no more to be said."

Even with Papa making that statement, Josh knew there would be ripples from what Matt had revealed that night. They just had to wait and see what happened.

The two sat on the chairs for over an hour and fell asleep where they sat. It was the sound of violent snoring that woke Josh in the middle of the night. He was the first to spot the flashing of police lights in the distance. Lights that traveled all the way down the road until they were parked right in front of Three Pecans. Following behind the cruiser was Matt's Oldsmobile.

MATT

Matt had sped off down the road with no destination or purpose. He was angry and frustrated. He just wanted to get away, needed to get away. If he had stayed put, he was likely to say something he would go on to regret, or at the very least receive a punishment that would help nothing.

The music had drowned out Matt's thoughts. One song after another, they rolled through the radio. Most of it was nonsensical static, but now and then Matt stumbled across a sweet spot. First it was "Hair," a song by The Cowsills that Matt could never remember any of the lyrics to, but he liked the beat. After that, the rest just faded.

He thought of another night where he disappeared into the darkness down a lonely road. That night at the pasture party with the Dodge boys. At the time, he thought nothing of it, but then he saw how freaked the rest of the family had been. The thought of disappearing down a lonely road once again just seemed stupid in Matt's mind.

His furious departure had resulted in a headache. Combined with the lateness of the night, Matt was growing feint. After an uncertain amount of time driving, Matt could feel himself beginning to lose control. Doing the responsible thing, he pulled over on the side of the road.

With no lights, mile markers or street signs in sight, Matt had absolutely no idea where he was. He wagered he had been driving for the better part of forty minutes, north by northwest or somewhere close to that direction. Matt felt a tinge of panic at the realization he did not know how to get back to Three Pecans. But after the moment of panic passed, he told himself that he would rest his eyes for a moment.

Matt did not remember falling asleep. He woke to the light of a policeman's flashlight.

"Well, shoot, I thought I recognized this car," the voice said before turning off his flashlight.

Only then was Matt able to look up at the man's face and see that it was his uncle, Frank LaCarpentera, sheriff's deputy of Robertson County. Uncle Frank was really Mama's first cousin but everyone called him Uncle Frank to save the trouble. The LaCarpenteras were farmers like all the rest in Highbank but Uncle Frank always seemed cut from a different breed. The story goes Uncle Frank liked the feeling of a gun in his hand a little too much.

Uncle Frank's presence told Matt just how far he had traveled from home. Matt saw that it was still dark outside, telling him that not much time had passed, but he still had no idea what time it was.

"What the hell are you doing out here at this hour?" Uncle Frank asked, leaning against the side of the car.

"Went driving, wasn't sure where I was, wasn't sure how to get back," Matt replied. "We in Calvert?"

"About a mile or two from it, yeah. Where were you going?"

"Nowhere. Just needed to get out."

"Wanna tell me why?"

Matt paused for a moment. "A family dispute. It's a bit of a long story. I just needed to clear my head."

Uncle Frank leaned closer. "Show me your eyes, will ya," he said, shining his flashlight in Matt's eyes again. He held it there for a few moments but clicked it off just as fast.

"Won't lie to you, son," Uncle Frank began, "I thought you were one of those hippies when I saw your car parked on the road. Thought you were here smoking grass or some shit."

"Nah, Uncle Frank, that ain't me," Matt said. "Wouldn't know where to find some even if I wanted it."

Uncle Frank called Matt a good boy and offered to lead him back to Three Pecans. Matt kindly accepted it and the two began the drive back southbound.

When the two arrived at the house, they spotted Mama and Papa asleep on the porch. Uncle Frank did not blare his siren, but he did flash the blue and red lights long enough for it to stir them awake. They could hardly believe what they were seeing as they stepped off the porch.

"Frank, is that you?" Mama asked.

"Yes, it's me," Uncle Frank replied. "Found Matty here on the side of the road. Don't be concerned, he's alright. Just got lost and didn't know how to get back. Made sure I got him home safe and sound."

"Well, we thank you, Frank," Papa said. "Matthew, go on and get to bed. It's late enough as it is."

Matt looked at Mama and Papa and then at Uncle Frank before heading into the house. Before he did, Papa held out his hand. Without having to say a word, Matt dropped the keys to the Oldsmobile in Papa's hands. The first of many punishments to come his way, Matt thought.

Even as he walked away, Matt could overhear pieces of their conversation.

"So, what's all this about?" Uncle Frank asked. "It ain't like Matty to drive off like that."

"It's uh, it's been a rather uneasy afternoon," Papa said. "Stuff with school we needed to discuss."

"Stuff with school? Hell, Matty's always been good about his schoolin."

"It's not about the schooling necessarily, but it's about school. Understand?"

"Somewhat. Anyway, didn't smell no drugs when I found him, so you ain't got to worry about that. No empty Jack Daniels bottles either," Uncle Frank said with a laugh.

"Well, that is good news to hear nonetheless," Mama said.

"Anywho, I best be off," Uncle Frank said. "Go easy on your boy, he's a good kid. Good night y'all."

Mama and Papa said their goodnights and soon retreated inside the house. They paused momentarily outside Matt's room but did not go inside to resume their conversation. The entire house just went to bed, putting the day's argument behind them.

Matt tossed in his bed for a while. Be it a result of his having taken a nap on the side of the road or from Matt thinking about any number of consequences that could come from his speaking out, slumber did not come easy. Matt imagined waking up and finding himself locked inside his room, only to be let out once he decided to not argue with Papa anymore. He also imagined waking up and finding all the letters gone or torn up, not a trace left. He was not sure if this seemed like something Papa or Mama would do, but he still imagined it.

Even so, once Matt did fall asleep, he dreamed of absolutely nothing. What did wake Matt was the first instance of light peeking through his window and shining into his eyes. There was a subtle chitter of birds, but no loud barking from Diamond that usually signaled the start of the morning.

Matt rolled over to look at his clock. Six in the morning, right on time. Matt took a moment to check that the letters were still under his bed where he had stashed them and then got to his feet to dress. Yet, when Matt went into the hall to brush his teeth, Mama stopped him.

"You can wait till your brothers have gone," Mama said as she flipped one of three eggs on a frying pan.

She was making egg sandwiches with wheat bread and slices of cheddar cheese. Mama's trick was to toast the bread, lay the cold cheese on the bread, and then let the heat of the egg melt the cheese into the sandwich. They were a breakfast the boys could eat while on the go when they did not have the time to sit at the table together. Matt caught a glimpse of how many eggs she was frying and thought she was short by one.

"What was that?" Matt asked.

"I said wait till after your brothers have gone," Mama said. "They've got to go out, you're staying with us today."

"With you?" Matt asked, perplexed.

"With us," Susanna said, appearing from behind Matt in her nightgown and walking into the kitchen to assist Mama in preparing breakfast.

Susanna, stone faced yet still not entirely awake, set about preparing the peanut butter sandwiches that acted as the boys' lunch when they went out to work. There was no time for them to come back to the house for lunch, so they always ate on the bed of their trucks, usually underneath the shade of a tree.

Two sandwiches each, apples, crackers, a can of cashews and various nuts to share between themselves, and jugs of water that had been chilled the night before.

This time, there was no meal prepared for Matt.

"Papa's already gone out for the day," Mama said, coming back with a pile of clothes that had been drying on the rack outside. "You're to stay here and help us at the house. Josh will drive your truck. The two of them have already discussed it."

Matt knew there were going to be consequences from his speeding off. He half expected Papa to stand before him and list the consequences like Moses delivering the Commandments, but that was not Papa. Papa did not like confrontations. It was better to just make his decision and move on, or at least Matt assumed Papa believed this.

Josh and Tommy gave an expression of surprise at the news about Matt, but they did not voice their disapproval, nor did Matt wish them to. He preferred to deal with the consequences himself.

Once Josh and Tommy had departed, Matt ate a breakfast of scrambled eggs, crispy bacon, tangerines, and buttered toast along with Mama and Susanna. It was strange to be in that setting, like he was getting a window into a society he was never privy to seeing before. Susanna almost seemed uncomforted by his presence, as if with one step she might wander outside of familiar territory.

Mama had no such thoughts. She put Matt to work right away. Guiding him onto the porch, she pointed out how tall the grass had grown in the lawn. It had gotten to a point where it was so tall that when Diamond laid down, he would all but vanish, only to pop up at a moment's notice.

For hours Matt drove the lawn mower up and down the yard, the blades turning with every step he took, until every square foot had been trimmed. It grew to a point where it actually looked like a yard. What had been tall dark grass was now a thin, light colored surface. Birds would come down from the trees to pick at the fresh cut grass and whatever bugs might be turned into snacks. Diamond did his best to catch the birds but only managed to frighten them off. Some did swoop down to peck his head in retaliation though.

By the end of it, Three Pecans' front lawn reflected a home that people lived in and not an abandoned plantation house. Once Matt had cut that grass, he went into the garden and cut the grass in the garden. Granted, Nonna made sure the garden was neater, for lack of a better word. Once that was done, he went back through the garden and pulled as many weeds out of the ground as he could find. Only then did Matt allow himself to take a breather on the porch.

Matt could overhear a conversation going on between Mama and Susanna as he rested on the porch, drinking from his jug of water. Mama had removed all the sheets from the beds and had thrown them in a pile to wash later. The fresh sheets had finished drying that morning and now they were making the beds.

"No, not like that," Mama shouted from inside one of the distant bedrooms. "You've got to get them all tucked in on equal sides. See, now that side's gone pulled clean off."

"I did it like you said, Mama," Susanna said.

"No, you didn't. If you did, I wouldn't be telling you this right now. Now just stop. I'll fix it myself."

Matt listened as Mama continued to critique Susanna's skill at making a bed. It was strange. A part of him felt like he should have gone into the room to stand up for his sister or at least to see what was going on. But the other part was afraid. Afraid that Mama might turn her gaze and ferocity onto him. For that reason, he stayed put.

But he continued to listen.

He listened as Mama critiqued how Susanna was wearing a wrinkled dress, how she had not cleaned up a smudge on her skirt, how she had not properly washed her face, how she had yet to turn on the radio, and on and on and on. Matt could not believe his ears. Mama just would not be pleased with anything that was happening around her.

Eventually, they returned to the living room, and Mama took a seat in her cushioned chair. Susanna went to the kitchen sink and set about rubbing the first of several sheets on the washing rack, but Mama stopped her.

"None of that now," Mama said from the comfort of her chair. "Why don't you play something on the piano?"

Mama may have phrased it as a question, but there was no room for debate. Susanna had to push away dozens of pieces of paper that Mama had been writing on. The piano was transformed into Mama's makeshift desk.

Matt scooted himself closer to the door so that he could listen but without being seen.

He listened as Susanna played her music. Matt, never having touched the instrument before, had no idea why each key of the piano made the different sounds that it did, but it was pleasant noise. It reminded Matt of mass, for that was the only place Matt had ever heard such music. Even so, he could tell this was not the sound of a random person pressing down on the keys.

Susanna knew exactly what the piano would resonate if she pressed each key in a certain order.

Matt had no guess as to who the composer was. Some long dead French or German man whose name Matt would never be able to pronounce properly, he assumed. Regardless, he acknowledged they had made joyful noise. Yet what he could not get over was Susanna was the one performing.

Not once had she performed for the family, not even during Thanksgiving or Christmas when someone would have asked her to perform. Never had Susanna revealed this part of herself, yet it was clear she had worked on her craft and was no amateur, even if it was some secret.

Susanna played for ten minutes, long enough for Diamond to walk over to the porch and rest his massive head on the hardwood. With the laziest of motions, he licked the side of Matt's boot. It was only after Matt gently nudged Diamond away that he realized the music had stopped.

Leaning closer to the window, Matt could hear the sound of snoring in the distance. Tucking his head into the room, he saw that Mama was passed out in her chair, leaning to her left side as her limp hands clutched her newspaper.

Matt looked to his left and saw Susanna still sitting at the piano. She too had glanced back at Mama's sleeping position, then at Matt. She stood up and walked outside to join him on the porch.

Susanna looked down at his reclined position. Rather than join him on the surface of the porch, she took a seat in one of the rocking chairs. Susanna didn't look at Matt. She just looked out past the garden and over the railroad tracks.

"You're very good at that," Matt said, looking up at his sister.

"Thank you," Susanna said, still looking away. "I guess it's a blessing you made Papa angry. The yard was in a terrible state."

"Yeah, I guess that's one good thing to come out of this."

"You'll never see Mama pushing a lawnmower up and down the yard, that's for sure."

"True."

Matt paused, listening to the cicadas for a moment.

"Why haven't you played the piano with the rest of us around?" Matt asked.

"No one ever asked me too," Susanna answered.

"Yeah, but if you're that good I thought you'd wanna show everybody."

"You only think I'm good cause you've never heard anybody else play."

"I've heard the people in mass."

"Yeah, and that's about as good as I am. I'm not one to boast. It's just a skill you learn. No different than driving a car or tying your shoes."

Matt seemed surprised that Susanna would brush aside something she clearly had worked on perfecting. Even if Matt had never touched the keys on a piano, he knew Susanna was not doing something anyone could do on the first try.

"Ain't ever heard you practice, though," Matt continued.

"You ain't ever been housebound before," Susanna commented. "Mama has me taking lessons at St. Joseph's every Tuesday. I go practice while she's running errands."

"You haven't ever talked about them."

"Haven't cared to. Only doing what Mama says. She says she wants me to play for the Church one day. Maybe be the music director."

"You haven't talked about that, either."

Susanna shrugged her shoulders. "Doesn't really mean anything to anyone else."

"But if it's something you want to do?"

Susanna didn't respond. She just continued to look out past the pecan trees and the gravel road. She squinted her eyes as the light from the sun warmed their faces. Matt thought he could read his sister in that moment. The piano was not an object of her affection, it was just something she did. Like she said, just like tying shoelaces. It was something she could do, not necessarily something she loved to do.

"I have to say, Matt, I'm surprised by you," Susanna said.

"What do you mean?" Matt asked.

"Driving off in the middle of the night. Keeping all those letters a secret. Standing up to Papa. I thought that was behind you. It's not you."

"What do you mean it's not me?"

"You don't cause strife. You're always doing what Mama and Papa told you to do, no questions asked. Sure, you might grumble, but you did the work. What changed?"

Matt had to push himself up onto his hands before responding to this query.

"What changed? What changed is I'm being offered something for my hard work and Papa wants to completely ignore it."

"But why would you speak out?"

Matt paused. "What?"

"You heard me. Why would you speak out?"

"Why wouldn't I speak out?"

"If you knew Papa would react the way he did."

"But I didn't."

"But you did. This wasn't something Papa knew about. It was news from outside the family that Papa had no control over. You shook things up, and Papa doesn't like not being in control. That and you went against the Aggies."

"Jesus Christ," Matt said in a whisper.

Even though he did not shout the curse, they both paused for a moment to make sure Mama had not been listening in on them. Had she heard Matt curse, there would definitely have been a punishment. To their relief, they could still hear the sound of her snoring.

"I did not go against the Aggies," Matt said, still keeping his voice calm.

"But that was all Papa heard," Susanna said. "You kept mentioning how one of those schools could be the right fit. To Papa, that meant A&M wasn't the right fit."

Matt leaned his head back against the side of the house, letting Susanna hear the thud of his head against wood. Had he been with Josh or Tommy, he might've screamed in frustration, but not then. He let out a deep sigh as if he was an exhaust pipe.

It was then that Matt went into his argument about how he did not know if A&M was the right school. He hammered home the point that he had not once traveled to the campus or had any idea what he would want to study once he got there.

"Just study what Papa studied," Susanna said, calm after hearing Matt's statement.

Matt clenched his hands together in an exaggerated attempt to keep himself from screaming.

"But that's the point," Matt said. "Why can't I decide what I want to study? Why can't I find out what I want to do?"

"Because it isn't what Papa wants," Susanna said, a cold air swiping across her stoic expression. "Papa's provided for everything we have. When have we ever gone a night without something we needed? It's not cause Papa's rich, but because he's been responsible and knows what we need. They've done that, we should just do what they say."

"That's why you play the piano and let Mama talk to you like that?"

Susanna paused, turned to Matt and chuckled at him.

"Don't be all righteous. Mama talks to us all like that. She talks to me like that every day, y'all just never noticed. There isn't a point fighting with either of them. You aren't gonna change their minds. It's just better to do what we're told to do. It's worked out so far doing it this way. They know what's best for us."

Matt shot up to his feet. He stepped over toward Susanna so that he could look down at her but was also in the doorway to the house. He took a moment to glance at Mama, still asleep in her chair. Matt leaned forward and whispered as he continued.

"They know what is good for us, to a point," Matt said. "They know how to make sure we're taken care of and how to make a life, in this setting. Only this place. They don't consider an alternative. This is all they know."

"It's all any of us know," Susanna replied.

Matt took a step back. He leaned against the doorway, staring at Mama as she continued to sleep in her chair. Then he looked back at the side of the house, at Diamond rolling on his back in the fresh cut grass. He looked past the train tracks. Nothing but farmland for miles.

"This ain't the life for me," Matt said. "You know, sis, I don't think I'd ever thought about it until a few weeks ago. Like, I would have been content with all that this is. Then, I don't know. Like a seed got planted. A tiny chink in the armor . . ."

"An ounce of doubt."

"Yeah. That's all I needed."

"What're you saying? You had an epiphany?"

"Hell, those are supposed to be world shaking. I think I'd have noticed. Nah, this was more like not realizing something had been there the entire time."

"And what did you see?"

"That I'm not a farmer."

Susanna just continued to rock in her chair after Matt said his peace.

"Don't think that news will thrill Papa when he hears it," Susanna said.

"No, probably not," Matt said, leaning against the side of the house.

"Don't you know all this is supposed to go to you one day?"

"One third."

"Whatever. Papa's been grooming you. It's clear as day. Don't think you get to drive two cars just cause you're the oldest."

Matt sighed. He knew she was right. Even if Papa had never made some grand statement about how he was grooming Matt to take over the farm, but it was clear. It was always "Matt, take your brothers . . ." or "Matt, you and your brothers . . ." Matt was always leading the trio in Papa's eyes. It would be wrong to say Papa was old-fashioned. Rather, that was the only fashion he knew.

Maybe it was archaic to have so much emphasis on the oldest son taking over, but that was how they were. The entire family had been like that for generations. That was why Nonno had so much sway over all the happenings. The last one to be born in the old country.

Matt was starting to fancy himself a trailblazer. A rock in the middle of a free-flowing stream. Even if he was dreading the conversations that were soon to come.

"Well, I don't even know why we're standing around talking about it," Matt said. "Nothing I say is going to change Papa's mind. Or Mama's."

"You just now realized that?" Susanna asked with an appropriate amount of sarcasm. "Just don't be thinking about doing anything extreme."

"Like what?"

"No, sir, I'm not giving you any ideas. Just don't do something that's gonna infuriate somebody. It ain't worth being a firebrand if it cuts you off from your family."

"Firebrand?"

"Yeah. Look it up in your Funk & Wagnalls. It doesn't matter. My point is, don't end up alone on a hill with no one to help you."

At that exact moment, the Union Pacific train blazed down the tracks. Matt and Susanna had not heard the train's horns or any sound of the locomotive's arrival. Usually, they could hear the train coming from two miles out. Regardless, it blazed past Three Pecans and made every part of the white house leap off of the ground.

The grass itself rattled and Diamond shot up to bark at the train as it clattered past, each wheel clicking as it rolled over the tracks. Matt and Susanna heard muttering and looked inside to see Mama stirring awake. Whether it was the train's horn or the shaking of the house, Mama was now waking up and it for sure was a rude one.

Matt made eye contact as if to say, "She's up," and they both walked inside.

"You alright, Mama?" Matt asked as he gripped her right shoulder.

"Yes, yes, I'm fine," Mama said, sitting up in her chair. "This darn house. Rattles like the earth is opening up with every little bump. Drives me crazy. Nonno and Nonna never have this problem."

"Well, we're closer to the railroad than they are," Susanna said.

"Yeah, but it's this house. Ain't built right," Mama said.

"Well, maybe there's something we can add," Matt said. "I mean Papa did build this house himself."

"You think there's something to fix this house? I don't believe it," Mama said. "Shoot, my daddy built our house when I was your age. It never rattled."

"Well, I'm sorry, Mama but this one does," Matt said. "If you wanna find out how to fix it, that's another conversation."

"Uh huh," Mama said, standing up from the chair.

Now that Mama was up, she gave Susanna the task of washing the set of sheets they had stripped from the beds that same morning. Together, they stood at the sink as hot water poured from the drain to make a soap bath in the sink. Little by little, they ran the sheets over the washing board, making a rhythmic grind with each up and down motion.

When Matt casually asked what he could do, Mama guided him to the pile of trash that was collecting in the bin. Mama commanded Matt to take out the trash and take care of the rest in the back.

Matt did as he was told and pulled the plastic bag out of the bin. Tying the strings into a knot, he took a moment to grab the tiny packet of matches that Mama kept by the candles that sat on the windowsill.

"Take two of the gas containers with you," Mama said with her back to Matt and her face to the sink. "I need to fill up the Cadillac."

Matt stopped to put the matches in his pocket.

"Why not let me just drive the Cadillac to the gas pumps?" Matt asked.

Mama looked back at him with an expression that said Diamond would start talking before Matt got to drive any type of car again. Matt somewhat expected that response, but the question was still worth asking. He did not see the point of filling up two gas containers just to empty them into the Cadillac when he could drive the Cadillac to the pumps.

Regardless, Matt had lost, so he picked up the two gas containers when he went outside. The pieces of red plastic sat on the porch outside with the caps screwed tight. No one was about to bring them inside. No need for bits of gasoline to drip onto the living room floor.

Same sentiment as dirt on boot heels.

Matt stepped off the porch with the trash bag in one hand and the gasoline containers in another. Matt could hold one container with just two fingers. Diamond was nowhere to be found, but Matt did not mind that. He was able to pass through the side gate with ease as a result.

Matt stepped through the gate and heard a mooing sound. He looked behind him to see the old white bull. The beast had craned its neck so that it was looking behind himself at Matt.

"Don't know what you've got to cry about," Matt said. "You've got the easy life."

Matt deposited the trash bag he was carrying in the very center of the lot road. The front gate was closed, so it didn't look like he would be blocking anyone's path at that time. He did find it odd to be in the lot and to not see his Ford truck sitting in the distance. There was no telling where Josh and Tommy would have been at that moment.

It did feel strange to be away from them, but he figured that would be his entire life soon enough.

Matt turned back around and opened up the cabin. The closet shaped structure, which may have been an outhouse in the olden days, rested right next to the paddock holding the three horses. Luke's Horse had wandered over, curious at the new arrival. Even the horse knew it was strange for one of the boys to be near the house at that hour. Luke's Horse chomped on his grits as he watched Matt intently.

Matt opened the door and had to cover his nose from the stench of how many bags had been stuffed in. At first, Matt thought there were five bags. That number increased to seven. He was not sure how they had crammed so many inside, but there they were, all strewn across the ground.

For Matt's sake, he was thankful that none of the bags split open and spilled their trash over the floor. Soon enough, they were all stacked in a radical pile that resembled a mound of rotten ground beef, more so than bits of common plastic and other trash.

"How the hell did this happen?" Matt said under his breath.

Matt heard mooing again and saw the old white bull was still braying at him. If he craned his neck any further, the bull might snap it off. Matt could not figure out what it was the old bull could have wanted.

He then picked up the two red gas containers and walked over to the middle of the yard. On opposite sides of one of the paddocks where Papa kept the broken tractors were two gas pumps. They were made of sharp metals but with perfectly smooth surfaces. They were colored bright brown and shiny, almost like red wood.

On them was the label Sinclair Oil Corporation, a company whose logo was a bright green Brontosaurus that was also labeled Dino. Because of that, the boys called it Dino Gasoline. "Fill it up with the Dino," is what Tommy would say when he saw the Cadillac or the Oldsmobile were low on gas.

They were gas pumps just like any other you would see at a station. Nonno always made sure someone was out to wash and polish the pumps, so they looked neat when the trucks came by to fill up the underground tanks. Sometimes that task fell to the boys. Regardless, Nonno didn't want the oil men thinking the Ruggirello farm was a place of disorganization. Matt was sure they would still have filled up the tanks, regardless of what it looked like. People didn't refuse money.

Nonno saw the tanks as a worthy expense, just like the diesel tanks. Why have everyone in the family rushing into town to fill up their cars, and rack up unnecessary miles, when he could pay a fee to have tanks for the entire family to use. Nonno was very giving in that way, at least in regards to family.

Matt unscrewed the caps of the two containers and, little by little, filled them to the brim with gasoline. Matt had to catch himself at one point as the gasoline containers went from weightless to several pounds. He would not be able to carry them with one hand like he had been.

As he filled them up, the sick cows in the adjacent paddock brayed at him. Their braying only led to the old white bull braying louder. Matt thought back to the five-legged calf. The calf and its mother had been brought back to the pasture weeks prior, the fifth leg shriveling up with each passing day. Still, Matt just about had it with animals making noises at him.

He shuffled his way back over to the mound of trash and began pouring some of the gasoline onto the pile. It was not so significant an amount that Matt would consider refilling the containers, but it was enough.

Matt took note of where the wind was blowing and made sure to stand where it did not blow into his face. Keeping his back to the main gate, Matt took out the packet of matches and lit one, holding it in his hand for a moment before tossing it onto the heap.

Matt watched as the pile billowed into a flame the moment the match touched the trash. Every ounce that had been touched with gasoline transformed into fire and just as quickly spread to the rest of the trash heap. Matt took a moment to feel the heat on his face. Even in the Texas summer, there was something different about the presence of a fire. Had he done his task a few hours later, Matt would have witnessed a mini bonfire in the midnight sky.

Then came the stench of spoiled food and soiled paper towels as the flames began to decompose the contents of the trash bags. The insides began to refry, and the stench filled the air and became intoxicating to the nostrils.

Matt no longer feared being smacked by the flames. He was more fearful of a putrid smell that would latch itself to him and never let go. Avoiding the smell may have been inevitable, but he still walked as far back from the fire as he possibly could.

Matt walked until his back was against the entrance to the yard. A pair of chains wrapped around the two gates and a lock kept it all secured tight. The gate and fence were both painted white but had long since been overdue for a paint job. They were now milky white and had become chipped all over. Matt ran his hands along either end, stretching himself out like he was on a crucifix, and rubbed against the pipes. He looked at his hands and they were covered with bits of chipped white paint.

The sound of braying got Matt's attention one more time, even if he knew its source by this point. Matt closed his eyes, took a deep breath, and then pushed himself off the fence.

"Alright, what is it?" Matt asked the old white bull as he walked toward it.

The old white bull brayed as Matt looked down at him. The old beast's knees were so bad that it could not have moved away if it wanted to. It was scared early on. Didn't like humans being so close if it wasn't feeding time, definitely didn't like being touched. Then one day, Tommy and Andy came by and started rubbing its back even if it didn't want them to.

It huffed at them and pushed his head forward, but his horns had long since been sawed off, just like the Aggie fight song. Even so, the old bull gave up fighting their presence. Maybe it knew it was better to just be alive than have a quick bolt gun through the forehead. Who's to say.

Now the bull had a trough for cattle feed and a basin for water, all within reach of its long neck. It also rested on a large patch of hay so it always managed to nibble on that for a snack now and then. However, this time, Matt noticed that the basin for the water was empty. There were still bits of food left, one of the hands always made sure there was food, but the basin was empty.

Matt inspected it and found a dent on the upper left side. He presumed that the old bull had knocked it over in its clumsiness. Even though the basin was now right side up again, what water was left was down at the bottom and out of reach. Any frustration Matt had for the bull was gone.

"Jesus, no wonder you wouldn't let up," Matt said, leaning down to look closer at the basin. "Throat's probably turning to sand just sitting in this heat. Gimme a sec."

Matt turned around and walked directly across the yard to the pipe and hose set up on the far end. The pipes were connected directly to the slough, the man-made drop-off that collected rainwater and acted as a natural water source for some of the cattle. It had also become home to ducks that would often be seen wading in the water. As far as Matt knew, there were no fish in the slough. The pipes drained their water directly from the slough, be it to wash a tractor or to fill a jug of water. Matt's task was closer to the latter.

Filling the bowl to the brim, the old bull inched closer and closer at the sight and sound of water. He licked against his big thumping nose as he anticipated the water rising to the surface. And rise it did. Matt made sure the basin was totally full and checked to make sure there were no holes in the basin. With none present, he strolled back and turned off the faucet, curling up the hose as he did so.

Looking back, he saw the old bull dunk its face into the water. The old bull started drinking so fast that it looked like it was smacking its face against the water in happiness rather than drink it. Gallons and gallons went down the old bull's gullet.

"Yeah, you're happy now," Matt said as he looked down at the old bull.

For a moment, he wondered if the bull would come up for air, but he knew the animal was smart enough to do that at the very least. He heard barking and looked over to see Diamond sitting on the grass, panting on the opposite side of the fence. Matt leaned into the basin and flicked some of the water at Diamond. Diamond reacted in a playful way, and Matt grinned.

"You'll get yours in due time," Matt said.

The old bull groaned, and he gave Matt a look to say he did not appreciate Matt sticking his hands in his water bowl. Matt looked back with an expression to say the old bull should be more grateful. It likely did not hit home.

At that moment, Matt felt an odd sense of calm pass over him. Matt didn't think about the old bull, the burning pile of trash or anything having to do with the letters stashed under his bed. Absolutely nothing.

Then the most ear-piercing lighting crack resounded across the sky. It caused Matt, Diamond and the old bull to all look toward the sky at that same instant. Diamond barked, and the cows mooed off in the distance. Matt immediately looked toward the sky. Somehow, he had failed to notice the darker clouds. They faded from gray to black across the sky.

The rain was not over Three Pecans yet, but Matt could spot the shade of rain falling to the earth off in the distance. The coal black clouds attached to it told him it was going to be raining for some time. It was only a matter of time before it hit them.

Matt looked at the cattle and knew they would be fine. Cattle had a fascinating thing of crowding together under a tree and laying down until the rain had passed. The old bull might get cold at a point, but he would survive. Diamond would have to hide underneath the house. If the rain got heavy, he would climb up onto the porch, but never inside the house.

The pile of trash looked like it would have mostly burned by the time the rain started, but Matt wasn't too worried. What he did think about was the topped off barrel of water that rested in front of the old white bull. He looked at it and thought about how it was going to start pouring rain soon.

"You really were crying for nothing," Matt said.

MATT

The workday ended early that day. At the sight of rain clouds, there was a mad dash to every field in order to close the wells that had been opened. This was a day where everyone rejoiced. The rain would irrigate the rows and need time to drain the following day.

Tomorrow, they would check all the fields to make sure they were draining properly. They might check on the cows, but rain always signaled a lighter workday.

The Ruggirellos and the hands did their best to close the wells and hurry to their homes before they got soaked. Josh and Tommy parked Matt's truck out front and dashed through the garden to get home. In that 15 to 20 seconds, they were soaked through. The rain was pouring so heavily that they could not see the train tracks from the front porch.

Diamond had climbed atop the porch for the shelter of the canopy. He had abandoned the old bull, but his calm brays were a sign of contentment. He was definitely hydrated at this point, Matt thought.

Josh and Tommy were in such a hurry to get inside that Tommy did not even see Diamond resting on the porch. The giant dog, all soaked and matted with mud, leapt up at Tommy and knocked him onto the porch. Diamond licked his face, but Tommy could not feel the difference between the rain on his cheeks and Diamond's slobber.

Josh was about ready to step through the door when Matt stopped him with a "Hold it." Matt, completely dry, walked over and laid towels down that led into Josh and Tommy's bedrooms.

"Boots off," Matt said. "Don't be dragging mud in here. Go into your room and get changed. No need to get the floor wet."

Josh looked at Matt with more than an annoyed expression. He could hear the tone Matt was taking, trying to imitate Mama by telling them what to do. Josh knew Matt was right, but it bugged him to hear it from Matt's mouth.

They both kicked off their boots and scurried into their shared room. Matt turned around, putting a bucket down where a drip was coming through the ceiling. Luckily, it was not in the vicinity of the television set or the radio. Last thing they needed was an electrical shock to go through the house.

Matt stepped into the dining room and to Mama, who was looking over one of the aforementioned letters. Once they had secured the house's protection from rainwater, Mama had asked to look at Matt's letters again. Mama wanted to go over them once more as she still was trying to grasp what the National Merit Program was.

She had been looking at the letter from Texas. The enemy, Papa might say. Papa never trusted a T-sip. Something about their work ethic, he once said, nothing grounded in reason. It all went back to football.

Either way, the numbers spoke to Mama. Texas was one of the schools offering a full ride over four years. Mama took one look at the numbers and knew it was a sum the farm could never produce.

This was her reaction with each letter. With every piece of paper, she looked at the numbers and her eyes would grow wide, as if she was zooming in with binoculars. There was not one detail Mama left uninspected.

"They sure did send you a lot of letters," Mama said. "Can't deny that."

"No one at school would've thought I was this popular," Matt said with a slight chuckle, taking a seat beside Mama. "Do you ever think about what you would've studied?"

"Oh, gosh no. I wouldn't have had time for that. Had all of you to take care of."

Mama then looked off at the corner for a moment, at a spot in the room where they placed a bucket to catch rainwater.

"I have thought about how your papa has that petroleum engineering degree. Graduated from a five-year program in three years. Oh, I was so proud when that happened. But he's never really used it. I sometimes wonder what would've happened if he had."

Matt watched as Mama let out the smallest of sighs. There was a glimmer in her eye. Matt was all but certain she was daydreaming. Perhaps about a life where Papa wasn't a farmer. Where they all lived in a nice house in town. Where they did not spend every day in the burning sun. A life where they never had to struggle. Matt could see it.

Josh and Tommy soon came out dressed in t-shirts and slightly cleaner pairs of blue jeans. Tommy had come out without wearing any socks, but that was only until Mama caught sight of his exposed toes. Mama shot up from her chair, noticing another spot where water was dripping into the room.

"This darn roof," Mama said. "It's gonna be weeks before we get someone to come fix it. Wouldn't have that problem if we were closer to town."

Mama said that last bit in a hushed voice so that the children did not hear, but Matt still heard it.

"Where is your papa?" Mama asked when they joined her at the table, putting aside the letters for the time being.

"I'm not sure," Josh said. "We weren't near him when the lightning first struck."

"Thought all the hair was going to fall off my body — it was so loud," Tommy said.

To be fair, Tommy didn't have much hair to lose. Not that he was lacking, but little had grown in. What he did have on his head was always kept at a close buzz, all the boys were given buzz cuts, it was easier to clean that way.

"Did they say over the radio that he was checking the Little Brazos?" Josh asked, looking at Tommy.

"It wasn't the Big Brazos?" Matt asked Josh, picturing how high the river might have grown with all the rainwater.

"That's what I'm asking you for."

"Well, why do you think I'd remember?"

"You're the one that's been out there in the truck all day!"

The room seemed to get smaller as they raised their voices. Their fear was palpable. Fear from confusion at not knowing where Papa was. Not knowing what was beyond the curtains of rainwater.

"Stop it, you two," Mama said from the other end of the table. "Can't hear myself think with all this rain, don't need you two giving me a greater headache. Joshua, hand me the phone."

Josh stepped into the hall and retrieved the landline, a phone that had an elastic cord which could stretch to every corner of the house. Sometimes, the boys might find Mama taking a phone call in one of the bedrooms. Sometimes she would be out on the porch. Either time, the cord was wrapped around a wall or stretched across the living room, but it never snapped.

Sometimes, they would make bets as to when they thought the cord would snap. There were no winners in the contest.

Josh took the phone off the latch and handed it to Mama. With her instructions, he dialed the number for the Big House. Nonna answered and when Mama asked to speak with Nonno, he came to the phone. While Papa was still away, at least Nonno had made it back safely.

The boys watched as Mama spoke back and forth with Nonno. Matt finished drying the dishes and slipping them back into their places on the shelf just as Mama hung up the phone.

"It was the Little Brazos he went to," Mama said. "Nonno knows that's where he went, but he hasn't seen him since."

All the boys looked at Mama, but she was just staring back at the table. She was far from content, but she was not one to speak up about her concerns. Another thunder strike soon resonated throughout the farm.

Tommy stood up from the table and walked over to the door. Peering through the screen door, he looked at the lot and how all the paddocks were soaked through. The old white bull seemed rather relaxed being doused by the rain.

He also noticed the mound of rubbish in the middle of the lot. A look of horror flashed across his face as he imagined the stench.

"Do you think the farms might flood?" Tommy asked.

"Possibly," Matt said. "It's definitely a storm."

"Mama, didn't the Bottom flood years ago?" Tommy asked.

"It did, when your Papa and I were just children," Mama said. "It was raining hard that day too. Just wouldn't stop. But the Bottom used to flood all the time, now they've got ways to drain it. It won't flood. The farms will get well and wet, but they're not going to flood."

"Hope Papa hasn't gotten stuck," Tommy said.

They all had fears about Papa. That the Mustang had stalled, that it had flipped on its side, that Papa had fallen into the water, any number of scenarios. It was incredible the terrible things people could think of when they feared the absolute worst.

Yet there was also a sense that as long as none of them voiced their fears, they would not come true. That's all they were, fears, nothing grounded in anything of substance. Yet Tommy had opened the threshold.

"I'm sure he's fine," Mama said, looking over at Tommy. "You watch. He'll come trudging up those steps any second. Probably going to make a mess when he does so, so have some towels ready for him."

They weren't sure what else to do but have all the dry towels they had by the door and at the ready. They would end up using them to clean up drips from the ceiling by the time Papa got home.

Matt took one look at Mama and knew she was trying to stay positive. She didn't know how Papa was, and she was as afraid as any of them.

He couldn't remember what Mama said her family did in Highbank when the Bottom flooded years ago. He wasn't about to ask now and have her stir up all kinds of unpleasant memories. But he did remember what happened to Papa.

This was back in 1938 when Nonno owned a convenience store, a place he sold as soon as he was offered the Carson Farm. Nonno said he hated working in that place.

On the day of the flood, Papa, twelve years old at the time, was working at the store by himself. Nonno had to drive into town to run errands, but it was so long ago he could no longer remember what he was fetching. No one thought it was going to flood that day, they just thought it was raining hard. But the waters rose and rose and by the time they all realized what was happening, it was too late.

Nonno was stuck in Bryan, unable to get back to the Bottom. Nonna and her children had managed to climb onto the roof and stay above the water. When the raining stopped, they tried their best to signal for help to anyone they saw in the distance. What was certain, Nonna had other people around her to help.

Papa was all alone.

Not one customer had come in the entire day and once the flooding became serious, there likely was not another soul within twenty miles of the store. As Papa put it, he panicked, froze for a great while until the water was past his ankles. There was no way to get onto the roof from outside and there was no latch to get to it from the inside.

So, standing on a makeshift stack of crates, Papa used a machete and cut a hole in the ceiling big enough for him to squeeze through and got onto the roof. It took the water three days to recede to the point where the roads were drivable again, but it took a day and a half for a boat to get to Papa.

They found him slightly dryer than when the rain started, but still soaked to the bone, damp. His knees had all but stuck to his chest from how long he had clutched them together. Papa was shivering and unresponsive, so the story goes, but the people got him on the boat and got him back to Nonno and Nonna.

Papa never talked about the flood. It was everyone else who had told the story to the boys. But obviously, it wasn't something anyone would just brush off, let alone a twelve-year-old.

Papa was always thankful when it rained. It was a blessing from God to help the crops grow, he thought. But Matt always took note of the way Papa prayed when it started to rain, the way he would grip his hands together so tight. Matt thought Papa was praying in thanks for the rain, but also praying for it not to flood again.

"The radio," Matt said, raising his voice after a prolonged silence.

"Come again?" Susanna asked.

"The ham radios in the trucks," Matt said. "Wherever Papa is, he's probably still in his truck. So, we can reach him on the ham radio."

"No, I don't like it," Mama said. "I don't want you boys going back out in this weather."

"But he's right, Mama," Tommy said.

"Come on, Mama, we just wanna be sure he's alright," Josh said.

Mama looked up at her sons. The worry was starting to creep across her face. It wasn't often that they could read Mama like an almanac, but this was one of those times.

She gave permission to Matt and Josh, wanting them to tag along in case the other got hurt. They weren't traveling far, just to where the Ford was parked, but the weather made them dress like they were going to war. They put on two layers of shirts and then put on their hooded raincoats. They didn't have any waterproof pants, so they put on their dirtiest pair of jeans and opted it was worth the sacrifice. They did have galoshes though, so their feet would stay dry.

They dashed out the door and down the stone steps. Diamond barked at them but did not have the energy to chase after them in the rain. Still, they made sure to close the gate behind them to keep Diamond from running out.

Even as torrential rain fell upon Matt's Ford, it did nothing to wash away the mud and dirt that had become caked onto the hood and the sides. The rain was as effective as the boys trying to wipe off a spot of dirt with a rag they wetted with their own saliva. It only managed to make things worse.

Either way, they both dashed to the truck and reached for the handles. In an odd moment, Matt and Josh had both gone for the driver's side. Matt had done it out of habit, Josh had done it cause he had been driving all day. Acknowledging the pointlessness of having an argument while standing in six inches of rainwater, Josh climbed into the passenger seat.

The windows had been rolled up earlier in the day, but the rain had done nothing to cool the interior. This was the one weather condition where the windows were rolled up. Whether it was burning hot or freezing cold, the windows were down. It was the only way to get any circulation. Still, they were not about to let the interior of the truck become soaked during a rainstorm.

Matt immediately reached for the radio in the center of the dash and switched it on. Static came across instantly.

"Is that good?" Josh asked.

"It would be a bad sign if we heard nothing," Matt said. "Now let's hope somebody's listening."

Matt clicked on the button of the communicator and began to speak into it. They called for Papa to answer if he was there. They asked him to respond, to confirm where he was and how he was. Matt and Josh took turns speaking into the radio. Perhaps they thought multiple voices might urge him to speak, wherever he was.

Their panic only strengthened during the periods where they waited for a response and heard nothing. Images of a truck underwater or flipped on its side blazed into their minds, but they did not mention them to each other.

"Papa," Matt said, waiting a moment but hearing nothing. "Papa!" He waited again, still nothing. "Dad, we know you're out there somewhere. If you're hurt, if you need help, tell us. We'll find a way to get to you."

Matt closed his eyes and clenched the communicator close to his chest. Josh was worried that Matt was going to snap the communicator off the wire. As he closed his eyes, Matt kept uttering the same demand in his head. Say something. Say something.

"Come on, Papa," Josh said under his breath. "Come on. Come on. Please."

Josh then noticed just how tight Matt was gripping the radio. Matt's face was clenched, almost as if it was going to fold in on itself from tension. The rain was falling harder than ever now. Each passing second seemed like the pounding of a drum. Then, right when the rain seemed like it would crescendo, Matt pulled the communicator up to his face.

"Answer, God damn it!" he shouted, much to Josh's surprise. "We know you can hear us! So, say something! Tell us where you are! Speak up!"

And with a strong flick of his wrist Matt flung the communicator onto the floor of the truck. With the rain still pouring down, Josh stared at his brother. The fire in Matt's words left Josh in a state of confusion. It was an act so aggressive that he would have thought it impossible to have come from Matt.

135

Josh did not confront his brother about what had just happened. He chose to turn his attention to the radio. He picked up the communicator and held it close. They still heard static so Matt's actions had not damaged the machine.

"Come on, Papa," Josh said, without any of the anger Matt had shown. "We're here. Talk to us."

Matt had looked away at this point. He had turned his entire body toward the driver side window and was both resting his chin on his hand and pressing his forehead against the window. The glass fogged with each passing breath. Matt felt water trickle down his temple but he could not tell if it was rainwater or sweat.

He saw no point in turning around. He could hear the static. All they had heard was static. There was nothing else they could do. Yet then, as if the rain had stopped all at once, the static ceased.

"Little Brazos," a feint voice came from the radio.

Matt whipped his head around to look at Josh, who was just as surprised as him. They looked at each other to be sure they had heard the same thing. They had.

"Little Brazos," the voice said again with a long pause in between phrases. "Tree line. Bridge out."

Without any hesitation, Matt took the radio from Josh's hands and replied, "We're coming."

The message had been clear. Papa had gone to the Little Brazos to check on the cows in the pasture. The voice was feint and hard to hear but they were certain it was Papa. They recognized the mumbles. He sounded uneasy but not hurt. He was well enough to alert them that the bridge was out.

Yet when Matt turned the keys in the ignition, his Ford would not start. It would honk, grind and clatter, but it would not start. Three times Matt did this but each time it was fruitless.

"What did you do to my truck?" Matt asked, almost shouting at Josh.

"I didn't do anything," Josh said. "It's probably all the rain clogging something up."

"Dirty old beast," Matt said as he turned the keys again.

"Do you think he's hurt?" Josh asked. "I could barely hear him."

"We can barely hear him at the dinner table," Matt said, still failing to start the truck.

"Just quit it, will you. It ain't starting, and we can't get a jump in this weather. Bound to shock ourselves to death."

Matt pulled the keys out of the ignition and tossed them onto the dash in frustration. Leaning back in his chair, he rubbed water off of his forehead as he heaved a breath through his nostrils.

"Come on," Josh said. "Let's go get Nonno. He'll know what to do, and we can use his truck."

Josh went to open the passenger side door but missed something Matt said due to the rain blocking the noise.

"What was that?" Josh asked, closing the door to better hear Matt.

"He said the bridge was out," Matt said.

"Yeah, he did," Josh said, not sure what Matt was on about.

Without warning, Matt leapt out of his door and sprinted toward the yard. He did not even attempt to grab the keys to the Ford.

Matt's hood flew backward as he ran, soaking his entire face and letting about a gallon of water start to slip into his shirt. Regardless, he did not trip over his galoshes and swung his legs over the fence into the yard and sprinted toward the horses' paddocks. The old white bull brayed at him as he returned to the scene from earlier.

An overwhelming sense of clarity had come over Matt. He did not think how the others would react, he just acted. He moved so fast that he did not even stop to check if Josh had followed him. If Josh had shouted something at him, it had been drowned out by the rain.

Luke's Horse was somewhat confused by Matt's arrival. He looked rather calm standing in his keep as rain dripped into his water bucket. Matt raced to the saddle, sitting on the side of the railing and ripped it off.

Matt was in such a hurry to saddle the horse that he forgot to put a blanket on the horse's back before putting on the saddle. Matt heard Luke's Horse groan as he tightened the rough leather around his torso, but he thought it was a natural reaction.

Matt did have to fight the horse to get the bit into its mouth and the reins tied tight, but Luke's Horse did give in. It was an easy choice for Matt to pick Luke's Horse as opposed to the other two. Luke's Horse was the one Ignacio rode on the rare times they got to ride. He had seen how quick the animal could move and trusted he would travel the fastest, even in torrential weather.

There was always a mystery about what Luke's Horse had been before coming to the Ruggirellos. Maybe he was a prized racehorse who had been stolen, only to be hidden in the most unlikely of locations. Matt once thought the horse was the descendant of horses a cowboy might have ridden on in the last century. The only thing they did know was the horse was strong and it was fast.

Matt guided Luke's Horse toward the exit of the stables but the horse started to panic at the sight of pouring rain. Matt held him by the reins until the horse calmed down and looked directly into Matt's eyes.

"Look, I know you don't know me, I know you don't like how it looks out there, but you gotta trust me," Matt said, continuing to look into the horse's eyes. "We've gotta get somewhere, and I need your help to do it. So, come on!"

There was no way of knowing if anything Matt said got through to Luke's Horse, but he pulled him forward regardless. Climbing onto the saddle, Matt kicked Luke's Horse in the sides and they shot off. It was then that Matt realized how cowboy boots had a greater grip than other footwear as his galoshes threatened to slip out almost instantly. Matt had to stay focused to avoid falling out completely.

He was not wrong with his predictions. The horse was fast, faster than all the others. Matt did not know what an actual mustang looked like, but in that moment, it felt like he was riding on top of one.

The hood of his rain jacket flew off, and it took all of eight seconds for them to race from one end of the yard to the other. The cows sitting in their lot brayed at them as they passed, disturbed by the sudden jolt of energy.

Matt could make out only a sliver of the road in front of him, but the road was there. Even with all the rain pouring down, the gravel roads had not turned into mush. The rain was so thick that Matt could not see either of the farmhouses but he quickly put that out of his mind. The Little Brazos was eastward. Matt knew all he had to do was travel on a straight path, so he did.

The rain turned into daggers on his cheeks as they raced through. It was as if the rain was now falling sideways, as if nature was spitting in Matt's face. The hooves of the horse became smothered with soaked gravel and kicked dirty water onto his face every time it stepped into a puddle.

Between the rain, the muddy water, the dirt, and the grunting of the horse, everything started to numb around Matt. He could not think of anything, he could not hear anything, he could barely see anything, he could no longer feel the rain because an entire layer of water now covered the surface of his skin. Matt wanted to let go of the reins and lean forward, to wrap his arms around Luke's Horse's neck and let the animal guide him to whatever destination he deemed worthy of traveling to.

But he did not do that.

Despite everything going numb, Matt did not let go of the reins. He knew that as long as he traveled down that single farm road, he would make it to the Little Brazos.

Matt looked to his left and right and saw that all the rows had indeed filled up. The rainwater splashed through the rows and onto the road, in some cases drowning a great number of the planted cotton.

Matt tugged on the reins as he made an effort to retake control of his steed. He remembered Papa's warning that the bridge was out. The last thing he wanted was to ride head strong into the open ravine and go hurtling toward certain injury along with the horse.

Matt counted down the rows in his head, trying his best to remember when the fields would abruptly end and the river would appear. If his thinking was right, it would be coming up soon.

Even with his heart beating rapidly, Matt used all his strength to slow everything down. The sound of the rain returned to his ears at a steady rate. Luke's Horse chuffed and brayed, reacting to the tug of the ropes. Matt knew the bridge was close, so he squinted through the rain to see where it would be. Even if the bridge was out, finding it would give Matt a sense of where to cross. If he crossed the Little Brazos at any which point, he would have to battle through bushes and uncarved roads, in addition to the rain, while trying to find Papa.

Matt recognized the ground around him. The bridge was going to be right in front of him. Yet when he looked forward, he did not see the shattered remnants of a broken bridge. He saw the bridge itself in perfect condition. Matt pulled Luke's Horse to a complete stop once he saw this.

Still gripping the reins, he slid off of the saddle and stepped in front of the horse. Matt kept looking to see where the holes were. They must have been there; the rain must have kept him from seeing them. Taking caution, he stepped forward, keeping Luke's Horse behind him as he pulled him with the reins. He brought them to where they were right in front of the bridge without being directly on it.

It was completely intact. The wooden bridge was soaked through and looked as rickety as ever, but it was intact. They all thought the bridge was going to snap one day just from the weight of any one of the tractors or trailers, yet somehow it remained, even through a rainstorm.

"I don't get it," Matt said to himself, wetting the inside of his mouth in the process.

He looked further out. He could see the pasture and the fences, the cattle guard that kept the cattle from walking into the fields, and he made out the black shapes of the cattle themselves all huddled together in various spots.

"Where are you?"

Matt scanned to his left, past the bushes and fences and to what he thought was a tall set of trees. The same trees they would sometimes sit under on a hot day to eat their lunches.

There it was. The Mustang. Sitting underneath a tree like it was any common day. The lights were off and the windows were up. Or were they? Matt couldn't tell. He thought they were, but all he really saw was darkness. Still, he was sure that truck was The Mustang, it was unmistakable. Why it was stationary in such a storm, he could not say. Either way, he knew he had to get to it.

Matt stepped forward, feeling the strength of the bridge for himself while also trying to be as light as possible. There were no sounds as if it was going to collapse, so he took a chance and led Luke's Horse onto the wooden structure. He made a complete stop once the horse was totally on the bridge. When they did not fall through and were satisfied that they would not fall through, Matt continued on. He did not dare climb back onto the saddle, that would tip the balance against them, but he did not stop moving. Yes, Matt took his time, keeping his eyes on the bridge to make sure neither of them took a false step, but he did not stop until they were on the total opposite side and their feet were planted on dirt and gravel instead of wood.

It was then that Matt looked back at the river and saw that the water had risen. It was now two-thirds of the way up, but it had not totally flooded over. Maybe it would flood eventually, but not then. Matt put it out of mind. He turned his attention back to The Mustang. The tree it rested under was at a slight incline, demonstrated by the water streaming down into the Little Brazos.

It was not far away enough to warrant getting back on the saddle. In truth, Matt did not think he could get a strong enough footing now that the saddle was soaked and his galoshes were wet.

Regardless, he pulled on the reins and guided Luke's Horse up the hill with him until they were right up alongside the truck. Matt lost his footing twice, but he never fell over. If he had, he might have gone tumbling all the way into the Little Brazos.

Matt made his way to the driver's side window and wiped away as much water as he could. More water fell in its place the moment he did so, but Matt kept wiping to get a look at whoever was inside, knocking to see if he got an answer. There was someone in there, even if he could not make out all the features. Matt went around the truck and tied Luke's Horse to one of the low-hanging branches under the tree. Marching to The Mustang, Matt opened the door, saw Papa sitting there in the driver's seat and climbed inside.

Matt relished the silence in that period as he took his time to catch his breath. He wiped his forehead and ran his fingers through his hair. It did nothing to actually dry him as his hands were also soaked—they were starting to wrinkle as a result of not wearing gloves, but the phantom action helped Matt calm himself.

It was a horrific sight to look out the window and be able to see absolutely nothing from the pouring rain. If he was at home, in his bed, the rain would have been the most soothing sound as sleep overtook him. But out in the rain, exposed to the elements, both freezing from the cold and sweating from the humidity, it was disturbing.

Matt thought Papa would speak first, if not to console him, to chastise him for being so foolish to come all the way out there on horseback in such weather. Then Matt remembered who his father was.

Matt could have sat there until the rainwater flooded the valley and reached up to the windows and Papa would still not be the first to speak or suggest that, maybe, they should get out of the truck. Matt slowly looked to his left and saw that Papa was staring out the driver side window. Judging from the angle, Matt thought he was looking at the Little Brazos if he could see it through the rain.

Matt breathed in the greatest amount of air his nostrils had ever consumed, so much that his nostrils burned when they stretched to grasp even more air. Once his nostrils and lungs were filled, he released them back into the truck with a huff that resembled the engine of a train letting off smoke. It caused Papa's head to turn just slightly, caught off guard by the rough noise.

"What are you doing out here?" Matt asked, succeeding in getting Papa to look his way. "We have the entire Gulf of Mexico falling down on our heads and you're out here, alone. What's going on?"

"Bridge is broken," Papa said slowly, as if the words had to be coerced out of him.

"No, it's not. I just walked across it. Maybe you thought it was, but it isn't."

"Rain's falling. River will flood. Have to stay on high ground."

"That's b . . .," Matt stopped himself, thinking cursing at that moment would not help anything. "That's wrong. You shouldn't be out here. Mama won't say it but she's worried about you."

"Went to check on the cows," Papa responded, taking his time with each response. "Wanted to be sure they were alright. Got stuck."

Matt glared across at Papa. His blood was boiling. To him, Papa's actions seemed idiotic. He went to check on the cows and not his own family. Matt could not see the logic.

"You went to check on the cows," Matt said under his breath, not expecting a response but just saying it as if to make it clear to himself. "Is the truck dead?"

"What?" Papa asked, slightly turning his head toward Matt.

143

"Is that truck dead?" Matt asked, raising his voice. "My truck was dead, that's why I took the horse. So is The Mustang dead?"

Papa was mumbling something—perhaps the phrasing of The Mustang confused him, but his reaction was not speedy enough for Matt. He looked over and saw that the keys were still dangling in the ignition. Inching over, Matt reached for the keys and turned them.

After three churns from the engine, The Mustang roared to life. Hot air blew through the vents, which Papa and Matt promptly closed, and the headlights shone out in front of the truck. The Mustang still shook and the engine roared, but even with the rain pouring down it was in perfect condition, or as perfect as The Mustang could be.

Matt leaned back in his seat dumbfounded. Papa just looked forward at the keys as they dangled. Papa had been sitting there for hours when he could have driven home.

"Can't get in the water," Papa mumbled. "In the water, we drown. Can't get in the water. People drown in the water. Bridge down. Can't get in the water."

Matt watched as Papa continued to repeat this phrase to himself. It was clear he was saying it only to himself. He made no attempt to look at Matt or to make sure he was understanding what he was saying. Between Papa's repetition and the grinding of The Mustang's engine, Matt could feel a headache growing, as if his skull was tightening like a wrench.

"Papa," Matt said, rubbing his forehead. "I understand your concerns for the cows. I understand the water, but you cannot stay here. The farm has not flooded. The Brazos has not flooded. You can't worry about the crops today. You have to worry about the rest of us."

Matt received no response from Papa.

"The truck is working," Matt continued. "The bridge hasn't broken. You can get home. We can get home."

"Bridge will break," Papa said. "We stay here. We wait it out. The rain will stop eventually. Help will come eventually."

Matt heaved in another large breath before responding. He had not thought about Josh or Nonno or Uncle Andrew until that moment. He had rushed off so quickly that he had not told Josh to follow after him or seen if Josh had gone to fetch Nonno. Simply put, he knew nothing and saw danger in waiting around for hope that might not come.

"Damn it, Papa! Enough of this! That may be your decision, but your decision is wrong. We cannot stay here. I know the fields are safe. We can get home without trouble. But there's no telling what damage this rain could have done to the hill. And then there's the lightning. We're so close to that tree we're daring to be hit. Now I've heard you out, but hear me out. We are going home!"

Without waiting to hear Papa's response, Matt reached over and turned the keys once more, listening as The Mustang roared to life. Matt continued by reaching over and rolling Papa's window down. This did elicit a response from Papa, mainly one of shock from the water hitting his face, but he did not chastise Matt. Or at least he did not have time to as Matt had exited the passenger side door.

Untying Luke's Horse from the branch of the tree, and thankful the horse had not run off, Matt climbed back on top of the saddle. Risking the wet conditions, Matt preferred to be on top and in a position of control. Gripping tight, he led Luke's Horse to the driver side door and to Papa's now soaked face.

"Follow me across the bridge," Matt said. "Trust me. It will hold."

Matt guided Luke's Horse back around so that they were traveling down the trail back to the bridge. He had rolled down Papa's window so that he could see what Matt was up to. He knew the windshield wipers had long lost their usage, if they ever worked.

145

Luke's Horse clopped down the hill. Even without Matt's guidance, it wanted to make sure its footing was firm before stepping forward. It did not think falling into the Little Brazos was too exciting of a concept either. Step by step, they made their way down the hill and were standing in front of the bridge once more.

They did not cross right away. Matt held the horse steady and looked back at The Mustang. It was still sitting there, headlights beaming toward nothing, window still rolled down. Matt was too far away to see Papa's expression, but he was sure he was staring right at him.

Matt held his gaze for almost thirty seconds. He would not break it. This was not a fight where he would give in. A fight where he was rewarded with the sound of wheels turning and the sight of The Mustang coming down from the hill. Matt watched closely, wanting to be sure Papa did not lose control and go tumbling down. That never happened.

Seeing him approach, Matt guided Luke's Horse onto the bridge and walked little by little until they were in the middle of the bridge. Matt knew that Papa now saw the bridge was still intact and could support one man and one horse at the very least.

Perhaps it would have been safer for Papa to have gotten out and abandoned The Mustang, but he didn't. Matt thought Papa was not about to step out of The Mustang and expose himself to the rain. He feared what Papa's reaction would be to touching the water.

Matt also wanted Papa to use The Mustang. The bridge had always supported it before. It was going to support it now, even in torrential rain. Matt wanted Papa to see that.

It took a few moments of hesitation, but Papa did guide The Mustang across the bridge at a true snail's pace. Regardless, Matt, Papa, The Mustang and Luke's Horse all made it across the bridge without any threat of tumbling into the gradually filling Little Brazos River.

From there, their journey was simple. Matt and Luke's Horse walked forward with The Mustang's headlights guiding them. There was no need to sprint now that Papa had been recovered. By now, they did not feel the rain from how wet they had become. Matt did not even hear the rain falling anymore. He knew it was still falling, but he could not hear it.

He could only wonder what Papa was thinking. He could only hope that he had recovered from his episode. But Matt was comforted with the sight of the headlights. As long as they were shining, he knew Papa was following.

The second set of headlights, this pair coming in front of them, alerted them to Nonno's impending arrival and the knowledge that they had made it home.

TOMMY

Papa, Matt, and Josh sat in a circle, sneezing at each other. Papa in his chair, Matt and Josh on the sofas. Tommy watched from the corner as he saw whose snot traveled furthest to the center of the room.

Summer colds were not a common occurrence in the Ruggirello household, but running out into a rainstorm changes that.

The family was always stuck inside after a rainstorm, but a flood was another matter. After a normal storm, the boys would drive around and help see if any rows were overflowing. If they were, they would break open the ditches to let out water. After a torrential storm, nothing could be done, even the roads were flooded.

In the meantime, all they could do was sit around at home.

"Living with a bunch of fools," Mama said to herself, not caring if they could hear her from the kitchen. "Running out in the pouring rain, getting lost, can't find way back home, foolish. Could've gotten yourselves killed last night. Could've gotten washed away and we wouldn't have known a thing. How 'bout you tell someone where you're going the next time you decide to go running off into the fields. That goes for all of y'all. Tell me you're gonna do one thing and the next I'm sitting here without any clue what's going on."

Mama ended her sentence by shoving yet another bowl of chicken broth into Papa's hands. Bowls to Matt and Josh soon followed. They had lost count of how many bowls, their throats were well and warm from the broth but there was no relenting from Mama. Nor were there pieces of chicken to add flavor to the liquid meal.

Tommy was the only one of the bunch who had remained dry after racing home and getting a change of clothes. He had seen how frantic and worried Mama had become. She was not the cursing type, but she said just about every other word she could say.

Tommy was doing his best to stay out of her line of sight. As far as he was concerned, nothing good was going to come out of her mouth if she had something to say. Even so, the rest of the day reverted into everyone sitting in their respective corners of the house and reading various things.

Josh was reading a copy of *AutoWeek*. It was not often that a copy would come into his possession. There was no chance of him acquiring a subscription either, but Josh would read his issues from cover to cover. Not only did he read the articles, but he enjoyed the photos of all the new models coming out of Detroit.

Matt was reading *The Outsiders* by S.E. Hinton. It was one of the books Matt had to read during his junior year at Hearne. Matt would normally go to the Bryan library for his schoolbooks, especially the novels, but *The Outsiders* stuck with him once school let out.

Mama was in her chair, flipping the pages of *Gone with the Wind* once again. Tommy peered across and saw that she was midway through the first half of the book. In truth, they had never seen her reading the last pages of the book. They thought for sure she had finished it once upon a time, since she had talked about it as if she had, not that the boys remembered many of the details.

Tommy crept behind her and noted the page. Mama was on page 231. He kept that in the back of his head.

Papa had tried to turn the television on. All Mama had to do was chuff to alert him of her displeasure. He tried to turn the radio on and was met by the same chuff. It grew to the point that it ticked Mama off and led to her shuffling back into the kitchen, retrieving a random old newspaper and tossing it onto Papa's stomach. Papa let out a little groan at the paper landing on him, but it was not long before he unfurled it and began to read.

Tommy had not seen where Susanna had gone. She had probably gone to her bedroom to sleep. Apart from Mama, no one else was going to bother her that day and there were very few tasks she could do, given the weather and everyone's lying about.

Tommy had snuck off to his room and was fiddling with one of his MatchBox cars. From time to time, he would lean out of his window and scratch Diamond's head. The giant dog had dried his fur after being soaked by the rain and was now lounging under Tommy's window.

The entire household seemed almost in a daze, like none of them knew what to do without work in the field. They were unaccustomed to all being at the house at the same time. The blazing past of the Union Pacific line was about the only thing to cause any commotion.

At the very least, it got Tommy back on his feet. He had no destination or goal—he just thought to check in on everybody. They were exactly where he had left them, sitting in their spots and reading. Tommy walked to the kitchen and picked up an apple, stopping to peek at what page Mama was on. She was on page 240. Evidently, she wasn't rereading the same page again and again, but she was taking her time.

It was only then that Tommy glanced over at Papa to see that he was no longer reading some unknown issue of *The Hearne Democrat*. Mama had never put away the letters she had been reading the night before. Unless Tommy was mistaken, he was sure this was Papa's first time reading any of the offers Matt had received. Everyone in the family had now taken a look at the details.

Tommy could not gauge Papa's reaction. His face was always stoic and wrinkled. Tommy could not tell if he was surprised, disgusted, pleased, or confused. Regardless, the arguing was far from done.

A phone call from Nonno came not long after that. It was revealed he too had the sniffles. Nonno asked how they were and Mama gave all the details in her usual manner, full of sass. Mama relayed the message that Nonno wanted Papa to come over. Mama wanted none of it, saying he needed to stay home and eat his broth. Tommy had never seen something equivalent to a look of fear cross Papa's face, but the mention of more chicken broth did cause his eyebrows to wiggle. Nonno insisted that Papa come speak with him. Mama could only fight Nonno's wishes for so long but was swayed with an assurance that Nonna would be making her own soup.

Either way, she told Tommy to accompany Papa to the Big House.

"If he goes and topples over on the way there, you either catch him or you come back and get me," were her parting words.

Papa did not make a fuss about being sent to the Big House. He groaned as he got up from his chair, more likely from soreness than illness, donned an A&M baseball cap and galoshes, and headed out the door. Tommy did the same, but had to rush in order to keep up with Papa.

The grass was still wet, and the trees were dripping water from every leaf. The garden had been ruined. Mama had spent the morning pulling out as many vegetables as she could salvage. Those that were salvageable had been taken inside, washed and left to dry. Anything that had been recently planted or had not grown to an edible size was ruined. Mama was frustrated but it was a loss they could overcome.

Trailing Papa, Tommy noticed that he had stuffed a couple of Matt's letters into his back pocket. It did cause Tommy to worry just a bit. There was no way of telling what Papa would do with them.

They made their way up the driveway, going through the back door adjacent to the courtyard and stepping into the kitchen. There they found Nonno and Nonna standing by the island and preparing lunch.

"Ah, mio figlio has arrived," Nonno said, finishing his second sandwich. "Come in, come in. Have you eaten?"

"Um, yes, Violet saw to that," Papa said, standing straight up at the front of the kitchen.

Tommy looked up and saw a sign of relief across Papa's face. It was relief that chicken broth was not being prepared. Papa was never one to refuse whatever meal was put in front of him, but he would voice his displeasure at certain meals. Even if Papa had eaten every crumb off his plate, it was no guarantee that he actually enjoyed the meal.

"Hello Tommaso," Nonna said. "Happy to hear you stayed dry last night."

"Yes ma'am," Tommy replied. "Mama said to keep an eye on Papa, so here I am."

"Keep an eye on him?" Nonna said. "Yes. After last night, I'm not surprised. If you'd've done something like that I'd have hidden your truck keys."

"I'd have ridden a horse," Nonno said, laughing as he nudged Nonna with his arm. "I didn't know Matteo was a vaquero."

The boys did not ride the horses often, but they all knew how to ride. Still, none had ever ridden in the fashion Matt had the night before.

"Surprised me too," Papa said, growing uncomfortable with the topic at hand.

"That boy was in such a hurry last night," Nonno said, spreading out more turkey. "He had tightened the saddle so much that there were cuts on its belly. Nothing serious though, just unfortunate."

Nonno and Nonna finished preparing their sandwiches, and Nonna reached into the refrigerator to pull out a jar of pickle spears. She pulled out one for each of them. Nonno grabbed a packet of crackers and plucked seven each, for him and Nonna.

Nonno also retrieved two grapefruits and proceeded to slice them in half. Tommy watched as Nonno took out the special, tooth-like spoons that scooped out the red gelatinous fruit and juices. Nonna slapped him on the arm for eating the grapefruit before his sandwich. Nonno just chuckled and licked the juices from his fingers.

"Come on then," Nonno said, picking up his plates and heading toward the table. "Come sit with us."

They sat at the circular table that sat in the corner of the kitchen, diagonally from the marble island. It was deceptive in size. At first glance, one would think those seated there could not move their arms from how tight they were seated. But once you sat down, you realized everyone could fit.

There was a chandelier hanging from the ceiling, bronze painted with electric bulbs in the shape of candles. In truth, there was no space for the chandelier, but the chandelier remained.

There they sat and ate and talked. Tommy did not say much. Granted, he was not sure what to say. He did manage to disguise his lack of talking by chewing on both the crackers and his portion of the grapefruit. Nonna asked him if their house had been damaged at all but he was able to report that nothing had been harmed. Even the old white bull was still in its same spot.

It wasn't until the sound of spoons against dishes resonated that everyone realized the eating was over. All they could do now was talk.

"Tommaso, why don't you help your nonna with the dishes," Nonno said, smiling.

Tommy hesitated for a moment and then nodded without saying a word. Their task did not take long. They rinsed the dishes with water and soap and then left them on the rack to dry.

Afterward, they went into the room overlooking the courtyard. Nonna had pulled out her rosary, a colorful creation of purple beads, and began her prayer.

Tommy was not sure if he was supposed to be doing something or if he should even be there. So, he curled his feet up on the sofa and gave the appearance that he was taking a nap. Maybe he meant to take a nap, but he also kept an ear open for Papa and Nonno's conversation.

"È stato stupido da parte tua ieri sera," Nonno said.

"Sapevo cosa stavo facendo," Papa said.

"Non hai detto a nessuno cosa stavi facendo?"

"Non c'è stato tempo."

"Bah, stronzate!"

Tommy was always thrown off whenever someone in the family started speaking Italian. Not in the sense of phrases that he heard all the time, but drawn-out conversations where he heard words he had never heard before.

It was a genius tool in terms of parenting. How better to keep your conversations secret from your children or grandchildren than by speaking in an entirely different language? Papa did not speak Italian around his children, it was never his first language. He and Mama knew it from talking to their parents as children, but they had been taught to speak English first.

Tommy could not say for certain what exactly Nonno and Papa were saying to each other, but from what he knew and how they were talking to each other, he could presume.

"How could you let yourself get stuck like that?" Nonno asked.

"I wasn't stuck," Papa said. "I was perfectly safe."

"Your family thought otherwise. Obviously, your son thought otherwise too."

"He was unwise."

"He was worried. Don't act like you never worried."

"I worried plenty in '38."

Nonno sat up in his chair, rubbing his mouth as Papa's words sunk in. That put an end to the back and forth. Papa rubbed his hands together and took a deep breath.

"He took a big risk going out there," Papa said.

"No doubt."

"But I gotta hand it to him. He got it done. I froze up, but he got me out of there."

"The boy grew up fast."

"Without me even realizing it."

Nonno took another deep breath.

"What's going on, Paulo?" Nonno asked. "The whole lot of you has had the oddest of expressions on your faces."

"Huh?" Papa asked, genuinely confused.

"You, your boys, even Violetta, you've all just had this look like something's weighing you down. What's going on?"

Papa paused for a moment. Tommy had a feeling that he was stopping to see if he or Nonna was listening. He took the added step to look away and close his eyes as Papa looked over, hopefully disguising the fact he was awake.

When Tommy opened his eyes, he looked over to see that Papa had taken out the three envelopes he had brought with him. He and Nonno were now hunched over, clearly whispering the details and not taking any chances of being overheard.

"Oh, that's stupendous," Nonno said in English, forgetting their unspoken decision to speak in Italian and almost shouting on top of that.

The slip only lasted for a moment. Their conversation quickly reverted back to Italian, but Tommy still tried to follow along.

"Why have you kept this secret for so long?" Nonno asked.

"I don't like it," Papa said. "Matthew kept this secret from us for some time."

"Did he say why?"

"He said he wasn't sure how we would react."

155

"So he was being cautious."

"And why would he be cautious?"

Nonno looked over at Papa with one eye almost closed from squinting.

"You remember that time you wanted to buy the Colson Farm? How you thought it would be better to have a part of land closer to Waco and I agreed with you," Nonno said, to which Papa shook his head in response. "Remember how crushed you were when the Colsons wouldn't sell?"

"Wouldn't sell to us," Papa mumbled out the side of his mouth.

"They didn't sell either way, but you were hurt because you had been thinking about all you could've done with that farm. It's the same with Matt. He likely started thinking about all types of things when he got these letters. So much so that he was afraid to say anything for fear that you might put it down."

Papa rubbed his face and held it for five seconds, blowing hot air out of his nostrils.

"These are some serious numbers," Nonno said. "How many letters did you say he got?"

"A lot," Papa said. "Can't remember how many."

Nonno held up one of the letters.

"Southern Methodist University," he read. "I don't know about the Methodist bit, but I might brag if my grandson went to a rich boy school like SMU."

"Don't brag, gives the wrong impression. And you don't know anything about SMU."

"That's true," Nonno said, holding his hands out. "But neither do you."

Papa sighed.

"I'm giving these a closer look after last night."

"And why is that?"

"I may know nothing about these schools or these scholarships, but if Matthew knows enough to take charge like that, maybe I should give these another look."

"You don't look so certain."

"I don't know."

Then there was a pause between the two. It caused Tommy to sneak glances back and forth at the two of them. What he saw was Papa taking in several breaths, hesitating before he spoke next. When he did speak, it was again hidden from his ears. This time, Tommy had no inclination as to what they might have said.

"Non voglio perdere i miei ragazzi," Papa said.

"Non vuoi perdere i tuoi ragazzi o non vuoi perdere il controllo?" Nonno asked.

"Non voglio un'altra Isabella."

Nonno leaned back for a moment. Judging that his next words all but ended their discussion, Tommy felt confident he knew the meaning this time.

"Well," Nonno said, "there are moments you have to have faith in your children. You're still young as a parent, but I think you know this. Perhaps now is a moment for you to have faith in Matteo."

And that was that. Papa took a few moments to sit there in silence and take in the entire conversation, and then they were off. He called Tommy back to his side and thanked them both for lunch before deciding to get back to Three Pecans before any more rain dripped from the sky.

Tommy had done his best to piece together the type of conversation they were having and the exact words they had used. He had spotted Matt's name a couple times in the conversation, but given the letters, that was no surprise. Tommy had a feeling this was the day. The time they would know what Papa was going to do about everything.

Neither of them were shocked to find the family had been stationary. Not a soul had moved from the spots they were in since the time they had left. Papa, not bothering to give any pre-warning or ask for everyone to put down whatever they were reading, just spoke the moment he stepped through the door.

"I've made my decision," he began.

This did catch everyone's attention. They were not all aware of just what exactly he meant or what he had said, but they were sure to pay attention. Everyone sat up in their chairs, alert and attentive. Susanna finally came out of her bedroom to hear what was going on.

"Tommy, go get me a chair," Papa said.

Tommy did so, and Papa took a seat near the front of the room. All eyes were on him, just as they always were.

"This whole business caught me by surprise when Matthew first brought it up," Papa said. "A lot of numbers, a lot of confusing names and titles. It was a lot. I thought it would be better to just not get involved with this National Merit Scholar business. Then last night happened."

Tommy watched as everyone seemed to lean closer.

"Last night, I froze. I can't describe it any other way. Matthew didn't freeze. He took a risk. It may have been dangerous, but he took the risk. I'm here cause of that. I have to respect that. So, if this National Merit Scholar *thing* is something he feels we should look at. Lets."

Tommy looked over just as Matt's eyes grew wide with the announcement. Obviously, he was surprised to be hearing this, they all were surprised to be hearing it. Yet the look was more like Matt thought he had heard wrong at first, only to realize that his ears had not failed him. Even so, he remained seated in his chair, hands clenched as he listened to Papa.

"Now there are conditions," Papa continued. "I know your argument has been you don't know about any of the schools, including A&M, and I'll admit to that. But many of these letters are from places we have never heard or ever been to."

"Not unheard of, Paul," Mama chipped in.

"Well, either way, we haven't been to them, and they're too far to travel too," Papa continued. "If you'd been having thoughts of going to Pennsylvania or wherever, Matthew, you're going to have to put those thoughts aside. If you can narrow a list of schools in Texas you want to visit, we can work that out."

Matt did not know how to react to this news. Tommy watched him shuffle in his seat as if he was going to stand up and go hug Papa, but that did not seem right. Maybe he was going to shake his hand, like they were gentlemen making a deal. In the end, all Matt did was bow his head.

"Thank you, Papa, I mean it," Matt said.

"I know you do," Papa said. "Now take tonight to figure out where you wish to go . . . except Texas."

"Papa," Matt said, pleading.

There was silence among the group. Everyone knew there was no love lost between Papa and the University of Texas, but it was all related around football. Papa had taken his hatred for the Longhorns—for it was a hatred—and their constant beating of the Aggies, into every facet of his life. If someone was from UT, he called them cheats and untrustworthy.

"You did a brave thing yesterday, I commend you for it," Papa said, avoiding eye contact. "But that is final."

Matt drew his head back and blew air out of his nose, but he voiced no protest.

"Come up with your list tonight, and we'll go make visits next weekend," Papa said."

Matt cocked his head in confusion. He looked to Mama and everyone else in the room as if they too were confused. They were. Regardless of their opinions of the schools, one weekend seemed too short a time frame to see anything of consequence.

"Next weekend?" Matt asked.

"That's what I said," Papa said.

"Don't you think that's a kinda short window?"

"It's what it is. It has to be next weekend cause the week after is the Fourth of July, and we need to get this handled as soon as possible."

"How come?"

"How come? Matthew, in case you've forgotten I still need you to work the farm and these months are the most important. Despite all this going on, you still have a responsibility. We'll make our visits and then that's that. Now I've made my decision."

Papa gave no chance for anyone to speak out against his decision. Tommy saw that Matt clearly had thoughts but was unable to say them. Even Mama had an expression that said she thought Papa was moving things rather fast. Papa was still getting his way, Matt knew it, Tommy knew it, they all knew it.

The only person Tommy did not see react was Josh. He retreated back inside his room. Matt went back into a stoic demeanor. He might have gone for a drive had he still had his keys, but in his chair he remained. He did ask Mama if he could help with anything, but when she had no task for him, a rare occurrence, Matt proceeded to slink further and further into the sofa.

When Tommy went to bed that night, a part of him did think that they had seen the end of it. Maybe this was as much as they would do about Matt's scholarship offers. Maybe this was a moment they would look back on in a few years' time. Not a moment they would laugh about. A moment where they would think, "What if this had gone differently?"

Everyone's footsteps were heavy as they went to their rooms. There was static in the air. As if being so close to each other was disrupting their bodies. No one was at ease, still.

It struck Tommy that the next day was Sunday. They had not talked about Church at all. He wasn't sure if they were still expected to go. They were recovering from their colds, but they all just felt down, low energy. Would they skip mass? Tommy didn't think such a thing was possible.

160

Either way, he was awake when he heard the shuffling of feet and the creaking of wood on the porch. Tommy could tell it was Papa without laying eyes on the figure. His stride was unmistakable. The wood only squeaked when Tommy walked on the porch. It groaned when Papa walked across.

Papa took a seat in one of the rocking chairs and rocked back and forth, letting his seat creak against the side of the house. Tommy heard Diamond's whining but the noise was quickly silenced. Tommy, wanting to see what was going on, crept out into the hall. Making his way to Papa's chair in the living room, he sat below the adjacent window so that he could see out but not be seen.

What he saw was Papa scratching Diamond's neck. For as harsh as he always was toward the dog, apparently, even Papa liked Diamond's presence.

Tommy then heard another pair of footsteps making its way around the porch and toward the rocking chairs. They were heavier than his but lighter than Papa's.

"Mind if I sit with you?" Josh asked outside, speaking softly so as not to wake up the rest of the house.

Tommy rolled back to the window to listen, dragging his ear as close to the windowsill as possible. There was no response from Papa, but the sound of a second rocking chair let Tommy know that Josh had sat down.

For a minute, that's how they remained. Sitting together, swatting mosquitoes and watching the empty train tracks. Tommy knew the silence wouldn't last, and eventually Josh started to talk.

"Look, I've not been the biggest fan of how Matt's handled the scholarships he's gotten," Josh began. "I've told him that, and now I'm telling you. I thought it would've been better to take the scholarship from A&M and move on. I just don't see a need for the rest of this or what else he could get out of it. But we're where we are now, you've made your decision and I support it. It's best to get it over as soon as possible. But I do think you're rushing it."

"I had a feeling something was coming," Papa remarked, dry.

"I get you want Matt to go to A&M, I think it's the right thing as well. But if you rush through all the other schools, you're just going to make him bitter."

"Well, let him be bitter now, he'll get over it. All we're doing is visiting. It's my call what school he ultimately goes to."

"That it is. Don't think we're not grateful for all you've done."

"I have to remind myself sometimes."

"Well, we are, but that doesn't mean Matt won't be bitter if you rush this."

"So, what would you have me do? Abandon the farm for an entire month while we drive all across the state looking at schools when we could be doing actual work?"

"I'm not saying abandon the farm, just let go for a moment. And not for a month, but for a week. Go look at the schools and be back before the fourth of July."

"An entire week? I can't abandon the farm in the middle of the summer."

"Papa, we have more than enough people. Yes, some of us might have to do double duty in some places, but we can do it."

"I don't know about that."

"Papa, you're still in control. Don't forget that. You're in control of the farm, and you're in control of what happens with Matt and the rest of us. It would be wrong to prioritize one over the other."

"But then I'd just be neglecting the farm to focus on Matthew."

"But you wouldn't be neglecting it. I'd be here."

Papa took a long pause after hearing Josh's proposal. The sound of the chair smacking against the side of the house reflected his brain thinking over the proposal. Then the rocking stopped.

"You?" Papa asked, almost dumbfounded.

"Yeah," Josh replied.

"What makes you think I'd do that?"

"Cause you've taught us well. I know when we need to get up, which fields to check, how to open the wells, how long to wait before seeing if they need to be closed, what to look for to see if the cows need to be fed. I know everything that needs to be done apart from how to change blades on a harvester, you ain't ever taught us that."

"Y'all too young to be messing with them."

"Well, they can wait. But the rest you can trust in me. I can look over our fields, I promise that."

"And you'd do this for your brother? Did he put you up to this?"

"No," Josh said, blowing out hot air after the fact. "I care about the farm, Papa. I want to see it taken care of. I know one day I might have my own land to look after. What better time to learn than right now? You can take Matt to go do his thing, and I'll stay here to help look after the farm."

The two sat together in silence for a good while after that. Long enough for the Union Pacific line to pass by them one more time. That may have been a partial distraction, but the silence still continued afterward. Josh knew there was nothing more he could say. He had made his case, and now it was time for Papa to make his decision one way or another.

The decision did not come that night.

JOSH

Josh was kept up at night thinking about his offer to Papa. He wasn't having second thoughts, but he knew how unpredictable Papa could be. Walking into the kitchen for his morning meal, he saw the tension had not evaporated. Josh watched as Tommy and Susanna lumbered into the room as if they had never used their legs before. No one made eye contact with anyone, nor did they speak.

Even Mama came out of her room in her robe and slippers, hair all in a mess without any curlers.

This was by far the longest they had spent any morning in their pajamas. The only other time they wore pajamas this long was on Christmas Day, a day they knew was nowhere in their near future.

By this point, they would normally have showered and climbed into their suits and dresses. The rain had stopped, but the Ruggirellos still acted as if their house had flooded. As far as they were concerned, they would be going to a later mass if at all.

Papa was the last one to join the gathering, wearing the long socks that stretched all the way to his knees. His arrival had been strategic. He made sure everyone saw him come into the room. Everyone except Matt, who was still in his room.

Mama, acknowledging the oddity of the morning, made a simple breakfast like a normal day. Scrambled eggs, fried bacon, and biscuits. If someone wanted fruit, they had their choice of bananas and tangerines from the fruit bowl. Everyone poured themselves glasses of water.

Josh, Tommy, and Susanna reflected on how strange it was to be eating on a Sunday morning. They could not remember the last time they did not fast on a Sunday. Their stomachs grumbled at the smell of food. All the discipline they normally held on Sundays evaporated with the scent of bacon grease and biscuit crumbs.

Matt's arrival was timed almost to the instant Mama finished cooking and prepared everyone's plates. Whether this was intentional or not, Josh could not say. His first guess was that it was a coincidence as Matt was focused on the six pieces of paper he had folded into his hands. The smell of food was a genuine surprise.

"Morning, everyone," Matt said, as if he was about to start a speech. "It wasn't exactly easy, but I was able to narrow down the list. I still say one weekend is . . . too short of a time frame, but it is what it is. So, I've worked it down to four."

Matt laid the papers on the table so that everyone could get at least a glimpse of the schools he had chosen. Baylor University, Texas A&M University, Southern Methodist University, and the University of Houston.

"I know these four are sorta, all over the place," Matt continued. "But the schools have a variety of degree programs that I want to know more about. Some more hands on, some more intuitive. It might be difficult for one weekend, but here's what I say. I say we use Friday to visit A&M. I know that's more than the weekend, but A&M's right around the corner, and we can get it out of the way. Saturday we can drive up to Waco and visit Baylor in the morning, then keep going to Dallas and check out SMU. Then Sunday, we can drive to Houston. Might even be able to visit Aunt Josephine and Uncle Tony."

Aunt Josephine was Mama's closest sibling, confidant, favorite person to talk to on the phone, and maid of honor at her wedding. She had married Tony Calabrese in 1950 and moved to Stafford, where Tony owned a chain of convenience stores.

"It's a lot, but I respected your order and left UT off the list," Matt said. "So how bout it?"

Silence stretched through the kitchen. Even with Matt's reasonable proposal, no one was sure what to say. Josh knew what they were all thinking, but it was not their place to say. Now, they had to wait once more for Papa to make his decision. For all they knew, Papa could have stood up and declared Matt only had one day to visit any of the schools.

Josh dared to glance over at Papa. Papa was staring right back at him. He did so out of the corner of his eyes, so it was not obvious to all that he was staring. One by one Papa reached over and looked at the documents. He had read the letters and offers before. Papa knew every detail to the penny. Josh assumed he was stalling. Or maybe he was reminding himself about all the details.

"Good, Matthew," Papa said, stacking the papers on top of each other.

Papa put the papers down and turned his gaze from Matt to Josh, but just for a moment. Josh knew what was happening. Papa was reflecting on their conversation.

"But I've changed my mind on some things," Papa said. "We will instead use this upcoming week to go look at these schools."

"The entire week?" Matt asked, more than surprised.

"That's what I said," Papa responded. "If you're so adamant on visiting these schools, then okay."

"You mean it?" Matt asked.

"I do," Papa said. "I haven't had time to work things out for this week, but we'll leave on Saturday morning, make the visits and be back before the fourth. That's my decision."

Matt took a pause.

"Does that mean we could look at more schools?" Matt asked.

Papa hesitated for a moment. "Yes, but be reasonable."

Matt nodded his head.

"In the meantime, Josh will be staying to help work the fields."

The others were not quite sure how to react to that part of the announcement. It was not so surprising that Josh would stay behind. It did not make sense for the entire family to travel across the country when they could be working. But they noticed an added sense of importance to Papa's statement. It was something they needed to hear, not something they just assumed was going to happen.

Even so, Josh caught Matt's expression for a moment. One surprised, then constipated look on his brother's face. An ounce of doubt.

...

Once all that had been settled, the day continued like a normal Sunday. Due to their sloth behavior in the morning, they were unable to attend mass until 11 a.m. Someone would have thought they had cursed the cross the way Mama was acting. As far as Josh was aware, there was no law saying parishioners had to attend the morning mass.

Perhaps Mama thought if they attended the early mass it would gain them favor.

There were ripple effects into the rest of the evening. Since they went to a later mass, they were unable to help Nonna with any of the cooking or provide any desserts. As a result, the rest of the family did not wait for them to get home before they started eating. Nonna was a kind soul and prepared leftovers for them to heat in the oven, but Josh and the others had to sit in isolation while they ate their food.

Well, not isolation per se, but there was an element of un-ease to be eating at a table that had just been used for a much larger and warmer meal. Josh, Matt and Tommy did find themselves unknowingly eating faster than they normally would. This was for sure a result of Andy and his siblings treating themselves to slices of pecan pie and vanilla ice cream. Looking around the room, they realized everyone was treating themselves to pecan pie and ice cream. This made the boys try to rush through their serving of spaghetti and meatballs, made with the Ruggirello family suga.

It is hard for anyone to focus on a nice meal that has been prepared when sweets are just an arm's length away.

The boys rushed through the spaghetti and meatballs, mopping up the suga with bits of garlic bread in the process. They came to realize they ate too fast. They could feel their stomachs pinching on their insides as they stretched to fill more space. All it did was make them groan and become uneasy. Now they no longer craved any pecan pie or ice cream. They could not bear to swallow another ounce of food.

Still, that did not stop them from being sent to deliver food to the hands. Nonno was not about to have them make the same mistake and wait till Monday to make their deliveries. This time, Matt, Josh, and Tommy were sent to deliver the food themselves. Nonno and Nonna held no sympathies for their aching stomachs.

Matt did his best to speak to Epefanio and Ignacio in broken Spanish, but they took the food regardless. Big Jake and Jim were outside their houses, pulling out weeds and mowing grass between the two lots.

There, they noticed a woman was leaning out the window of Big Jake's house. They had never let eyes on her before, but she must have been Liza. Big Jake's daughter looked as skinny as a telephone pole compared to him. Liza sat on the windowsill watching them work.

Yet the boys noticed Jim kept stealing glances at Liza. He seemed to be grinning, but she didn't return the gesture. She seemed annoyed by it. When Big Jake approached the truck to take his container of food, Jim stood up straight and looked at Liza for the entire time it took Big Jake to return. Big Jake handed Liza the food, and she disappeared back into the house. None of the boys confronted Jim about his staring when he came to take his portion.

When they made it back to the Big House, everyone was all cheerful. Nonna and Aunt Gertrude kissed Matt on the cheek and Uncle Andrew and Nonna shook his hand with firm grips.

"Proud of you, son," Uncle Andrew said.

"What an accomplishment," Aunt Gertrude said.

"The pride of the family," Nonno whispered beside Matt's ear.

One by one, they all gathered together in the smoking room, sitting on the various sofas and chairs. Many of the children found themselves comfortably sitting on the floor, Indian style, as the teachers used to say.

Josh did not have to be an expert to see what had happened. Whether Papa had revealed it willingly or had it pulled out of him, the whole family now knew that Matt was a National Merit Scholar. Given their excitement, they had worked out that, one way or another, being a National Merit Scholar means money comes into your hands.

Josh glanced at Papa. He was not frowning with disappointment, but he was not smiling widely with the others, either. Papa may have confirmed the news, but it must have been Nonno who had spilled the beans. Tommy had told Josh about how he had listened in on their conversation.

They all asked Matt questions about how he had been named a scholar, when he learned, what it means, and ultimately that one big question.

"Well, what school are you going to go to?" Aunt Gertrude asked.

Matt hesitated for a long while, glancing at everyone as he balanced what his response would be.

"I don't know yet," Matt answered. "I received over thirty offers. It took a lot of time to go through it all. I've narrowed it down to a few."

"Oh, which ones?" Nonno asked, intrigued.

"Well, A&M, obviously," Matt began. "Houston, Baylor, SMU."

Truth be told, there was no excitement for any of the schools he named apart from A&M.

"Well, those are great schools," Aunt Gertrude said, meeting sharp gazes from the others. "They are."

"Is it just those four?" Uncle Andrew asked.

"At the moment," Matt answered.

"Well, I'm sure you wanted to narrow the list down," Uncle Andrew said.

"Yes, many of the schools I had to look on a map to find," Matt said. "Josh and Tommy can vouch."

"Made a whole map of where all the schools were," Josh said. "Hadn't heard of half of them."

"Sometimes those are the best ones," Nonna said. "The ones that not everybody knows about."

"Perhaps," Matt said.

"So, which one will it be?" Uncle Andrew asked, continuing to prod.

"Well," Matt began, clapping his hands. "I'm not sure yet. We're to start visits next weekend."

The entire group uttered words of excitement. Granted, the majority confirmed how much Matt was going to love A&M. Still, they assured him that he should cherish the opportunity. It was clear that all in the room understood the significance of what was happening to Matt. Those gathered around the sofas, and the fewer that had the opportunity to attend college, never had the option of a second school.

Josh did not add much to the conversation. He and Tommy just sank into their respective seats on the sofas. Eventually they slid themselves down onto the floor and stretched their legs, and their stomachs, out on the floor. There was no need for them to not be uncomfortable. They were not the ones being interrogated.

Eventually, the boys did receive their portions of pecan pie and ice cream. Even with bulging stomachs, the dessert was still sweet on their tongues.

The family had been talked out by the time they returned to Three Pecans that evening. Everyone retreated to their respective parts of the house. Some watched the television, some took naps, but overall, they just wanted space from each other. They had about had their fill of Matt and his revelations. All they wanted was to think about nothing at all.

Even so, once they had eaten a simple, but grateful, meal of meatloaf and bread, the three boys found themselves gathered on the porch outside. Tommy had gone out there to brush Diamond's hair—what little good it would do. Josh had come out to read his *AutoWeek* magazine. Light from the sun was scarce, but the light from his bedroom proved more than sufficient.

Tommy's grooming had turned into petting Diamond's back. Tommy would rub his hands through the dog's great mane, and then Diamond would cry when he stopped. Soon, it became Tommy dodging Diamond's jaw as he tried to nip at his hands.

Josh was enjoying reclining in the chair, rhythmically thumping the chair against the side of the house as he read the magazine. He found himself rereading an article about the 24 Hours of Le Mans. Again and again, memorizing every detail about the impossible race. Josh found himself daydreaming about what it would be like to drive an actual race car, to drive as fast as an airplane engine. Josh had never driven anything faster than a beaten down Ford.

He was pulled out of his daydream by the sound of boots clicking against the porch. Matt had come to join them.

"Well, there he is," Josh began, "the man of the hour."

Matt just chuckled and shook his head. He did not speak at first, he just held up a single finger to his mouth once both Josh and Tommy were looking at him. Matt then reached into his bedroom window and pulled out a bottle of Coca-Cola.

Josh laughed at the image of his brother comically holding up a single bottle of cola. Papa was not a fan of them drinking the "sugar water," said it made them weak and lazy. That may have been true if they over indulged, but the boys still tried to sneak a drink whenever possible. Josh assumed Papa couldn't tell the difference between Coca-Cola and alcohol.

"Want one?" Matt asked, gesturing to both of them.

"Why not," Josh said, closing the pages of his magazine.

Matt reached back into the window and pulled out two more bottles from an unknown space under his mattress.

"They're cold," Josh said, shocked as he held the bottle. "How'd you keep these cold?"

"Oh, I only just got them," Matt said, cracking off the cap against the wind sill to hand Tommy the other bottle. "Nonno gave them to me after lunch. Said he could either share them with me or with y'all. His way of celebrating."

Tommy grabbed his bottle and took a long swig. Diamond got his share and licked the condensation from the bottle. Tommy sighed when he was done, always appreciative of a cola. It reminded him of drives to the grocer on a Saturday afternoon.

For a while, they all just sat there, sipping on their drinks without any worries. They knew the silence would end eventually. Silence for the Ruggirellos was never peaceful. It was just build up before someone in the family said what they were waiting to say.

"So what's it going to be?" Tommy asked.

Matt looked down at him, confused. "What do you mean?"

"Well, you picked those four cause you thought you only had a weekend," Tommy said. "Now you have a whole week. Are you going to stick with the four or add any?"

Matt closed his eyes and rubbed his nose. "I don't know," he answered. "It was hard enough picking those four. I had thought about Tulane, but Papa did help out by limiting my choices to the Texas schools. Besides, I couldn't see myself moving out of state right now."

"So what were the schools you were on the fence about?" Josh asked. "Maybe they're worth looking at now."

"Well, I thought maybe Texas Christian," Matt said. "I don't know much about Fort Worth, but the letter says the campus is green and full of trees. Had good degree plans though. If I'm going to be in Dallas, I might as well take a look. The one I went back and forth on was Rice."

"Rice?" Tommy asked.

"Yeah, Rice," Matt said. "The place where JFK made that speech about going to the moon. 'Why does Rice play Texas?' Rice."

"Why'd you go back and forth about it?" Tommy asked.

"Well, it wasn't the money, they offered a full ride," Matt said. "It's in Houston so the location didn't bother me. Rice calls itself the Ivy League of the South."

Matt then took a minute to explain what the real Ivy League was to Tommy. He quickly realized the prestige that such a group seems to carry.

"They wrote that only the top students in the country come to Rice," Matt continued. "The top teachers, too. At least that's what they claim."

"So, why don't you want to go there?" Tommy asked.

"It's not that I don't want to go," Matt said. "Yeah, I'd love to have the best teachers I can get. But it came off as very elitist. I feel like I'd get there, and I'd be like 'What am I doing here? Do I belong here?'"

"Sounds like it's on the list, then," Josh said, pulling his left knee up onto the seat.

Matt turned himself so that he faced Josh. He noted an amount of sass in Josh's voice. Nowhere near as much sass as Mama could pile up, but it was still there.

"Sounds like there's something you want to say," Matt said.

Josh flashed his palms. "Not that I can think of," Josh said. "But the way you're talking about that school tells me you want to see it. You want to find out if you belong."

"Yeah, you're right," Matt said, "but that's not the only thing on your mind."

"I think I've said all I need to say."

"Evidently. How you convince Papa to let you run the farm by yourself?"

"All I did was offer myself. I see it as my doing you a favor."

"Do you?"

"You'd be stuck with a weekend trip if it wasn't for me stepping up. Now you've got all the way to the fourth."

"Yeah, I realize that. Though it seems more like you helped yourself just as much as you helped me."

"Oh please, Matt. You've got the entire family talking about what school you're going to go to and how great these scholarships are. You're going to be jealous right now?"

"I'm not jealous."

"Oh yes, you are. Even though you're getting everything you wanted, you don't like that little bit of attention I got."

"Cause you're breaking from us."

"What?"

"Let's not pretend Papa is thrilled about this. He's allowing it to happen. Yet while he and I are going up and down the state, you'll be back here taking care of his precious farm. You're trying to show Papa that he can rely on you more than the rest of us."

Josh abruptly stopped the argument tennis. Tommy had not said a word. He was now standing in the front yard, watching them talk across from their chairs. They were not shouting, despite the anger in their voices; they did not want to be heard by Mama or Papa. Diamond could feel the tension, as well. The dog had cradled itself between Tommy's legs, prone on all fours.

Josh took his time to finish his bottle of cola before chucking it into the grass. He made a mental note to go pick it up later.

"You never listened to my advice before," Josh began, "always second guessed me. Now I did this one thing and you can't just sit back and be grateful. Yes, I'm trying to show Papa he can rely on me. I'm trying to show I'm a good worker. That I can wake up one morning and know the tasks I need to accomplish.

"Papa knows you can do that. You always get the tasks. Now you've shown you're one of the smartest guys in the Bottom. I don't want you thinking you're better than either of us. We're all the same in this family. Maybe Papa will be impressed by my work, but that's nothing you can control. Let me handle my business, you go find your school."

Josh departed from the porch and went inside to his bedroom. Matt and Tommy had no more words.

TOMMY

"Buongiorno, nipoti," Nonno said as he walked through Three Pecans' front door that Friday morning.

The boys were all sitting around the table eating a breakfast of bacon and eggs. Tommy and Josh both had their forks in their mouths when Nonno stepped through the door. Even though they had warm food in their stomachs, they were still groggy in the early morning hours. The sun was only just coming over the horizon.

"A gorgeous meal, Violetta," Nonno said as he walked over and kissed Mama on the cheek. "Keeping an eye on her, Susanna? Making sure she doesn't slip?"

"Yes, Nonno," Susanna said as she flipped a piece of bacon in the frying pan.

"What are you doing here, Nonno?" Tommy asked.

"Why I'm here to get you three, of course," Nonno said.

"We're riding with you today?" Josh asked.

"No, there's been a change of plans," Nonno said.

The siblings all looked across the table. They looked at each other and they looked back at Mama. Papa had left early that morning, as he normally did. This change of plans was clearly something he had not anticipated.

"What are you talking about?" Mama asked.

"Well, with Matt beginning his college visits tomorrow, I thought we'd start a day early," Nonno said. "I thought A&M is right around the bend, so why don't we make a day of it?"

Nonno's proposal was like an entire world being opened to them. A family venture. Such a thing did not exist in the Ruggirello household. Even when they drove down to Houston during rodeo season, it was not to watch the bull riders, it was to check on the cattle to see if any were worth buying. Travel was always just another form of business.

"All of us?" Tommy asked.

"Of course," Nonno replied, full of jolly. "I thought it might be a good chance for you all to get a feel for the university."

"Have you told Paul about this?" Mama asked.

"No, I haven't," Nonno said, turning back to the boys. "That's our first task, fetching your father."

Nonno winked at them as he said so. They all allowed themselves to grin and laugh out of their nostrils. Mama did not seem too thrilled, but she did not put up a fight either.

The boys had the advantage of not having gone to work yet. Meaning they had not had the chance to sweat through any of their clothing. While their non-workday wardrobe was only slightly changed from their workday attire, they found it significant to be wearing it on a Friday in the summer.

On school days, they wore white undershirts with collared button-down shirts that were either checkered or single colored. The shirts were all of a brown or dark red variety. They did not own any brightly colored shirts. For school, they would wear khakis and tan shoes that they felt were moments away from slipping off their feet.

Tommy was so averse to wearing socks with them when he first got them. He thought they would work perfectly fine with just his bare foot sliding in. Mama was not about to let him go to school with the tops of his feet exposed.

But when they were not going to school and when they were not working, they let themselves relax. Blue jeans. Always blue jeans. They made sure to separate the work jeans from their leisure jeans. They made sure to rotate the jeans they wore during workdays. Mama taught them never to waste the clothes they owned.

The boys never wore shorts. They did not own any shorts. If they had shorts, their legs would burn. If their legs burned, they would be unable to work. No shorts.

They also got to wear t-shirts. Tommy wore white t-shirts most of the time, but all three of them owned t-shirts of white, blue, red, and yellow. Josh had a fondness for wearing a jeans jacket over his yellow t-shirt. Josh never said why he fancied the look, but Tommy assumed he thought he looked like Paul Newman or Steve McQueen. Josh may not have been blonde-haired, but he wanted to look cool.

But what the boys showed off the most on their days off were their boots. Their work boots were designed in the shape of cowboy boots, but they were not the real thing. Those boots were dirt brown, did not bear any flashy designs or distinctive click of the boot heel. They were not boots anyone cared to look at. Nor were they boots that anyone looked forward to wearing.

On Sundays, the boys always wore black dress shoes. On their non-workdays, they got to wear the fancy boots that had been gifted to them two Christmases ago.

The Ruggirellos fell into that Texas cliché of having a fondness for Western movies. If John Wayne had a new film out, it was almost a duty to attend a viewing. Steve McQueen films were more so an urging of the boys, but Papa loved his westerns.

So two Christmases prior, Nonna had the idea to gift all her grandsons authentic cowboy boots. These were not knock-off boots someone might find in a common store—these were Lucchese. The best of the best. Boots that the slick-haired gamblers wore in the movies. Pristine leather and intricate designs.

The boys would walk around in their boots for hours, just listening to the click of their heels. But they did not mistreat their prized possessions. Whenever they wore their boots, the first thing they did when they got home was to rub them down with boot polish. They wanted them to be in prime condition whenever they would be worn next.

Needless to say, they were in prime condition when they put them on to follow Nonno out the door. Mama and Susanna were not about to be left behind during the outing. Susanna may have had the secret desire to go, but Mama's unwillingness to be left out of the college decision making was what sealed their trip.

The boys gathered around Nonno's truck as he hailed Papa on the radio. Their conversation droned on as the boys looked down the road, spotting Uncle Andrew driving toward them. When he turned into the Big House's driveway, they knew he was joining them on the venture. Uncle Andrew and Andy were both dressed in casual clothes as well. The adults were wearing the closest thing they owned to everyday shoes, but the boys were all wearing boots.

Cowboys. Or at least they fancied themselves as such.

Nonno had to talk to Papa for a long while. It did not sound like Nonno was being truthful about why he wanted him back at the Big House. It also sounded like Papa saw no reason in his coming back to the Big House, as he was already hard at work.

Tommy thought he overheard Papa ask where all the other trucks were, that he had not seen anyone else out in the fields. Nonno eventually won out, and The Mustang rumbled around the farm roads before depositing itself back in front of the Big House.

Papa sat in his chair staring at everyone. Confused by their fresh faces and clean clothes, he did not speak. He was not going to ask what was going on, his expression asked as much. Nonno, still jolly, was the one to make the announcement that they were driving to A&M for the day.

With the boys all drifting closer to the road, Papa pulled Nonno and Uncle Andrew aside. It sounded, unsurprisingly, that Papa was not pleased. He seemed to argue against the entire family abandoning the farm for an entire day and that there would be detriments to the work they would not be doing.

In the end Papa deferred to Nonno, retreated back inside Three Pecans to quickly wash — there was no time to thoroughly shower — change clothes and join the others. Matt, Papa and Mama rode in Nonno's car. Josh, Tommy, Susanna and Andy rode with Uncle Andrew. They were both driving Oldsmobiles.

"Did Nonno tell you he wanted to do this?" Tommy asked.

"Of course, he told us yesterday," Uncle Andrew said. "I'm assuming he didn't tell y'all."

"Uh uh, surprised us this morning," Tommy said.

"That's why Papa had already gone off, didn't know any better," Josh said.

The boys were quiet for the majority of the car ride. They were still groggy to a point. Josh did take advantage of the head rest to catch a few more minutes of sleep.

Uncle Andrew did his duty as co-tour guide on their drive to the university, a tour that started once they turned on Highway 21. On the right side of the road, they passed a long, abandoned field with broken barbed wire fences and a large barn whose roof had caved in. These were barb wire fences three layers thick, impossible to jump over.

"I can remember when I was y'all's age, we'd come up here to visit your papa when he was at school," Uncle Andrew began. "There were camps set up all along here. POWs from Italy and France. Army shipped them back her to go to work."

"Work what?" Tommy asked.

"Mostly stuff for the army. Sewing uniforms, piecing together bullets, some of them even put together fighter jets. But a few of them got sent to work the farms."

"Y'all let a bunch of prisoners work the farms?" Josh asked.

"Had to, the military ordered it. Y'all got to remember, the war was an effort by everybody, not just the soldiers. They needed us to produce crops, so we did. If they wanted us to use POWs, we did. Nonno saw it as what it was, more hands to work the fields. He welcomed it."

"Did you talk to them?" Tommy asked.

"Hah, no, I didn't get close to them. Nonno kept a close eye on them, but we got lucky that most of the POWs sent to us were Italian, so Nonno was able to openly talk to them. Also gave me a chance to practice my Italian."

Uncle Andrew explained that before and after the war, the field house had been used as one of the training grounds for the Corps of Cadets. Every day, the cadets would be bussed to the area for drills. Sometimes they would spend the night in the area, but not every night.

A&M had been founded as a military college. Both Papa and Uncle Andrew had been members of the Corps of Cadets while they were students, they had no other option at the time. Yet neither of them had experienced war. Uncle Andrew had been held in reserves for Korea, stationed at a base in California but was never sent abroad. Papa came within one year of being sent to the Pacific to fight the Japanese. Then came President Truman and the atom bomb.

"It was after that, when Rudder became president, that girls were allowed to attend the university," Uncle Andrew continued. "I can't remember if he's letting them join the Corps or not. The Corps is still there, still many men signing up, but now the school is completely co-ed. It's probably for the better."

"You think Matt's gonna join the Corps?" Andy asked, sitting in the passenger seat.

"I don't know," Uncle Andrew replied. "Probably not. Don't get me wrong, he'd get a lot out of the Corps if he joined. Teaches you teamwork and discipline, about the fruits of hard work. But I think your uncle's already taken care of most of that already. No, Matt's going to end up in some role where he's responsible for a great deal of people. But the military? I don't know."

"Well, ain't he going to come run the farm after Uncle Paul?" Andy asked.

"Has he said that? Your uncle, I mean?" Uncle Andrew asked.

"No, but it's seemed that way," Andy said.

"Boys? Susanna?" Uncle Andrew asked, looking at Josh and Tommy in his rear-view mirror.

"Nothing's ever been specified," Susanna said. "But there's been hints."

"Huh," Uncle Andrew sighed. "Well, I guess only time will tell."

When the grass fields and wood fences started to transition into gas stations, barber shops and fast food chains, the boys knew they had reached Bryan. There was no great sign announcing the split between Bryan and College Station. One just drove down one road and then another and before long they were at the intersection of Texas and University with the campus not a hundred yards away.

It was a sprawling creation. Once a massive ranch of thousands of acres, just like the rest of the city. There was still a great deal of hills and grass fields but gray stone buildings now stood where barns and ranch houses once rested.

They passed by several dormitories on the way to the university's front entrance. The dormitories were square brick structures of seven floors. Air conditioning units jutted out of every window like pimples to the building's skin.

Tommy was unimpressed. All the buildings were like that. Simple, rectangular shapes with few distinguishing features. Even with trees littered throughout to add color, they did not hide the ugliness of the buildings. Papa once said there were statues of generals and famous alumni further in the university, but they would have to get out of their cars for that.

Eventually Uncle Andrew, following Nonno, drove the car down the sloping road that passed the stone walls with the wording "TEXAS A&M UNIVERSITY" carved into them. It was a sight not uncommon to them. It was a sign telling them they had, once again, entered hallowed ground.

At the very end of the road rested a long rectangular build-ing, very different from those they had passed. This one had pillars and a flat roof with a shade of light brown rather than cloud white.

They did not bring the cars into the parking lot in front of this building. That would have been the reasonable thing to do. Where else to begin the tour than at the very front of the univer-sity? But Nonno, or someone, had other ideas. Instead, they took a left and ventured through the university roads.

They passed several more colleges and dormitories, as well as trees and grass fields. There were a few students taking summer courses, but the majority of people they saw were cadets march-ing around the campus.

Uncle Andrew told stories of his cadet days and how rough the officers trained everyone. But he also shared fond memories of the classes he took and people he met. The boys only half listened.

If anyone was deserving of a grand narration it was Matt, Tommy, Josh, and Susanna all said in their heads. But they both looked at the car ahead of them and saw it was not driving at a leisurely pace. Maybe they were regaling Matt with stories, but they were driving too fast for him to take in anything significant about the scenery. It would be incorrect to say they were speed-ing, but they were driving as fast as the roads would allow.

"I knew it," Josh said as Uncle Andrew guided the car around another corner.

What he saw off in the distance was that oh so familiar struc-ture of stone, bleachers, grass, and one well-groomed collie. Kyle Field, the home stadium of the Texas A&M Aggies football team. Once just a simple plot of land with a ring of seats around white chalk markings of a 100-yard field. Now, it was an ever-growing piece of steel and stone that seated up to 48,000 people.

The Ruggirellos did not make it to every game, but they did listen to each broadcast on the radio. If the Aggies lost, Mama and Papa would talk about it for a week as if they were in mourning. If they won, they would still talk about it for a week. Never longer than a week, though. At the end of the week, they had to focus on the next game and its emotional trauma.

Just two years prior, the university had added 7,000 seats. Soon, the seats would be up so high that the football players below would look like mere specks.

The Ruggirellos had been cheering the maroon and white of A&M since before Papa had ever set foot on the campus. Theirs was a love rooted in the year 1939.

War may have been starting over in Europe, but a thirteen-year-old Paul Ruggirello was fixated on the Aggies. Every Saturday, he would race to the family's radio set to hear the play-by-play. Every Sunday, he would go on his own to find a newspaper about the previous day's game. Papa wanted to know every detail. Every player, every play, every score, every reaction, all of it. Papa couldn't get enough.

Papa had been loyal to the Aggies, since they were the local team. Baylor was still somewhat of an effort to get to. But that year planted a seed that had grown into a ravenous fandom.

Papa had not thought much after the first week. An opening day win is not the most uncommon thing in the world. But then they won again, and again, and again. Before long, the Aggies found themselves ranked in the top 10 of the Associated Press Poll. From then on, Papa wanted to know what everyone had to say about the Aggies. He wanted to know what people expected them to do. He needed to know that his thoughts of how high they could climb were not unwarranted.

It all billowed to the point where it erupted on Nov. 30, the Thanksgiving weekend game against Texas. The Aggies were 9-0 and ranked No. 1 in the nation. Anxiously sitting at home, listening to the radio, Papa did something he normally would never do. He acted on impulse.

With the game still an hour from kickoff, Papa shot up from his seat at the house, ran to one of the trucks, and raced to the stadium. Uncle Andrew was with him, of course.

"I was only ten years old at the time," Uncle Andrew said. "I had a feeling we were going to get in trouble for taking the truck, but I was for sure not going to be left behind for that big a game. I told myself whatever the consequences were, they would be worth it. We get there, we left a note to let Mama and Papa know where we had gone, but we get there and the place is full. There is not an open seat in all of Kyle Field. But we found one ticket taker who made an exception for us. He couldn't give us a seat, but he let us stand on the entrance ramp to where all the seats were.

"Your papa was still taller than me back then. I couldn't see anything. I heard all these roars of action, but couldn't see. So, after pleading, your papa put me on his shoulders so I could watch the game. Even he was having to get on his tiptoes to see certain things, so together we relayed the information to each other. I'll never forget that day."

Papa and Uncle Andrew watched as the Aggies shutout Texas 20-0 to end the regular season a perfect 10-0 and remain ranked No. 1 in the nation. On January 1st the Aggies played Tulane in the Sugar Bowl and came out on top 14-13, ending the year a perfect 11-0 and the consensus national champions. But in Papa's mind, the Texas game was what sealed the title.

From then on, no one in his house would cheer for anyone except the Fightin' Texas Aggies.

Despite all the memories that the stadium drew for the Ruggirellos, it was not their final destination. Instead, they drove to about a mile away from the stadium. They drove to a set of fields that were untouched for the majority of the year. When they were in use, they were not normally accessible to the public. That day, there was an exception.

This was a field that was sometimes used for club soccer competition, but at the moment was used as the football team's practice area. It was early in the offseason. The new recruits were still hard at work reviewing playbooks before they ever got a chance to touch the ball.

The summers were spent for conditioning. Years ago, they would travel to some small town in West Texas; now, they just conditioned at home. All Tommy knew about conditioning was that the players would run up and down the field again and again until everyone on the team had thrown up. He was convinced he was seventy percent accurate on that assumption. Tommy had seen the Hearne football team condition, and that's exactly what he saw. Why wouldn't the Aggies do the same?

This day turned out to not be a regular conditioning session. While the players were in t-shirts and shorts, with their helmet being the only scrap of uniform on their bodies, they were running drills with each other like a normal practice despite no coaches being in the area.

This was an independent practice that the 12th Man Foundation had spread the word about. As a result, over seventy people came to sit on a pair of bleachers set up to watch the practice. There, the Ruggirellos gathered.

They parked their cars on a field of grass that had been turned into a parking lot by other cars. They all lined up together like a circus performer was going to try and leap his horse across the entire row.

"Nonno, what are we doing here?" Matt asked. "I thought we came to look at the school?"

"We are," Nonno said. "I made a call to the university the other day, and they told me about this here practice. I thought it would be a good place to wait."

"Is this really necessary?" Papa asked.

"No, but I think we should enjoy," Nonno said with a smile, patting Papa's arm.

They sat there among the crowd watching as the quarterback completed passes and the running backs ran their drills. The defense was limited in their ability to make plays, what with no pads

THE BOYS IN THE BRAZOS RIVER BOTTOM

and no interest in hurting their own offense. But the defensive players still found time to grab hold of the backs again and again.

Even though Tommy was enjoying the day out, he was questioning just what they were doing there. Matt was supposed to be visiting A&M's campus and learning about the classes he could take. Comparatively, watching a meaningless practice seemed like a waste of time.

Tommy glanced over at Matt and Papa. For once, they seemed to be of one mind. Both of them wanted to be doing something else other than watch football practice.

Some men were walking around the bleachers and offering popcorn to people. Tommy was confused as he saw no popcorn machine in sight. From their age, they looked like they were students, possibly sophomores or juniors trying to make a quick dime.

Tommy knew better than to ask for popcorn, but when a second man came with a backpack full of chilled Coca-Cola bottles, he couldn't resist. Nor could the rest of them. Nonno, Uncle Andrew, Tommy, and Andy all clamored for a bottle. Matt, Susanna, and Josh took theirs reluctantly but did enjoy them. Papa was the only one to abstain.

Papa looked as if the skin was going to slip off of his bones. He sat in his spot, upright with a straight back and his hands gripping his knees. Tommy was sure there were bruises the size of fingerprints on his kneecaps.

"Would I be right to guess y'all are the Ruggirello family?" a voice called from behind them.

All nine of them turned to see who had called. A man in a three-piece suit, maroon tie and navy fedora was walking toward them on the grass hills. It was not common for them to speak to any man who wore such a suit. Such men were not churchgoers, let alone farmers.

The only man Tommy had ever seen dress like that was Tom Landry of the Dallas Cowboys, and that was only a picture in a magazine. Yet down he trotted, dirtying his black shoes in the wet grass regardless.

"Yeah, that's us," Papa said.

The man in the suit approached Papa and shook his hand.

"Ron Smith," he said. "I'm from the admissions office. I'm to be your tour guide this afternoon."

The man was smiling between every word he said. Clown-like, Tommy thought. There was something disingenuous about his pleasant demeanor. Tommy noticed Matt rubbing the back of his neck. Perhaps he had his suspicions as well.

"Ron, if I didn't know any better, I'd say you were in the oil business, judging by that suit," Nonno said.

"Well, sir, that was my past life," Smith said. "I was digging up oil in Midland for a while. Then went to Houston to manage a couple refineries. Now I'm back at my alma mater trying to give back."

Papa looked away after hearing Smith's backstory. He was never fond of the get-rich-quick attitude among oil men.

Smith went around to every person in the family and shook their hands, doing his best to remember everyone's names. Then it got to Matt.

"Ah yes, you're the one with the scholarship offer," Smith said. "Any thoughts about going to your father's alma mater?"

Matt hesitated.

"Only that I'd like to see more of it," Matt said. "To learn as much as possible before the day's end."

"Sounds like a plan," Smith said. "I won't bore you with Kyle Field, I'm sure you've heard the stories, but let's get started."

Smith turned his back on the family and started heading toward the university. Nonno, Mama and Papa followed. Matt glanced back at his siblings, not looking too excited about their tour guide, but soon followed the others.

For Tommy and the others, they all remained and watched the football team practice. They could only enjoy it so much. It was hard to enjoy the motions of football without any stakes, without the risk of injury or even the chance of claiming victory.

"That man was a cardboard cutout," Susanna said.

"Huh?" Tommy asked.

"He's a stiff. I didn't buy one word about his backstory."

"Why not?"

"Just struck me as something a tour guide would say to show how 'big and successful' you can be if you come to their school. It's all just stories. Who goes and makes a load of money in the oil industry and then goes to work for their college?"

"Maybe he lost it all?"

"Then he's an even worse spokesperson."

Tommy couldn't help but agree with Susanna. Ron Smith struck him as another one of the Aggie faithful who wanted nothing more than to sing the praises of their university. Tommy saw nothing wrong in that, but he imagined Matt's exhaustion with such people.

It did start to seem senseless what they were doing. They had not escaped the heat, as they were still sitting under the sun. They were not working, but Tommy was not sure if he would call their actions relaxing. The Coca-Cola helped. The players in front of him hazed over, but all Tommy thought about was the drink in his hands. When his bottle ran dry, it was like a tub of ice water had been doused over him.

Turning his attention back to the practicing, Tommy continued to sip at his Coca-Cola bottle. Once it was finished, he tossed it onto the grass in lackadaisical disappointment.

"Quarterback takes the ball under center," a voice said in front of Tommy, almost a whisper but still audible. "He rolls to his right. Defense coming after his head. Has an open man over the middle and overthrows his target! Well, the play was there, but the moment was squandered. Special teams will be coming out to punt now . . ."

The sound of the man's voice increased the longer he talked, but Tommy was not sure if he was actually getting louder or if Tommy was listening harder. Either way, the voice came from a man sitting by himself on the third row of the bleachers. Tommy looked around and he seemed to be the only one hearing what the man was saying.

Josh was staring off into the distance. Uncle Andrew and Andy were having their own conversation, like a pair of mirrors, but Susanna had noticed the man too. Together, they slid down a couple rows.

"Hey mister, who're you talking to?" Tommy asked.

The man turned around. Tommy saw that he was a young man, about 25. He wore jeans and a long sleeve plaid shirt. In a word, he looked normal.

"Nobody," the man said. "Myself, if I have to name someone. You could say I'm talking to everybody."

"Talking to everybody?" Tommy asked.

"Yeah," he replied. "I'm assuming you heard me talking through the plays just then."

"I did. Like a radioman."

"Right on the money."

"You're a radioman?" Susanna asked.

"No. I'm practicing."

"For what?" Susanna asked.

"For myself. Gotta get good at it before anyone'll give me a shot."

"So you want to be a radioman?" Tommy asked.

"Right on the money. Take a look here."

The man pointed toward the field and the practicing Aggies. They were all lining up for another drill and the radio man told Tommy to pay attention.

"Quarterback takes the snap. He drops back. Linebackers coming through the gaps. He hands it to the running back. It's a draw! He's got acres of space! Fifty, fort-five, forty, thirty-five, thirty! They finally bring him down at the twenty-five! That is a Fightin' Texas Aggie first down!"

Tommy did not look at the man. He never broke his gaze on the drill. The man had perfect timing. Less than half a second after the play had commenced and the radioman was saying a perfect description of what was happening. Tommy was amazed.

"If I wanted to be really good, I'd be sure to use their names," the radioman said. "It's one thing to see a jersey number, but another to know the name of the player. People at home want to hear who it was that makes the game winning play or who commits the costly penalty. Parents at home who can't travel to games want to know if their boys are making plays. Names are important."

"Then why didn't you use any of their names just then?" Tommy asked.

"Cause I don't know any of them. Edd Hargett and those boys have gone and graduated. Last I heard, Hargett was preparing for the NFL."

Edd Hargett had been the quarterback for the Aggies up until that past season. While the '68 team was disastrous, Hargett's time with the Aggies was highlighted by the team's improbable victory over Alabama in the Cotton Bowl in 1967.

"I was at that game," the radioman said.

"You were?" Tommy asked, full of intrigue.

"Yes, indeed. Friend of mine was photographing the game for the *Dallas Morning News*. He managed to get me on the sidelines for that game."

"You saw Bear Bryant?"

"Couldn't miss him. Not with that houndstooth hat. Didn't dare go near him. But I saw the whole game from ground level. Saw Ken Stabler, he's in Oakland now. God, what a day."

Bear Bryant had coached the Aggies for four seasons in the fifties. Now he was off winning national championships at Alabama and Gene Stallings, who played for Bear at A&M, was the head coach of the Aggies. The Cotton Bowl was the first time Stallings went up against his old coach. It was also the first time the Aggies had ever beaten the Crimson Tide.

"The student beat the mentor," the radioman continued. "Couldn't believe my eyes."

"I don't think anyone could," Tommy said.

"Yep. That day was like, an epiphany for me. Everything became as clear as day."

"You knew you wanted to be a radioman?"

"Well, maybe not that clear. But I knew I wanted to be involved with Aggie football. I didn't want to let go of that roar of the crowd."

Susanna, rolling her eyes at hearing yet another Aggie obsess over the Cotton Bowl victory, butted in.

"So why radio?" she asked.

"Play-by-play. It's called play-by-play. But why? Well, I saw the radio commentators as having the best seat in the house. Not only can they see everything, but they get paid to be there."

"So, that's what you're practicing for? You're trying out for A&M's radio team?" Tommy asked.

"No, I need a bit more credits to my name before doing that," the radioman said. "I'm auditioning for the local station. Help with covering games like Bryan, Hearne."

"That's where me and my brothers go to school," Susanna said.

"Yeah, Hearne?"

"Yep," she answered.

The man then held out his hand and Susanna shook it.

"Jack West," the man said, finally revealing his name.

"Susanna Ruggirello."

Jack West then held out his hand to Tommy.

"Thomas Ruggirello. Brothers call me Tommy."

"Well, Tommy, try to remember my name. Maybe you'll listen in on a Friday night and hear me calling plays. Hopefully one day you'll hear me calling the Aggies for real."

"If that happens, I'm sure everybody will know your name."

Tommy and Jack West spoke for a little while longer after that. Both were too polite to the point where they did not know when to stop talking. Tommy told Jack West how his family had come with Matt who was looking at the university, explaining that the rest of them were farmers and would not normally have a day off. Jack West admitted that he too was an A&M alum, although he was originally from Corpus Christi. Jack West was confident Matt was going to find the university to be as high standing as anywhere else.

Tommy left out the National Merit Scholar detail. Had he been told, he was not sure how Jack West would have reacted.

MATT

Matt said little about what he thought of the A&M campus. In truth, he could not get over the figure of Ron Smith. Here was the man who was supposed to sell him on why the university was a great fit for him, Matt thought. Yet all Smith did was dish out the same rhetoric Matt had been hearing from his family for 18 years. Everything the man said went straight through Matt's ears.

As expected, most of the degree programs centered around the engineering and agricultural fields. Stuff Matt was growing less and less interested in studying. Matt wasn't sure how to say it, but he had a craving for something he knew nothing about.

Papa may have been taken aback by the impromptu visit to his alma mater, but he kept good on his word. Come Saturday morning, Matt, Papa, and Mama all loaded into the Cadillac and headed north to Waco.

The path was familiar enough to the family. Waco was the big city compared to Bryan. The city had a similar make to Bryan. Nothing but open fields on the drive up through Highway 6, then homes and streetlights and a downtown with one country version of a skyscraper. What Waco had beat on Bryan was the greenery. Once a driver reached the city limits, they saw a great number of green trees that added color to the town. Yet in the end, both towns were full of shops to take advantage of traffic passing through.

Matt and the others had traveled to Waco a handful of times to watch the Aggies play the Bears, but they had never seen the campus. Baylor's football stadium was three miles southwest of the campus itself.

Baylor stood out from the rest of Waco. Crossing over the Brazos River, Matt was once again drawn to the greenery of the setting. A deliberate attempt to make the Texas town acceptable to outsiders. A city within a city. Driving down Third Street, the Ruggirellos took note of Moody Library before wrapping around Baylor Avenue and getting a glimpse at the dormitories.

Matt did feel a sense of grandeur walking around the campus. Even more so, he was impressed by the degrees available, anything from social work and philosophy, journalism and history, as well as any type of language Matt could ever wish to study. Matt saw Baylor was a place to study the mind, whereas A&M was a place to study the land.

Matt started to imagine himself living in Waco and going to Baylor. At the very least, the place would be beautiful to look at every day. Plus, it was reasonably close to home, meaning he could ask for help at any time. Still, he did not say any of this out loud.

...

The trio spent the night in Waco, dining on Dairy Queen as one does when traveling through Texas. They woke up at seven in the morning to receive mass at St. Mary's, thankful to have found a Catholic church in the Baptist community, before making the drive to Dallas.

Matt slept through the first hour of the drive and then experienced the horrifying sight of Dallas traffic. The highway was clogged like cotton balls as hundreds of cars were vying to get into the metroplex. For two hours, they inched along through traffic, long enough for Matt to have taken a second nap—had he chosen to.

The pace was so monotonous that Matt didn't feel any sense of excitement when the ranchland turned into tall skyscrapers off in the distance. They drove right past Cotton Bowl Stadium, but Matt so desperately wanted to get out of the car that he was unfazed by the historic facade.

SMU and TCU were separated by only 40 miles of distance. Dallas and Fort Worth may be two different cities, but where one began and another started was a mystery. Matt's mood had already soured as a result of the traffic ridden drive, but his spirit only dampened the longer he toured both universities.

Both campuses were sharp contrasts to the skyscraper ridden downtown areas of Dallas and Fort Worth. SMU and TCU's campuses were full of lush green trees and bright green walkways. The buildings had domes and archways and were likely modeled off of government buildings in DC. It was all pleasant to look at, but Matt kept thinking about how it all reminded him of Baylor.

Granted, the three universities were not identical, but the designs were similar. All three stood out from the crowded downtown areas of their respective cities. All three had bright green settings with elegant buildings designed to reflect the history of the school and the famous alumni who have passed through.

Matt felt short of breath when they got back into the car to go find a hotel. He had spent so much time thinking about these schools, exhausting himself over how to get Papa along with the idea. Yet he laid on his bed, staring at the ceiling, feeling almost worse than when he started.

None of the schools had screamed out to him. None of them felt like home. None of them felt like places he could be successful. Matt asked himself, if all the schools were exactly the same, how can he justify going to any of them?

As Matt ran through these thoughts, delaying sleep for as long as feasible, he started to envision his attending A&M after all. He saw an image of him walking onto the campus with the proverbial tail between his legs.

JOSH

For Josh, Tommy, and Susanna, the days without their parents were like most other days. They woke up early in the morning, showered, ate breakfast, and went to work. The main difference was Nonno waited for Josh and Tommy before he set out. He wanted to talk with Josh in person to discuss which fields he was going to inspect. Josh did not take it as Nonno did not trust him or Tommy to do their job. Rather, it was Nonno's doting personality seeping into Josh's work. Nonno knew this was a big week for him.

Susanna was more than capable of preparing meals and keeping the house in order. In truth, with half of the family gone, Three Pecans became an extremely hollow space. Were it not for the television set being on, there would have been no noise in the entire house. They could circle one corner and not see either of their siblings if they were not in a particular place. They did not say it, but the silence made them uncomfortable.

On Sunday morning, all three were cleaned and dressed before Nonno or Nonna could call their names. When Nonna found the three of them standing by the back door and dressed in their Sunday attire, they looked like the loneliest souls in the entire state. Like children from a tale who are just desperate to find a home.

They all rode together to Sunday mass. Even with Mama and Papa gone, the congregation was still overwhelming. Mr.

DiRusso came up to speak to Nonno. He inquired why Papa was gone, as he was not one to miss church. Ever.

There were long debates about where a Ruggirello plot began and a DiRusso plot ended. Eventually, a fence was put up but even that far from settled the debate. It was amazing how heated grown men could get over simple square acreage. Then again, that square acreage was likely a great deal of cash down the line.

Either his speaking to Nonno was a courtesy or Mr. DiRusso was looking for chances to scheme.

Sunday lunch commenced like all the others. Baked Ziti was the meal. Another dish where they threw all the ingredients together and stuck it in an oven.

"I hope the visits are going well," Nonno said.

"Knowing Paul, they're likely blazing up and down the state to get it over with," Uncle Andrew said.

"I wouldn't mind if Matteo ended up in Waco," Nonna said. "He wouldn't be too far away from home."

"True, it would be better than Dallas," Nonno added. "The few times we've gone there, it's always felt so . . . loud. Waco might be nice."

"Though I've heard things about the Baptist community," Aunt Gertrude said. "It might be tough for Matt to adjust."

"Obviously A&M would be best," Nonno said. "You all know it, and it's the closest of all."

Josh found relief that the rest of the family did not interrogate him on any topic. They just talked about their own opinions on the subject. He did find it amazing how steadfast they were on their negativity toward other schools. They all knew where their allegiances lied.

Lunch was ended prematurely by what must have been a broken power line. All at once, the kitchenware and the lights in the house uttered a loud buzz and fuzzed out just as fast. In shock, the Ruggirellos uttered curses many of them would only ever say in their heads, never out loud. They all felt the urge to shame someone for cursing, but the darkness protected the sinners. It was likely those seeking to shame had themselves cursed in the shadows.

They would later learn that a telephone pole had been knocked over some ten miles south of the house. A truck full of used tires had made a sharp turn, trying to avoid a speeding car that did not stop at the intersection. The truck swerved and the right side ended up lifting off the ground, tipping the weight too far to one side and sending the truck crashing to the ground. Sliding to a halt, the truck knocked over the telephone pole and all the wires connected to it. Every home going northbound lost their power in an instant.

The speeding car never did stop to see the crash.

Uncle Andrew took the lead and went driving to find out just what had happened. He would be the first to find a crash and make contact with a policeman to get a telephone crew out to the location. The rest of them went to work lighting every candle Nonno and Nonna owned and opening every window in the house so they had some sort of circulation.

Once that was done, they all went to their respective homes and did the exact same thing.

Josh, Susanna, and Tommy went about opening their windows and lighting what candles they could find. It did not do much to give them light, so they retreated to their rooms for naps. Yet as night crept upon them and hunger returned to their stomachs, they all acknowledged the need for light.

"Go check up in the garage," Susanna said. "There should be two or three oil lamps up there. Don't know when they were last used but should still work."

"You sure the floor will hold?" Josh asked.

"Well, if you fall and I hear you scream, I promise never to send you up there again."

Josh did not respond to her claim. He just grabbed Tommy by the shirt sleeve and led him to put on his work boots and gloves.

The second floor of the garage was a storage space where shovels, axes, spare tires, gardening tools, and any number of equipment the family needed could be found.

The two oil lamps were sitting on an old desk that also contained beaten up ledgers and glass jugs originally filled with iced tea. Josh grabbed one, ignoring the cobwebs, and handed it to Tommy. The second one he grabbed himself. But as Josh turned around, he saw how Tommy reacted to a noise behind them. There had been a rustling.

"You hear that?" Tommy asked.

"Yeah, what was it?" Josh asked, still facing Tommy.

"Not sure. It came from back there."

Josh stepped forward with hesitation until he was standing in the doorframe of the second room. Josh could just make out the shape of something moving in the distance. An animal. Taking a gulp, Josh lifted his flashlight and clicked the button on.

What the light revealed was a white feathered barn owl.

That owl took one look at the boys and flew straight at them. It flapped its wings and hooted, sending the boys running out of the garage, so frightened that they shouted words and phrases they never would have uttered out loud. They were lucky that the owl failed to scratch or bite either of them.

Josh and Tommy looked at each other, swearing they wouldn't be going back up there anytime soon.

They stormed back inside Three Pecans without any thought of tossing their boots off. They dropped the oil lamps in front of Susanna and she just looked back up at them.

"Did I hear a scream?" Susanna asked.

"Don't matter what you heard," Josh said. "Just light the damn lamps."

Susanna did, pulling open the glass pane to pour fresh oil into the lamp. Striking a match, she held it over both open spots until a flame was struck and then put the glass back over the flame. Turning the knob, an orange glow filled the room and gave them all the resemblance of an illuminated home.

Susanna was preparing a simple but large meal of sandwiches and crackers. The sliced bread grew smaller and smaller as Susanna chipped away at the mold on the edges. Josh was hesitant at the sight of molding bread. She prepared two sandwiches for each of them, stuffing the slices of bread with mayonnaise, ham, turkey, pickles and sliced cheese. Absolute monstrosities.

Josh and Tommy weren't even that hungry. Nonna's meal had been enough for them, as it had been for most Sundays. Susanna was trying to stay on top of things. The power outage meant the refrigerator had also lost its power and no longer cooled the contents inside. Susanna took that to mean all the meat and cheese and milk inside was in danger of going bad, therefore they needed to eat large portions that night.

The three were sitting at the table, eating their sandwiches, savoring the beautiful monstrosities with every bite. Then, around 7 p.m., all the lights turned on all at once. None of them said a word, but their stomachs continued to grumble.

None of them remembered leaving the radio on before the power outage, but they could hear the machine buzzing to life in the hall. Susanna took Josh and Tommy's plates of uneaten sandwiches and stuck them in the refrigerator. They all knew they could not eat another bite, so they would eat them later. Even Susanna was so food fatigued that she did not bother to put plastic wrap or aluminum foil over the sandwiches.

Josh and Tommy shuffled their way into the living room and took their seats. Josh took advantage of Papa's absence and sat in his cushioned reclining chair. Tommy remained on the floor, laying on his back. But before that, he fiddled with the radio until he found something interesting.

They were only going to be half listening to whatever was put on, but they wanted something to pass the time. They ended up settling on what sounded like a baseball game, one of the national broadcasts. As they listened closer, they realized it was NBC's broadcast of the New York Mets and the St. Louis Cardinals.

Josh had not kept up with the baseball standings. He was not one to keep up with much about sports, never saw the point. Josh did not enjoy how ravenous people got over something as simple as a sport. He was certain everyone and their niece were betting on games, which he knew was illegal.

Matt was the one who kept up with baseball. Once Papa was done reading the paper, Matt would always go to the very back and read the scores of all the MLB games and see who was leading the divisions. From what Josh had overheard, the Mets were playing decently, and they had never been anywhere near decent before.

Josh half listened to what was going on in the game. It sounded like the Mets were winning. The announcers kept describing hits, but there were never any cheers from the crowd. Josh worked it out that they were in St. Louis. Given the prolonged silence, he also worked out that the Mets were kicking the Cardinals asses.

Tommy found himself paying close attention to the way the announcers spoke. He thought back to the way Jack West spoke, it was similar. Perhaps he would hear him on the radio one day, Tommy thought.

They were both certain that they ended up falling asleep listening to the game, for about two hours later they were rudely awoken by the sound of a car rolling into the garage and Diamond's alert barking.

All three of them craned their heads toward the back door. They could hear footsteps coming up the stone walkway and up the steps. Susanna craned her neck out the kitchen, Tommy craned his neck from the floor and Josh all but looked at the door upside down from the comfort of the chair.

All at once, Papa, Mama, and Matt stepped through the door. They did not look excited, downtrodden, thrilled, or disappointed. They just looked tired. Tired and relieved to be home.

Papa seemed least likely to talk out of all of them, though that was unsurprising. He walked over to his seat in the living room, took one look at Josh and then walked over to sit in Mama's chair. They all sat there in silence, exhausted for various reasons, reclining in their seats.

Josh seemed certain that Papa was going to ask him how the crops were, how he had managed working on his own, what he still needed to do. He assumed there would be questions on any number of things to find out what he had done wrong or what Papa needed to fix. Perhaps he knew he couldn't ask these questions. If there was a problem, Papa would feel compelled to come back to the farm and work. He couldn't do that. Papa was a man who kept his word. He couldn't abandon the college visits, not now.

"This is a surprise," Josh said.

"Hotel's A/C broke," Papa said. "Decided to head back. Who's playing?"

"New York," Tommy said, still laying on the floor.

"Really?" Papa asked, sitting up.

The mention of New York seemed to have given him a shot of energy. Enough to make him sit up in his chair, at least.

"Always did enjoy listening to the Yankees," Papa said. "That was the one team we all pulled for. My brothers and my uncles, I mean. We could sit around and listen to an all Italian outfield. Papa Paul heard their names one time and said, 'That's our team. That's our people.' We can always pull for the Yankees. Who's winning?"

"The Mets, Papa," Josh said, looking to his left. "It's the New York Mets. Not the Yankees."

"The Mets?" Papa asked, confused. "Who in the world are the Mets?"

"They're a new team. Newer."

"They added another team in New York," Papa said to no one in particular, looking off at the wall. "Just don't seem right. Why would anyone cheer for another team in New York?"

"Give a listen, they aren't," Josh said.

"Cause they're in St. Louis," Tommy said. "Ain't no New York fans in St. Louis."

"You got one right here in Mumford, Texas," Josh said. "Why wouldn't there be any in St. Louis?"

"Fine, no Mets fans in St. Louis," Tommy said. "Clearly there's a difference."

"Another New York baseball team," Papa said, continuing to mumble to himself.

Josh knew about Papa's affection for the Yankees. They all knew about his love for the Yankees. This was not something he kept close to the chest. The Yankees were the only organization, entity, personality, or deity that could cause Papa to take a leave of absence from the farm. It only happened once but it was a notable occasion. It happened in Houston just before the start of the 1965 MLB season.

Facing off against the Astros in an exhibition series, the Yankees were to help debut the Astrodome to the world. The winningest team in the history of baseball bringing all the world's attention to the stadium they dubbed The Eighth Wonder of the World.

Within a day, Papa had made the announcement that he had purchased tickets. They were all going to be traveling to the Astrodome.

They dressed as if they were attending church. Mama and Susanna wore white dresses while Papa and the boys dressed in black suits with red ties. There was notably a lack of orange and blue. They were not there to see the Astros.

They left early, took photos of the stadium, attended the game and drove back to Three Pecans that same day. It was a rare moment where the entire family traveled to a location that was not church, the market or an Aggie sporting event. Of course, it wasn't the entire family. Tommy had been left at home.

There was never an explanation given. Tommy was left behind while the others went traveling. Nonno had assumed Papa thought Tommy was too young to go with them, but Papa never said so. They were still driving the Cadillac, so there was room in the car. Maybe Papa couldn't afford that many tickets? But he didn't say so. Nor did he ask who had the most interest in going to the Astrodome. All he said was they were going and who was to come along.

Josh later admitted he was impressed by the stadium's architecture. The lighting in the domed ceiling particularly interested him. In regards to the game, he could not remember who had won or anything grand about the two teams.

Even Papa, who had been so excited about the Yankees, never made any remark about what it was like to see the fabled Bronx Bombers.

But Tommy noticed. Tommy took note of how everyone acted. Took note of everything that was said. Even though there was the picture in the news clipping, Tommy tried to paint a picture of what the Astrodome looked like. The forbidden structure.

"Matt, you out there!" Tommy called out, still laying on his back.

The sound of creaking bed springs resounded through the walls, alerting Tommy that Matt was sitting up in his bed. The creaking of floorboards told them he was walking into the living room.

"What is it?" Matt asked.

"Are you still going to Houston?" Tommy asked, still looking at the ceiling.

Matt walked over so that he was leaning against the doorframe.

"Yeah," he said. "We're heading there tomorrow. Just wanted one more night in our own beds first."

"You going to visit the Astrodome?" Tommy asked.

That silenced everyone in the room. They were mistaken, but they also thought the radio fuzzed out at that moment. Tommy was certain that all five of them suffered a flashback moment at that time. And in it, they all remembered the one soul that was left behind at home during the big event.

"No, we weren't," Matt said, pausing for a moment. "You want to come along."

"I'm thinking about it," Tommy said.

"No, not necessary," Papa said, eyes closed and barely awake. "You should stay, help your brother."

"I barely help as is," Tommy said. "I ride around, I carry a shovel, I turn a valve, I groom a horse. Nothing I do is crucial."

"So you say," Papa said.

"All I'm saying is I want to see Houston," Tommy said. "If you say no, you say no. But I'm voicing the fact I would like to see Houston."

Their conversation ended at that time. Both from fatigue and from the fact the conversation was at a dead end. Tommy could say no more, Matt and Josh could say nothing to help. The ball was once again in Papa's hands, and he was snoring in his chair. Tommy would have to wait and hope that Papa remembered anything of what was said in the last few minutes.

Before he went to bed that night, Tommy was told to pack his bags.

MATT

It's a terrifying feeling to be sitting in the back seat of a car, helpless to do anything, while the driver continues to veer to one side of the road and the other, each time waking up just before the car scrapes along the concrete shoulders.

That was the feeling Matt and Tommy felt as they sat in the back seat of the Cadillac. It was Mama's car but Papa took over during long distance trips. There was a directness about the way he drove. Papa had a destination whenever he got behind the wheel, and he would not stop until he reached that point. If someone became hungry, it was their fault for not bringing a snack. If someone needed to pee, they'd better hold it.

One time, Tommy had to pee after only ten minutes of a two-hour road trip. It took a great deal of pleading to get Papa to stop. It was the realization that the back seat could've been ruined had Tommy urinated on it. So, Tommy got to relieve himself on the side of the road.

But the monotonous act of getting up, driving several hours, stopping to visit schools and then driving for several more hours had caught up with Papa. He could not fight back the fatigue any longer. Mama was in the passenger seat, holding a wet cloth to her forehead as she combated a headache. She too found Papa's swerving to be dangerous, but she was indisposed herself.

It grew to the point where they stopped at the McDonald's in Hempstead after taking the exit onto 290. They did not go into the McDonald's to eat, or even get drinks through the drive-thru, but they did get out and stretch their legs.

Mama questioned Papa to see if he was fit to drive. When Papa responded, his mouth stretched into a great yawn. It was early, but Papa was one to be fully awake by that time of day. Finally Mama was the one to say that Papa would not be driving anymore, telling Matt to take over. Tommy asked if he could sit up front with Matt. She took a moment to think about it, but did surrender her seat. She had grown dizzy sitting in the passenger seat and closed her eyes shut when she climbed into the back.

"Wake us once we reach Cypress," Mama said. "We'll tell you where to go after that."

"Yes, Mama," Matt said.

Traversing through the Texas countryside was easy if one was traveling to the major cities. It amounted to getting on a highway, driving for at least two hours and then exiting at the desired location. That was the case with Matt driving down 290 toward Houston. All he had to do was not veer off the road and he would reach Houston in a matter of time.

As expected, the drive was much smoother with Matt behind the wheel. While no one is capable of keeping a car perfectly straight, he, at the very least, kept the Cadillac from swerving outside the lane. That smoother drive helped both Mama and Papa calm down. Within fifteen minutes, they were both snoring in the back seat, although to Matt it sounded like they were snoring into the back of his ears.

He had a thought in his head throughout their snoring, he just tried to figure out when the right time would be. When an eighteen-wheeler blazed past them with the loudest engine that had ever been placed on God's green earth, and did not wake up Mama or Papa, he knew then was the time to try.

"Tommy," Matt said, fiddling in his pocket. "Turn the radio on, but make sure the volume isn't too high."

"Oh, you gonna put on KTSA?" Tommy asked, excited.

"Nah, I've been waiting for a chance to use one of these," Matt said, pulling out an 8-track tape from his pocket.

"I've been wondering why you had a brick in your pocket," Tommy said, before leaning forward and turning on the radio.

Tommy swiftly turned the knob, so that there was silence, then turned it the opposite way so that the sound was audible but not overpowering. Matt followed suit and stuck the 8-track tape into the stereo. A moment of silence spread throughout the car as the stereo switched from radio waves to the 8-track.

The silence lasted for three seconds, then the sound of light guitar plucking and a kick drum crept out of the radio. The music lasted for about thirty seconds, setting the mood, then came the scratchy lead vocals of Dennis Edwards and the rest of The Temptations. "Runaway Child, Running Wild."

The Temptations were one of Matt's favorite groups. The 8-track he had just plugged into the stereo had some of their greatest hits, ranging from the classic era to the current one.

Matt and Tommy did not fancy themselves like the little boys who had run away from home in the song, but they kind of felt like it. They were in the driver's seats after all. They could have gone anywhere they wanted to. But they also didn't know what was out there to go to.

Matt clearly wanted something to calm his nerves. A little bit of music could go a long way. If it meant Mama and Papa waking up and taking away his 8-track, Matt decided it was worth the risk.

They ended up making it all the way from "You're My Everything" to "Ain't too Proud to Beg" and from "My Girl" to "A Love I Can See." Not once did Mama or Papa speak up to get them to turn the music off. Though it was a sad moment when the 8-track clicked off, needing to be rewound now that all the songs had been played.

"What're their names again?" Tommy asked, reclining in his seat. "Not Aunt Josephine and Uncle Tony."

"Uncle Leon and Aunt Tina," Matt said.

"And which one owns the whole goods store?"

"Uncle Tony."

"But they all live across the street from each other?"

"Right."

"But they don't talk to each other?"

"As far as I know."

"But we have to go see both?"

"Right?"

"Why?"

"Cause it would be improper not to."

"Improper to see one and not the other or not see them at all?"

"Yes."

Mama had not sprung this detail on them, more so that she reminded them of their familial duty. Her Uncle Leon and Aunt Tina both had moved to Stafford at different points years ago and had started families. Stafford rested to the southwest Houston area, but was its own city. Every time they traveled to Houston for any reason, they made visits. Quick visits, just to say hello and catch up. Sometimes they had dinner but not often. Mama had reminded Papa of this necessity and there was no way of getting out of it. Now that Grandpa, Mama's father, had passed away, there was added pressure to make these visits.

The visits were easy enough once they did get to Stafford. Almost identical in topics. They talked about Matt's scholarship offers and how they were in town to visit the two universities. Tommy was always sitting off to the side, happy to be along, but no one asked why he was there. Aunt Tina asked how Mama's siblings were and she told them. She revealed that they had a large gathering planned for the Fourth of July. Something she discussed even further when they shuffled off to Aunt Josephine's house. They talked with that openness that all sisters have.

Traveling to Stafford was out of the way for their journey, but the short visit was worth the months of criticism that would follow knowledge that they did not pay a visit. The Vitales could hold grudges just as much as the Ruggirellos.

Matt had done his part in getting them to Stafford, but the drive became far more stressful once they reached Loop 610. The roads became narrower and narrower the closer they came to Houston. They shrank so tight until it was just two lanes without any shoulders to pull out on in case of a flat tire or any sort of emergency. The path went from calm drives with joyful music on the radio, to bumper to bumper traffic, with the radio having been switched to a local news station. Papa made them do so once he and Mama had awoken, both fully rested from the journey.

Tommy had this look on his face as if to say he had never seen so many cars in one place. He hadn't. Tommy assumed there had to have been a brutal accident for traffic to have been so backed up. There wasn't. They moved at snail's pace but there was no sign of carnage or a wreck once they finally got moving.

What they did see were cranes and construction workers building new highways and tearing down old ones. They had been there four years earlier when Matt and the others traveled to the Astrodome and they would be there four years later. Houston construction was a never-ending project with no end in sight.

Somehow, they could not say how, but somehow, they did move into the loop after a period of time. The number of cars never lessened, nor did their pace pick up, but they moved. Tommy did not cry outright when he realized that to get to Stafford meant they had to go outside the city, meaning they would have to go back into the city eventually, that made him groan.

Matt was ready to give back control of the car once they had made their visit in Stafford. He shared no thrill at traversing through Houston traffic. He had seen the horrors of Dallas traffic, but had not been asked to drive through it. Now, Matt had to take on a different animal.

Papa drove them back inside the city limits and made their way to Southwest Freeway. Another jam-packed freeway, but not one that looped around the entire city. Papa did end up going too far toward their uncertain destination, which led to him taking a wrong exit and them being further delayed.

Whether it was his intention or out of frustration, Papa ended up exiting onto the feeder road and pulling into a Dairy Queen. The fast-food joint was jam-packed with people piling through the drive-thru. Many of them likely did not have time to sit and eat, but the slowness of the drive-thru mirrored that of the highways. In the end, no one in their cars had time to eat in any fashion, they just did not know it yet.

But Papa had given in to the headache-inducing horns of the traffic, as well as the sheer claustrophobia. Together, the four of them exited the car and went in to eat a lunch of burgers, fries, and milkshakes, the common meal of any Dairy Queen attendant. Matt noticed a look of shock come across Tommy's face as his eyes grew wide.

Matt looked behind him and saw that out the window was a view of the Astrodome. He could make out the shapes of roller coasters and other rides that made up the neighboring AstroWorld theme park, but the dome was clear as day. Tommy's mission had been accomplished. Even if they weren't going to see a game, he had laid eyes upon the beast. He knew he would see the inside one day.

Once they had rested their legs, as well as eaten their fill, Papa continued the drive a shorter distance to an unassuming hotel just outside the loop. There, they checked into a room, dropped off their bags, and headed back to the car just as quickly as they had arrived. Matt, and his nerves, agreed with the action. They had come all the way, so there was no reason for them to stop.

Matt was delighted once he realized the path to Rice University no longer meant entering the highway. The path included several narrow two-way roads that seemed to crunch and expand every other mile. Their journey was only a handful of miles, but the amount of cars and traffic lights prolonged their venturing. Perhaps this was the reason Papa avoided cities, Matt thought to himself.

But Matt took in their surroundings the further they drove. While the concrete sidewalks never wavered, the sights of gas stations and storefronts eventually gave way to more and more trees. In the middle of such a dense metropolis, lush green trees were popping up all around them. Just when Matt thought about the previous green campuses he'd seen, the trees started to curve and reach across the road. They had formed a pathway, guiding the cars down the road, sunlight just barely breaking through.

It came to pass that Papa mistook, or never realized, what road he was on. He was certain it was the right path, but his slowing down told Matt that Papa had his doubts. Papa and Mama were bickering about that fact at that same moment, which resulted in Papa taking a right turn when he shouldn't have. Nothing catastrophic occurred, but it took them down a neighborhood of houses and nowhere closer to the university.

Papa ended up on a one-way street that dead-ended, so he turned left. Peering out the right passenger window, Matt got his first glimpse of a notable landmark. It did not shock his world with its elegance or size, but he recognized the sight from pictures, Rice Stadium. The gray stone stadium nestled in the western side of the university. Matt took one look at it and thought back to Kennedy's speech.

It was then that Matt realized that the trees did not stop at the entrance to Rice University. The 300-acre campus had them littered throughout. Matt remarked that the campus was smaller than all the others they had seen to that point. Yet at the same time, the greenery was not overpowering. There was room to move, Matt thought.

Whether by intention or accident, Papa ended up going in and around the campus several times. It was not a prolonged drive, but it allowed Matt to get a glimpse of the various buildings and even more trees. Like the other schools, Rice was its own village inside Houston. Yet unlike Waco or DFW, Houston felt easily accessible from Rice's confines. Rice was there, fully functioning, but Houston was just a few yards away, full of potential.

Matt came to realize that Papa was not driving around and around for sightseeing purposes. It was for his inability to find a parking lot. Mama was the first to speak up about how they were still driving and that she wanted nothing more than to get out of the car. That seemed to bring clarity to their situation, as Papa found a parking lot only a few minutes later.

The four of them stepped out of the car and continued to take in the lush green around them. It was then that Matt got a good look at the design of the buildings on the campus. Matt thought everything was very castle-like, right down to the arched hallways and orange-yellow tinted stone walls.

A series of hedgerows led the way through an archway off in the distance. It gave everything a regal appearance.

Everything was clean. That was Matt's overwhelming thought. Everything was clean, extremely clean.

They marched their way into the first building they approached, not knowing if it was the appropriate building to be going into or not. In luck, there was a welcome desk and a clerk sitting behind it.

She took one look at the four arrivals and, likely, deduced they were not from Houston or anywhere nearby. Matt thought the clicking of their boot heels gave that away.

"Can I help you?" she asked.

Papa leaned his arm on the desk.

"We're here for a tour of the campus," Papa said.

The woman hesitated, mouth agape. Matt assumed she knew nothing about a tour of any kind.

"When were you scheduled to receive your tour?" she asked.

"We didn't," Papa said.

"Oh."

"My son has a scholarship offer to this school. We've come to have a look."

Matt examined the woman's further confused face. Nonno may have been the one to call ahead to A&M and schedule a tour, but Papa had not followed his example. It was the same with every campus they had visited to that point. It would have been such a simple gesture that he could've done at any time. Papa must not have agreed, or he had never thought to do so at any point.

"Give me one moment, and I'll find someone to help you," the clerk said. "Have a seat in the meantime."

The four found themselves awkwardly sitting on a bench for an uncomfortable amount of time. They could see people they assumed were students, writing in books at desks in far-off corners, but they did not approach them. Mama grew more and more uncomfortable the longer they sat. She started talking about a small shopping center they had passed while circling the university. It must have been less than a block away from the university itself.

Eventually, a man appeared through an arched doorway on their right-hand side. He was not dressed in a three-piece suit like Ron Smith. Instead, the man arrived in blue jeans, a gray button-down shirt and a sports coat, as well as black shoes. Matt thought he looked relaxed, but sophisticated.

"Welcome all," the man said with a cheerful smile on his face. "You all must be the family looking for a tour guide. Look no further!"

"Yes," Papa grumbled, standing to his feet. "Paul Ruggirello. This is my son Matthew. He's the one with the uh, scholarship offer."

"Ah, excellent," the man said, holding out his hand for Matt to shake. "My name's Steve Gibbons, I work in the admissions department. Pleasure to meet you all."

"Pleasure," Matt mumbled.

"Well, I must admit your arrival caught us all off guard, but let's get underway."

Gibbons was a very positive tour guide. He was the type of gentleman that always had something to say. The dialogue never stopped and the conversations only lulled when Papa or one of them had to respond to a question.

Gibbons ran through the congratulatory speech over Matt's receiving the National Merit Scholarship, yet rather than go straight into all of Rice's degree plans, he went into history and setting of the school. He discussed how the founder, William Marsh Rice, wanted a university for "Letters, Science, and Art" and how famous people like Howard Hughes once walked its halls, leaving out that Hughes dropped out of the school before receiving his degree.

"And of course, I have to tell you about President Kennedy's speech over at the football stadium, but I'm sure you all knew about that already," Gibbons said. "It's the first thing most people bring up when they get here. But if y'all are a sporting family, the football, baseball, and basketball arenas are all within a short distance of each other. There's even grounds for recreational sports like cricket and rugby."

Matt had no idea what Mr. Gibbons was talking about when he mentioned those last two sports.

Mr. Gibbons also made mention of West University, the historic center full of shops and cafes filled with anything a person could desire at any moment. People would drive from the far edges of Houston just to go to the West U shops, Mr. Gibbons claimed.

The knowledge of West U peeked Mama's interest. This had been the shopping center she had asked about earlier. Upon realizing this, she informed Matt and Papa that she was going to visit a coffee shop and that they should come to her once the tour was over. Papa did not fight her, understanding that Mama had also been exhausted from the consecutive days of travel.

She made Tommy come with her. He wasn't thrilled about it as he was inquisitive about the rest of Rice, but he still found joy in exploring West U.

"So what do you do for a living, sir?" Gibbons asked Papa.

"Agriculture," Papa answered. "Should be a good crop of cotton this year."

"You own a lot of land? Any cattle?"

"Yeah. Mostly crops, but we have a good amount of cattle."

"I can remember I was at the Rodeo a few years back and at one point they let loose thirty some odd calves and had a bunch of high schoolers chase after them. Something about the Youth Farmers Association, that doesn't sound right but something like that. It was crazy to see. Is that what you want to go into?"

The question was directed at Matt, and it caught him off guard. Both because he had only half paid attention to Mr. Gibbons' story and half because he did not know. He had spent so much energy focusing on earning the right to visit the schools that he never stopped to think what he wanted to do at any of them.

"I . . . I've sorta gone back and forth on it," Matt answered. "Sometimes I feel I want to do stuff with my hands. Other times I want to do stuff with my brain. I guess I really don't know."

"Well, that's alright," Mr. Gibbons said. "That's the beauty of college, you get to find out what you want to do."

Matt did not completely believe Mr. Gibbons. He thought he should have some idea of what he wanted to do. Use college as a springboard to a career, or at least that was the idea.

"Here at Rice, we set up students for success as undergrads and later as graduate students," Mr. Gibbons continued. "We have schools of Engineering, Music, Humanities, Natural Sciences, and Architecture. In among those are numerous concentrations. I'm sure you saw in our letter we call ourselves the Ivy League of the South?"

"Yes, I did," Matt said, hesitantly.

"Well, that's exactly right. We prioritize in recruiting the absolute best students in the south and keeping them here in the south. Why go off to some Ivy League school you've never heard of, in a place you're unfamiliar with, when you can be in a city like Houston. It's honestly one of the best things about Rice. We provide top-level learning environments with top professors and top classmates. Then you're right next to the medical center and the museum district to learn more about any field you could want to cover. My point is, there are options for what you want to do once you get here and those options aren't limited to the 300 acres."

A cool breeze swept over the fields and ended up shaking many of the trees in front of them. The breeze resulted in a swaying motion that made the trees look like they were dancing. It was a calm, momentary distraction.

Matt still had many questions. Mr. Gibbons was saying flowery words, but he knew to expect that. The man was trying to sell the school to him after all. He was not going to let Matt leave without thinking Rice was his go to destination. But Matt still wondered if he would fit in at Rice. He wondered what he would do at the school. How he would handle being so far away. How he'd be able to make friends. Matt had always been a bookish kid that did well in school. It got him to Rice, but it didn't bring many friends with him. He would be in an enormous city without virtually anyone to call upon.

Matt took a moment to think about whether he would be standing there had he not been offered the scholarship. He didn't think it was likely. That was something he began weighing. What schools could he go to if he didn't have the scholarship?

Yet despite those worries, Matt could feel a tingle running up his spine. He started to realize that picking where to go to college was not wholly about what school offered the best classes. There was going to be a moment where Matt just knew which place was the right one.

The tour continued and Gibbons showed Matt the dormitories and recreation centers, as well as the respective buildings for each college. Every one of them had an aesthetically pleasing design that contrasted with the military simplicity of A&M's architecture.

Gibbons wrapped everything up by giving Matt a large packet of documents and instructions on who to contact if he did choose to decide on enrolling at Rice. Papa and Matt had made it clear that no such decision was to be made that day.

They both walked back to the Cadillac, and only once they were inside did Matt make a comment.

"I don't think I want to visit UH anymore," Matt said.

Papa paused.

"Hmm, okay," he said. That was that.

TOMMY

The trees had a cooling effect on their walk. Tommy assumed it was in the mid 80's that afternoon. However, the tree canopies had formed an umbrella along the sidewalk that did not allow the sun to touch the earth. Their path was a cool 72 degrees that was even further chilled by the wind tunnel the trees created.

They walked two blocks away from the university, through the gateway that the trees created, stepping into West U's shopping center.

Mama took one glance at the shops and knew immediately that they made the right decision to walk. There were parking spots all along the street, but not a single one was open. The long-bodied cars stretched into the sidewalk and out into the street. Passersby had to swerve every time to avoid damaging their own car. But West U lived up to its billing.

There were clothing stores with fashionable suits and dresses. Another store displayed a vault of shoes, from sneakers and sandals to high heels and cowboy boots. There was a record store that Tommy was sure Matt would have gone into had he been with them. There was a Whataburger, crammed into a space between a hot dog joint and a candy store. Along with several other food joints, there was a restaurant that labeled itself as the source for all-things chocolate. Tommy was not sure what it meant, but he began to picture a variety of everyday foods coated in liquid chocolate, as well as common chocolate one could buy in a grocery store. It made his stomach tighten, even though he wasn't hungry.

As advertised, there were numerous cafes and coffee shops all around the block. Tommy knew West U was only a series of squares, but it still had a maze-like feeling how there seemed to be something new around every corner. Mama eventually settled on a café titled Fabian's. It was a cozy, dark wooded structure where men and women were sitting around, reading books, writing in journals, smoking cigarettes and, of course, drinking coffee. Some were eating croissant sandwiches or grilled cheeses, but all were drinking coffee.

Without telling Tommy what they were doing, Mama stepped inside, went right up to the counter, and bought a cup of coffee with cream and a blueberry muffin. The muffin was for Tommy.

Together they sat at tables set up outside, sitting in the shade as they watched people and cars pass by. Mama had done this to avoid the cigarette smoke that had formed a cloud against the ceiling inside. Mama did not criticize those who smoked, but she did not understand why someone would smoke inside and disturb others.

Tommy ate his muffin, peeling it apart with his fingers while gazing at further shops across the street. There was one stop with a white banner and two red crosses, one going diagonally and another like a crucifix. It was a Union Jack flag. There were other shops across the street, as well as what looked like a Jewish deli on the street corner, but this shop with the Union Jack flag interested Tommy more than the others.

"Whatcha looking at?" Mama asked, turning toward Tommy.

"That shop over yonder," Tommy said, pointing.

"Which one?" Mama asked, turning.

"That one with the funky red, white, and blue flag."

"Oh. That's the English flag."

"Oh," Tommy responded, no more informed than he was before. "What do you think it is?"

The shop had the words "Baker Street Bookstore" labeled on the top beam. Bright gold letters over a dark green surface. He could not see what was beyond the tinted windows at the front.

"It's a bookstore," Mama said, bluntly. "Can't you read as much?"

"I got that part of it," Tommy replied. "But what's the deal with Baker Street? We're not on Baker Street."

"Well, your guess would be better than mine. Finish up and we'll go take a look."

Tommy had not considered wanting to go inside the bookstore. Yet now that the possibility was before him, he smiled at the thought and all but swallowed his muffin. Together they crossed the street, leaving their dish and mug on the table at the coffee shop. They walked to the bookstore, Tommy glancing up at the Union Jack for a moment, and stepped through the front door. It was then that they got a proper look at the interior.

Baker Street may have looked like a tiny shack from the outside, but inside it appeared to have miles upon miles of bookshelves. From left and right and down one aisle after another, bookshelf upon bookshelf leaned against one another. Above the bookshelves would be markers of "Fiction" "Nonfiction" "Poetry" "Fantasy" "History" "Suspense" "Religion," any number of categories that a book could be considered.

It looked to Tommy like every book that had ever been printed was somewhere inside Baker Street Bookstore. He did not even know so many books existed. To be fair, Tommy was sure he could not name more than ten books, and that included The Bible. But he looked up at Mama and saw her eyes glow.

He was sure she had never seen that many books either, but Mama loved to read. Without saying a word, she started walking up to the bookshelves and running her hands over the book spines. Tommy read what names he could see. Austen, Byron, Doyle, Spenser, Wordsworth. All names foreign to Tommy. Foreign in the sense that they were unfamiliar. Tommy saw no names that sounded Spanish or Italian, though there were a few French ones like Hugo or Verne. In contrast, when he saw names like le Carre or du Maurier on another aisle, he would be surprised to learn these people were English.

Tommy resigned himself to the fact that he knew nothing about books or the people who made them.

Mama had not said a word. She just walked from one bookshelf to another, taking a look at two or three books at each location, fanning the pages open to read a paragraph, and then putting them back in their place. The books themselves had been crammed together so tight that no air existed between one book and another. Tommy did not see anyone else in the store and wondered if anyone ever actually bought the books. Maybe they just did what Mama was doing, walking around and examining them, but with no intention of buying anything. At least Tommy assumed Mama didn't intend to buy anything.

Still, she seemed joyful, if not overwhelmed by all the options in front of her.

Eventually, they came to one particular aisle. Here, Mama found a copy of *Gone with the Wind.* This seemed to calm her down. Something she knew that she had a good understanding of. Yet Tommy feared they were going to spend the next four hours standing there as Mama read from the book for as long as she pleased. He knew she wasn't going to buy it as she had her own copy, but there was no telling how long she might read for.

But to Tommy's relief, she put the book back and continued running her hands along the bookshelf.

"I wonder," Mama whispered. It was so quiet that Mama may have thought she hadn't said it out loud, Tommy thought.

Mama's hands continued to wander until abruptly stopping in the W section. She scanned up and down the shelves, making a face as if she was trying to tug at a memory that was now little more than a shadow. Then, like a pellet from a gun, Mama shot her hand to one book and pulled it from the rack.

Mama looked at the front and then flipped it over to read the back flap. Tommy looked up at the book's cover. *Forever Amber* by Kathleen Winsor.

"What is that, Mama?" Tommy asked.

"This? Was a book that the priest at my church condemned when I was a child," Mama said.

Tommy looked up, shocked that Mama would pick up such a book.

"How come?" Tommy asked.

"It's scandalous," Mama replied. "The priest said it's about a woman who seduces men to move up in society. I think she seduces a priest in it, as well."

"You think?"

"Well, I never read it. Wasn't allowed to. But . . . have I not told you about this?"

"Nope."

"So. My father, your grandfather, he loved movies. Fascinated by them. Mama never understood what he enjoyed, but he loved going to see them. Now, yes, he'd take us with him sometimes, but it was not uncommon for him to go by himself. So, years ago, before I even knew your papa, they made a movie of *Forever Amber*. And the priest in Highbank, he warned everybody about it. Said that nobody was to go into town and see the movie. Said it would be a sin just to see it.

"Well, one day my papa drove into Bryan to pay our taxes. He left like he did every year, and we all expected him back that afternoon like normal. But by the time Mama had prepared dinner that night, Papa was nowhere to be seen. We waited and waited and waited but Papa still wasn't home. It got to the point where my brothers wanted to get in a car and go looking for him. Your aunts wanted to call the sheriff, report that Papa was missing. And then, once the sun had set, he came home. Perfectly fine."

"Well, where was he?"

"He'd gone to see the movie! He'd gone and paid the taxes and then went over to the movie house! There we were worried sick, and he'd gone to see a movie. Mama couldn't believe it. It was so stupid. But it must've been a good movie."

Tommy had no comment to make. He did start to laugh at the ridiculousness of the story, of the character of the maternal grandfather he never knew. Papa Joe had passed away when Tommy was just a baby. Yet all the stories he had heard painted a very jolly figure, not unlike Nonno in that regard. Still, Tommy appreciated getting those bits and pieces of information describing who he was.

Mama then looked to her right and saw there were a few chairs set up next to a lamp planted against the wall. It was one of several reading stations throughout the bookstore. Mama wandered over to the chair and started reading the book.

"Go on and take a look around the place," Mama said. "I just want a few minutes to see how it reads."

Tommy had heard this before. Just a few minutes to get some reading in. A few minutes might turn into three hours. Tommy didn't protest, he just turned and walked to a different part of the store. He wandered aimlessly, not knowing what types of books interested him or what were considered good books to read. He did see one section of sports books. Tommy thought about seeing if they had anything on the Yankees, but that thought dissipated. It was not the same to read about sports as opposed to watching the games.

Near the front of the store was a shelf of books with the sign labeled "Best Sellers." There were no signs of second-hand usage, no wear and tear. Many were thick and hard covered. Almost no paperbacks. Tommy took a quick look at the names on the spines and covers.

"Vonnegut. Roth. Crichton. *Slaughterhouse Five. Portnoy's Complaint. Andromeda Strain.*"

Tommy had no reference for who these people were, what their books were about, or even why people were buying their books. No one in the Brazos River Bottom was reading these books, yet here they were, best sellers. Tommy thought for a moment that he did need to read more. Apart from school textbooks, newspapers and car magazines, Tommy didn't read at all. So, he continued to scan the shelves to see which one of these best sellers would be worth picking up.

He ran his finger over each and every book, sometimes pulling one out to read the back flap but more often than not just passing over. For whatever reason, Tommy's curiosity just was not peaked by those he saw or read about. Then he found one author whose name was different from the others.

Puzo.

It was a simple name. Short and to the point. Not unlike Roth, but this was no Jewish name. This was an Italian. This was one of us, Tommy thought. So he pulled out the bright red book titled *The Godfather*.

He flipped open the first page and silently read the first sentence.

"Amerigo Bonasera sat in New York Criminal Court Number 3 and waited for justice."

Tommy did not look away. He kept reading. There were names like Bonasera. Johnny Fontaine. A baker named Enzo. Americans, everyone, but Italian-American. Linked to that distinction. They all lived different lives, but they all had struggles they needed to overcome. To overcome their struggles, they all turned to the same man, someone called Don Corleone. The titular Godfather.

Tommy figured out very fast that this was a book about Italian-Americans. All their eccentricities, their large families, their unique sounding names, all of it. It may have been set in New York, another place Tommy could not imagine visiting, but this large family and the way they spoke to each other hit home with him. He kept reading and found himself looking at the pages of a grand wedding taking place at an almost castle-like home. All the while, there were backdoor conversations going on with this Don Corleone. Tommy kept reading, not fully comprehending what was happening but unable to put the book down.

He never found a chair to sit down in. Tommy remained standing by the bookshelf and leaned against it whenever he needed to rest his legs. Tommy was just getting to pages about a man named Sollozzo when he heard the chime of the bell that alerted someone had come through the front door. He had no inclination as to the time. Nor did he bother to look up.

"Thomas? Is that you, Thomas?" a woman's voice asked.

Hearing his name was the one thing to cause Tommy to close the book. He did not put it back on the shelf. There was no chance of him leaving the store without the book. Still, he was confused who might be calling for his name.

Tommy looked up to see a woman in her late forties with two daughters by her side. One girl looked to be about Matt's age, the other was closer to Josh's age. The woman was smiling at him. It was not a frightening smile, but it was a nervous one. A smile that implored for Tommy to remember who she was. Tommy had no memory of this person before him.

"You've gotten so big," the woman said. "You were just three years old the last time I saw you."

Tommy stepped two feet forward, hoping the light might jog his memory. It did not.

"I'm sorry, miss, do I know you?" Tommy asked.

"Oh Thomas, it's me, your Aunt Ella," the woman said. "I'm sorry, I should've said that. I recognized you, but that didn't mean you recognized me."

It all came flooding back to Tommy. Nonno's eldest child. The lost daughter. The forgotten aunt. Gone away to Houston, seldom heard from. Unknown marriage, possibly failed marriage. Never in Mumford long enough to create lasting memories.

To see them standing before him now was as if a single character from any one of the books around him had hopped off the pages and casually tried to start a conversation.

"What are you doing here?" Aunt Ella asked.

"Mama!" Tommy shouted, not caring who else in the store he may have shocked by his call.

It was not a call done out of fear, but necessity. There wasn't anything frightening about Aunt Ella, but he knew he needed to alert Mama about what was happening. Mama came around the corner not fifteen seconds later. It took her a moment to notice Aunt Ella as well, but she was just as surprised once she did.

"Isabella?" Mama said, perplexed.

"Hello, Violet," Aunt Ella replied. "So good to see you again."

"Yes, likewise," Mama replied, cautious.

"I was just saying how long it's been since I'd seen Thomas," Aunt Ella said. "This is a happy surprise."

"What're you doing here?" Mama asked.

"Just window shopping for the most part," Aunt Ella said. "I picked up the girls from school and they wanted to go shopping. I felt today was as good a day as any. I didn't think to run across you two."

There was an uncomfortable pause between the five of them, where Mama was not sure what to say.

"What brings y'all to the city?" Aunt Ella asked. "Are you two alone?"

"No, Paul and Matthew are here as well," Mama said. "We've come to look at the school."

"Oh, Rice? Is Matthew going to attend Rice?" Aunt Ella asked.

"It's possible. I have to say I don't know what his thoughts are, he's there right now."

"But you didn't go with him?"

"Well, we heard these stores were here, so I wanted to take a look. It's also a welcome break from looking at all these schools."

"Have y'all been to a lot?"

"Too many, I'd say."

"Any idea where Matt will go?"

"I've juggled with that question all week. I still can't see Paul sending Matt into a city like this all by himself when he can send him to A&M, a place he knows, a place not far from home and for half the cost."

Tommy wasn't sure what Mama meant by "half the cost." Matt was gonna go to school for free wherever he ended up going. But had Papa just been playing along? Were they going to disregard all the trips they were making? Tommy worried about how Matt would react to hearing so. He thought back to the night Matt sped off down the highway. That night he feared if he'd ever come back, Tommy did not want to experience that again.

"How long are you all staying?" Aunt Ella asked.

"Just for the night, at least that's what I was told," Mama said. "I always think we have a set schedule and then, out of the blue, we're going an entirely different direction. So, who knows. I know we're staying tonight so I can tell you we're staying tonight."

"Well, I only just thought of this now, but would you all like to join us for dinner?" Aunt Ella asked, pausing in between sentences from an overpowering nervousness. "There's a cafeteria south of the loop we've been meaning to try. I wager it could fit the whole family."

Aunt Ella laughed at her last remark, a small chuckle, but Mama did not. Mama could only muster a small grin. Mama knew she was dangling into dangerous territory. Aunt Ella was estranged from the family, and Mama had no authority to unestrange her. Nor could she think how the others would react to knowing she had met with Aunt Ella.

"Oh, where has my mind gone!" Mama exclaimed, almost slapping herself on the forehead. "We won't be staying that long cause we can't. We have to get back and prepare for the Fourth of July."

"Oh yes," Aunt Ella said, as if she too had forgotten the date. "That is this week, isn't it?"

"Yes, we're having a big gathering in Highbank. It's an all hands-on deck sort of thing."

Aunt Ella smiled and looked away for a moment.

"I'm sure it'll be great," she said, smiling at Mama before looking away again.

Tommy then glanced out the window of the bookstore, himself wanting to look away from an uncomfortable situation that was far from clearing up. As he did, he caught sight of the Cadillac passing by the street. The windows were only tinted on the outside, so Tommy was able to catch the faintest glimpse of Papa and Matt passing down the street.

He drew Mama's attention to their presence, and all five of them shuffled out the door. Papa was driving slow enough for Tommy to race down the sidewalk and signal for them to turn around. A parking space just happened to open up outside of the bookstore and Mama fended off three oncoming drivers to let Papa pull into the spot.

"When they told us about these shops, I didn't expect it to be such a maze," Matt said to Tommy as he stepped out of the car. "We've been circling for at least ten minutes trying to find a spot."

Tommy didn't respond. Instead, he gestured toward Aunt Ella. The sight of Matt's eyes squinting and then growing wide with a look of confusion told Tommy that he remembered her. It was the same expression that he saw on Papa's face on the opposite side of the car.

"Ella," Papa said, taking a long pause. "I'm surprised to see you. I . . . apologize for not calling ahead, I just didn't think we'd run into you."

"Oh, it's alright," Aunt Ella said in her passive, but clearly bothered, way. "I've just been talking to Violet about why you're here. Congratulations Matthew, Rice is an excellent school, and you'd be great there."

Matt opened his mouth to respond, but Papa cut him off.

"We haven't made that decision yet," Papa said, stern but calm.

"I see," Aunt Ella said.

"We've been looking at a lot of schools this past week," Matt said. "There's a lot to consider."

"We're all just tired, is all," Papa added. "We need to be getting home."

"Yes, I'm sure, back to the fields and the pastures," Aunt Ella said, as if she was visualizing them from a memory. "Should be a happy Fourth of July."

Papa did not respond. He just looked at his sister for several moments. Tommy assumed she could not have changed so much since the last time they saw each other, but Papa looked at her as if he was familiarizing himself with every curve of her face. Tommy could not see any anger or frustration on Papa's face. He could not see any signifiers to tell him how Papa was feeling, period. Papa and Aunt Ella were just there. A meeting that to all present seemed so strange to be happening.

"Boys, would you mind waiting in the car with your mother?" Papa asked, slightly turning his head to look at them. "I just want a word with your aunt."

Tommy and Matt nodded and took their spots in the backseat. There would be no listening to Motown on that car ride, but that was not what was on their mind. They watched as Mama took her seat and then as Aunt Ella sent Grace and Chloe down the sidewalk to what looked like a bakery. Aunt Ella and Papa then stepped off to the side and leaned into each other to talk.

Considering Papa was already a mumbler, the boys knew they were not going to catch a smidge of anything he was saying to their aunt. But they watched closely.

When they stopped talking, when it was clear their conversation was over, they both looked calm. Papa was not frazzled, and Aunt Ella seemed content with whatever he had said.

Papa remembered his manners and kissed his sister on the cheek before climbing in the car with Mama and the boys. Aunt Ella waved to them as they left, and both Tommy and Matt waved back.

The boys did not speak up. No matter how curious they were as to what had been said, they feared asking at the wrong time and never receiving a response. Tommy guessed what was said. A warning to not come by the Big House anytime soon. They remained silent on the ride to the hotel. It was only once Papa had driven beyond the narrow roads and onto wider lanes that Mama spoke up.

"So, what was that about?" Mama asked.

Papa glanced to his right to look at her before responding.

"She asked if I could send a message to Papa."

"What message?" Mama asked.

"To ask if she can come home to the farm. She said she'd like to be there for the Fourth of July."

"In Highbank?" Mama asked in loud surprise.

"No, she wants to be there with Papa and Mama."

"But that's not all she wants."

"No, I think she does want to come back. Come back home. As to what she hopes to do, I don't know."

Mama paused, looking out the window, reflecting on all that had been said and transpired.

"So, what are you going to do?" Mama asked.

"The only thing I can, I'm going to tell Papa."

And that was that. Papa and Mama would delay the consequences of running into Aunt Ella for a later date. Like many other things, they would wait to speak to Nonno. Whenever in doubt, talk to Nonno. Again and again.

"What's that you got there?" Matt asked, looking over at Tommy.

It was only then that Tommy looked at his hand and saw the book gripped between his fingers. Tommy had been right. They had walked out of Baker Street Bookstore with books in their hand and no one did anything to stop them. An innocent mistake with the distractions.

Tommy handed over the blood-red-covered book and gave Matt a quick rundown of *The Godfather*.

"I haven't read far enough to know what the whole story is, but it's about Sicilians here in America," Tommy said. "New York Sicilians, but still Sicilians. There's a whole bunch of people that need help and they all go to the same person. I think it's a family story, I got to a bit about a wedding. Kinda sounds like us."

Mama kept turning around to look at Tommy as she overheard his descriptions.

"What're you talking about?" Mama asked as she turned around. "Let me take a look at that."

Matt handed over the book without protest. Mama would be reading *The Godfather* for the next three days.

"What's the other one?" Matt asked, gesturing to the book in Mama's lap.

It was a paperback copy of *The Swiss Family Robinson*.

JULY 1969

TOMMY

The family's return to Mumford had the feeling of the earth splitting asunder.

Everything seemed normal on the drive up. Papa likely feared the worst had happened to the farm in their absence, Matt thought. But there were no fields afire or coyotes stalking the cattle. Everything appeared normal from the car window.

They only began to think otherwise once the Cadillac was parked in the garage. All eight of their ears perked up at the same time. They thought they heard music. Not piano or anything classical, rock music. Nothing like Mama or Papa would listen to. The sound caused both of them to speed their way onto the path and into Three Pecans.

Matt and Tommy walked slowly behind them, having to pull everyone's luggage and stopping to pet Diamond on their way up the stairs. As they grew closer to the house, they could hear the music clearer. It was Paul Revere and the Raiders. Matt couldn't remember the name of the song, but that drum set paired with those guitar strings was unmistakable. Matt found himself humming along to the beat, but he soon stopped himself. There was no reason that sound should've been coming from Three Pecans.

They stepped inside to find the music coming from the radio. No one was around it, but the music was so loud that it could be heard from every corner of the house. Without thinking twice, Matt turned down the sound and then flicked off the machine. Turning around, Matt saw Susanna standing by the kitchen sink, a dish in one hand and a soapy sponge in the other, looking at the four of them standing in the hall.

"Oh," Susanna said, looking stunned and unsure of how to start talking. "Hello, everyone."

If it hadn't been for the music playing, no one would have thought anything was strange about the image. But the music, and the fact it was Susanna listening to the music, had Mama and Papa on edge.

"What's going on?" Mama asked in a high-pitched tone that some might call a shout. "Why was that music playing?"

Susanna mumbled for a second and shrugged her arms. "I had felt like listening to music, so I turned on the radio," she answered.

"And so loud?" Mama asked.

"I needed to hear it over the water," Susanna said. "I'm sorry. I didn't think you all would be home so soon."

Mama had a look of complete confusion. She let out a great huff before storming into the master bedroom. Matt knew what Mama was thinking. Mama thought she had a firm grasp of who her daughter was, who her most loyal helper was. Mama was now having to realize that Susanna had secrets, that they all had secrets.

Where Susanna had first heard Paul Revere & The Raiders, they did not know. None of them had ever taken her to a concert, nor had she asked to attend one. She likely heard it when she was away at summer camp years ago, Matt thought. An annual excursion that Mama ended when Susanna told a story about how scorpions had fallen from the ceilings in their cabin one day.

Papa had looked annoyed by the loud music but did not appear as if he was about to burst, like Mama did. He followed her into the master bedroom. Matt hoped he was going to calm her down.

"That was different," Matt said.

"I'm more surprised I found a station that broadcasted it," Susanna said, going back to washing the dishes.

THE BOYS IN THE BRAZOS RIVER BOTTOM

"What station?" Tommy asked.

"Umm, I think it was 550? KTSA San Antonio?" Susanna said.

Matt and Tommy turned to look at each other. It was like their whole world had changed. They could stay at home and listen to KTSA. They didn't know when they would get that chance, but just having it available intrigued them. Needless, they sympathized with Susanna.

"Where's Josh?" Matt asked.

Susanna turned around and looked at him like his question was unimaginably stupid.

"Out on the fields, obviously," Susanna said. "You do realize it's the middle of the day? Just cause you lot were exploring doesn't mean we've been lounging. Josh's been getting out there and working, just like he said he would."

"How's he doing?" Matt asked.

"You mean in the fields? Not sure exactly," Susanna said. "But each day he comes back covered in sweat, beet red, totally exhausted. But he's working."

Susanna turned back around and finished wiping down two more dishes before putting them on the drying rack.

"So. How was Houston?" Susanna asked.

Matt and Tommy helped themselves to glasses of iced tea from a pitcher in the refrigerator and sat at the kitchen table. They talked to Susanna about driving down. They discussed the traffic, Matt discussed what Rice was like, and Tommy dropped the news that they had run into Aunt Ella. This was what caused Susanna to stop cleaning the dishes and join them at the table.

The thought of Aunt Ella coming back for the Fourth, only a few days away, and possibly coming back permanently, did come as a surprise.

"You think Nonno would let her?" Susanna asked.

"I don't know—I can't see why he wouldn't," Matt said. "What has she done wrong, actually?"

"Picked the wrong husband by the sound of it," Susanna said. "Maybe that's enough."

"She looked . . . sad," Tommy said. "Just sad, I don't know how else to say it. Like a kicked dog."

"Yeah, like seeing us gave her a bit of hope," Matt added. "We'll just have to wait and see what Nonno says."

Susanna shrugged her eyebrows, "We might be waiting for a while if that's the case."

Before Matt or Tommy could ask, they heard a door open and close at the end of the hall. They heard Papa's thumping footsteps before they saw him come back into the kitchen.

"Susanna, your mother's on the bed in her room," Papa said, matter-of-factly. "She says she has a headache—be sure to give her a cold cloth and help unload her bag. I'm going to speak with Nonno."

"That's what I was just about to tell them, Papa," Susanna spoke up, stopping Papa from turning around and walking out the door. "Nonno and Nonna are in town, at the hospital."

Papa swiveled back on his pivot foot to look at Susanna.

"What?" he asked, puzzled.

"Nonno's at the hospital in Bryan," Susanna said.

"What for?" Papa asked.

Susanna then told all the details. Nonna had been preparing cupcakes for the Fourth of July celebration. She had all the ingredients set out on the island but found that she did not have enough flour. Nonna had no idea how it came to pass that she was so low on flour, but quickly sent Nonno out to fetch some. This would've been around six in the afternoon.

Nonno drove to a grocer several miles south bound and bought the flour without any trouble. But coming home, Nonno passed a median in the train tracks where a hooligan in an all-terrain vehicle came over the ridge and dashed out in front of Nonno's truck.

Swerving to avoid hitting the boy, the sudden jerk of the truck caused it to flip upside down. It did not roll, so Nonno was saved from a possibly fatal injury, but his left hand had been completely crushed.

Nonno always drove with the windows down and his left hand gripping the roof of his truck. It was something Nonno did without thinking. It ended up being his doom as once the good Samaritans that lived along the road went and helped Nonno up, it was clear that every bone in his hand was broken. Nonno was sent straight to the hospital and had to have surgery done on his hand.

"They literally put him back together with wires and everything," Susanna said.

"Wa . . . why didn't anyone call to tell us this?" Papa asked.

"Nobody knew where you were staying, so we didn't know where to call. So, we didn't."

"Someone could've called. Someone could've gotten a message to us."

"I think it's alright. Nonno seemed in good spirits when we saw him yesterday."

"How's he look?" Matt asked.

"He's got a ring of wires through every bit of his hand," Susanna said, grimacing with her teeth as she said so. "But apart from that he seemed normal."

"And what about your uncle? Where's he?" Papa asked.

"Don't know," Susanna said. "All I know is Nonna's gone into town to fetch Nonno. He was discharged today."

Papa shut his eyes for a moment, taking a deep breath to compose himself. Matt and Tommy both saw his hands were clenched.

"Very most. I'm going to find your brother," Papa said, turning around and heading out the door before any more news could be shared.

Matt and Tommy didn't think twice about it, they jumped out of their chairs, and followed Papa out the door. They did not think to put on their work boots or change out of their casual wear, dirtying their shoes, jeans and t-shirts the moment they climbed inside The Mustang. It was only once they were inside the truck that Papa turned to see them sitting with him.

"What're you doing?" Papa asked.

"Going with ya," Tommy said.

Papa looked like he was going to interrogate them, like he was going to ask why they weren't in Matt's truck or off doing some other assignment. Papa could not think of anywhere else they should be, so they hitched a ride. It was just strange for him to have anyone else in that hulk of a machine they called the Mustang.

Tommy did not even think about turning on the radio.

He and Matt remained silent. Rather than attempt a conversation, they let the sound of the engine and rolling tires fill their ears as they drove down the fields. They saw other trucks off in the distance, likely Big Jake and the rest of the hands at work. To the north, they saw glimpses of Uncle Andrew and his Aggies but they were not close enough to strike up dialogues.

Papa was looking for signs of wrongdoing. Signs that Josh had failed at his work, if any of the hands had slacked off or if an outside force had come to do them harm. They didn't see Josh, but they did see something further north on the farm. There were about four trucks, all circled within a square mile of each other. Now, they were far away, but Papa didn't recognize these trucks.

Whether it was the music or the news about Nonno, Papa was on alert that afternoon. Something in his bones told him that those trucks were not supposed to be there. So, moving The Mustang faster than either of the boys thought was possible, he sped off toward the trucks.

There was a group of men. They were wearing blue jeans and white jackets and appeared to be measuring the earth with a variety of tools. There was a variety of other equipment in the beds of their trucks, odd devices that one never saw on a farm.

There were two men digging into the soil and depositing them into containers, marking them with permanent markers to distinguish them. Papa saw this happening, and all but flew out of The Mustang when they arrived in the area. The boys were thankful that Papa had remembered to put the truck in park before hopping out.

Papa walked right into the center of these men and started waving his hands around like he was cornering a cow. He did not shout, for Papa never shouted. There was question if his lungs had the capability of shouting. But he called for them to stop and by all appearances, they were hearing him.

Instinctively, Matt and Tommy stepped out with him.

"Whatever you're doing, you have to stop this now," Papa said to the men. "You are trespassing on private property. I'm giving you all the chance to leave before contacting the police, but you all've got to go."

"Paul!" Uncle Andrew's voice called out.

Papa looked to his left and saw Uncle Andrew walking from the far side of one of the white trucks. There were so many trucks together that they had not even noticed Uncle Andrew's truck parked alongside all of them.

"Paul, it's alright," Uncle Andrew said. "They're here on my invitation."

"Your invitation?" Papa asked. "What about . . ."

"Papa knows they're here. I told him days ago that they were coming. I told him before the accident."

"Well, just who are these men?"

"They work for Chevron."

A wave of realization washed over Papa. Tommy thought back to the rocks Andy and Uncle Andrew had showed him. Remembering how vocal Andy was that they had found oil, that Uncle Andrew was going to be rich. Tommy recalled how easily he threw off Andy's comments as fever dreams. People didn't find oil in the Bottom.

What Papa and Uncle Andrew had discussed, in regards to the rocks, was a mystery to them. Yet Uncle Andrew must have received positive news on the sample he had sent off.

"You're oil men?" Papa asked, looking at the men.

"They're geologists," Uncle Andrew said.

"We're taking mineral samples to perform tests," One of the men said.

"I know what you're doing," Papa said, all but saying he too had a Petroleum Engineering degree. "You're looking for signs to see if there's crude oil somewhere beneath the surface."

"Paul, they've already tested the soil on my land," Uncle Andrew said.

"On your part of the land," Papa rebutted. "It's Papa's land, the family land. Don't be misusing your words."

"Come on, Paul, you know what I meant. They're all but positive there's oil under the ground. They've checked all over the land I work. I wanted them to check the rest of the farms too."

"But you came to this decision by yourself."

Uncle Andrew stiffened his back a bit. He may have been the younger brother by three years, but he had a good two inches on Papa. It showed in that instant.

"I did. I decided they should look and Papa gave us his approval," Uncle Andrew said.

"Yet I knew nothing of this," Papa said.

"You weren't here."

"I'm here now. Obviously, I was going to come back. Why were you in such a hurry? Did y'all pressure my brother?"

"No one pressured me. I decided not to wait."

"Why? Why couldn't you wait?"

Uncle Andrew sighed through his nostrils. "It's not that I couldn't have waited, it's that I chose not to. What's the point? Why wait when there could be something so lucrative?"

Papa stepped closer to Uncle Andrew to speak so that only he could hear, at least that was his intention. Matt was able to overhear just enough to make out what Papa was saying. It was still a mumbled whisper, but there was clearly anger in the voice.

"You're acting greedy, Andrew," Papa began. "If there's oil on this land, as these people claim there is and which you believe, that means it's been there long before we got here. Probably before the Carsons too. Yet you felt compelled to let these people get to work. You let your mind think about all the money you'd make.

"And you're right, it would be substantial. A pump jack on every farm, pump out as much as possible before anyone else in the area can catch up with you. These people would pay a great deal to use our land, not to mention how much they'd pay for every barrel filled. That's not what bothers me, though it does frighten me.

"I cannot imagine what it would mean to own so much. I cannot imagine what one would do with so much. How one might change once they had such. I hope I would not change if oil was found here. I hope I would see it as just another resource. To put it back into this land that's given us everything. If it's there I would use it, but I would not run for it. That's what bothers me. You're running toward it. I see that now. You're sprinting without seeing what you're running toward."

Papa stepped away and said a few more words to the men from Chevron. It would be wrong to say he gave his approval, but he gave them permission and then headed back to the truck. Matt and Tommy shuffled their way back to The Mustang as well, but they were still quivering.

They had never seen Papa talk like that. They were trying to figure out if he was angry or just strong-voiced. He never shouted, and they thought all angry men shouted. Yet they could not ignore the look on his face. Like he could kick down a steel fence with one thrust of his foot. They did not say a word. But Papa kept talking.

"I've probably never told you boys how I could've been one of them," Papa said, eyes focused on the road.

Tommy did not care to correct Papa that he did know his backstory.

"Could've ended up like them, testing other people's lands, looking for oil," Papa continued. "My friends in the Corps called me a fool for turning down the job. Told me I could've been rich. Had a comfortable life. Never worried about anything. You know what I told them?"

The boys knew they were not actually supposed to reply.

"I told them I already didn't worry about anything, that all we had here could provide for us."

Papa had never made this speech before, but it felt familiar to them.

"Yeah, I would've made a lot of money, but it would've been at someone else's expense. I would come onto their land and drill and they would be paid for it, we'd all be paid for it, but then that's that. You drill a hole on that land and that's it. It can never be used for anything else ever again. I'd be coming in and defiling land that may have belonged to families for generations. Land that had supported families, seen children grow, brought fortune to those who had never had it. All of that would be gone in a matter of months. All for an immediate profit."

Matt no longer feared Papa's reaction. He had only been afraid due to his unknowing how he would react. Now that he had seen it, all he thought was that Papa looked extremely sad. The kind of sadness that befalls somebody when they simply do not understand why something was happening. It was the same reason why babies cry when they hear a crash. They are just so overwhelmed with everything around them that they cannot help but cry. Papa did not cry, but he was definitely pained.

Papa did not say another word for the duration of the trip. Matt and Tommy remained silent as well. They each wanted to make comments about Papa but did not dare say them, not even in a whisper to one another. Matt and Tommy had questions about the oil men from Chevron. They couldn't visualize what was going to happen. They had seen pumpjacks on the road to Houston but had never seen their implementation. Tommy pictured dozens of men and machines working for months to set them in place. Then there would be this machine that had not been there before, endlessly pumping up and down night and day until every last drop was pulled from the earth. It was a crude, ugly image.

Whether it was in a feverous rage or a confusion as to what else to do, Papa kept driving. They passed by every field on the farm, even those Uncle Andrew was responsible for. Tommy had the illusion that they were still looking for Josh. They weren't. Papa did keep an eye on the irrigation wells, all were open and appeared to have been open for their proper amount of time. Josh had done his work. Still, they kept looking. Papa did not stop until every last farm had been checked.

Matt started to think Papa was trying to make sure no other changes had been made to the farms. Papa needed assurance that the majority of things were still in order. He and Tommy were just there for the ride.

When Papa was done checking the farms, they went east to the Little Brazos. Here, Matt made himself useful and opened the gate for them to enter the pasture. The cows stirred when they heard the familiar roar of the engine. A handful came right alongside the truck, close enough for Matt to scratch at their heads.

They quickly retreated with annoyed moos once they realized there was no feed of any kind. Papa just sat there, watching them all, surveying every head before him. There were a few calves that appeared to have been born in the past few days, but nothing to cause worry.

"Huh," Papa uttered, his first word of any kind in over an hour. "That's strange."

"What?" Tommy asked, feeling safe to ask the simplest of questions.

Papa pointed out toward the field with his forefinger, hands still gripping the steering wheel.

"That big bull over yonder, you see it? The one strutting around the others," Papa said.

Matt looked forward. The bull was unmissable. The animal was tall, flat backed and full of muscle. Its muscles rippled with every step of its mammoth legs. It held its head high as if it liked to remind the others he was in charge.

"That ain't our bull," Papa said, flat toned.

Matt and Tommy looked up at Papa at once, both raising their eyebrows.

"That there's a Charolais," Papa continued. "We don't own any Charolais. So, unless Nonno, or your uncle, went and bought a new bull between the time we left and the time Nonno had his accident, that ain't our bull."

"You sure it's not one of ours?" Tommy asked.

"Positive. Ain't got our brand," Papa said.

Matt looked again. Papa was right. The rest of the cattle had the same brand on their left hind hips, a cursive letter R whose ends connect in the circle of the branding iron. The Charolais did not have it. They could not see a brand of any kind.

"What're you going to do?" Matt asked.

"Right now, nothing," Papa said. "I don't have the men or the tools to get rid of it. Even if I did, I don't know who I'd give it back to. It's no harm to us if he stays in there a few days."

"What if someone does claim it?" Matt asked.

"If someone claims it, I'll give it back," Papa said. "For now, I'll leave him be."

With that inspection done, they turned around and drove to the Big Brazos lot, checked on the cattle there and then got on the highway to visit. Yet it was turning onto the highway that they passed Nonno's 1958 Oldsmobile. Nonna may have been driving it, but the car itself was unmistakable. Papa wheeled The Mustang around and followed it back to the Big House.

Together, they followed Nonno and Nonna back into the house. Matt and Tommy ogled at Nonno's wired-up hand, even if it was far from polite to stare so intently. Nonno was playful about it, thrusting his hand forward like a claw about to attack them. Papa, not cracking a smile, sent the boys back to Three Pecans to fetch Josh. Papa had guessed correctly that Josh had been all over the farm and had gone home for a rest.

Matt and Tommy found Josh passed out face first on his bed. His shirt was wrapped tight to his body from all the sweat. Tight enough for them to see his ribs.

Mama was outside plucking figs from the trees and had headed off to the Big House to bake fig cookies. Susanna was left behind to stir a pot of suga. In their absence, Mama had hurried together the concoction of vegetables, tomato sauce, tomato paste and water and now Susanna had to keep stirring it for the next several hours.

The fig cookies and the suga would be Mama's contribution to the gathering for the Fourth of July.

"Mama's gone?" Matt asked Susanna, still looking at Josh passed out on the bed.

"Yep!" Susanna hollered back.

"Wake up, Josh!" Matt yelled at the top of his lungs not one second later.

Josh hopped onto his hands and knees like his soul had been harpooned back into his body. He uttered surprised gasps as air rushed back into his body. Josh turned around and leaned up on his arms like planks. Still sweating, he looked up at his brothers as he took several deep breaths.

"What?" Josh asked, confused. "What time is it?"

"When did he get back?" Matt hollered back to Susanna.

"About 30 minutes ago!" Susanna hollered back.

"You've been asleep for 30 minutes," Matt said, in a calm voice.

"Is something wrong?" Josh asked, looking like he could pass out at any moment.

"We're all over at the Big House, we came to fetch you. Come on," Matt said before heading toward the door, Tommy in tow.

Josh fell back on the bed for a moment, heaved a sigh that rocked the bed and followed his brothers.

"You look dead," Tommy said.

"See how you feel, organizing all this by yourself," Josh said.

"Didn't Uncle Andrew help you?"

"At first. But once the day got started, he had his own business to handle. The hands checked on the farms I told them to, but I kept losing track on where to send who and I had to go reopen wells that had been closed prematurely. They all seemed in a bad mood for some reason. Like they all had thorns in their feet."

"And you don't know why?"

"Not a clue. Then Nonno had his accident. So yeah, by myself. You'd be exhausted too."

"Wait till you hear this," Matt said as they walked through the side door.

The sight before them would have been so common as not to comment on it, apart from the fact Nonno had a hand that was 65 percent steel and only 35 percent bone. Papa and Nonno were sitting at a table talking, while Mama and Nonna were cooking sweets. By all accounts, normal.

And so, it came to pass that Papa voiced his grievances about not being told about Nonno's injury or Uncle Andrew's decision to bring men from Chevron to look for oil on the farm. Papa repeated almost the same speech about the indecency of violating land that Matt and Tommy had been privy to just a few hours prior.

Nonno heard all Papa had to say, giving his calm headed advice as he continued to pick at his hand, something the doctors told him not to do. Nonno shared the opinion that Uncle Andrew saw a money-making venture before them with minimal out-of-pocket cost. For that reason, he gave permission to the geologists.

"This is not the end of our way of life," Nonno said. "Just, another part of it. You are viewing this in too apocalyptic a sense."

"I understand that it can be profitable," Papa responded.

"Then why do we keep talking about this?"

"Because it's not proper!" Papa said, slamming his hand on the table to provide emphasis. "Ruggirello Farm and Sons. That's us. That's our company. Andrew and I, with you, making decisions together. Remembering the importance of a handshake. This is a divide."

The boys' backs all stiffened at Papa raising his voice, an impossibility they had thought. Even if it was not a shout, it was the loudest Pap had ever spoken. The boys went back and forth, thinking if Papa was being selfish, or if Uncle Andrew had been wrong by not consulting him.

Yet in that moment they all remained silent. Papa informed Nonno about Aunt Ella and her desire to come home. Nonno looked surprised, but did not outright say his answer to her request, only that he would speak with her later. After that came more silence. Silence that was broken by shouting from outside the house.

"Mr. Paul! Help me, Mr. Paul! Mr. Paul!"

Everyone turned and looked at one another. The shouting continued, a call for help that grew louder and louder. It was coming from the street. Then came the sound of a gunshot. A loud one, like a car backfiring. Papa recognized it as a shotgun blast.

Everyone ducked except for Papa, who looked out the window to see the commotion. A second voice soon came from outside.

"Yeah crawl, just like a maggot! Should've never turned my back on you. You think you could lay hands on her? You're more of a fool than I realized!"

"Don't do this, Jake! We did what we did but this don't have to be how it ends."

"Yes, it does!"

It was Jim and Big Jake. Matt caught a glimpse out the window as Jim tripped coming up the driveway. Jim was crawling backward with Big Jake trudging toward him, shotgun in hand.

They would later learn that Big Jake had found Jim in the act with Liza. Whether it was consensual or not was always up in the air. Regardless, the sight had sent Big Jake into a rage that saw Jim fleeing for his life.

All the Ruggirellos cowered, not one thinking of running out to help Jim. They were more fearful of Big Jake's shotgun finding an unintended target. Tommy was aghast. He had always thought Big Jake was so jolly a figure, yet the man in the driveway was out for blood.

Big Jake moved with the same precision as the bullet he would fire. His eyes remained fixed on Jim the entire time. His hands steady. Having missed his earlier shot, he knew he only had the one left. Granted, the birdshot of the double-barreled weapon almost ensured Jim would be hit.

Still, Big Jake's aim was true. So true that he never saw Papa come from behind him and grab the barrel with his left hand and step in front of him.

"I ask ya to step aside, Boss," Big Jake said, straightening his back to look at Papa.

"Can't let you do this, Jake," Papa said. "Drop the gun and walk away."

"Boss, that scum there's done a wrong."

"And this ain't a right. Let go of the gun and walk back."

Tommy observed all of this from the window. Papa stood there as still as any of the tractors with their engines turned off.

Big Jake straightened the shotgun once more, now pointed right at Papa's chest. Yet Papa did not move. Jim remained cowering behind him, but Papa did not move.

Tommy could not see Papa's face from his vantage, but he imagined he was giving Big Jake the fiercest of stares. A stare fierce enough to move even the likes of Big Jake.

After a good minute of tension, and Big Jake's face curling with anger and frustration, he let go of the shotgun. Without another word said or curse thrown, Big Jake turned around and shuffled back the way he came. With the shotgun hanging by his side, Papa turned around to face Jim.

"Thank you, sir," Jim said, huffing for air.

"You can spend the night at The Wagon Wheel," Papa said, stoic faced. "No doubt Jake will wring your neck if you go back to the house, but you and him don't work here anymore. I don't care where you go, what you do, but you don't live here anymore."

Matt and the others all watched on from the window, hearing every word of Papa's declaration. Jim said nothing as he departed. Thankful to be alive, but nothing more.

Papa took the shotgun, aimed it toward the sky at an angle, and fired. A great blast resounded as the pellets went into the darkness. The blast would've killed him had Big Jake fired. Now all were safe.

The old white bull brayed loudly at the sound of the shot. Papa sighed, as if thinking the bull was the one thing that had not changed.

JOSH

Entering the Highbank House on a holiday had more in common with entering a war zone than visiting family, Josh thought. Some family gatherings feel as if everyone is pressed against the walls due to lack of space. On the Fourth of July, there was no extra space.

The Highbank House was an architectural feat. While it did not have the multi-floor grandeur that was found in a state house from an old money family like the Russells, it was an achievement. One hundred feet long from end to end, spotted wallpaper, cross wind windows every five feet, a spacious living room, dining room and a newly added dishwasher. The dining room in the house was the closest thing anyone in the family had to a dining hall. One room with a fifteen-foot dark wood table that could seat up to 30 people if necessary.

Most importantly, the house contained four massive bedrooms. One master for the husband and wife and the rest for all ten children to find a bed. For that was the primary purpose of the house, a home for all ten of the Vitale children to live together.

It was Giuseppe Vitale who masterminded the Highbank House. To his friends, he was Joe. To Mama's children, he was just Grandpa, sometimes called Papa Joe. Grandpa was a farmer, like everyone else who immigrated from Sicily to Texas, but he had a drive to elevate himself. Some may have gone away, moved to the city, tried to find a different line of work, but he didn't.

Instead, Grandpa opened a grocery store that treated all of Highbank and the traffic going to and from Waco. That little grocer allowed him to meet many influential people that needed gasoline or any number of things. One such person was a man by the name of Tom Connally, who was a member of Congress at the time.

Mr. Connally's wife was from Marlin, another town in the Bottom, so he was passing through on the way to her home.

Grandpa would never say what exactly he and Mr. Connally spoke about, but only months after their first meeting, Grandpa found himself named Postmaster of Highbank. Yes, there are loftier titles, but it was a government position, the first in the Vitale family. The position brought more money than farming ever did and cemented Grandpa's importance in the Highbank community.

Grandpa had passed away in 1953, so all the Ruggirello children ever knew of him was the stories they heard from Mama or their aunts and uncles. These large family gatherings, like the Fourth of July, were means of remembering him and what he provided for all the Vitales.

Including Aunt Josephine from Stafford, the Ruggirellos had five aunts (Bianca, Margaret, Daisy, and Benetta) and four uncles (Jim, Thomas, Joshua, and Joseph Anthony, who everyone called J.A.). All of them had struggled as children, finding spaces in the tiny homes and trailer houses Grandpa had moved them into. The Highbank House was meant for all of them to have a home to come back to.

"I was the baby," Mama said. "I was born in that house. That house is home. Never did have to do no chores. Had my pick of the rooms. I would watch my siblings get into fights and see who would get in trouble and be able to tell who I'd have to share a room with that night."

Aunt Bianca was the oldest and was the first to marry. As Mama put it, they were all born within two years of each other and once they started marrying, they all got married within two years of each other. In total, there were 34 Vitale grandchildren, including the four Ruggirellos. Among their cousins were the Calebreses, the Scruppulos, the Devinos and DiMarias, as well as Uncle Walt and Aunt Christine's respective families, who didn't have an ounce of Italian blood to their names.

The names of Matthew, John, Joseph and a number of other figures from the New Testament could be heard shouted by many cousins and their connected families. Italians were notorious for recycling names of family members.

The four mingled about while uncles were placing giant American flags on the side of the house and cousins planted miniatures in the front lawn. Tommy would be seen running with dogs, as well as cousins, around the house. Matt would find a table with the older cousins and play card games. Susanna would wander off and lounge about on beds and sofa—the boys never knew what she talked about with her cousins. Josh despised it.

Too often he found himself standing against a wall, dodging smaller and taller children alike, not knowing where to start conversations with any of his aunts and uncles, nor did he look forward to the questions he might get asked about school or his health or any other interests going on.

It was accurate to say Josh did not enjoy crowds, but it did not help that on the drive up, Papa had done nothing to improve his spirit. Josh had borne the criticism of not having called Papa about Nonno's injury or the Chevron people. Josh knew, in Papa's eyes, he had failed.

Josh knew to expect no statement of approval from Papa. It was a struggle to get him to say anything as simple as "Good job." Yet Josh could read the silence that surrounded Papa. The way he tucked his head and would sink into his chair. Papa was displeased and would not turn his head Josh's way.

Mama disappeared into the crowd of her nieces and nephews the moment they stepped out of the door. Her first stop was to Grandma, who sat in a luxurious green chair by the window, but after that, she could be spotted moving throughout any corners of the house and grounds. Papa disappeared without a trace.

Josh surveyed whatever he could see happening. The kitchen was a bustle as casseroles were placed into ovens to reheat, water was boiled for pasta and fried chicken was flipped in the pan. The largest pot Josh had ever seen sat on top of the stove. All ten Vitale children had prepared their own helping of suga and had deposited it into the bowl. The amount of pasta they were about to cook could feed an entire army platoon.

By this point, an entire fleet of grandchildren had gathered around Grandma as she told stories. Josh presumed it was about the flood. They had heard about the flood a lot. Highbank was a community that flooded every year. There wasn't a single well on any of the farms, as the community relied on natural irrigation from the flooding. Lately, most of the farmers had transitioned to ranchers, increasing their cattle herds by the hundreds to take advantage of the lush grass that grew after a rainfall.

Uncle Jim was one such man. Uncle Jim was the only sibling who still lived in Highbank. Everyone else had moved away, albeit some further than others. He kept the 100 acres that made up the old Vitale farm, but lately had stepped into the business of cattle competitions. Using medicine and exact diets, Uncle Jim was breeding champion cattle for the Fort Worth Stockyards. Or at least that was the end goal.

Josh took advantage of the grandchildren gathering and stepped outside. A long white table, large enough to seat all 40 plus of them, was seated in the grass. Silverware was being placed, but the only food was a series of sliced bread loaves, the kind of bread that pulled apart with just the smallest of movements.

"Ragazzini!" a voice cheered out.

This call could've been to anyone, but by chance, Susanna, Tommy, and Matt were beside Josh and they all turned instinctively. They turned to see a woman with ink-black hair and fresh curls come toward them and embrace all three of them at once in the mightiest of hugs before kissing each of them on the forehead.

"Hello Aunt Benetta," they all said in unison.

"So good to see you all, as always," she said, still smiling. "Just couldn't go any further without hugging y'all. Why, if it weren't for me telling your mama to reply to that letter, the four of y'all might not even be here."

This was how Aunt Benetta greeted them every time they saw her, but it was true. When Papa was a young man, he had no skill for relationships. He still had no great skill for cultivating intimacy, but it was no different with Mama. They had stood together at Aunt Josephine's wedding, but Mama took no notice of Papa. He took great notice of her.

Rather than come up to her or Grandpa, Papa instead wrote a letter expressing his desire to see Mama. She, hardly remembering Papa and already having a boyfriend at the time, was ready to throw the letter away without a second thought. It was Aunt Benetta who convinced Mama to give Papa a chance and write back to him.

They never learned the details of why that other boyfriend fell out of the picture, or what his name even was, but Aunt Benetta was the one to kick-start their relationship. Therefore, Aunt Benetta could argue that without her, Matt, Josh, Tommy and Susanna might never have been born.

As quickly as they gathered, the four dispersed just as fast, finding cousins to talk to and wanting to further walk about the house. They moved so fast that Josh did not even see where they went off to.

A black Labrador came up to Josh and climbed up to hug him and lick his face—quite like what Diamond would do at home. Josh did not know which cousin the dog belonged to or if it had wandered from a neighboring farm, from the smell of all the food being cooked. Either way, he shooed it away and walked toward the river.

Josh came to the edge of the bank and peered down. Several trees towered on each side of the river, the common result of Texas sunlight and flooding waters. The house was built on stacks of cinder blocks, meaning it would be untouched if the waters ever rose again.

The sound of voices caught Josh's attention, and he looked to his right to find Uncle Thomas and Uncle Joshua talking to each other. They had not noticed him, but he listened in on their conversation.

"When are the LaCarpentera's supposed to be here?" Uncle Joshua asked, taking a sip from his bottle of Lone Star.

"After sundown, once all the fireworks start," Uncle Thomas said.

"Sounds about right, can't have fireworks without them now."

"No, we cannot."

"You still trying to get Uncle Frank to deputize you?"

"Trying to, ask him about every time I see him."

Uncle Thomas then pulled out a revolver from his pocket. It was short-barreled, not like the nickel plated .45s you would see in a John Wayne movie or on the cover of a western novel. But it was a gun, no doubt about it.

"Frank gave me this here .22 to practice with," Uncle Thomas explained. "Said I need to have good aim."

"How'd you think your students would react to learning you've gone off and joined law enforcement?" Uncle Joshua asked.

"Hopefully, they'd see I was living out a dream of mine."

Mama once said that Uncle Thomas had read too many books about lawmen and crime fighters. He had always desired to go into law enforcement, but Grandpa would never allow it. Even after Uncle Thomas had settled into a teaching role at Reagan High School, the alma mater for all the Vitales, the dream did not die.

"Am I right remembering that Uncle Joe LaCarpentera was shot to death?" Uncle Joshua asked.

"Well, died from a gunshot," Uncle Thomas responded.

"Right, they found him at their grocer? Closer to the Bottom?"

"Yeah, New Year's Eve. Coldest night I can remember. Uncle Frank and Uncle Carlo found him slumped over on the floor."

"Right. Thought he had pneumonia or something and only realized he'd been shot after they removed several layers."

"Yup. Died in the truck before they could get him to a hospital. Never did find who did it."

"Really?"

"Yep. From what I heard, Uncle Joe was whispering a name to Uncle Carlo in the truck right before he passed, but Carlo couldn't fully make out what he was saying."

"You think whoever it was tried to steal some of the Devino moonshine? Weren't they storing some of it in the grocer?"

The Devinos had a bit of notoriety to them for their work during Prohibition. Already owning a handful of grocery stores, the Devinos started making moonshine out of their homes and making backdoor sales at the stores. No authorities ever came looking for them, so the Devinos never stopped.

Once Prohibition ended, the Devinos opened liquor stores in Bryan and Waco and no one was worse for wear.

"Can't say for certain," Uncle Thomas said. "But I won't forget that night for a while. Jim and I searching for the shooter all through the night with the Scruppulo boys. It was like we were chasing a ghost."

Uncle Thomas stopped to take a drink from his bottle.

"What brought this to mind?"

Uncle Joshua made a gesture with his Lone Star.

"The gun," he said. "Just popped into my head."

Uncle Thomas put away the revolver at that time, deciding to put it away until the fireworks later on.

Josh slinked off around the house and past the giant lawn table. The platter of bread had shrunk two layers since his previous stop. Passing it, Josh found a much smaller round table had been set up underneath a fig tree on the right side of the house.

There, he found Matt and Tommy sitting with Uncle J.A. and Aunt Daisy playing cards. Josh recognized the game: Scopa. A simple game, though Josh could never remember how to keep score. In plain terms, four cards were placed in the center of the table and everyone tried to pick up as many cards as possible, be it from matching pairs or from possessing the sum of multiple cards. If someone managed to clear all the cards in a single turn, that was called a Scopa.

"Scopa!!" was the resounding call from Tommy as he won the latest hand from the table.

"Little brat got us again," Uncle J.A. said with a smile.

"Oh shush, you've just got to get a better hand," Aunt Daisy said.

"Don't think I'm alone in that regard," Uncle J.A. said as he tallied up the scores on a piece of paper. "At least I'm beating you."

Aunt Daisy looked back, aghast. Tommy and Matt only chuckled.

"Uncle J.A., do you think about the war a lot?" Matt asked.

He looked up at his nephew from the corner of his eye as he passed out the cards.

"Well, I would say I think about it every day," Uncle J.A. said.

Everyone in the family knew about Uncle J.A.'s enlistment in World War II. He was part of a whole generation of men that enlisted right after the attack on Pearl Harbor. He admitted that he expected to be drafted into service as he was not in school, having left A&M to help work the family grocer after Grandpa had fallen ill, and was not working in a vital enough field to remain at home.

Uncle J.A.'s decision helped him avoid the draft and choose his path in the war. Having a natural skill for mathematics, Uncle J.A. found himself assigned to the Army Air Force and shipped off to Midland to train as a bombardier. He would go on to serve in numerous successful missions in Europe, including the D-Day invasion, but was shot down over France and was held in a Prisoner of War camp for the remainder of the war.

"And we didn't know until much later," Aunt Daisy explained, jumping into the story. "The Army delivered a letter telling us that his plane had been shot down, but it didn't say anything about whether he had been killed or if he had landed safely. All we knew was that the plane had been shot down. We were all stunned. I don't think Daddy ever did recover."

"He was definitely weaker when I did make it home, that's for sure," Uncle J.A. said. "They tried to shoot me out of the sky when I was falling in my parachute. I did my best to look dead in hopes they wouldn't shoot me. For whatever reason, they didn't shoot when they took me prisoner, just put me in with a dozen other soldiers who'd bailed out of their planes. All of us went to the same camp. But I survived, I guess someone was looking out for me that night."

Uncle J.A. told stories about escape attempts by fellow prisoners, even claiming that his Stalag was the one that the film *The Great Escape* was based on. No one ever checked to verify this fact, but it might've been true. Other stories included the putting together and breaking apart of a radio every day in order to hear coded messages from the Allies. Uncle J.A. even joined a baseball team while in the Stalag as a means to stay occupied. The first time he ever swung a baseball bat was in Germany.

What puzzled the boys was that Uncle J.A. never sounded afraid in the stories. Like he knew he was going to survive despite being in dangerous territory. Perhaps he knew the Allies would reach them eventually. Perhaps he relied on faith that the Germans would not execute their prisoners. Maybe he was lying through his teeth. They didn't know and the boys never would ask.

260

"Is there a main memory you think back on when thinking about the war?" Matt asked, picking up a card from the table.

"You know, Matthew, from time to time I think about London," Uncle J.A. said. "It was after D-Day and my team had been given leave to visit the city. It had been heavily damaged during the Blitz; some buildings were blown completely in half. It felt like nobody was in the city. We were able to walk into normally busy restaurants and be seated without waiting. We walked right up to the gates of Buckingham Palace without anyone crowding around. We didn't see the King or Queen, but we knew they were there. It was enough to see the Palace itself.

"But we had our pick of where we wanted to go in the city and eventually, we went to this nice retail store, I can't even remember the name, and found this nice pair of black boots with fur lining on the inside. I could never have afforded them, but the workers gave me a discount for being a soldier. Stepping into those boots was like being hugged by a mama bear. I had never been so cold as it was in Europe, but I had never worn boots so comfortable as those. I told my buddy that those boots were going to see me through the war.

"Well, I wore those boots on every mission and every day I was at camp, including the night I was shot down. I don't know how it happened, but as I was falling to earth, the boots came loose on my feet and scattered into the wind. I had to march to the POW camp barefoot in the cold mud. I'll probably never find as good a pair of boots as those. That's what I think about when I think about the war. Boy, they were a nice pair of boots."

"SCOPA!!" Tommy called again, returning everyone's attention back to the card game on the table.

"Oh gosh," Aunt Daisy said. "You've gone and let the nephew win again while you were telling stories."

Uncle J.A. just shrugged and continued to play the card game.

Josh continued his milling about the house and grounds without any aim or destination. His plan was working to perfection. Not a soul had stopped to interrogate him or even ask for his help preparing food or tables. When he took a chance to glance inside the house, he found all the beds filled with sleeping children and all the sofas occupied by passed out uncles.

Before long came the call that food was ready. Rising to their feet with the speed of cannonballs, Papa and all the uncles shot out of their slumbers and entered the kitchen to retrieve whatever tray of food was presented before them to carry out onto the lawn table. On that table were lasagnas, some with meat and the others with spinach, a cheese and potato casserole, a great bowl of spaghetti, freshly sauced, an assortment of fried chicken, a bowl of Italian sausage, meatballs, ground beef and boiled eggs for the pasta, an extra bowl of suga to apply more sauce to the pasta, five blocks of freshly grated parmesan cheese, three pitchers of water and two pitchers of sweet tea, although more than one uncle still had bottles of Lone Star in their hands.

No one was instructed on how to seat themselves, but all 40 plus of them piled together. The wives would sit across from their husbands and the children would sit next to one or the other. Each family did this until each seat was filled. Grandma was seated at the head of the table where Grandpa would have sat. Josh looked down at her. She looked happy.

They all said grace, their voices resounding like a choir from their sheer numbers, and commenced with the feast. For the first ten minutes, no one could hear a word said that wasn't from the person directly next to them. The sounds of chomping teeth, forks and knives clattering against plates and the barking of dogs at children's feet created a drowning noise that deafened all in attendance.

Even so, story after story was shared between cousins, between aunts and nephews, and between uncles and nieces. Whoever was on their shoulder, that person had a story to tell.

262

Mama was by far the loudest, never wanting to be outdone by her siblings. She never seemed to lose energy when they visited her childhood home.

Once everyone had finished their meals, and some had finished their seconds, and the suga had been mopped up with buttered bread, dessert was presented. Three pecan pies, two apple pies and an option of chocolate cake, each served with a generous slab of vanilla ice cream.

Everyone claimed they couldn't eat another bite once the main meal was finished, yet they all made room for dessert.

Once that was eaten, and all the men had unbuckled their belts, Grandma made a sign that she wished to speak. One by one, everyone silenced themselves.

"I cannot put into words how happy it makes me to see you all together," Grandma began, soft-spoken but audible to all. "In every one of you, I see your father. It feels strange with him not here, but I know he would be just as proud as I am to see all of you here, all healthy and happy. We're not one year removed from the news of the earthquake. That was . . . it was a sad day to know my childhood home had been destroyed. But it gladdens me to see the home and family we have created here. Chin Chin!"

All the adults resounded with "Chin Chin!" and drank from their drinks in celebration.

Grandma was talking about Poggioreale when discussing the earthquake. It had just been the last summer when they all received the same news: Terremoto. That was the first word at the top of every letter. Terremoto.

Poggioreale, the home village of every Italian family in the Brazos River Bottom and the surrounding areas, was struck by a 5.5 earthquake on January 14, 1968. Over 200 people died and thousands were displaced from their homes. From what the Ruggirellos and Vitales were told in letters, the town was to be rebuilt in a different location several miles away, but Poggioreale, as their grandparents had known it, was gone. A ghost town in every sense of the phrase.

There was wailing throughout the Bottom on that day. Everyone desperate to learn of relatives who had perished or who had been displaced.

The grieving had passed. Now they celebrated.

It did not take long for news of Matt's status as a National Merit Scholar to reach his aunts and uncles. The interrogation soon followed; a conversation Josh proceeded to drown it out. He was sick of it.

Josh would not deny it. He was tired of hearing the same conversations about how smart Matt was and how great an accomplishment it was that he had earned these scholarships. Tired of hearing everyone saying that Matt was always going to be the one to earn such distinction.

It started to press on Josh that no one was talking to him or attempting to talk to him. It was an odd thought for Josh. All that time, he had been doing his best to avoid talking to people. He took note of what everyone was saying, but he had no interest in taking part. Yet now he felt bitter. Why wasn't anyone wanting to talk to him? Why did no one want to strike up a conversation? Why was no one curious how he was doing? Josh started to ask himself these things.

Even so, no one noticed Josh's head start to hang low.

…

An hour passed, with the platoon of cousins lingering around the house and grounds. A handful had placed blankets on the grass and were lying about as the sun began to set. Pretty much everyone found a place to lay about to finish their desserts and digest their dinners.

Josh had wandered inside, deciding to take a nap on one of the many lounge chairs. He was fortunate enough to find an unoccupied seat by an open window. That window looked out to the front of the house, where Matt was talking with Mama on the stoop. Josh looked away, but leaned his ear to the window.

"You think you've made up your mind about all these schools?" Mama asked.

"Just about," Matt said.

"Let me ask you this. What do you feel would be the biggest thing you'd gain?"

Matt bit his lip for a moment.

"Exposure, I think. I'm curious what it's like to live somewhere other than home for a stretch of time. Don't know how I'd feel about it, but I think I need to learn."

Mama scratched at the back of her neck. The sun was setting right into their eyes, so their squinting prevented Josh from reading into their expressions.

"Want to see what's out there, huh?" Mama asked.

"Maybe," Matt said, still indecisive.

"That's one thing we can't replace, memories. I look at all the people here, you all. We can all move wherever we want to go to, but all the memories come back to this place."

"Would you ever move back out here?"

"Nah, I can't see that. I love this house, I love my family, but there's nothing out here, nothing I could see myself doing in Highbank. Your grandma's here, but if she wasn't here, I don't know if we'd still come up."

"I guess you're right."

The two took a moment to catch their breath, watching a couple of cousins run past with tiny American flags in their hands.

"That's what I wish I could've given y'all," Mama said. "A home where you had time to make friends."

"We have friends in Hearne," Matt said.

"A place you have to drive to. I imagine a house in a neighborhood where y'all could go to school and just be kids. When I was little, I had my family for company. But as they got older and moved out, I saw how lonely it can be out here."

"Have you talked to Papa about moving into town?"

"I keep putting it off," Mama said with a sigh. "He always said he needs to be in the country. Needs to be able to work the farm. I don't see why he couldn't do that and also have a house in town."

Mama then added a sentence that possibly was not meant to be heard. It was under her breath, as silent a whisper could be. Yet Josh managed to get a piece of it.

"Not like he's around a ton to begin with," she said.

Matt didn't respond to the last bit. Josh wondered if he heard it, what he was thinking, but he did not react.

"Well, Papa is a stubborn one," Matt said. "But it's a nice idea."

"I just look around at my sisters," Mama said. "All of them have been better off since they moved to town." She sighed again. "I don't know."

...

That night, a honking horn in the distance drew everybody's attention to the front of the house as a car pulled up in an unavoidable fashion. Cheers rang up from both the Vitales and those who stepped out of the station wagon. The LaCarpenteras had arrived.

Dozens of family members went up to greet their cousins. New life had been injected into the party. Yet not long after that came the announcement that Aunt Josephine and Uncle Tony and their three kids were leaving. Despite urges from many for them to stay the night at one home or another, Aunt Josephine and Uncle Tony insisted that they wanted to get back to Stafford that night. Their children were not enthusiastic about the retreat, but Josh took the opportunity.

"Mama, may I ask Aunt Josephine if they can take me home?" Josh asked.

"What, you want to leave?" Mama asked. "It's not even time for fireworks yet."

"If I'm being honest, Mama, I've felt overwhelmed all day. And I'm still tired."

Mama looked up, a little confused. Mama looked forward to the crowds. She had grown up around a bevy of people and felt out of place in the Ruggirellos', comparatively, tiny home.

Mama leaned over to whisper to Papa what Josh had said. Papa looked down at Josh for a moment, but only a moment. Before long, Josh was climbing inside the Calabrese's car and back down the farm road with them.

TOMMY

It happened like clockwork.

Just as the sun would creep over the horizon and moonlight would fill the sky, there would be the sound of a firework miles away. From the top porch of the Highbank House, they could see a glimmer of the rockets going up and scattering into a million shiny pieces.

Firework after firework shot up into the sky. Soon after that, pop rocks, firecrackers and sparklers were placed into the hands of the children and tiny explosions of various shapes began to scatter around the lawn. Not long after, Uncle Jim and Uncle Joshua wheeled a set of seven red rockets that ranged from three feet to five feet in height. One by one, those too were shot into the sky. Everyone watched as red, green, and yellow embers cascaded down to the earth like a rainstorm of lightning bolts.

Everyone laughed and cheered as they watched the fireworks. Many of the children laid down in the grass to look up at the light show. But the LaCarpenteras took their spot on the front porch. Uncle Frank LaCarpentera led them all as they aimed their pistols into the sky and fired with the wild yips of coyotes.

Shot after shot, they fired their guns. The pistols shooting off with a fiercer blast than any of the rockets. Still, the spectacle did not disappoint. Always a sight to behold.

Someone inside the house turned on the radio to a station playing patriotic music. Some of the cousins started singing

"You're a Grand Old Flag," but most of the party took joy in watching the sparks in the sky. That was enough.

Just as fast as it started, the festivities seemed to wrap up just as fast. Just as the barrage of fireworks appeared to be endless, they fizzled out to mere sparks. No more fireworks came from The Highbank House or from any of the surrounding towns. The sparkles burnt out and all the pies had been eaten.

Many of the children had slinked off inside the house to claim their beds for the night. The aunts and uncles would have to settle for blankets on the floor. The Ruggirellos opted to depart.

The five that remained each went up to Grandma, who was still awake in her comfiest chair, kissed her on the cheek, and thanked her for her hospitality. They said goodbyes to whatever relatives were still awake, but before long, they were loaded inside Mama's Cadillac once again.

All was well on the drive home. Papa drove, wide awake despite the late hour. Matt, Tommy and Susanna all sat in the back and slept on the half-hour drive to Mumford. Yet Papa did not pull up to Three Pecans upon reaching home, he pulled up to the Big House.

Papa saw that Uncle Andrew's car was still in the driveway, but there was also a car Papa did not recognize. The lights were still on inside, so Papa chose to investigate. He told none of this to Tommy or the rest of them, but they knew his mannerisms enough to work it out.

Tommy took one step out of the Cadillac and heard a great scream echo through the house. There was nothing comical about it, nothing similar to being scared by a cheap prank. This was someone in pain screaming from inside the Big House.

He could not remember the last time he saw Papa run, but Papa ran into the house when he heard the scream. He dashed up the driveway and into the kitchen, and the others followed close behind.

It was Nonno. He was dressed only in his night clothes but he was standing over the kitchen counter screaming at his wired-up left hand. Nonno screamed in Italian, he screamed in English. He uttered every curse one could find in a dictionary, curses the boys did not even know existed, curses that only Sicilians knew, curses only farmers said. Devilish words, but the words that only someone in true pain would dare to shout.

Again and again he repeated the curses, stopping Papa and the boys in their tracks. Then they looked on in horror at the realization that Nonno was holding wire cutters in his right hand.

"Figlio di una cagna fili," Nonno cursed through clenched teeth. "Caro Dio, abbatti il bastardo che ha pensato a questi."

"Woah, Daddy, woah," Papa said, waving his arms in the air as if he was approaching a bull. "What are you doing?"

"My hand! It's on fire!" Nonno said, letting out another scream. "It's these wires!"

"What?"

They could hear shuffling from the other room.

"What on earth is going on?" Uncle Andrew asked, entering from the smoking room.

"Daddy says his hand's on fire," Papa said.

"It feels like I shoved my hand in fiery coals," Nonno said. "It's these damned wires."

"When did this start happening?" Papa asked Uncle Andrew.

Tommy thought back to the previous night and how Nonno had never stopped fiddling with his hand. They had thought nothing of it, they had never expected it to become this bad. Uncle Andrew confirmed that Nonno had still been fiddling with his hand but had not seen anything to suspect Nonno was hurting.

"You thought nothing of it?" Papa asked after hearing Uncle Andrew's reply.

"I didn't know what to think! How am I supposed to know what a hand full of wires feels like!" Uncle Andrew replied, raising his voice to defend himself.

"Maybe if you'd have paid better attention, he could've gotten help by now!" Papa said back.

"Stop looking for a fight, we need to do something," Uncle Andrew said.

"Oh, dear god!" a voice shrieked.

Everyone turned to see Aunt Ella standing in the living room. She too was in nightclothes and must have been stirred awake by the screaming. A wave of confusion and anxiety swept over the group as they realized Aunt Ella had been permitted home. They didn't see the girls with her, but they must have been asleep in the guest bedroom.

The boys looked over at their papa. His face was blank, like he had been to a person's funeral and had come home to find them standing in his living room. Aunt Ella's presence made Papa dizzy about everything happening around him. He felt neither joy nor anger. Just confusion.

Aunt Ella's arrival caused a long enough distraction for the majority of the group to miss Nonno slip from Papa's grasp and clip at the wire connecting his thumb to his index finger. It took three clips, each sending a ripple of pain, but Nonno snapped the wire in half and proceeded to pull it from its holding place.

This seemed to be the moment that one would think the screaming would occur. It was the total opposite. Dead silence all around. Everyone couldn't believe what they had seen. Nonno had pulled a wire right out of his thumb in about the complete wrong way anyone was meant to remove said wire. All they could do was stare as blood trickled out of the open holes in his hand.

Tommy expected Nonno to topple over from shock or blood loss, but he didn't. Nonno just stood there, looking at his hand, as if he was surprised at what he had done. Nonno was now gripping his wired hand with his right hand. He was doing his best to keep his thumb and the rest of his hand from crumbling in on itself.

They would later learn that Nonno's hand had become infected by the wires, hence the pain he was feeling that night. But in that moment, Nonno went from feeling excruciating pain to feeling absolutely nothing. Nonno was afraid that in his haste, he had severed a nerve or a crucial ligament.

Luckily for him, Nonna appeared from their bedroom, dressed in a nightgown but totally calm, went up to Nonno and wrapped his bleeding hand in a washcloth.

"Andrea," Nonna said, addressing Uncle Andrew by his Italian name. "If you're all done, go start your car and drive us to the hospital."

"Yes, Mama," Uncle Andrew said before trudging out of the house with his head down, not bearing to make eye contact with anyone in the room.

Nonna guided Nonno out of the house, whispering to him in Sicilian in what sounded like the most harsh and condescending words.

They all waited till they heard Uncle Andrew turn the keys in the ignition and drive off down the road. They were like statues, paralyzed over what they had seen. Only once the car was gone did they turn back to Aunt Ella.

Papa looked at her and said something, but it was so low of a mumble that no one could make out what he had said.

"I'm sorry?" Aunt Ella asked, herself unclear what Papa had said.

"I said, so they let you come home," Papa said.

"Yes, we uh . . . we arrived this afternoon."

"Are uh, are you intending to stay?"

Aunt Ella gave a forced smile. "I'd like to. I didn't say all I wanted to say with Daddy tonight. I hope he's alright."

"So do I."

They paused in their dialogue. Mama did not speak up, nor did Matt or Tommy. Aunt Ella and Papa even looked like they didn't want to talk to each other. It was like Papa had to say or do something, anything, to stop him from thinking about what had happened to Nonno.

"Well, I think it's best if we head home," Papa said, barely audible.

"Yes, we shall see you tomorrow," Aunt Ella whispered. "The girls are asleep in the back."

Papa nodded and began to turn but Aunt Ella stopped him.

"Say hello to Josh for me," Aunt Ella said. "I saw him head out, but he never came by."

Papa looked back at her, eyebrows angled.

"What?" he asked, now audible to everyone.

"He was dropped off at your home earlier, but then I saw him head out into the fields."

Aunt Ella just looked at the Ruggirellos as they struggled to grasp what she was saying. Not because of its context, but the story it was revealing. It did not make any sense to them. If Josh was anywhere, he was at home, in bed. There were no lights on at Three Pecans. They took that as Josh was asleep, not that he wasn't there at all.

One by one, they all turned and funneled out of the door. Not one of them said a good-bye to Aunt Ella. Most of them still did not know what to say, so they said nothing.

They struggled to keep up with Papa, whose stride seemed to lengthen with each passing second. It was as if he was speed lunging rather than power walking. Mama ended up in the rear while Tommy managed to stay on Papa's heels.

Diamond leapt onto all of them as they passed. The dog might as well have jumped against a brick wall, considering how hard he bounced off of Papa's shoulder. Papa's thunderous feet trampled inside Three Pecans and flicked on every light switch in every room. Josh was nowhere to be found.

Papa checked the rooms without stopping. He entered, turned on the light, and scanned the room as he continued to pass through the next entry. It was dizzying to keep up with. Still, he found nothing. Without stopping, Papa headed out the back door and into the garage. Tommy and Matt managed to reach the garage just as Papa had pulled open the large wooden doors and walked inside.

Sure enough, the Mustang was parked right where Papa had left it, but Matt's Ford was vacant. Matt soon followed and saw it for himself. They all knew nothing good could come of it.

For some reason, Tommy had the initial thought that Josh had ran away. He had not taken the chance to see that all of Josh's personal belongings, including his collection of *Auto Week* magazines, were still in the room. Josh, at the very least, was still on the farm. Where on the farm was the larger question.

They mentioned the possibility that Josh had gone to close the wells. It was possible, but it was foolish. Josh was too young to go out at night alone, Papa declared. All it took was one instance of falling asleep behind the wheel and one's truck would cascade into a ditch or a row or flip over completely.

Regardless, none of the wells were supposed to be open. Papa had been convinced to take, yet another, day off from working the farm. It was the main reason he had been so anxious at the party. Even with the familial festivities going on, all Papa thought about was how every day he was not working in the fields was one more day he wasn't providing for his family. Of course, he never voiced these concerns, but the boys learned how to read it on his face.

Mama, all but talking to herself, continued to talk about where Josh could be or what he could've gotten up to. She also questioned why Nonno or Nonna had not said anything, forgetting for a moment that Nonno was rushing toward a hand surgeon at that very moment. She continued talking, but Papa had stopped listening.

He had seen that The Mustang was still present and within moments was climbing inside, swinging his legs into the seat as if he was climbing a horse. Tommy and Matt attempted to climb inside, but Papa looked at them and uttered "No." That was that.

They went ahead and opened the gates to the farm roads and followed the taillights as they grew further and further away. Tommy and Matt walked slowly without saying a word, wanting to keep an eye on the truck, wanting to keep track of everything that was happening.

But then the truck stopped. The truck stopped and for twenty seconds remained idle in the middle of the road, rocking back and forth from the engine.

It was Josh. He was standing there in the middle of the road. Covered in dirt and hair matted. Filthy.

The foolishness had taken place after all. While they were back celebrating the Fourth of July, Josh had driven into the fields and opened the wells on the home farm. It would have been a short period for irrigation, but Josh wanted to show he knew how to look after the Home Farm. Even as day turned into night, Josh remained in the fields.

"I felt I had more work to be done," Josh later told them.

In his efforts to check all the fields, Josh ventured over the Little Brazos to inspect the well-being of the cattle. Yet after Josh had opened the gate to enter the pasture, he drove three feet forward and rolled over a stump of mesquite that burst the truck's front tires.

Stunned at what just happened and unable to stop the cattle from wandering out of the pasture and into the adjacent cotton field, Josh began to shake at the realization of his errors. He honked his horn in a desperate attempt to halt the cattle's advance, but he could not move fast enough to close the pasture gate.

Without anyone or anything to help him, Josh walked home and was about to reach Three Pecans when he came across Papa on the farm road.

Papa listened to Josh's story without saying a word. Everyone else made comments, but Papa waited until Josh was done. Once he had heard the story, he had Matt and Tommy get in The Mustang with him and together they pulled the truck out of the river and back to the Yard.

By far the most unnerving thing, Tommy thought, was the fact that once it was all over, Papa went to bed. He did not say a word. He did not give a speech. He did not utter punishments. He did not complain about right and wrong. He went to bed without a single word said. Mama said words, but not Papa.

It kept Tommy up into the early morning hours thinking about it. Nothing may have been said that night, but there would be repercussions for foolery.

MATT

The Ford ended up needing two new tires as both of the front tires had flattened by the mesquite thorns. That resulted in Papa making another negotiation with Sullivan, but afterward, Three Pecans gave the appearance that its inhabitants had taken a vow of silence.

In the morning after Josh's accident, no other words followed.

Papa remained in a deathly silence from morning till night. He gave no instruction as to what the boys should do or what Josh's punishment would be. Nor did Papa question Josh for his rationale behind running off. Papa remained quiet. That worried them more than anything.

Whenever Papa was upset, he did not yell or scream, he got deathly quiet. He would walk around and do his daily routines, but in total silence. The longer the silence lasted, the more upset Papa was.

There would be no outburst when the silence finally ended, whenever that would be, but Matt feared what would be said once Papa did resume talking. The silence stretched longer than any other period of silence they had seen from Papa. Whatever was going to be said on the other side of it wouldn't be good for any of them.

All three boys had ridden with him to purchase the tires. Along the way, they had passed Sullivan's house.

It was a common house like any other they would see in Bryan or Hearne. They passed it every time they drove to town. Not once had they stopped to look at what was there. This time, Papa brought The Mustang to a halt just as they passed Sullivan's.

Papa did not look at the boys or back at the house. They all had seen it. They questioned what they had seen. A few thought they were imagining things, as if they were sleep deprived and a dream had slipped into the daytime. Papa cocked his head to the side, questioned these thoughts in his head, and then went to turn the truck around.

The four of them peered from the opposite side of the street at Sullivan's house. There, like any other vehicle, was an M4 Sherman Tank. The hulking piece of dark green metal and tractor belt appeared to be in working condition without any sign of wear and tear. Papa had no idea why Sullivan had a tank at his home or how he had come to possess one, but he could tell it was the real thing. To describe the feeling among the Ruggirellos, it was odd. It was like a dream after all. It was something none of them ever expected to see in The Bottom.

They remained there for a good while, and then continued driving. They didn't even talk about the tank. They didn't know what to say. They could mention how absurd it was. Maybe they would say how cool it was to see a tank that maybe General Patton led into battle. The tank had more than likely never seen combat, given how fresh its parts looked, but they still imagined.

Instead, they said nothing as Papa continued down the road. When they reached Sullivans, the boys were tempted to ask about the tank, but they said nothing. At home, the three of them were responsible for jacking the truck up and replacing the tires. Papa remained at a distance to oversee the procedure.

They hoped he would come to their aid if an accident occurred with the jack, but they did not risk finding out.

On Saturday, the boys were kept confined to the house, Mama's instructions but Papa's commands. Mama put them to work cleaning the house and washing clothes, but their main task was the garden. They picked every fruit and vegetable that was ready to be picked and then re-sowed the soil. With twelve different bags of seeds at their disposal, each weighing twenty pounds, the boys delicately planted seed after seed along the rows before topping everything off with a light layer of water.

It was more exhausting than they expected. Matt started to feel a creak in his back from leaning over for so long. They would rather open and close wells any day rather than plant seeds one at a time.

The task was meant to keep them occupied all day and it did. Yet even once Papa had returned and they had eaten dinner, the boys still were kept at home. Even Matt was not permitted to work the night shift.

"Not tonight," was all Papa said when he saw Matt donning his work boots.

Matt was caught off guard, but Papa's decision was in line with everything else happening.

Sunday came and the Ruggirellos all gathered for church, even Aunt Ella and her girls. There was chatter among members of the congregation about Aunt Ella's presence. They all noticed people glancing at her, but none approached to hurl curses. None approached to welcome her either.

Gathering at the Big House for lunch, they all got their first glimpse at Nonno's re-wired hand, now with proper medication to prevent another flare-up. Nonno still found himself knocking over cups of water, forgetting he now had no use of his left hand. Nonna looked tired.

Uncle Andrew shared an update from the Chevron people. They had signaled out a spot of land further north on Uncle Andrew's plot. There were still tests to be done and plans to be configured, but that would be where they would build the first pumpjack.

He then announced one more surprise. The Chevron men had gone to the hill overlooking the Little Brazos. Matt noticed Papa clench his hand in frustration. Technically the land belonged to all of them, not just Papa, given that it was land meant for cattle and not crops. There was a clearing on the hill, free of any trees, where the Chevron men wanted to plant a second pumpjack.

"Badger One, they told me it'd be called," Uncle Andrew said.

No one at the table talked about the matter beyond that. No one talked about figures or when the pumpjacks would be put in place. It seemed clear that Papa would agree to their desire to put an oil well on that hill, but he did not desire to talk of it that night.

There was the question of where Papa would find new hands now that Big Jake and Jim had been dismissed. The two of them had left the farm, as instructed, without any further issue, but they left a major hole in the workforce. Big Jake was known to open and close a well with the ease of flipping a light switch. They would miss that skill, but there was no excuse for what they had done.

Uncle Andrew offered to send a couple of the Aggies to work for Papa while he searched for new hands. Papa declined the offer.

"I'll take care of it," was all Papa mumbled.

After dinner they all departed, sharing only the mildest of pleasantries with the rest of the family. The boys could tell Papa wanted quiet and wanted to be alone. He would get neither at the Big House. So, they departed as soon as they were fed.

They all trudged back to Three Pecans and Tommy made sure to put food in Diamond's dish before going inside. Papa went to his chair first thing, likely to have a food coma, but Matt stood in front of him to get his attention.

"Papa, don't you think we need to talk about some stuff?" Matt asked.

Papa just looked up at him.

"Like how we're gonna organize tomorrow?" Matt continued. "If we're not gonna use Uncle Andrew's Aggies, then we need to work out a plan."

"Ain't nothing for you to worry about," Papa said, calm as ever.

"I still say we need to talk about it, though. We've got a lot of land and fewer people now, so why don't you tell us where you want us to go. I mean, am I still working the night shift?"

"No, you are not."

Josh and Tommy looked over at that moment. It was happening.

"Okay then," Matt said. "So where do I go? Where do we go?"

"I'm surprised with you, Matthew," Papa said. "Just days ago, it seemed like you wanted nothing more than to get away from this place."

Matt turned his head at that moment. The words came out in Papa's usual low voice, but they cut deep. Anger that had been repressed was now starting to billow.

"Yes, yes, so excited to visit Houston and that nice school," Papa continued. "Nothing like The Bottom. Nothing like A&M. You liked it cause it was shiny and new. I know it. It's no different than your uncle becoming infatuated with the oil under the ground. This I know."

"But," Matt began.

"Sietete!" Papa responded before allowing another word to be spoken. "You all will stay here and help your mother with whatever she needs. I'll find new hands. Y'all will stay put."

Papa sat up in his chair as he said these words, as did Josh and Tommy upon hearing them.

"You will not drive the Oldsmobile and you will not drive the Ford, unless asked," Papa continued. "You may seek work from your grandparents, but you may not go into the fields. Help around the home, help around the garden, but not the farms."

"Why are you saying this?" Matt asked.

"Y'all need to work on listening. It may be a lot of work for me in the short term, but y'all need to stop taking it for granted. This work isn't a chore, it's a necessity."

For a moment, Matt did question if this was a bad thing. Was it wrong to no longer have to wake in the early hours and to spend entire summer days in the hot sun? But that wasn't it. They weren't being freed from having to work, they were being placed in confinement as if they were criminals.

"And just how long is that to be the case?" Matt asked.

"As long as necessary," Papa replied.

"Papa, that's just unfair," Josh said, entering from the kitchen. "You can't just lock us up here."

"You won't be locked up, but you'll remain here," Papa replied. "You'll stay until you can learn to follow orders again. You're still boys. Boys who think they know better than men who've been doing this for decades. I won't have it."

"Papa . . ." Josh continued.

"Sietete! Sietete! It's been said. You have your instructions, now you follow them. That's the way things are. It's time you all understood that."

Papa stood up from his chair. Like cubs around a wolf, the boys instinctually sat down. They knew they were beaten. They didn't like what they were hearing, but nothing else could be said. They had to defer.

Mama and Susanna had been in the kitchen this entire time. They could only look on with blank expressions at the news. Their faces provided neither criticism nor comfort for the boys.

"And Matthew," Papa said, stopping on his way to the bedroom. "I've made up my mind. A&M is the best fit for you after all."

JOSH

The boys never traveled further than the half square mile that made up Three Pecans and the Big House. The keys to all the vehicles were kept in a lockbox under the kitchen sink, a lockbox that only Mama and Papa had keys to. They could travel as far as their feet could carry them but no further.

The silence that they had feared from Papa had entered into their very being. They did as they were told, completed every task without any complaint or moan, but they did not speak to each other. They shared no stories about the latest baseball games or shows they had seen on TV, not even comments about random news they had heard on the radio.

Not a word.

Tommy felt an energy around the three of them that had not been there before. They always argued about something. Brothers argue. This was different. This seemed like a threshold had been passed. Some grievance committed but left unspoken. Tommy feared aggravating it if he tried to speak to either of his brothers, yet he was also left uncertain of any remedies.

From time to time, Matt and Josh would glare at each other from across the garden or across a room. They rarely stood next to each other, let alone talked. They didn't need to talk. Josh knew Matt saw him as the problem. Josh owned up to the fact that he went out without supervision and messed up—there was no way around that. But Josh saw himself with clean hands when it came to Papa's decision to send Matt to A&M.

In Josh's eyes, Matt had let his imagination get the best of him. The real world had come crashing back into his life, and now Matt was looking for someone to blame. The only one to blame was Matt, Josh thought.

That was how they interacted. They worked with distance between each other, often with Tommy as a buffer. Over dinners, Mama did most of the talking and everyone else would talk when she asked a question. Papa would make comments about work that still needed to be done on the crops.

Josh wondered, if there was still work to do then why not let them go to work? Even if Papa was trying to make a point, to show his strength, the crops were still going to be hurt as a result. Was that worth the risk?

Come Saturday, Mama had made plans to attend a bridge club in Bryan. She thought it would be a good chance to run a few errands as well, so she asked Josh to come with her to help. There didn't appear to be any ulterior motive to her selection. There was no sense that Mama was trying to cause some much-needed separation from Matt and Josh, but Josh jumped at the chance.

Of course, once they reached Bryan, Josh quickly became bored at the idea of sitting in the corner of a beauty shop while Mama and four other ladies played cards at the table. Bridge club meetings could last several hours, so Josh asked permission to walk over to the Dairy Queen. Mama gave it.

Josh intended to walk to the Dairy Queen, that much was true, but he never made it there. To get to it, Josh had to pass by the local movie house. The property was formerly a traditional theater where traveling companies performed shows. Then A&M built a performance hall for the Corps of Cadets, and all those traveling companies started paying the university to use its facility instead. As a result, the old theater was transformed into a movie house to bring in all the moving picture shows.

Josh didn't take note of what movie was playing, but he thought it would be a good way to pass the time. That was until

Josh stuck his hand in his pocket and realized he had no money. They never carried that much money to begin with, but Josh could find nothing but a couple of dimes in his pockets.

He did not give up so easily.

The movie house sat on the corner of the block and while the entrance was on the main street, the attendees would exit onto the side street. People would come out 30 at a time every few minutes. Sometimes fewer would come out, but it was clear that while people were exiting, Josh could slip inside without anybody noticing. And that was exactly what he did.

The congregation of mostly college students all wandered through the doors, many of them discussing the film they had seen, and headed to their homes without any thought. Josh was able to slip in like a sheep entering a paddock. He found an aisle seat in the third row, wanting to avoid any suspicion from those coming through the main entrance. He took his seat, crossed his legs, and did not say another word.

The next thing he knew, Josh was watching a film about two hippies on motorcycles driving around the country. One rode this tall bike with American flag colors all over it. The other had a thick mustache and long hair that blew in the wind. Josh thought to himself, they don't look like anybody I've ever seen in my life. Definitely not like anyone in the Bottom.

They rode all over the country, living off the land, sleeping with hippies, running away from rednecks, and traveling to New Orleans. Theirs was a life free from the land, unshackled by any job or family other than the family they made on the road.

A tinge of envy crept into Josh's chest.

The film was called *Easy Rider,* and he made a note to remember the title.

Josh exited out of the movie house like every person who had actually bought a ticket. Now he understood why they were talking so much.

Spotting a clock through a storefront window, Josh worked out that Mama would have been wrapping up her game by that point, so he hurried back to the bridge club. When asked where he had been, Josh lied and said he went to read in the library. He made no mention of *Easy Rider* or the fact he had seen a movie at all. No one asked about Dairy Queen either, so Josh never incriminated himself.

He helped Mama with her errands like she asked, and they returned home like a normal trip. Yet on the way home, Josh started to take note of the vehicles sitting in the farmers' backyards, be they broken-down or in working condition. He was hoping there might be something there he had not noticed, or had noticed and had not cared to remember.

No one questioned Josh about his changed demeanor or the fact he seemed cheerful after being so glum. It was simple. Josh had a new goal. A personal one.

Matt and Tommy did not say anything as it seemed like their work was moving along at a smoother pace. Papa still did not let them go into the fields, but they were allowed to drive Nonno on his errands when he asked. Truth be told, Nonno could have driven himself with one hand, but Nonna would not hear of it. If Nonna had her way, Nonno's foot would not hit a gas pedal for an entire year.

It was on one such drive that Nonno turned to his right, and said "What in the world?"

It was the Sherman tank that they had seen the previous week.

"Stop the truck, Giouse," Nonno said. "I wanna take a look at this."

Josh did as he was told and brought the truck to a halt right in front of Sullivan's house. He then went around and helped Nonno out, making sure to grab the good hand before helping him up. Nonno, as casual as ever, walked right up to the fence and peered out at the tank.

"What a sight," Nonno said. "To think, your uncles used to ride around in something like that. Incredible."

"Yeah," Josh replied. "It's something."

"You ever thought about the military?"

"Me? No. Can't picture it."

"That's good. All we hear on the news is people dying for nothing. Absolutely nothing. Stay in school, get good grades like your brother. That's what I say."

Josh had only been half listening to Nonno. It was true Josh did not think about the military, he did not think about the war in Vietnam at all. It was just something that was happening, something they were living through.

Once Nonno mentioned Josh should be like his brother, Josh completely checked out. He took a long glance at the tank as Nonno continued to talk. Josh imagined climbing onto the tank, peering inside, maybe even giving it a drive, although he doubted the engine actually had gasoline. Still, it was impressive seeing the machine up close.

It was then that Josh started to look at the other items in the lot. There were a bunch of whitewall tires that looked freshly polished. Two pickup trucks with a variety of gardening equipment in the beds. Several other pieces of machinery, likely from broken-down cars and tractors, but Josh soon drew his eye to an item in the far corner of the lot.

It was a motorcycle. A dark metal, almost black design. Sleek and low to the ground. Round light bulb on the front. Cushioned seats. Tight handles. It looked nothing like the choppers ridden in *Easy Rider*, but that was all Josh could think about. A motorcycle in a land where motorcycles didn't roam.

The sight of it drew Josh to remember a conversation with Sullivan from one month ago, back when he accompanied Papa to Sullivan's store to look for tires. He had mentioned the motorcycle, mentioned Josh coming to have a look one day. He had thought nothing of it then, but now he was a thousand times more interested.

"Ah, I see my home is becoming a tourist attraction," Sullivan said as he stepped out of his house. "Like what you see?"

"I'm more surprised that such a thing is here to begin with," Nonno said. "How'd you come by that there machine?"

"An ad in the paper," Sullivan said, probably lying. "It's a collector's item. They don't build them anymore, they're out of date. Most of them are getting donated to museums, but this guy was selling a few. I wouldn't say I've thought about owning a tank in the past, but when the chance to own one arrived, I jumped at it."

"And it's legal? It's safe?" Nonno asked.

"Oh perfectly," Sullivan said. "There's no gasoline in the engine, so nothing is flammable. No gasoline means it can't be driven. Even if it could, there's no shells to load it with that would make it a danger to any of my neighbors. They don't seem to believe me when I say it's no danger. These people think I'm gonna drive through their homes or something. It's laughable."

"Perhaps," Nonno mumbled.

"Well, Mr. Ruggirello have no fear, the police have already inspected it," Sullivan said. "I even called them when I ordered it. I showed them it's immobile. Nothing but a shell. Like I said, a collector's item."

Nonno looked away from Sullivan and back at the tank.

"Fascinating," he whispered.

It was then that Josh took a chance and asked about the motorcycle. It was indeed the one he mentioned beforehand.

"I'm trying to find a buyer," Sullivan said. "I think it's worth a fair price. I can't ride them anymore. Lost my balance after an injury."

Sullivan then tapped his left leg, the one he limped on.

"But there's no thrill like riding on one of those down a highway."

Nonno held up his wired hand.

"No more excitement for me in my life," Nonno said, smiling. "Come on Joshua, we should get going. Thank you, Mr. Sullivan."

"My pleasure, Mr. Ruggirello," Sullivan said.

Nonno headed back to the truck, but Josh stayed behind to share words with Sullivan. He asked about the motorcycle, how much he wanted for it. Josh asked if someone could pay it off in installments. Sullivan said if the man was trustworthy, he could agree to it. And that was all that was said. Josh made no promises and Sullivan did not goad him. Josh just got in the truck and drove off.

Then came the night of July 20. The moon landing.

All everyone had heard on the news that week was how the United States was going to be the first country to put a man on the moon. The astronauts had launched on Wednesday and on Sunday they were making their descent onto the lunar surface. Just like every other family in the country, the Ruggirellos had gathered around the television set to watch the descent. Even Papa.

The video broadcast around the country was grainy and they could only just make out what the astronauts were saying. Still, the Ruggirellos never broke their gaze from the screen.

The footage on screen made them think it was already nighttime, but by the time the lunar module touched down it was just 2:30 in the afternoon. Even so, the energy made them feel like a whole day had passed.

It seemed like everything had changed. The world was different now. A man had left the earth and set foot on a moon. Life would now be categorized as having happened before or after the moon landing. No one felt this more than Josh.

The Ruggirellos had been so focused on the television. They all remained to watch Walter Cronkite guide them through what was happening and how historic the moment was, but not Josh. Josh had asked permission to go help deliver the Sunday dinners to the hands. The moon landing had prevented the traditional family gathering, but Nonna had still prepared casseroles. Papa heaved a sigh, relenting to the moment. It looked like Papa found no joy being confined to the living room, Josh thought. So, Papa unlocked the lock box and handed over the key to Matt's Ford.

Josh was not telling a lie, he did go and deliver Nonna's casseroles to all the hands at their homes. He just wasn't telling the whole truth. For after he had finished his deliveries, Josh turned back down the highway and returned to Sullivan's house. Convincing the man to step away from his television set, Josh asked about the motorcycle.

Sullivan was hesitant to make a deal with Josh, still a child in his mind. Yet Josh had figured out how to talk with Sullivan. He knew Sullivan would not pass up the chance to make a profit. Josh weaved around to a price he believed was manageable. During the school year, Josh worked as a grocer at Brookshire Brothers in Hearne and planned to give Sullivan a payment every week until he had paid off the motorcycle. With a handshake to seal the deal, Sullivan helped load the motorcycle in the bed of the truck and with it, Josh headed home.

Josh purposefully hid the motorcycle in one of the tractor sheds in the yard, throwing a tarp over it for further disguise. Josh knew Papa would've turned the motorcycle into scrap metal had he found it in the garage.

That next morning, Tommy was awake by six like any normal day. Yet this time it was not Diamond's barking or the sound of a train passing that woke him. It was the sound of a sharp buzzing noise that was growing louder and louder. Something miles down the road that was headed down the highway.

Tommy went out onto the front porch and watched as Josh flew past on his black metal motorcycle. He had not even realized it was Josh. The wind was blowing so hard that all of Josh's hair looked like it was being pulled back on a string. Even in the warm morning, he wore his denim jacket, needing something to protect himself from the wind chill. Yet he enjoyed every second of it. If there were any doubts, they were dismissed by the Aggie whoop Josh bellowed out as he blazed past Three Pecans.

"What the devil is that noise?" Mama shouted from inside the house.

Soon, all four of them were standing on the porch to see what was happening. All except Papa, who had already gone into the fields.

Josh did not hear her shout. He rode all the way to the intersection and back, twice whooping past Three Pecans as he blazed down the road. It was euphoric for him. He did not think about Papa's disappointment with them or his arguments with Matt or even what was going to be said in the coming minutes. All there was, was the road and it was pleasant.

Still, even Josh knew it couldn't last forever. So, surrendering to the fates, he drove the motorcycle back into the yard and parked it at the side of the garage. The old white bull mooed at him as he did so.

"You don't like it?" Josh asked sarcastically to the bull.

"Joshua, you get in this house!" Mama shouted from the top of the steps.

Papa may have never been the shouting kind, but Mama was unafraid to let her voice rise to a sharp edge. Removing the gloves he had been wearing, Josh trudged inside the house, remembering to remove his boots before he did so.

"What is that?" Mama asked, standing in the kitchen with Matt, Tommy, and Susanna sitting at the table.

"It's a motorcycle," Josh said.

"And what do you think you're doing with it?"

"Going for a ride."

Josh glanced over at Matt. He looked like he could not believe what Josh was saying, let alone doing.

"Where?" Mama asked.

"I wasn't going anywhere," Josh said, being honest and not defensive. "Just up and down the road before the day started."

"The thing's a death trap waiting to happen," Mama said.

"It's perfectly safe," Josh said. "I have my license. I paid for it. I can ride it."

"You paid for it? How?"

"With my money. Money I've saved."

"Where on earth did you get an idea like this? Is this from all those magazines you've been reading? I knew those were no-good, so stupid."

"It's nothing like that. Only been thinking about it for a week or so."

Mama continued to grow frazzled, gasping for air as she searched for her next response.

"I just . . . I just don't understand it," Mama said, more to herself than to anyone else.

Mama was starting to pace around the room, her breaths growing longer and deeper. It was actually a concerning sight. The simple act of breathing had become laborious.

"All of you go outside," Mama said. "I need to think. Just go out on the porch and stay there."

Josh, not wanting to give the illusion that he was running off to his motorcycle, waited until his siblings had exited the room before following them. He was not about to give Mama another scare. He knew that much.

They all wandered onto the porch, taking their respective spots in rocking chairs, on the floor, or leaning against the beams. Diamond was in a barking match with the old white bull, keeping them from hearing what Mama was saying to herself inside.

Mama may have grown frazzled, but Matt was ready to burst.

"I guess you think you're some big shot now," Matt said.

"Now that's uncalled for," Susanna said.

"Don't go putting words in my mouth," Josh said. "I bought a motorcycle; I rode a motorcycle. That's all that has happened."

"And you've made a scene," Matt said. "Mama could be having a heart attack right now 'cause of what you've done."

"An unwarranted worry," Josh said. "I know how fast I was going. I was never not in control."

"It just takes one mistake, Josh. You know that. Look at Nonno," Tommy said.

"Hence why I'm not driving like a madman," Josh said.

"Beg to differ," Susanna mumbled, low enough that no one else heard her.

"Why'd you even get a motorcycle?" Tommy asked. "Thought you were trying to save your money, buy a Shelby one day, get a real Mustang?"

"I had an urging," Josh said. "Motorcycle was there, it was attainable. The Shelby was always going to be a dream."

"Just stop this right now," Matt said. "We know what you're doing. You're causing a scene so that all the attention is on you. Even if it's negative attention, you want everyone to be focused on you and what you're doing. It's the same reason you went working in the middle of the night, and it's the same reason you're doing this now."

Josh straightened his back against the beam as he looked across at Matt. He turned his head toward the front yard and spat into the grass. That was his response.

"I don't think you have any place to talk about running off in the middle of the night," Josh said.

Tommy and Susanna both looked at Matt. His face was flushed and his hands were white from clenching. He looked like he wanted to hurl the rocking chair at Josh, but he didn't. He wouldn't.

"And I think you're still stuck in the past," Matt said. "It's been three years since that night, but you're making excuses for something that happened just two weeks ago."

"Don't you think Papa's just gonna take it from you?" Tommy asked.

"It's possible, likely even," Josh said. "But when I saw it just sitting in the yard, I had a thought. If I could feel the rush of riding it, to feel the wind smacking against me, feel my blood pumping, even if it was just for a moment, it would be worth it. So I did. Maybe that will be the only time I ever get to ride it. If it is, I'll accept it. I'll always have that moment. The memory of that rush. That thrill. It was pretty sweet."

They all just looked at him. It was a look that asked, "Who is this and what has happened with our brother?"

Josh, sliding onto the floor, looked out at the grass, and saw a weed sticking out. He reached down, plucked it, and stuck the weed between his teeth.

"We live in a new world," Josh said. "A man has gone to the moon. If I want to do something like ride a motorcycle, I should have that chance."

It was then that the others realized Josh was miming the motion of smoking a cigarette. Something they had never seen him do before.

"I'll admit it, yes, I was sick and tired of everything I was hearing," Josh continued. "Everywhere we go, hearing nothing but my brother the National Merit Scholar, my brother the brightest among us, my brother with the bright future. Being told to be more like my brother. Not so subtle comments letting me know I could never reach as high as Matthew Ruggirello. Bullshit. Absolute bullshit. You know who you never listened to? Me. You know who told you visiting all those schools was a waste of time? Me. And look at you now. You thought you had the world at your feet. And after all that, you're still going to A&M, just like I said. I've been right all along."

The air was silent among the siblings after that. No one had a rebuttal. Matt knew Josh had been right. He had predicted Papa's way of thinking every step of the way. Matt had to live with that.

AUGUST 1969

MATT

"Now I'm tired of telling you this, that ain't your bull and you know it ain't your bull," Mr. DiRusso shouted from his side of the fence on the Little Brazos pasture.

He and his hands had driven up to the fence that Papa had repaired weeks ago. Now the DiRussos were inspecting the cattle to find supposed lost property.

"You're welcome to come get it, but don't you dare cut that fence," Papa shouted from the driver's seat in The Mustang. "You cut that fence and I'll tell the sheriff you're trying to steal my cattle."

"You no-good liar, you're the one stealing cattle!" Mr. DiRusso shouted. "That's my Charolais bull right there, clear as day. We paid good money for it and you went and took it."

"Now Francis, you know that ain't true," Papa said. "For starters, that bull don't got a brand on it."

"It's my bull."

"You can say it's yours and I won't disagree, you're certainly talking like it's yours. But you can't go calling me a thief, you've got no proof."

"I've got my Charolais bull sitting in your lot."

The Ruggirellos were never sure what took the DiRussos so long to come looking for their Charolais bull. Perhaps they thought it's lingering in the neighboring pasture was too obvious a place to look. Even so, after weeks had passed, they came looking for the bull and found it on the Little Brazos.

The two patriarchs yelling across the field at each other had some semblance of a debate from the old west days. Someone could have transplanted their words onto any number of old cowboys from days gone by. The only difference here was they were sitting in enormous pickup trucks instead of saddled horses.

"You stole my bull and you're going to return it!" Mr. DiRusso continued.

"I did no such thing," Papa responded. "I was in Houston when your bull hopped that fence. My son can attest to that. I even had to get a new post to fix the one he broke."

"Then why haven't you brought it back?"

"It ain't got no brand! Don't be attacking us when someone on your side didn't do their job. And besides, I've got no business moving a bull that fit. I'm liable to get some calves out of it."

"Calves you owe us."

"No, I don't. That's my cows that're impregnated. Now you can bring your men to come get this bull, but you ain't taking anything else."

The air got low between their two trucks at that moment. Neither of them had guns on their hips, but the danger still lingered. Both were resourceful enough to do damage to the other.

"Very well," was Mr. DiRusso's final response before driving his truck further down his pasture.

In a few days, the DiRussos would come by and retrieve the Charolais but a few months from that day, a handful of white calves would start showing up in the fields.

"Dile a tu gente que vigile la cerca," Papa said to Epefanio and Ignacio, who were also in the pasture that day. "No quiero que intenten algo sospechoso por la noche."

"Si patron," they replied.

Papa had been stubborn, but he was not a fool. The task of managing his half of the 3,000 acres would have been impossible with his dwindled roster of hands. As a result, he sent Epefanio to bring in a few more hands, four more to be specific. They were quiet fellows that kept to themselves. The boys thought it was odd to see the workhouses filled so quickly after Big Jake's departure. Big Jake was the only person they had ever known to have lived in that hut.

Even so, Papa's imprisonment of the boys could not persist. He needed the numbers.

Matt, Josh, and Tommy were all sitting on the trailer that The Mustang had been carrying. The trailer was full of feed for the cattle. Three hay bales had been placed in opposite corners of the pasture but the feed was to provide a bit more protein in the cattle's diet. Anything to make them beefier come time to slaughter.

The boys stood in the flatbed trailer and shoveled the feed into each trough Papa drove past. The cattle would hurry up to them and start eating, but it was nothing like when they were fed cotton seed. Post-harvest, there would always be truckloads of cotton seed leftover from the crop that they would then feed to the cattle.

The stuff was like the sweetest candy to the cattle. In the past, they had seen cows jump over one another to try and get closer to the cotton seed, all just for one more bite. It was incredible, violent stuff. That day was mellow in comparison.

They finished distributing the seeds, and Papa turned the truck around to head for the exit. They would make the long drive to the Big Brazos pasture to feed the cows there. Along the way, they passed Uncle Andrew's home at the Orange Grove. Lately, Uncle Andrew had started planting pecan trees. Papa would not say so, but it irked him.

Matt glanced over at Josh from time to time. They had been right about the motorcycle. Papa took one look at the machine and had a parking brake put on the front tire. They didn't know where he got the parking brake, but Papa had one. They were a little surprised he did not outright destroy the machine, but that one day had been the only time Josh rode the motorcycle.

Even so, his antics had not stopped. Josh still did all the work he was told to do, but he decided he was going to grow his hair out. While Matt and Tommy each got their traditional buzz cuts, Josh was growing the first strands of what would become a mane of hair. Just like Dennis Hopper, Josh thought to himself.

Papa did not give a great outburst like after Josh had rolled the truck. Papa just locked up the bike and that was that. Matt did recall that same night that Papa wandered out onto the porch by himself. He was all alone except for Diamond and the old bull, but apart from a few errant noises, there was total silence.

The only words Matt heard come out of Papa's mouth was the Hail Mary. Papa said a complete rosary from memory before turning back to bed.

Matt had followed into line with the others. In appearance, it was like he had reverted to before earning the National Merit Scholarship. Matt had locked his lips and did as he was told, but it was not as before. Matt may have been silent, but he had not stopped thinking about Papa's decision since that fateful night.

He knew he needed to speak. It would eat at him for years, if not the rest of his life, if he did not say anything. He just didn't know when to speak.

Tommy had said very little in the weeks since the accident. Even so, he was keeping a close eye on how his brothers were interacting. No one had seen him do it, but Tommy figured out that Josh was sneaking out to smoke cigarettes. All the sweat and dirt that gathered up from a day's work seemed to mask the smell of smoke that otherwise lingered on his clothes.

They continued onto the Big Brazos, crossing the cattle guard and making two stops. First at an enclosure where they kept the older calves that were ready to go to market. They filled their troughs as the calves brayed at them and then moved on past another cattle guard to the larger pasture. Whereas the Little Brazos pasture was sloped at the base of a hill, the Big Brazos was perpetual flat grassland. The cows always had enough to graze on, the feed was just a bit extra.

The herd headed toward The Mustang the moment they heard its engine growling. The boys all stood to attention at the sound of the cattle braying. They were to shovel the remaining feed into a series of tires on the ground, while also keeping any of the cattle from eating directly out of the trailer.

Yet the tall grass had hidden a hole in the ground that had formed from past rainfalls. The Mustang passed over the hole without the tires hitting it, but the left tire of the trailer fell right into the hole and caused it to buck into the air. Tommy, who had been standing on the left side, went tumbling out of the trailer and onto the ground, flat on his back.

"Stop the truck! Stop the truck!" Matt and Josh shouted in unison, loud enough for Papa to hear them over The Mustang's engine.

Papa jumped out of the truck and saw Tommy lying on the ground, clutching his left elbow. Tommy's eyes were shut in pain and his mouth was open, yet not a sound came out. The cattle started to gather toward Tommy, curious about the figure that had come into their midst. Papa shooed them away like a shepherd and inspected his son.

Nothing looked broken from what Matt and Josh could see. Tommy was clutching his elbow but there was nothing visibly gruesome about it.

After a quick inspection, Papa hauled Tommy into his arms and went to place him in the passenger seat.

"Unhook the trailer," Papa said as he walked around the truck.

His command was soft enough that he had to raise his voice the second time for the boys to hear him.

"Unhook the trailer! It'll slow us down."

Matt and Josh jumped into action like a bee had stung their behinds. From opposite sides, they pulled out the pins that hooked the truck to the trailer. The trailer fell to the ground with a clunk.

Papa, who had never taken the keys out of The Mustang, heard the clunk and immediately started driving back the way they had come.

Matt and Josh, each standing behind The Mustang's rear tires, found their faces spattered with dirt and mud and, likely, a mixture of cow pies. Covered in filth, they watched as the truck sped off faster than they ever thought it could move. Papa had not thought to wait and let them climb in. They could hear him say it, "No time, no time."

Matt and Josh looked at each other, each covered head to toe in filth. So much filth that they could not move out of sheer disgust. The cows brayed behind them and they turned to see them eating straight from the trailer, exactly what they had been trying to avoid. They would be bloated by the end of the day.

Josh somehow found humor in the situation and reached into his back pocket. He pulled out a packet of cigarettes, stuck one in his mouth, and then lit it with a lighter. How Josh had come by the packet of smokes, they did not know. Yet there Josh was, puffing away in the middle of the field.

"What the fuck!" Matt snapped. "What the fuck! What the fuck is he doing! What the fuck are we doing! What are you doing? We're covered head to toe in shit and you're acting like nothing's wrong?"

Josh blew out another puff.

"There ain't nothing I can do about it," Josh said.

"But why! Why'd he leave us here?" Matt continued. "He couldn't have told us what he was doing? Does he think we're not concerned about Tommy? Is he not worried something could happen to us out here?"

Josh puffed again.

"He probably blames us," Josh responded. "Maybe this is his punishment."

"Throw cow shit on us?"

"Maybe he didn't intend it, but he probably isn't upset about it. He's probably going to say we should've kept a closer eye on Tommy, not let him fall off. Something like that."

"Why are you so calm?" Matt asked, catching his breath.

"Getting upset ain't gonna help anything," Josh sighed.

The cows brayed again and they looked back to see the trailer was almost empty of feed. There wasn't anything they could do. They figured it would be hours before Papa came back or another truck came along to pick them up. They had no way to lug the trailer back, so they started walking. The closer they got to the highway, the closer they would be to help.

All the way, Matt continued his fussing.

"I'd rather he have the guts to slap me in the face than do something like this," Matt continued.

"What're you on about?" Josh asked, growing confused.

"He's still on his high horse that we haven't done enough to make up for our wrongdoings."

"So you admit we both committed wrongs?"

"Your wrongs. I've done nothing wrong, but he doesn't see it that way. Still, every chance he gets, he's passive aggressive and keep us in our place."

"Is it working?"

"It's fucking frustrating, is what it is! I'd rather him be up-front about it than whatever this is."

"This feels very upfront," Josh said, looking at his mud-covered shirt.

"But it's not. He won't do it looking at us. He'll give us tough assignments or leave us like this, but he won't outright do what he wants to do. I'm sick of it. It's cowardly."

"You know what Matt, you can say all that, but it ain't going to change anything."

Josh's words did not carry any weight of criticism. Nor did they carry any of the anger they once held, any of the desire to prove Matt wrong. They were matter-of-fact. Josh said them because that was the way it was.

"Papa's like a boulder in a stream," Josh continued. "The world can throw everything it has at it, the water can storm over it, but it will never move. Papa is set in his ways. We're trying to move an immovable object."

Matt looked down at the ground, watching his feet as he marched step by step down the dirt road, shaking his head all the way. They walked in silence from then on. Matt wanted to question what was past the boulder, what was further downstream? But there wasn't any reason to ask.

Josh tossed his cigarette into the Big Brazos as they crossed it. The only advantage of the cow pies on their chests was that they hid the smell of cigarette smoke that otherwise would have surrounded Josh.

Eventually, they spotted Uncle Andrew's truck off in the distance. Seeing them covered in filth and hearing what had happened, he let them climb in the bed to bring them home.

"I wondered what Paul was racing down the road for," Uncle Andrew said as he dropped them off at Three Pecans. "I'm sure it'll all work itself out."

"Nuts," Matt said as he jumped off the side of the truck and headed toward the garden gate, only giving Uncle Andrew a backhanded wave as he drove off.

Susanna spotted them through the window before their feet had touched grass. They weren't going to try to walk in the house with cow pies on their boots, but Susanna was there to make sure of it. She stood on the porch with the hose and affixed it with a new handle and proceeded to spray them with cold water.

Daggers pierced their skin as she shot the water into their hair and down their bodies. Once their clothes were soaked, they stripped them off until they were only in their boxers, and then she continued to spray them. Matt and Josh were chilled to the bone by the end of it. And even then, they had to wait their turn to shower, meaning Josh had to sit outside with only a towel to cover his lower half.

Once they were cleaned, they relayed the incident to Mama. They thought the news had broken her as Mama began pacing around the house and huffing upon hearing the story. Her reaction was in response to the chance Tommy could be hurt. She made no comment about the fact Matt and Josh had been left behind.

They learned that Papa had rushed Tommy all the way to the emergency room at St. Michael's in Bryan. Papa was convinced that a bone was broken, but the doctors found Tommy in good health. There were bruises on his back and arm, but nothing was broken. Still, Papa questioned the doctors repeatedly about whether they were sure Tommy wasn't hurt. In the end, they wrote Tommy a prescription for pain medicine just to get Papa to leave.

When they got home, Tommy told Matt that he stopped hurting before they even arrived at the hospital.

By this point, the day was lost. There was no point going out again as none of the wells had been opened. Add on top how hectic the afternoon had been and everyone decided that the day was done, even Papa.

Yet after Papa and Tommy had relayed the story, Matt did not let Papa sit in his chair.

"Is there something you'd like to say?" Matt asked, looking down at Papa's feet.

"What?" Papa asked, confused.

"Would you like to say something? To us?" Matt asked, now looking at Papa's face.

"Matthew, I'm tired. I'm sitting in my chair now."

Papa put his big, crusted mitt on Matt's shoulder and moved him aside to sit down. Papa's act was not violent, Matt just could not fight against Papa's strength to stay in his way.

"You don't have anything to say?" Matt asked.

"Matthew," Mama said, from the kitchen, trying to get him to settle down.

"Not at this moment," Papa said.

"You don't?"

305

"You're the one who seems to have something to say."

"I'm trying to jog your memory back to a few hours ago. There isn't something you feel like apologizing for?"

"I've been with Thomas all afternoon."

"Jesus Christ," Matt sighed, rubbing his temples.

Mama snapped at Matt's curse, but he did not care that he was heard. The curse was genuine, it came out of exhaustion.

"You left us," Matt finally said. "You left us in the middle of a field, covered in shit, without any indication of where you were going or when you would be back."

"Did I need to? You got home all the same," Papa said.

"You should have, though. You don't know what could've happened."

"Your brother was hurt," Papa replied, still monotone voiced. "He was the priority."

"You couldn't have waited five seconds? You wanted to rush off. You deliberately wanted to leave us there."

"No, you sound like the DiRussos. Nothing but unfounded claims."

"I'm sick of it, Pa!" Matt snapped.

Everyone in Three Pecans may have been fiddling with their own individual tasks at that moment. But when they heard Matt's proclamation, all turned to attention. Even Diamond did not dare bark.

"We're not your hands," Matt continued, blowing smoke out of his nostrils. "We work for you. We do the jobs. We do every task given to us. But we're not the hands. You cannot . . . ignore everything we say. You can't ignore our suggestions or make us think it's pointless to speak up to begin with. You're not teaching us. You're telling us what to do like we're pawns on a chessboard. You put us down every chance you get. We never feel a sense of accomplishment for what we're doing. We're not doing anything. We don't get to do anything. We've never gotten to do anything. All we do is work for you and you belittle us, you shackle us.

"I can already hear what you're going to say. Don't think I'm ungrateful for everything we have. None of us has ever not appreciated what you, what Mama, what Nonno and Nonna have done for us. We get it. And do not say I should've been there for Tommy. I know that. None of us wanted that to happen. But it was an accident, you need to see that and not place blame.

"Acknowledge us. Hear us. Support us. Listen to what interests us, talk to us about what we want to do. Treat us like people. I don't know how many ways I can say it. It just . . . it just can't go on like this. You don't care about us. I didn't want to say it, but I see that now. You don't care about us or what we need or what we want to do. We're resources to you. We're resources for the farm. That's all we are. Isn't it?"

Papa had long stopped looking at Matt. The television was off, but Papa kept his gaze on it. He couldn't look Matt in the eye. Not then. And it was the silence that said everything.

Matt stood there, feeling as if he had just finished a marathon. His chest heaved, sweat trickled from his forehead, and he could feel his knees quaking. He couldn't quite believe he had said what he had wanted to say. Three years' worth of thoughts had come out in that one moment. An exhausting, hurtful moment, but a moment that needed to be said. Odd enough, Matt struggled to remember what he had said just moments after saying it.

He did not stand around waiting for a response. He turned and headed for the rear door and went straight for his truck. They all sat there and listened as the keys were turned in the ignition and the Ford pulled out of the garage.

MATT

It was a stroke of luck that the lockbox containing the truck keys was open, otherwise Matt's departure from home would have been abruptly cut short.

Climbing into his truck, Matt saw that the key to The Wagon Wheel was attached to the ring. Acting on impulse, he swung by and retrieved a bottle of Wild Turkey. A strange nostalgic feeling swept over him.

Matt drove eastward, over the Little Brazos and up to the clearing at the top of the hill. A makeshift fence had been set up around a large square area in the center of the hill. Some tractors were set up inside the fence, but no substantial work had yet to happen. Matt parked right next to it.

Stepping out of the truck, Matt wandered to the edge of the hill so that he could look out over the entire Bottom. He reckoned he could see all the way to Hearne from that high up. Sitting down, Matt began to drink. He drank with no rhythm and to no end. He drank until the sun had finished setting and he could see a pair of headlights coming up the hill.

It was a truck, no doubt, but Matt had to wait to see who was behind the wheel. The truck came up beside Matt, but his vision was blinded by the headlights of his own truck. Matt had never taken the keys out of the ignition. Bobby Gentry's "Fancy" was playing over the radio. Matt could make out two feet stepping out of the truck, but when the figure came into view, it wasn't Josh or Papa or even Nonno or Uncle Andrew. It was Aunt Ella.

"Where'd you get that?" Aunt Ella asked, gesturing at the bottle of Wild Turkey.

"The Wagon Wheel," Matt replied.

"I forgot about that place. We didn't have it when I was a kid. I'm sure I would've made a few bad habits."

Matt paused, still surprised to see Aunt Ella standing there, and held out the bottle to her.

"Don't want to start a bad habit now, either," she said.

Still, she sat down next to Matt, who let the bottle plop down on the ground.

"What're you doing here?" Matt asked.

"I caught Josh when he was coming down the road," Aunt Ella said. "I had heard the shouting from the house, and I wanted to help."

"So, where's Josh?"

"He's still in the truck."

Matt looked back and could just make out the silhouette of a figure behind the wheel.

"He didn't want to come out?" Matt asked.

"He thought you needed to hear someone new," Aunt Ella said.

Matt never had a deep conversation with Aunt Ella. He remembered he was 12 years old the last time he had spoken with her for a prolonged period of time. Yet there she was.

"What're you doing up here?" Aunt Ella asked.

"I couldn't stay home," Matt said. "I couldn't. I felt like I couldn't breathe. Like my head was going to explode. I needed to get out."

"Yes, but why here?"

Matt looked at the fence set up by the Chevron men.

"I thought about this spot," Matt said. "This is where it's going to be, right? Gopher One? An oil well in a place where oil was never pumped before. I thought about this place, so I decided to go see it."

"It's not anything yet," Aunt Ella said.

"Yes, but in a matter of months, it will be. Everything will change. Soon, Uncle Andrew will have one, then Papa will have this one, then another and another. They'll pump out every bit of oil they can."

"I'm not following."

"Things change. The land will always be here. Papa is right about that, but what's on the land will change. Is changing. We're changing, I'm changing. He doesn't see that."

"Is that what led to the outburst Josh told me about?"

Matt sighed. "I don't know what that was."

"You don't?"

"No. I hadn't rehearsed it, hadn't thought about it. All I wanted was an apology, an acknowledgment. When I didn't get it . . . that happened. Hell, I doubt it did any good."

"Then why'd you say it?"

"I think I had to. It was like hot water boiling over a pot. Couldn't keep it any longer. You know what it is. At this moment, this very moment, I feel I have a good grip on who I am. I'm not sure about what I want to do, but I know who I am."

"And who are you?"

"Not a farmer."

Matt felt like a levy had broken as he said those words. They came out as calm and flat as any other words, but they carried the weight as if he had screamed them from the top of the hill they were sitting on.

"I'm not a farmer," Matt repeated. "I've said that a few times, but now I'm sure of it. We've always done the work. We always did as we were told. We knew we were doing good. That's what Papa wants us to be. He wants to keep the farm alive. He wants us to keep supporting the family. Not once has he asked what you or I wanted to do or let us do anything that wasn't related to farming during the summer."

"So, what do you want to do?" Aunt Ella asked.

"I don't know. That's the problem. I've never had the chance to learn. During school, we work in the classroom and in summer, we work on the farm. We've never been allowed to be anything else. Maybe if we had, I'd know. Now, maybe it's too late. I can say all this till I'm blue in the face, but if it was ever going to change anything, the moment's long past."

Aunt Ella sat there looking at her nephew. The nephew she barely knew, a piece of a family that was drifting away from her every day.

"I think all that is good," Aunt Ella said. "Maybe you don't know who you are, but you've lived enough to know who you aren't. But can I tell you something?"

It was not often that anyone asked permission to share their thoughts, they just said them. So, Matt shrugged his shoulders and Aunt Ella continued to speak.

"Your papa didn't want me to come home—he told me so. Well, he asked me not to. Worried I'll be a bad influence, which is fair. When I was your age, I felt like I could do anything. Daddy was never too strict about his expectations. I wanted to go off and see the world, so I did. I went into the world, but I left my family behind."

Aunt Ella paused for a moment, looking at the ground, before looking up again.

"I had some fun, but I made even more mistakes. I'm trying to right those wrongs, I'm trying at least, I'm trying. But I know the damage has been done. So, what I say is this. You go find out who you are. You answer the questions you have about yourself, but don't push your family away. I went out to figure out who I was, but I left them in the rearview mirror. I was a stranger to them when I needed them the most. You're fighting now. Maybe you'll always be fighting in some way. Still, I've realized we can't replace our family. There will come a moment when you want them by your side. Let them be there."

Matt had not broken his gaze on Aunt Ella the entire time she spoke. She was crying.

...

Papa never did confront Matt about his outburst. Matt was right, it had not changed anything. They all still got up to work every day and made sure the crop was fertilized from sun up to sun down.

Matt had sat there with Aunt Ella until the lights to his Ford shut off. The engine had died. Breathing out a little curse, Matt had followed her into the truck, where Josh was still sitting. It was unclear how much, if any, he had heard of Matt's proclamation. Together they drove down back to Three Pecans, stopping by the Big House momentarily to let Aunt Ella out. The three of them held fingers up to their lips to signify they would not tell Papa of her activity.

The next day, they went up and put a new battery in Matt's Ford and continued to work as if the incident had never happened.

Weeks passed and the summer heat grew to its highest. July turned to August. Like every year before it, the tiny buds that had remained tiny buds for months prior, bloomed into white balls of cotton that seemed to grow with every sunrise.

There was no greater sign of a blessed crop than bulging cotton. Cotton so plentiful that one felt like ignoring the thorns and leaping onto them as if they were as soft as the clouds in the sky.

The cotton was a blessing. Reward for months of toil and hard work. A guarantee that the farmer could provide for his family for another year. Harvest was the one time the boys could guarantee seeing Papa smile. As the tractors entered the field and harvested the tons and tons of cotton, he could always be spotted with a smile on his face going up and down the roads.

Within a few more months, the cotton would be harvested and sent to the Reffino Gin to have the thorns separated from the flowers. The Reffinos would give the Ruggirellos a price as to what they could sell the cotton for. If Nonno thought they could find a better price, then they would take the cotton to market in the coming weeks. But for the boys, their work was done.

Now the focus was on school.

The boys may have been a part of the majority of the work, but they would not be able to see it through to the end. It was the same every year. Just as the tractors started getting pulled out of the barns for arguably the most satisfying job of the year, the boys would be taken into town with Mama to purchase school supplies.

Josh still acted in his leisurely, relaxed manner, but Mama, through constant begging, convinced him to cut his hair. Mama had conjured up the story, which could have been true but was never verified, that male students of Hearne High School were not allowed to have their hair go lower than their eardrums. Josh was in danger of scratching his shoulder blades.

Josh ruminated on the revelation for a handful of days but gave into the request after Mama's constant pestering. He did not go into town and receive a buzz cut like Matt and Tommy did, but he did allow Susanna to cut his hair so that it no longer went past his ears.

Still like Dennis Hopper, Josh thought to himself.

Apart from this wrinkle, little had changed in the family dynamic. Dinners with Nonno and Nonna were regular. Nonno, whose hand had fully recovered from the accident, had helped Aunt Ella purchase a home in Bryan. Grace and Chloe would start school there in the fall, but they too would join the dinners as well. Matt noticed a hint of frustration in Mama's eyes over Nonno buying the house, but she never vocalized it.

Gopher One's ignition was an inevitability and Uncle Andrew provided constant updates about his own pumpjack and the other areas Chevron believed that oil could be struck.

Papa was still his stoic self, but Matt had no further outbursts. Even so, Matt listened every night as Papa ventured out onto the porch to say his Hail Marys. Each night, Papa's voice grew lower and lower.

Eventually came the first day of school. Matt, Josh and Susanna dressed in their school clothes, ate their breakfast, and climbed into Matt's Oldsmobile. Mama was to drive Tommy to the Mumford primary school after they had gone. For Papa, nothing had changed. He had still risen before all the others and had gone to work in the fields.

Matt had turned on the radio, but no one was listening to the random tune coming out of the stereo. Josh and Susanna were looking to the left and right, watching the fields roll past the windows. Matt had lost himself as one does driving down the road.

All of them were calm, relaxed. Their heads were filled with absolutely no thoughts. Not even what was to be done once they got to school or how they would interact with friends they had not seen all summer.

They were so relaxed that none of them noticed the station wagon that shot into the intersection, clipping the back of the car and sending them spinning off the side of the road.

MATT

Matt was out. For how long, he was not sure. When he woke up, he could feel blood trickling down the left side of his head. Someone had hit them. Matt never saw the car, but someone had hit them. He slowly tried to move every finger, every toe, each arm and each leg. Somehow, nothing was broken. Everything was dizzy, Matt felt sore, but he felt no broken bones.

The Oldsmobile had slid into the neighboring ditch, a piece of some other farmer's cotton crop. The front of the car had wrinkled slightly, but most of the damage was to the rear. The left rear door was dented, the sight of the T-bone collision from moments prior. Had Susanna been sitting on that side, she might've been jettisoned through the opposite side of the car.

Then Matt looked to his right. Susanna was leaning against the back of Josh's seat. She was coming to, her forehead cut in two places. The crash appeared to have thrust her forward into Josh's seat. Josh was crumpled against the dash, blood trickling from his face at an increasing speed.

Dead. That was the first thought that shot into Matt's head. Josh was dead. He was looking at his body. Matt was sure of it. It froze him for a moment, but then he saw Josh's back heave as he took in a breath.

Cautiously, without breathing, Matt moved forward and sat Josh up. Josh was in a state between being asleep and being awake. With the pain he must have been feeling, all Josh's body could do was keep him asleep. Yet when Matt sat him up, every single one of Josh's teeth started to crumple to the floor.

In a complete reflex, Matt thrust his hand into Josh's face and held it tight, willing himself to keep Josh's jaw from falling apart. It seemed like they had been arguing just the day before, now Matt feared for his brother's life. His closest brother. His constant rival. The same person he could see himself arguing with for years to come. Yet now, everything could change in a moment.

"Wake-up!" Matt shouted. "Both of you, wake-up! Susanna, I need you to get up!"

With his hands preoccupied, Matt repeated the command again and again. It accomplished waking Susanna, stirring her to sit up and see the carnage before them. Josh started to stir as well, but Matt had to keep him from pulling away and risking damaging the jaw.

"Susanna, can you walk?" Matt asked.

Susanna looked over herself. "I think so. What happened?"

"Someone hit us. I need you to focus though. We need to flag someone down and get to a hospital."

"What're you going to do?" Susanna asked.

Matt hesitated, not wanting to freak Josh out too much, but he also wanted to be realistic.

"I'm going to make sure Josh's jaw doesn't fall apart," Matt said.

Josh shut his eyes and his arms twitched for a moment, possibly from pain but also from fear at what might happen. Yet after the twitches, Josh's eyes were still. He was focused on what they needed to do.

Susanna, ignoring the soreness flooding through her body, forced her way out of the car and up the slope of the ditch and to the side of the road. This was the first time she got a glimpse at who hit them.

The woman was on the opposite side of the road, standing by her car and looking at the crumpled exterior. Susanna didn't recognize her at first, but then realized it was Miss Russell, one of the mathematics teachers at Hearne. The same Russell who was a member of the old Russell plantation family.

Miss Russell, the aging, should-be-retired woman had evidently slept through her morning alarm and was speeding down the roads to get to work on time. Driving too fast, she ran right into the Ruggirellos.

Susanna headed the old woman no mind and instead peered down the highway. A single red truck was coming southbound, right toward them. Seeing no other cars or trucks coming close, Susanna stepped into the highway and waved her arms rapidly, fighting through the soreness to get the driver's attention. After doing this for a long while, the driver indicated with his lights that he was going to pull over.

In an ironic moment, the car was being driven by none other than Francis DiRusso, who still accused the Ruggirellos of stealing his Charolais bull even after it had been returned to him. Yet at that moment, he forgot all about the bull. He saw the wounded, frightened Susanna and did not think about her family.

"We've been in an accident," Susanna said. "We need to get my brother to a hospital."

Mr. DiRusso hesitated for a moment, still looking at the frightened Susanna, and then went to go check on Matt and Josh. He saw first-hand the damage that had happened and how injured Josh was. He could see that Matt was not about to let go of Josh's jaw, no matter how heavy his hands became.

Mr. DiRusso helped Matt and Susanna guide Josh out of the car nice and steady as to avoid any further damage. Bringing them to his truck, he placed Matt and Josh in the bed and had Susanna ride in the passenger seat. He gave all of them what few cloths he had in order to clean up their cuts as best as they could. Then they headed south.

The truck flew down the highway and on the way to Bryan. Matt knew there was no hospital in Hearne that could help Josh. They're only hope was to get him to St. Michael's, to experienced medical professionals, as fast as possible.

For the entire duration of the drive, Matt continued to hold Josh's jaw in place. Blood trickled between his fingers and onto their clothes, but he did not care. Matt knew he was the tourniquet. He knew his actions weren't doing anything substantial, he just hoped they were enough.

He lost track of time as they sped down the road, his hands becoming numb from applying constant pressure. The last thing he saw was the Emergency Room logo at St. Joseph's hospital. Then he passed out.

...

When Matt woke up, he found himself laying on a hospital bed. His cuts had been stitched up and his boots had been taken away. There was a brace on his left foot—maybe he had been more hurt than he realized.

However, the first thing he saw was Susanna in the bed across from him. She was sitting up, her stitches visible across her brow, talking with Mama and Tommy, who had made their way to the hospital. Papa was away, but Matt thought they said he was coming.

Susanna was crying, and Mama and Tommy had both wrapped their arms around her. The chaos of the last few hours had swamped over her. The realization that she could have died, that they all could have died. Coupled with Mama's affectionate embrace and the confusion over Josh's health, it overwhelmed her. All Tommy could do was continue to hug her as the tears flowed forth unobstructed.

It was at this moment that Matt let out a groan and forced himself to sit up. It would've been easier to remain motionless, but he needed to return to life. Consequently, Mama and

Tommy looked back at him like a corpse had risen. Then, Tommy threw himself at his brother, knocking the wind out of him once more.

Mr. DiRusso had called Three Pecans the moment Matt, Josh, and Susanna had been handed over to the doctors. After hearing the news, Mama had lost her balance and would have fallen to the floor had Tommy not been there to support her.

Mama was in such a hurry to get to the hospital that when they arrived, she almost forgot to put the car in park before stepping out. Tommy went with her, evidently going to miss the first day of school. Before leaving, she left a message with Nonna at the Big House about what had happened and where they were going. She could only hope that Papa got the message and came as soon as he could.

Now Matt was crying. Crying from the pain, crying from the shock, crying from relief that they had made it out. It was then that there was a knock at the door. A man in a white coat by the name of Dr. Zimmerman approached.

"I see the family's all here," Dr. Zimmerman said.

"Most of us, at least," Tommy said, glancing at the floor.

"Are you the one who stitched us up?" Susanna asked.

"No, that was a junior doctor, but I'm keeping close watch on all three of y'all."

Matt took a gulp. "How's Josh? Where is he?"

"Well, the front of his jaw is completely shattered."

All four of the Ruggirellos' faces stretched into stunned stares. A sight sharp enough to force Dr. Zimmerman to jump to the positive news.

"But I have to say, you did the right thing," Dr. Zimmerman said, gesturing to Matt. "Had you not kept your brother's jaw in place, there could've been permanent damage. He's going to need false teeth because of the impact against the dash. He won't be able to eat solid food for maybe a year, but you saved his life."

"Where is he now?" Mama asked.

"Upstairs getting X-rays," Dr. Zimmerman said. "If anything else is broken, we'll find it. We're worried we might have to pull some teeth down from the top of his mouth, but we don't know yet. For now, you two," gesturing at Matt and Susanna, "need to rest."

Mama followed Dr. Zimmerman's suggestion and forced Matt and Susanna to lay back down in their beds. Tommy took a seat in the chair adjacent to them. Mama stepped out into the hall to further discuss what was going to happen with Dr. Zimmerman. Matt felt numb, exhausted, and held no motivation to stay awake. The sleep that followed was glorious.

...

Tommy was the only one awake when Papa arrived at the hospital. Hearing the story, Papa did not faint or begin to cry, but Tommy noticed the most peculiar look on his face. Tommy wasn't sure how to describe it, but he knew it was different. It looked like Papa was out of breath. So much so that even he took a seat and waited for Dr. Zimmerman to come back and explain the situation.

When Matt and Susanna woke up hours later, well past lunchtime, a rare sight followed. Papa stepped between the two beds and wrapped his arms around the pair of them. Mama followed the gesture, but Tommy took note that Papa instigated the action. He held that position for a good minute.

They later learned that the police took away Miss Russell's driver's license, deeming she could not be trusted behind the wheel of a car. Papa also made sure to call Mr. DiRusso and thank him for what he did. Papa did not say how he would repay the debt, but he promised to stay in Mr. DiRusso's good favor. Mr. DiRusso did not brag about being a good Samaritan, he just did the right thing.

Matt and Susanna were sent home the next day with medication and strict instructions to follow. Every two hours, they had a pill to take. Mama ended up keeping them home the entire week to better keep an eye on them.

Josh ended up staying in the hospital for four days. When he came home, his face was all but wrapped in an iron mask of bandages, barely able to move. Dr. Zimmerman's prediction proved right as Josh would be unable to eat solid food for the foreseeable future. The bandages would have to remain for over a month while his face healed naturally, forcing Josh to be silent the entire time. Josh accepted his situation and decided to wait it out. Life would go back to normal eventually.

Yet what changed the most about Three Pecans was Papa. Papa did not do anything grand about the house or do more than was asked of him, but he was present. Papa decided to let Uncle Andrew instruct Papa's hands on which fields to pick. He knew Papa would return eventually, but it looked like Papa understood his need to be with his family. A silent, calming presence, oddly enough.

One such night, Tommy awoke to hear Papa out on the porch. He too had been hearing Papa's excursions onto the porch to say his Hail Marys. A new tradition at Three Pecans. Yet this time, Mama came out to join him.

"Do you find comfort coming out here alone like this?" Mama asked, sitting down in the creaking rocking chair.

Tommy noticed a shift in the way Mama spoke. It was not sharp or loud, it was soft. This was the way she talked to Papa.

"Sometimes I just need to be alone with my thoughts," Papa replied.

"I think you've been alone with your thoughts for 43 years."

Tommy could hear Papa breathe a deep sigh.

"I'm losing them," Papa said. "I'm losing my children."

"What're you talking about?" Mama asked.

"I'm losing them. I've been teaching them the way I thought was right. I kept trying to remind them of the importance of what we have here. But they don't feel at home here. This whole time, I've been pushing them away. I didn't think much of their outbursts. I thought it was just something they'd move past. But today . . . I almost lost them for good."

There was a long pause between sentences. Tommy thought he heard something that sounded like a whimper. It didn't sound like Diamond was with them.

"We almost did lose them," Mama said. "That's why we have to thank God they're still here."

Papa sighed.

"I always just wanted to keep them safe," Papa said. "They get these ideas about school and the big city, but they don't know who they'll meet, who might try to hurt them, what accidents might happen. At least here, here they're close. Here, we have some idea of what we're sending them into."

Mama rocked in her chair a couple times.

"That may be true," she said. "It was definitely true when you and your brother went to school. But…maybe things are changing and we're not catching on."

"What do you mean?"

"I mean, think about these oil companies coming in. You always had such a distrust for them, but maybe these ones are different. They're not threatening to take the farm away, they just want to use a small piece of it. Would that be so terrible, considering how much they're willing to give for it?"

"No, I suppose not," Papa answered after a long pause. "More money, for the right reasons, isn't a bad thing."

"I will be honest with you, Paul, there are times I wish we lived closer to town."

"You do?"

"Yes. I just think about how much more we would have access to. Better schools, better stores, better supplies, more people to be around."

"But what about here?"

Tommy could hear Mama's chair creak as she turned her head to look at Three Pecans. The home her husband hoped to give her. The place she was able to raise four healthy children. It would always be there. Always rooted to the Ruggirello land.

"This will always be home. In the summer, you and the boys will always come back here. On holidays, we will always be here. This is where we made a family, but we should think about the now. How can we benefit now?"

Papa sat up in his chair.

"Those oil companies, it's one more crop," Mama continued. "The easiest crop you'll ever grow. One more crop to feed your kids and put them through school, with or without any scholarships."

Tommy perked his ears up when he heard Mama mention the scholarships. It didn't seem natural in the conversation. Almost as if she was trying to guide Papa into thinking about it.

"Matthew," Papa sighed. "Head full of steam he's got."

"Yes, but he's changed," Mama replied.

"Maybe that's been the scariest thing of all." Papa sighed again. "But he did good. He saved Josh's life. I wish it had never happened, but Matt grew up in that moment."

"Maybe we just hadn't realized it."

Papa huffed out a sigh. "So, what should I do?"

"I can't tell you what to do. But I think you and him should have another talk. One more talk."

"Do you?"

"Yes."

Papa held Mama's gaze from their short distance from each other.

"Perhaps you're right," Papa finally answered. "Will you pray with me?"

Mama nodded her head and together they began to say the rosary. Tommy fell asleep with an extra tinge of excitement. A tinge of curiosity over what tomorrow might bring.

They woke up to find that the old white bull had breathed its last. Diamond whimpered from the opposite side of the fence at the old beast, crumpled on the grass. A peaceful passing.

Lightning Source UK Ltd.
Milton Keynes UK
UKHW020609301222
414606UK00017B/205/J